Mallory Kane has two great reasons for loving to write. Her mother, a librarian, taught her to love and respect books. Her father could hold listeners spellbound for hours with his stories. His oral histories are chronicled in numerous places, including the Library of Congress Veterans' History Project. He was always her biggest fan. To learn more about Mallory, visit her online at mallorykane.com.

Be sure to look for more books by Mallory Kane in Harlequin Intrigue—the ultimate destination for edge-of-your-seat intrigue and fearless romance. There are six new Harlequin Intrigue titles available every month. Check one out today!

Mallory Kane

SEARCH & RESCUE

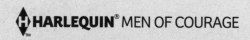

HARLEQUIN® MEN OF COURAGE

Recycling programs
for this product may
not exist in your area.

ISBN-13: 978-0-373-60977-2

Search & Rescue

Copyright © 2014 by Harlequin Books S.A.

The publisher acknowledges the copyright holder
of the individual works as follows:

His Best Friend's Baby
Copyright © 2009 by Rickey R. Mallory

The Sharpshooter's Secret Son
Copyright © 2009 by Rickey Ricks Mallory

All rights reserved. Except for use in any review, the reproduction or utilization of this work in whole or in part in any form by any electronic, mechanical or other means, now known or hereinafter invented, including xerography, photocopying and recording, or in any information storage or retrieval system, is forbidden without the written permission of the publisher, Harlequin Enterprises Limited, 225 Duncan Mill Road, Don Mills, Ontario, Canada, M3B 3K9.

This is a work of fiction. Names, characters, places and incidents are either the product of the author's imagination or are used fictitiously, and any resemblance to actual persons, living or dead, business establishments, events or locales is entirely coincidental.

This edition published by arrangement with Harlequin Books S.A.

For questions and comments about the quality of this book,
please contact us at CustomerService@Harlequin.com.

® and TM are trademarks of the publisher. Trademarks indicated with ® are registered in the United States Patent and Trademark Office, the Canadian Intellectual Property Office and in other countries.

Printed in U.S.A.

CONTENTS

HIS BEST FRIEND'S BABY

For Michael, for the usual reasons

PROLOGUE

THE COLD RAIN beat down on the white roses that blanketed Bill Vick's coffin, turning them yellow and soggy. The canopy flapped and creaked in the wind.

A dozen or so people had braved the weather to attend the graveside service, but Matthew Parker saw only one—Aimee Vick, his best friend's widow.

From his vantage point, several dozen feet away and partially hidden by trees, Matt could barely see the strands of brown hair that had escaped from beneath her hat to blow across her pale face.

Aimee didn't notice. She stood stiffly, her arms folded protectively across her tummy, nodding and smiling sadly as people filed by, offering their condolences one more time before they headed home.

Matt pushed his fists deeper into his pockets and hunched his shoulders against the bone-deep chill that shuddered through him. A chill that had nothing to do with the cold April wind or the freezing rain that poured off the brim of his Stetson.

Three days before, he'd done the two most difficult things he'd ever done in his life. He'd brought Bill's body home to Sundance, Wyoming, and he'd faced Bill's wife and tried to explain how a weekend adventure had turned into tragedy.

How, in the blink of an eye, she was widowed, and her unborn baby would never know his father.

Her utter shock and disbelief had been agonizing to watch, but he'd stood there, needing to see it. Just as he did now. He needed to share her grief, her pain.

Aimee wiped her cheek with a gloved finger, and bowed her head for an instant.

Matt's eyes stung. He blinked and looked at his watch. He needed to leave now. His flight back to the tiny border province of Mahjidastan was scheduled to leave in an hour.

For a few seconds, he debated whether he should speak to her. But he quelled the notion as soon as it surfaced. Seeing him would only hurt her more.

He'd known Aimee nearly as long as he'd known Bill, which was most of his life. He'd kidded Bill about not deserving her. She was generous and kind, and forgiving to a fault. She gave everyone the benefit of the doubt, until they proved they didn't deserve it.

Three days ago, Matt had proven he didn't deserve her forgiveness. She hadn't said it, but the look in her eyes had spoken louder than words.

If not for him, Bill would still be alive. He'd be safe at home with his wife, awaiting the birth of their son.

Bill's death was his fault.

CHAPTER ONE

A year later
THURSDAY 0900 HOURS

MATT PARKER STEPPED outside Irina Castle's ranch house, the headquarters for Black Hills Search and Rescue in Sundance, Wyoming, and headed for the helipad a few hundred yards to the east. He lifted his head and took a deep breath of crisp, fresh Wyoming air.

The day before, for the first time in a year, he'd set foot on American soil, on Wyoming soil. He was back home, where he belonged. He loved the Black Hills. Even though they'd tried to kill him and his three best friends twenty years ago, he loved them. They sustained him.

He'd done his best to track down any rumors of Americans in the remote mountain province of Mahjidastan, which was located in a disputed border area shared by Afghanistan, Pakistan and China. His objective had been to find Rook Castle, Irina's husband. But ultimately, he'd failed, as had BHSAR specialist Aaron Gold before him. And now Irina had called off the search.

As he circled the Bell 429 helicopter that was BHSAR Specialist Deke Cunningham's baby, another fellow specialist, Brock O'Neill, appeared in the doorway of the hangar.

"Parker," he said as Matt approached. The terse greeting was typical of the ex-Navy SEAL. He held out his hand and cocked his head—the only indication Matt had ever seen that the patch over his left eye bothered him.

Matt shook his hand. "Brock. How're you doing?"

"Hmph. Watch out. Your buddy's in a mood." Brock broke the handshake and headed toward the ranch house.

Matt suppressed a smile as he continued toward the hangar. For Brock, that was a warm greeting.

When he stepped through the open door, Deke was leaning back in his desk chair with his feet propped up, tossing a steel bearing from hand to hand. A small TV was tuned to a morning news show, its sound muted.

"Hey, Deke," Matt said. "Playing catch with yourself?"

Deke's feet hit the floor and he set the silver ball on his desk. "That goober I just hired overtightened a bolt and ruined this ball bearing. Brock offered to take him out for me."

Matt laughed.

"How're you doing?"

Matt took Deke's hand. "Been a while. Can't say I'm glad to see you."

"I know."

"Man, I hate this," Matt said, nodding back toward the ranch house. "The place feels like a funeral home. I didn't see Irina. How's she holding up?"

Deke shook his head. "She's trying to act like she's fine, but she's not. She's in bad shape." Deke wiped a hand over his face and then pushed his shaggy hair back. "She's in town this morning, talking to her accountant again."

"So it's true?" Matt asked. "All her funds are wiped out?"

Deke nodded. "All her personal funds. Damn Rook for not signing everything over to her when they got married. I'd like to kill him—" Deke stopped and clamped his jaw.

Matt snorted. "Too late. But it's not like he knew he was going to die."

"No?" Deke's brows lowered and his blue eyes turned black. "He spent his whole life stepping in front of bullets for other people. He had to figure one would hit him sooner or later."

"I don't get it. She's his wife—widow. Why doesn't she get his money?"

"It's all about the suspicious nature of his death. Just because they don't have a body—greedy bastards."

"Hang on a minute," Matt said as he glanced at the TV. "Turn that up."

Deke scooped up the remote control and tossed it to him. "What is it?"

"Check out the pink dress. It's Margo Vick."

"Bill's mother? Opening another Vick Resort Hotel?"

"Not this time. That's FBI Special Agent Aaron Schiff standing next to her." Matt hit the volume control.

"—I am personally offering a reward for any information leading to the kidnapper."

Kidnapper. Alarm pierced Matt's chest as Margo yielded the microphone to the FBI special agent. Among the dark suits, her brightly colored dress drew all eyes to her.

"We plan to hold press conferences on a regular basis, and we'll update the media as we have more information," Special Agent Schiff said. "Meanwhile, please let us do our job. Our primary concern is getting Mrs. Vick's grandson back home safe and sound."

"It's Aimee's baby. He's been kidnapped." Matt sat on the edge of a folding chair and propped his elbows on his knees, listening as Schiff answered questions from reporters. The cameras pulled back to reveal the front of the Vick mansion, located just outside Casper, Wyoming. Besides Schiff and Margo, several uniformed police officers stood on the marble steps, along with a couple of men in suits.

Matt's gaze zeroed in on a pale face behind Bill's mother. It was Aimee, dressed in something dark that blended with the suits and uniforms. Her eyes were huge and strands of hair blew across her face.

"There's Aimee." He didn't take his eyes off her until the camera switched back to Schiff. Then he shot up off the chair and paced, rubbing his thumb across his lower lip.

"There's something more going on here," he said as dread pressed on his chest like a weight.

"What—with the kidnapping?"

"About a month ago, my journal disappeared from my room."

Deke frowned and picked up the ball bearing again. He tossed it back and forth. "You mean on your laptop?"

Matt shook his head. With every passing second, pressure in his chest grew. "I keep notes in a small leather journal just for my use. I write my reports to Irina from my notes. You know, rumors of Americans in the area, anything I can glean about what Novus Ordo or his terrorist friends are up to, lists of expenses."

"You think it was stolen?"

He nodded.

"Okay. How does this have anything to do with the grandbaby of one of the wealthiest women in Wyoming being kidnapped?"

Matt glanced back at the TV, but there was a commercial on. "Work stuff wasn't all that was in the journal."

He turned toward the window, letting his gaze roam over the jagged peaks in the distance. "It's been a year since Bill died, and I haven't talked to her."

Deke didn't comment.

Matt rubbed his lip. "I just couldn't face her. So I was trying to compose a letter. A way to—tell her how sorry I am."

"I don't follow."

"Novus knows we've been searching for any clue that Rook survived his sniper attack. I've been followed ever since I got over there. I'm sure whoever stole my journal was sent by Novus, so now—"

"Now he knows how you feel about Aimee," Deke supplied. He set the ball bearing down and sat up straight.

"How I feel—?" Matt frowned. "Well, yeah. He knows about her baby and about me being William's godfather. And now Irina's stopped looking for Rook. What if Novus thinks she stopped because I found him?"

"And what? You think Novus had Aimee's baby kidnapped—"

"To get to me."

Deke blew out a long breath. "Kind of a stretch. Why wouldn't he have grabbed you before now if he thought you knew something?"

"Think about it. I've been in Mahjidastan for the past year, searching for information about the only man on the earth who could identify Novus Ordo. And before me Aaron was there for a year. There hasn't been a day since Rook disappeared off that boat that a BHSAR specialist hasn't been looking for him. Suddenly, Irina pulls me out and doesn't replace me. Novus didn't have a chance to get his hands on me. I left within four hours of Irina's phone call."

Deke gave a short, sharp laugh. "That's quite a conspiracy theory. But it makes sense—sort of. What now?"

Matt met Deke's gaze and set his jaw. "If Novus Ordo has taken Aimee Vick's baby to try and get his hands on me to interrogate me about Rook, I'm going to make it easy for him."

So far everything was working well. Not bad for a plan that had been put together in less than twenty-four hours.

The Vick baby was already in safe hands. The FBI was on the case. And, most important, Parker was acting exactly as predicted. He was inserting himself right into the middle of the kidnapping investigation.

A warm sense of satisfaction spread through him. It was immaterial whether Rook Castle was alive or dead. He had a larger goal. And finally, it was in sight.

He looked at his watch. Almost time. He had a telephone call to make.

THURSDAY 1430 HOURS

Aimee Vick paced back and forth across the living room of her mother-in-law's house. The room was crawling with FBI special agents, uniformed police officers, and technicians trailing spools of wire everywhere.

She looked at the grandfather clock for the hundredth time—or the thousandth. Two-thirty p.m. It had been eight hours. Eight miserable, terrifying hours without her baby.

When she'd woken up this morning and discovered that William was gone, she'd have sworn she couldn't survive eight hours without her baby. But she was still alive, and still rational—barely.

William Matthew was only seven months old, and she'd never spent a night without him. Hardly even an hour. He was her anchor, her life since her husband's death.

She didn't notice that someone else had come in the front door until she heard her name called.

She turned and found herself face-to-face with Matt Parker, her husband's best friend, her baby's godfather, and the last man on earth she expected to see.

"Matt," she croaked. Her voice was hoarse and sounded harsh to her ears.

The last time she'd seen him was a year ago, when he'd brought her husband's body home. He looked just as stricken as he had that day.

Her first impulse was to run to him and hug him. But she didn't. Her emotions were already in turmoil, and seeing Matt made things even more confusing.

She should be furious at him. After all, he hadn't shown up for Bill's funeral, nor for William Matthew's christening, even though she'd honored Bill's request to name him as William's godfather.

She'd spent a good portion of the past year filled with anger. At Matt for taking Bill skydiving. At Bill for going off and dying. At herself for not putting her foot down and refusing to let him go.

Matt looked down and rubbed the back of his neck. After a few seconds, he raised his head enough to meet her gaze. "Aimee, I'm so sorry about your baby. I've talked with Special Agent Schiff. He's agreed to let me help with the investigation—if you'll agree."

Aimee clutched at her abdomen, where the hollow nausea that had been her constant companion ever since Bill died was growing, threatening to cut off her breath.

"How did you get here?" She shook her head. "I mean, it just happened this morning—"

"It doesn't matter. I'm here. Will you let me help?"

Aimee looked at Special Agent Schiff, who nodded at her reassuringly. "I can't believe—I haven't seen you since—"

Matt's gaze faltered. "I know. I'm sorry, Aimee."

Aimee started when Margo laid a hand on her shoulder—a heavy hand. "Aimee, dear, why don't you get a glass of water?"

"Thank you, Margo, but I'm not thirsty." She tried to step away from her mother-in-law's grasp, but Margo held on.

"I'd like to speak to Matthew alone for a moment."

Aimee rubbed her temple, where a headache was gathering. She knew what Margo planned to do. She was going to tell Matt to leave. She could practically see the wheels turning in her mother-in-law's head. A lot of people in Casper knew that Matt had been with Bill when he died, and Margo didn't like the Vicks being the subject of gossip.

Appearances. They'd always been her main concern. The magenta suit she wore attested to that. Only Aimee and the owner of Margo's favorite dress shop knew that her first act upon hearing of her grandson's kidnapping was to have the suit rushed over in time for the press conference.

"Anything you have to say, you can say in front of me, Margo." Aimee stiffened her back and met her mother-in-law's gaze.

"If you're sure, dear." Margo turned to Matt. "Aimee is terribly distraught. I'd rather she not be upset further. Perhaps you should leave."

Matt raised his brows and gazed at Margo steadily. "I have every right to be here. William Matthew is my godson."

A godson he'd never seen, Aimee thought. To make matters worse, Margo had spent the year since Bill's death trying to coax Aimee to relinquish control of William's future to her.

I have the resources and the connections, dear. You don't.

Grief and fear and anger balled up inside Aimee, until she felt as if she were going to explode. She had to bite her tongue to keep from lashing out at both of them.

Aimee had loved Bill, but the six years of their marriage had been a tug-of-war between him and his mother. Now she was in the same position, standing between Margo and Matt.

"William is my child," she blurted out. "This is my decision."

Every eye in the room turned their way.

"Aimee," Margo said warningly as her fingers tightened on Aimee's shoulder. "Don't make a scene."

Aimee wasn't sure how she felt about Matt showing up after a year—almost to the day—since Bill's death, but she didn't doubt his ability. As a weather expert and survival specialist, rescuing the innocent was his specialty.

If anyone could save her child, Matt could.

"If Special Agent Schiff agrees, I want Matt here. It makes sense for him to be involved. He's trained in rescue and recov—" Aimee's throat closed on the word *recovery*.

"Rescue," she said as firmly as she could. *No crying.* She hadn't cried yet, and she didn't plan to start now. Crying never helped anything. She was afraid that if she started she wouldn't be able to stop.

Margo's dark eyes snapped with irritation as she drew in a sharp breath. Then, with a quick glance around the room, she consciously relaxed her face and nodded.

"Of course," she said stiffly. "I didn't mean to imply otherwise." Her grip on Aimee's shoulder loosened and turned into an awkward pat.

The shrill ring of a cell phone split the air. Aimee jumped.

It was him. The kidnapper.

She whirled, looking for her purse, and then remembered that the FBI had forwarded her cell to Margo's house phone. At that instant, the landline rang.

Special Agent Schiff motioned her over to the table, where wires and headphones and computers appeared to be piled haphazardly.

"Mrs. Vick—" Schiff said in a cautionary tone. "Remember what we discussed?"

She was going to have to talk to the man who'd taken her baby. Her stomach turned upside down. As she approached, a computer technician handed two sets of headphones to Schiff. Schiff, in turn, reached past her to hand a set to Matt. Then he donned the remaining set himself.

"Wait to see what he says," Schiff cautioned her. "Once he starts talking ransom, you insist it be delivered by a family friend—Parker. Don't let him bully you. Don't give in to any demands. *You* are in control, not him. Got it?"

Aimee had never felt less in control in her life. Her baby was in the hands of the monster on the other end of the phone, and she was being forced to bargain for his life. The phone rang again, the piercing noise sending terror slicing through her.

"On my count," Schiff whispered. "Pick up on three."

She nodded jerkily. Her throat was too dry to swallow. Her hands were shaking so much she wasn't sure she could hold on to the phone.

Schiff nodded at the computer tech, glanced at Matt, then held up a finger. "One," he mouthed to her.

A second finger went up. "Two."

Aimee bit her lip and reached for the phone. Matt stepped closer.

Schiff held up three fingers. "Three." He nodded.

She picked up the phone, her other hand pressed to her chest. "Hello?" she croaked.

"Hello, Aimee. Hello, Special Agent Schiff, and whoever else is listening."

Aimee stiffened at the kidnapper's menacing tone.

At the same time, Matt's shoulder brushed hers. Coiled tension radiated from his body like heat. He rested a hand lightly on the small of her back. Somehow, his touch gave her courage.

"What have you done with my baby?" she cried. "I have to know if he's okay."

"Your baby is perfectly safe for now," the harsh voice said. "It's up to you to keep him safe. Let's talk business."

"What do you want?" she asked tightly.

"Money, of course," the man replied. "Are you listening, Schiff? Because I will only say this once. I want a million dollars in hundreds. Don't give me any problem about the money. I am aware of who your mother-in-law is." The man's voice was cold and hard. "I don't want to hear excuses about needing time to get the cash together. Just do it."

Aimee felt helpless and lost. She could hardly make sense of what he was saying. She took a deep breath. "Let me talk to my baby," she begged. "He must be so scared. He needs to hear my voice."

"Shut up. You're not giving the orders. I am. Now here's where the exchange will take place."

He rattled off some numbers that meant nothing to Aimee. Out of the corner of her eye, she saw Matt nod at Schiff.

"Got it?" the man snapped.

Schiff sent her a nod.

"Y-yes," she said.

"Tomorrow at 1500 hours. Aimee, if you want to see your baby again, *you* will deliver the money."

Matt jerked. He shook his head fiercely at Schiff.

"I—I don't know," she stammered, her heart stuck in her throat.

"Family friend," Schiff mouthed.

"Wait. I can't come alone," she said as strongly as she could. "I—I'll need to care for William Matthew. I need to bring a—a family friend—"

"Schiff?" the kidnapper said. "What did I tell you? I will not say it again. Make it happen."

The line went dead.

"Dammit," Matt spat.

Aimee's throat closed and her eyes stung with tears. She swallowed them as the phone dropped from her numb fingers. "What is it? What's wrong?" she asked.

Schiff didn't answer her. "Give me those coordinates," he told the computer tech, who repeated the numbers.

"You said you're an expert in weather and survival," Schiff said to Matt. "Know where that is?"

"That latitude and longitude puts it north of Sundance," Matt muttered. He pulled a small device out of his pocket and pressed buttons. "It's about halfway up Ragged Top Mountain. Rough terrain. Plus we've got a late-winter storm building. Could dump a foot or more of snow before it's done."

He turned toward Margo. "Isn't Ragged Top where your husband's hunting cabin was? I think Bill and I went up there a few times."

Margo nodded stiffly. "That's right. No one's been there in years. I don't understand. What did the kidnapper say?"

"He's demanding that we bring the money to a location on the south side of Ragged Top."

"South—? That's—" Margo stopped, frowning. "Oh, dear." Her face drained of color.

It was only the second time Aimee had ever seen Margo shaken. The first was when she was told her son had died. Maybe her mother-in-law wasn't as cold and insensitive as she'd always appeared.

"What?" Matt demanded. "It's what?"

The woman blinked. "Nothing. It's just—it's so hard to get up there. Especially this time of year. I'd have thought—I mean how's he going to keep William safe up there?"

"I'll tell you how," Matt said. "He knows the area. I'd bet money on it, judging by the way he rattled off those coordinates. He knows Aimee can't go by herself."

Schiff raised his eyebrows. "What about you? Can you do it?"

Matt's jaw clenched in determination. "Yeah. I can do it. I've pulled innocents out of more remote locations than that. But this storm's coming in fast. By 1500 hours tomorrow, it'll be right on top of that peak."

Schiff frowned. "The weather service said it would be moving into this area late tomorrow night."

"Yeah, that's what they're saying." Matt set his jaw. "I'm going in alone."

Aimee stiffened. She knew he could do it. That wasn't the problem. He was a search-and-rescue specialist, trained in the Air Force. There was no one better suited to the job.

But the kidnapper had been very specific.

"Don't even think about leaving me behind, Matt," she said. "William Matthew is my baby. He needs me. When you hand over the money, *I* will be there to take him in my arms."

CHAPTER TWO

THURSDAY 1600 HOURS

AFTER COORDINATING TIMES and plans with Special Agent Schiff, Matt drove straight back to Castle Ranch. He needed to talk to Deke.

At thirty, Deke Cunningham was one of the most decorated Air Force combat rescue officers alive. His skill with a rifle was legendary. The only thing he did better than shoot was fly a helicopter.

Which was exactly why Matt wanted him on alert for the ransom exchange.

When he got to the hangar, Deke wasn't there. But at the door to his office, Matt saw something he hadn't noticed before.

The plaque hanging beside Deke's office door. It had hung in Rook Castle's office since the day he'd created Black Hills Search and Rescue, Incorporated. It was small and plain, with a simple message.

IN MEMORIAM
Vietnam Veteran and Combat Rescue Officer
Arlis Hanks, 1944–1990. Our pledge—to honor
your bravery by rescuing the innocent.

Matt touched the four signatures that were emblazoned into the bronze. Robert Kenneth Castle,

Deke Cunningham, Matthew Parker and William Barker Vick.

Irina must have given it to Deke. Matt nodded to himself. It was fitting.

He found Deke in Irina's office, sitting with her, Specialist Rafiq Jackson and Aaron Gold near a bank of windows that framed a view of the desolate, magnificent Black Hills. He nodded at Rafe and Aaron, and acknowledged Deke with a brief glance.

Irina smiled and stood to give him a hug. Rook Castle's widow was as vibrant and lovely as ever. Her blond hair glowed in the sunlight that streamed in the window. But behind her smile and the sparkle in her blue eyes, Matt saw a shadow of grief.

He couldn't imagine how difficult it had been for her to give up searching for her husband. She'd seen him shot, and watched him fall into the Mediterranean Sea. Even so, she'd clung to the hope that because his body had never been recovered, he might be alive.

Now, she'd given up. For everyone who knew her, and who'd supported her efforts to find him, that made it official. Rook Castle was dead.

"Irina," Matt said. "When you called me the other day, I didn't get a chance to say—"

She held up a hand. "I know. Thank you, Matt." A small, sad smile lit her face. "It's been more than two years. It's time I stopped living in a fantasy world. What's important now is rescuing Aimee's baby. All my resources are available to you."

He studied her face, wondering if Deke had told her about his theory that Novus was behind the kidnapping. He decided not to mention it. "I wanted to see if Deke could help me out."

"Of course. You two talk here. I need to check with Pam about my schedule. Rafe, Aaron, walk out with me."

After Irina left, Matt sat and propped his elbows on the table. He intertwined his fingers. "What's up with Rafiq? Did you talk to him about Novus?"

"He's listening in on activity around the Afghan/Pakistan/China borders. Chatter's way up in the region since Irina stopped searching." Deke rubbed his face. "Nothing concrete, mostly speculation."

"I'm glad we've got Rafe. It's good to have someone who speaks the language. Has he heard anything about what Novus is up to?"

"Well, you made big news when you left. Sounds like you're right. The chatter supports the theory that you left because you found Rook."

"Hmph. So much for my fifteen minutes of fame. I wish the chatter were right."

Deke didn't respond.

"What about you?" Matt asked him. "Are you on a case right now?" he asked.

"Nope. No case. Just hanging. I'd love to be out kicking butt somewhere, but I feel like I need to be here. You know?"

"Irina looks pretty good. How's she holding up?"

Deke shook his head. "It took a lot out of her to make the decision to stop looking for Rook. All this time she's lived with the image of him being shot, then disappearing into the Mediterranean. It was awful—" Deke's voice cracked. "I mean, it had to have been."

Matt didn't have to imagine. He had his own nightmares. His dreams were haunted by the sight of Bill Vick spinning helplessly as he plummeted to earth, trailed by the parachute that failed to open.

"What about Aimee?" Deke continued.

"Not good. And I'm afraid I made it worse, showing up like that." Matt stared at his clasped hands. "With her about to break, and the kidnapper's demands, I've got a real situation brewing. Can you be on alert for the ransom drop?"

"Yeah, sure. When is it? Soon, I hope. There's a doozie of a winter storm heading this way, and my bird's not fond of snow."

"I know. I've been tracking the front. I think it's going to blow in earlier than they're predicting."

"You should know. I still say you should hire yourself out to the local TV station as a weatherman." It was an old joke.

"Hair gel and a blue screen? I'll do that the day you become a rodeo sharpshooter." Matt couldn't help but smile. Then he got back to business. "The ransom drop is scheduled for 1500 hours tomorrow. Here are the coordinates the kidnapper gave us." Matt handed Deke a scrap of paper.

Deke snagged it and stepped over to an area map hanging on the wall. He tapped the point with his finger. "It's pretty high up, and isolated."

"Yeah. I'm going to take one of our Hummers. There's a maintenance road up the south side. It'll take at least two hours to get up there."

"I see it. But if you're right about the storm… Why don't I fly you up in the bird? It'd be a lot quicker."

"Because there's a complication. The kidnapper demanded that Aimee make the drop herself."

"The Hummer holds two passengers and it's heated. Coming back, we may have a baby."

Deke's brows shot up. "May? You don't think your kidnapper is going to turn over the kid?"

"That location gives me a bad feeling. How's he going to handle a seven-month-old, and make sure nobody gets the drop on him?"

"He'd have to have an accomplice."

"Right. That plus the storm—I don't like the odds. That's why I need you to be available. I want primary and secondary rendezvous points in case something happens and we can't use the Hummer to get out. Maybe even a tertiary." Matt paused and rubbed his neck. "The location he's picked is going to receive the brunt of that storm. He's got to know that. I have a feeling he's banking on it to cover his tracks."

"I'll have the bird ready to go."

"If you don't hear from me, head for the first rendezvous point. Be there by 0800. Here are the times and places I've got mapped out."

"Friday 0800 hours? That's sixteen hours. You're planning to ride out the storm up there? You could be blown right off that mountain."

"Thanks for that image. No. I *plan* to be back down the mountain in the Hummer with Aimee and the baby, safe and sound. The 0800 rendezvous is if we get caught by the storm or something goes wrong. If everything goes as planned, I'll call you. It'll probably be after dark."

"Just make sure you've got plenty of flares."

"Don't worry. We'll have flares. Do these times work for you?"

"Times are fine. And I see you're planning to move up toward the peak, rather than down."

"Right. I figure if we can't ride back down in the Hummer, we need to be heading to higher ground. The storm's coming in from the west. I'd like to try to stay either ahead of it or above it. Plus, your bird's not going to like dodging trees, so the fewer the better."

Deke nodded.

They quickly agreed on two alternate times and places, the second twenty-four hours after the first.

Plus a third, twenty-four hours after that, in case the storm stalled.

"One last thing," Matt said. "Take these coordinates. This is a last-resort location. It's an hour's walk south from the Vicks' cabin."

"The hunting cabin. I forgot about that place. You think you might end up there?"

Matt shrugged. "It's good shelter. We might need it, if we have to travel that far."

Deke stuck the piece of paper in his pocket. "No problem. I'll hang on to these."

"Thanks, man. I knew I could count on you." Matt stood.

"You know there's another way to handle this."

"Not really."

"Sure there is. Leave Aimee out of it. You and I go up in the Hummer, get the drop on the kidnapper and get the baby back safe and sound."

Matt sighed. "That would work—if one of us could pass for a medium-height, slender female. But there's another consideration. The baby. If everything goes well, which one of us is prepared to bring back a seven-month-old who needs his mother?"

He opened the door. "Have you ever been between a mother and her child? I'm not telling Aimee she has to stay behind."

Now Cunningham was involved.

He knew them all so well. Of course Cunningham would drop everything to help Parker. They were "brothers," after all.

It tended to get annoying, listening to the stories of their childhood friendship, and their oath to save innocents just as that broken-down Vietnam veteran had saved theirs.

He hadn't had time to sabotage Parker's equipment or vehicle. He'd had to trust Kinnard to handle that part of the plan.

His job was to make sure that when Parker needed help, it wasn't available. There were two ways he could handle that, but only one was a sure thing.

All he needed were some tools and a little private time.

FRIDAY 1430 HOURS

AIMEE BURIED HER NOSE more deeply into the high collar of her down parka. She'd rolled her balaclava up like a watch cap, ready to pull down over her face if she needed it. The vehicle was heated, but she was still cold.

The chill didn't come from the dropping temperatures outside, though. It came from her heart. As often as she told herself that William was safe, that the kidnapper couldn't afford to hurt him if he wanted his money, her heart remained unconvinced.

Matt's grim expression didn't help. He looked worried as he maneuvered the Hummer's steel snow tracks over the rough terrain. He glanced at her. "You okay?"

"Okay?" she croaked, then pressed her lips together. *Control,* she reminded herself. *It's all about control.* She had to hold herself together, for her baby's sake.

"If you're cold, there's a blanket under your seat."

She gave a harsh little laugh. "You think I'm worried about being *cold?*"

"Aimee, I know you're afraid something's going to happen to William. But I don't want you to neglect your own health. You're highly stressed and exhausted. You could become hypothermic without even realizing it. I need to make sure you're warm and comfortable."

"Well, don't. I don't need to be comfortable—I don't want to be. I just want to get up there, get my baby back and get home."

"That's what I want, too," Matt said.

She closed her burning eyes. *Control. Control.* She repeated it like a mantra.

"Dammit!"

She jumped and her eyes flew open.

"Sorry." His fingers tightened around the steering wheel. "I can't believe I let the kidnapper run the show. I should have jumped in and forced him to do it my way. It's dangerous for you up here."

"Where should I be? Back at home, all safe and warm? Waiting? No, thank you."

"Yes. Back at home, all safe and warm. I don't like putting you in danger. Plus, with you here, I can't do everything I'd be able to do if I were alone."

"Sorry I'm cramping your style."

"That's not—" He stopped and his jaw muscle worked. He kept his attention on the barely discernable path before them as the incline grew steeper, and the sky turned increasingly dark and gray.

Where they'd started out, near Sundance, spring was in the air, with new shoots of grass and fresh coverings of moss. As they'd climbed higher, the greenery turned brown, and patches of old snow dotted the ground.

Aimee hunched her shoulders in an effort not to shiver. Matt's hands were white-knuckled on the steering wheel. His face was expressionless, but his jaw was clamped tight. He looked the way he had the last time she'd seen him. The day he'd brought her husband's body home.

That memory spawned others. Like the argument she and Bill had a few days before that fateful day.

"It's just a weekend, Aimee. A guy trip. You're starting to sound a lot like my mother."

Aimee had yelled back at him. "Well, for once I agree with Margo. You have responsibilities here. Have you forgotten that I'm pregnant? That you're fighting cancer? Why would you want to waste even a weekend? You need to use your energy to get well. I need you to stay with me."

At that point Bill had gathered her into his arms and kissed her. "I'll be with Matt. He's safe as houses. Safer. He never takes unnecessary chances."

Then he'd looked down at her and a tender solemnity had come over his face. "Don't ever forget, Aimee. I trust Matt as much as I trust myself. More, maybe. No matter what happens, you can count on him. Ask him anything. He'll do it."

Those last words had been prophetic. Bill had asked Matt for something. Matt had obliged. And Bill had died.

The doctors had said it could have been months before the lymphoma took Bill. Long enough for him to know his child. But he'd stolen those last months from her and his son. And Matt had helped.

Then, when Aimee could have used a friend, Matt had disappeared for a year.

Bill had been wrong. She couldn't count on Matt.

"Aimee, tell me how it happened."

She started. "What? How it—?"

"The kidnapping."

"Didn't Special Agent Schiff tell you?"

He nodded. "But I'd like to hear what you remember."

Aimee closed her eyes and folded her arms. "I've been over it in my head a hundred times. I should have heard him. I should have woken up." She shook her head. "How could I have slept while someone came into my house and stole my baby?"

"William wasn't in your room, was he?"

"No. My doctor said that wasn't a good idea, for either of us. I shouldn't have listened to her. I should have kept him right beside me."

"Aimee." He put a hand on her knee. "Stop beating yourself up. You didn't do anything wrong."

His hand was warm. She could feel it even through her wool slacks and silk long underwear. She looked down.

He jerked away and gripped the steering wheel. "When did you realize he was gone?"

She was still looking at his hand. It was big and solid, with long, blunt-tipped fingers. "The sun was in my eyes, and I knew I'd overslept. William always wakes me up around five-thirty or so. He's such a sweet baby." She smiled. "He wakes up happy. I'll hear him through the monitor, cooing and laughing—" Her voice broke and her throat closed up.

He shot her a glance. "The sun woke you?" he asked gently.

"It was almost six-thirty. When I realized I hadn't heard him, I panicked. So many things can happen—"

"What did you do?"

"As soon as I realized I'd slept late, I grabbed the monitor. The camera points right at the head of the baby bed. But I couldn't see him. His bed looked empty." She took a shaky breath. "I ran across the hall. His bedroom door was open and I knew I'd left it closed. He wasn't there. He wasn't anywhere."

She felt the panic rising in her chest, heard it in her voice. Just like then. Had it only been yesterday morning?

"So I called 9-1-1."

"Schiff said there was no sign of forced entry. You're sure it was a stranger?"

Aimee frowned at Matt. "What do you mean?"

He spread his hands in a shrug without taking them off the wheel. "I just mean, is there anything specific you're thinking of when you say it was a stranger?"

She shook her head. "I just can't—it can't be anyone I know."

"Are you usually a sound sleeper?"

"No. Actually, I've been having trouble." Aimee thought about the past seven months since William Matthew's birth. All the nights she'd lain awake, worrying that something would happen to him if she went to sleep.

Dear heavens, something had.

"What about the evening before?" Matt drove steadily, watching the road and glancing occasionally into the rearview mirror. "Did you drink anything? Take anything to help you sleep?"

"No," she answered indignantly. "I would never take a chance like that with William. I gave him his bath and played with him a while, and then made myself some herbal tea and went to sleep."

Matt nodded and drove in silence for a few minutes.

Thoughts and images chased each other helter-skelter through her brain. What had she done? What had been different about that night?

"I didn't do anything differently," she said finally. "My life revolves around his, and his routine is pretty well set. I locked up the house and turned out the lights around nine, just the way I always do. I bathed him at the same time as I do every night. We played the same games we always play, then I put him to bed and went downstairs to the kitchen."

"So anyone who'd been watching the house could know almost to the minute what time you go to bed?"

Aimee nodded miserably. "Yes. My life is that ordinary. I make the same tea, use the same cup. Probably even the same spoon. I can't think of anything unusual—" She stopped. There had been one thing different.

"What is it?"

"It's—it's nothing. It *has* to be nothing." She was really twisted—or really desperate—to even be thinking what she was thinking.

"Tell me."

"This is awful. I can't believe I'm even saying it." She took a deep breath, preparing herself for Matt's ridicule. "The tea? It's a new blend. Margo bought it for me at the health food store. They told her it was good for insomnia."

Matt glanced at her, frowning.

"But, Matt, I've been drinking it every night for almost a week now."

"Is it helping you sleep?"

"Yes," she said. She hadn't really thought about it, but she *had* slept better this past week than she had in a long time. "It is. You don't think—?" Her breath hitched. "No. That's ridiculous. Margo wouldn't— Not her own—her only grandchild—" She stopped, horrified at her thoughts. During the first moments after she'd realized William was missing, she'd briefly considered that Margo might have planned it, but she'd dismissed it as impossible. She was his *grandmother*.

Matt glanced at her.

"No. She couldn't do that—could she?"

"You tell me."

"But it's outrageous. Not even Margo— I mean, yes, she's been complaining about how hard it is for her to get anything done through the Vick Corporation board since Bill died."

"What's that got to do with anything?"

"Bill left everything to William, just like his dad left everything to him. Remember when Boss Vick died?"

"Sure, that summer after we graduated from high school."

"Right. Bill was all set to go to MIT. He wanted to get his degree in aerospace engineering, then go into the Air Force, like you and Deke and Rook."

"Yeah. After his dad died, he changed his mind, and decided to go to the University of Wyoming."

"Right. To stay close to home. Margo convinced him that he had to run the business. Because when he turned twenty-one, the entire Vick Hotel fortune—and responsibility—fell into his lap."

"Bill controlled everything—"

Aimee nodded. "And Margo controlled Bill," she said bitterly.

"And now?"

"Now that Bill's dead, William stands to inherit all of it."

Matt looked at her questioningly. "What about until he's twenty-one? Who did Bill name as William's trustee?"

"Me," Aimee breathed.

"So you're the one who votes the controlling interest. That must rankle Mrs. Vick."

"I go to the board meetings, but I've never opposed a single decision. Why would I?"

"But you could."

Aimee shrugged. "I suppose. You think she did it, don't you?"

Matt glanced in the rearview mirror. "Think about it. What does she want? What does kidnapping her own grandson right from under his mother's nose accomplish?"

"Frightening me?" Aimee cast about for any possible explanation. "Making it look like I can't—"

"Like you can't take care of your own child. What would she gain if she had custody of William? She'd retain controlling interest in the corporation. But it's damn hard to get custody away from the mother. She'd have to prove that you're unfit. That you couldn't protect your own child in your own home."

She moaned under her breath. Hearing those words in Matt's carefully neutral voice made them sound true.

"Sorry," he muttered. "But it would explain a lot."

Aimee's face felt numb. Her *mind* felt numb. Intellectually, she understood Matt's reasoning. If he were right, her mother-in-law was setting her up to take William away from her.

His words echoed in her brain, taunting her with their truth.

You couldn't protect your own child in your own home.

CHAPTER THREE

AIMEE WAS STILL REELING, still trying to process the idea that Margo could have kidnapped her baby, when she realized that Matt's demeanor had changed.

Nothing outwardly was different. His hands still held the steering wheel in a tight grip at ten and two. His expression was carefully neutral, if a bit tight.

But tension suddenly crackled in the air, and it definitely came from him.

He'd gone on alert.

"Matt, what's wrong?" she asked.

"Wrong?" He glanced in the rearview mirror.

"Don't act like you don't know what I'm talking about. Something's wrong. I can tell. Did you see something?"

He didn't reply.

His sudden transformation fascinated and frightened her. Yesterday, he'd been the consummate soldier on a mission. This morning he'd acted more like a protector. She was his charge, his responsibility.

But now in the blink of an eye, he'd morphed from protector back to predator. He was a hunter, and he'd scented his prey.

She opened her mouth to ask him again when, without warning, he veered off the stark mountain road and stopped.

"What are you doing?" Fear raced through her.

"I'll be right back," he said. "If you hear or see anything while I'm gone, lie flat across the seat. The metal should protect you."

"Protect me? Matt—?"

"Do you understand?" He glared at her, his tone and the grim set of his face brooking no argument.

"Yes," she retorted.

He walked over to the edge of the graded area and stopped at the line of trees. For a couple of seconds, he surveyed the mountain road in both directions, then reached for his fly.

Aimee gaped. Was he—? He was! On the way to exchange a million dollars for her baby, he'd stopped to take a leak! She didn't know whether to scream or laugh. Was he so confident? Or so arrogant?

She reached for the door handle, prepared to jump out and yell at him for wasting time while her child was in the hands of kidnappers. At that instant he turned his head imperceptibly to his right, back the way they'd come. And she got it—his sudden transformation. His razor-sharp alertness. Her impression that she was watching a predator.

He'd detected a threat.

Her heart jumped into her throat and she twisted in her seat, looking behind them. But she didn't see anything. Of course, she wouldn't. Matt was ex-Air Force Special Forces. His skills and senses were sharper than an ordinary person's.

She watched as he took a step closer to the trees. The sight was awesome and frightening. The curve of his back and the set of his shoulders made her think of a leopard about to spring. Standing still, he might look like a regular guy, but when he moved—*oh my.*

Absently, it occurred to her that, although she'd

known Matt as long as she'd known her husband, Bill, she had almost no knowledge of his personal life or his background. He might as well be a stranger.

She hunched her shoulders, feeling fragile and human and exposed.

All at once the very air around her went still. Only the occasional snap of a twig or the rustle of bare branches in the wind broke the silence.

The nape of her neck prickled. Her pulse pounded in her ears. She didn't move, not even turning her head to glance at the spot where Matt had disappeared into the trees.

She wasn't sure how long she'd sat there, not daring to move, like a rabbit sensing a threat, when she heard it. *The crunch of twigs and rocks.*

Someone was coming toward the Hummer from the opposite direction.

Without hesitation, she threw herself down across the seats, avoiding the stick shift.

It was Matt—it had to be. *Didn't it?*

She squeezed her eyes shut as the footsteps came closer. Her fingers twitched. If only she had something she could use as a weapon.

Then the driver's-side door opened.

Panic exploded in her chest and she curled her fingers into claws. Fingernails were better than nothing.

"Aimee." Matt touched her shoulder. "Good job."

Relief washed over her. Her scalp tingled. She sat up and tried to hide her trembling nerves. "You sneaked up on me," she accused.

He slid into the driver's seat. "Sorry I scared you. I wanted to circle around, make sure we weren't being watched."

"I knew you saw someone. Why couldn't you have

just told me? I'd have been a lot less scared." She blew out a breath between pursed lips. "Who was it? The kidnapper?"

He shook his head and started the engine. "Can't be sure," he said shortly.

He was lying. But she'd already figured out that he would tell her just what she needed to know, and then only when she needed to know it—in *his* opinion.

Once she had William in her arms and they were safe back at home, she'd let him know what she thought about his gestapo tactics. For now, as much as she hated to admit it, his air of command, his complete confidence, and even his predatory edge, made her feel safe.

And feeling safe was dangerous.

Safety was what she longed for. But she'd learned as a child that trusting someone else to keep her safe was a fantasy. As the only child of older parents, she'd grown up with the weight of their health and safety on her shoulders.

When she'd married Bill, he'd promised to keep her safe, but he'd never been able to stand up to his mother. Then he'd promised her she could count on Matt, but he'd trusted Matt with his life, and Matt had let him die.

No. There was only one person she could count on. Herself. She had to stay strong, stay in control. In the year since Bill's death, maintaining control was the only thing that had kept her going.

Now, at the very time when it was more important than ever to hold on to that control for her baby's sake, she was tempted to relinquish it to someone else—to Matt—and the urge scared her to death.

She lifted her chin. She was *not* going to depend on Matt. Her baby trusted her to save him.

She would.

After another fifteen minutes or so of navigating the winding mountain road, Matt pulled over again.

"What is it?" Aimee looked in the passenger-side mirror. "Did you see something again?"

He shook his head. "We're five miles from the meeting point." He pointed to the GPS locator on the dashboard. "And twenty minutes from the meeting time. So this is where I get out. I'll circle around, while you drive the rest of the way alone. You've got the case of money. You've got the baby seat, formula, diapers and blankets. The GPS locator is programmed for the exact coordinates. It's a straight shot. Just stay on this road."

He pulled a folded sheet of paper from a pocket. "Here's a printout of the route in case something happens to the GPS. You just stay on this road. Now, let's go over everything one more time."

Aimee nodded shakily. "Please. I feel like I'm in some weird dream—like all of this is a nightmare and I'm going to wake up tomorrow morning holding William."

"With any luck, that's exactly what'll happen."

His words were kind, his voice gentle. Aimee had to clench her jaw to keep from crying. Time stretched out before her like an endless road. It would be hours before she'd be back home with William, safe and sound. Many hours and many opportunities for something to go wrong.

"Hey, Aimee," Matt said. He lifted a hand toward her cheek, then checked the movement. "It's going to be okay."

She lifted her chin. "Don't do that. Don't spout meaningless promises to me. I need to know what I'm up against. What if the kidnapper doesn't bring William? What if my baby's cold, or hungry—?" She bit her cheek. *Control,* she reminded herself.

"Whoa. You can't worry about any of that. And remember, being scared is normal. You're very brave."

"Oh, yeah. I'm the bravest woman on the planet, driving up this remote mountain to rescue my baby from a kidnapper." Tears stung her eyes and a lump lodged in her throat.

She was so *not* brave.

"Matt. I'm so scared." She touched his sleeve, and then squeezed the material in her fist.

A tender look softened his sculpted features. "Listen to me. You *are* the bravest woman on the planet. And—" He paused for a second. "Bill was the luckiest man in the universe. Aimee, I—"

"Don't—" She stiffened and held up her hands. "Please. Don't start. I have to think about William. I can't afford to get all emotional about what happened to Bill."

Matt's expression closed down. He nodded. "Yeah. Best to hate me for one thing at a time," he said flatly.

She caught what appeared to be sadness in his dark eyes before he averted his gaze. His words and the look surprised her. It wasn't like Matt to feel sorry for himself.

He shrugged it off and climbed out of the Hummer, pulling a daypack out with him. Then he leaned his forearms on the driver's-side door. "I put on the emergency brake. Don't forget to release it before you head out."

"I've ridden ATVs in these hills all my life. I can handle this Hummer."

He nodded matter-of-factly. "I've got my route planned out. Going straight up, it'll take me about fifteen to twenty minutes to reach the rendezvous point. If you drive no faster than fifteen miles per hour, we should arrive at about the same time, since this maintenance road snakes back and forth, and the terrain is getting rougher. Just stay on it. Don't get lost."

"I'll be fine."

"Aimee, I can't stress too strongly how dangerous this man could be. If anything—*anything*—goes wrong, you have to turn the Hummer around and head down the mountain as fast as you can. With or without William. Understand?"

"No. I don't understand. There's no way I'm going anywhere without my baby."

"Listen to me. I *have* to know that you'll do as I say. I promise you, you won't have to deal with him. I'm going to ambush him. I don't expect anything to go wrong, but if something does, I have to know you'll follow my orders. Do what I say. I can't do my job—I can't rescue William—if I have to worry about you. Your baby will be safe. I swear."

Aimee frowned, studying his face. There was something else—something he wasn't telling her. He wouldn't meet her gaze. Instead, he stared down at his clasped hands.

Suddenly she understood. "You don't think he's bringing William, do you?"

His head ducked lower for an instant. Then he straightened.

"Do you?" Aimee grabbed his hand before he could remove it from the car door. She held on until he bent down again. His dark eyes finally met hers—solemn, guarded.

"Oh—" Her heart cracked wide open and all her careful efforts at control spilled out. She shook her head slowly, back and forth, back and forth. "No, please, Matt. Tell me my baby's okay."

He reached out and brushed a strand of hair from her

cheek. "Aimee, I swear to God, if I have to die to make it happen, William will be back in your arms today, safe and sound."

THE MAN WAS lighter on his feet than Matt had expected, given his size and the bulky daypack strapped to his back. His clothes and pack were a winter camouflage pattern that blended perfectly into the patchy snow and barren trees as he moved.

And he moved well, silently as a woodland animal, alert to everything around him. An assault rifle—military grade—was hooked over one shoulder.

Matt could tell he was ex-military. Maybe even ex-Special Forces. That explained this location, the timing and the man's obvious comfort in his surroundings. Not many people knew how to glide silently through rough terrain, leaving almost no trail.

Matt would bet money that he was also a survivalist. He had to have trekked every inch of this mountain, or he wouldn't have chosen it.

But was he here alone?

Matt had no doubt that he'd seen sunlight glinting off metal in the Hummer's rearview mirror as the vehicle had snaked back and forth up the maintenance road. That was why he'd stopped, to try and catch a glimpse of whoever was tailing them. But he hadn't spotted anything.

Whoever was back there was good. Probably as good as the man in front of him. Impressively close to having Matt's own skills.

The question in Matt's mind was—were there two guys following him? This man could have followed them up the road and then cut through just as Matt had and beaten him to the ransom drop point.

But it was also possible that he had an accomplice, and the accomplice had followed them while this guy waited up here.

Matt couldn't afford to let down his guard, so until he knew otherwise, he assumed the kidnapper had an accomplice.

Matt had to watch his back.

He'd planned out as much of his strategy as he could. He, too, was dressed in winter camo and carried a small daypack. Besides binoculars, he was equipped with a compact MAC-10 machine pistol he didn't plan on using, a mini-tranquilizer gun and a few flexicuffs.

His intent was to surprise the kidnapper and immobilize him with the tranq gun. Once he had him restrained, he could definitely make it worth his while to reveal the baby's location.

He crouched, hidden by scrubby bushes, and observed the kidnapper through his high-powered binoculars. The man was positioning himself for greatest cover and widest angle of sight.

For a couple of seconds, Matt held his breath, listening for the Hummer's engine, but he didn't hear anything. It was nerve-racking, waiting up here, knowing Aimee was about to drive straight into the lion's den. All this would be so much easier if he didn't have to worry about her being hurt.

Matt shifted, examining the area around the kidnapper. He searched for signs of another person—someone whose job it was to take care of the baby. He used a careful mental grid layout he'd developed in the Air Force.

The controlled search made it impossible to miss a person, much less a vehicle, but all Matt saw was a set of tracks made by a one-man snowmobile. He saw no trace of the vehicle itself. The kidnapper had done a damn good job of hiding his vehicle and covering his tracks.

Matt's respect for him went up a notch, and his fear for Aimee's baby went up three. The suspicion that had planted itself in his brain from the first moment he'd seen the TV news, rooted itself more deeply, undermining his confidence.

If this man were simply a kidnapper, out to make a quick million, and if he'd come to make a good-faith exchange, then why didn't he have the baby?

Matt continued his grid search until he'd covered every square inch of visible land surface. He saw nothing that indicated anyone but the kidnapper had been— or was—in the area. He pocketed the binoculars.

Damn. He would hate to be right about this one.

Although the kidnapper seemed to be all about money, and Aimee's revelations about Margo's need to control the Vick Corporation made Margo a prime suspect, Matt didn't believe it.

A silent vibration started near his left knee. His cell phone. Grimacing, he shifted enough to pull it out of the cargo pocket of his camo pants. Keeping one eye on the kidnapper, he glanced at the screen.

It was a text message from Deke. He focused on the letters.

GOT PSNGR LIST OF YR FLIGHT. HAFIZ AL HAMAR, AFGH NATL, ON IT. SEE PHOTO. DC.

It only took a couple of seconds for the photo to come through. Matt cursed silently when he saw it. He'd seen that man before. He'd run into him several times in Mahjidastan.

Still watching the kidnapper, Matt keyed in a quick message back to Deke and, making sure the sound was off on his phone, hit SEND.

RECOG AL HAMAR FR MAHJID. TRACE HIM? MP

A sick certainty burned in the pit of his gut. Novus

Ordo had engineered William's kidnapping to get his hands on Matt, to interrogate him about whether Rook was alive. And that meant he wanted Matt alive. But Matt was sure Novus wouldn't blink at killing anyone who got in his way.

Matt had made a huge mistake by bringing Aimee up here. He should have come alone, or brought Deke or another BHSAR specialist.

If he was right about Novus, and he was becoming more and more sure about that by the hour, she and her baby were disposable pawns in an international terrorist's effort to protect his identity.

The kidnapper was on the move again. Matt pocketed his phone and cleared his mind. He needed focus and hair-trigger response. If he failed to return William Matthew to his mother's arms, he'd have plenty of time for regrets and unbearable sorrow later. His mission was to get the drop on the kidnapper and rescue Aimee's baby. He didn't allow the thought that William wasn't here to enter his head. He had to operate as if he were.

He crouched in a position from which he could spring in a fraction of a second, and let his senses feed him information. They were as clear as the mountain air. The smell of evergreen and the coming snow teased his nostrils. The tingling in his hands and face signaled the dropping temperature.

And the quickly darkening sky telegraphed the approach of the winter storm—early, just as he'd predicted.

The only sound Matt heard was the rustling of bare tree branches and evergreen needles in the rising wind.

The kidnapper raised his head, as if sniffing a scent on the breeze. He appeared calm and relaxed, and yet poised to react with swift reflexes.

Damn, the man was good.

A discordant hum rose in the distance. The Hummer. Aimee was almost here. The kidnapper swung the rifle from his shoulder and settled into a comfortable, balanced stance—observant and attentive—ready for anything.

Matt shifted, feeling the weight of the MAC-10 in its holster. He could get to it if necessary, but he didn't plan on using it. He held the tranq gun and the flexi-cuffs were looped through his belt.

The Hummer's engine grew louder, its steady roar filling the air around them. The engine's noise blocked Matt's keen hearing, but it also covered any noise he might make when he sneaked up on the kidnapper.

After an automatic glance around, Matt crept forward, until he was less than twenty feet behind the man. With his tactical-grade, compression-fit long underwear, he had far greater agility than the bulkily dressed kidnapper. He could rush him, sink a tranq dart in his neck and cuff him within seconds.

The Hummer crested the rise, and Matt's pulse kicked into high gear. He could barely make out Aimee's silhouette through the vehicle's tinted windows. As he watched, she slowed down, then rolled to a stop.

Stay in the vehicle. Make him come to you. He silently recited the instructions he'd given her.

He'd retrofitted a loudspeaker for her to use for any necessary communications. He'd warned her not to exit the vehicle until the kidnapper produced the baby. And, as he'd reminded her not twenty minutes before, at the first sign of trouble, she was to turn the Hummer around and get out of there.

Those were *her* instructions. But Matt had other plans. He had no intention of letting the kidnapper within twenty yards of her.

She inched the Hummer closer. The kidnapper shifted to the balls of his feet, holding the rifle loosely yet competently, like a pro. Another point in his favor and more cause for concern on Matt's part.

Matt made his move. He rose from his crouch and crept around the edge of the clearing, keeping the scrub bushes between him and the other man. Once he got into position, it would take him less than thirty seconds to get behind him, slip out from the trees at the last second, then grab and tranquilize him. In a situation like this, thirty seconds was a hell of a long time.

He'd choreographed every step ahead of time. He'd had plenty of experience with stealth from rescue missions he'd conducted in the Air Force and afterwards while working for Black Hills Search and Rescue. He knew how to approach an enemy and extract an innocent without detection. Given this guy's obvious expertise, he was glad to have the noise of the Hummer's engine as added cover.

He positioned himself directly behind the kidnapper. Staying low, he inched silently forward.

Then without warning, something hit him from behind.

With no more than a fifth of a second wasted on startle response, Matt whirled. He rammed his fist and shoulder into the attacker's body. As his knuckles encountered flesh and bone, he followed through, putting his whole weight behind the blow. But it wasn't enough. His attacker was quicker.

Matt went down—hard.

The man grabbed a handful of his hair and slammed his face into the frozen ground.

The blow dazed him. But the cold pressure of a gun

barrel pressed to the side of his neck brought him back instantaneously. Adrenaline sheared his breath and cleared his brain. He jerked just as a quiet pop echoed in his ear. Something sharp scratched his neck.

A pop. Not a bullet. A tranquilizer dart.

Damn! Even as the thoughts rushed through his brain, he torpedoed his elbow backward. With a breathy grunt, the man fell away and his tranq gun went flying.

Before he hit the ground, Matt whirled and grabbed his collar. With a renewed burst of energy, and using muscles he hadn't used in months, Matt heaved the man's bulk around, between himself and the kidnapper.

Pocketing his own tranquilizer gun, Mat slid the MAC-10 from its holster and buried its barrel into the flesh of his attacker's neck. He was tempted to rip off the man's ski mask, but to do that, he'd have to let go of the man or the gun.

"You nearly got me with your tranq dart, but believe me, this is not a tranq gun," he growled, scanning the area in front of him in case the kidnapper had heard them. "It's the real thing. And it will take your head clean off if you don't tell me who you are."

His answer was a blood-chilling string of curses, some English, some Arabic. Dammit, the kidnapper had to have heard him.

"Are you *Al Hamar?*"

The man's head jerked in surprise.

"So—you are. Did Novus Ordo send you?" Matt whispered, digging the muzzle of the MAC-10 deeper into his flesh.

His prisoner shook his head, but Matt saw the truth in the man's black eyes. "Tell me what you know about the kidnapping—"

The crack of exploding gunpowder hit his ears a fraction of a second before the bullet whistled past his head.

Matt ducked.

Al Hamar used Matt's own elbow trick to knock the wind out of him, then leapfrogged across three or four feet of ground, diving for his own weapon. The kidnapper shot again.

Matt aimed the machine pistol at Al Hamar. But something was wrong. He couldn't clear his vision. He bent his head and squeezed his eyes shut for an instant. Just as he did, a second bullet grazed his ear.

He swallowed a pained cry and his hand flew to his ear. It came away bloody. His bloodstained fingers trembled as he stared at the proof of how close the bullet had come. If he hadn't paused to clear his vision, it would have split his skull.

A high-pitched scream, barely distinguishable above the roar of the Hummer's engine, sent his heart slamming into his chest. It was Aimee. She gunned the engine and the vehicle shot forward, toward the kidnapper.

Aimee, no! What was she doing? *Turn around. Get out of here.*

The kidnapper aimed at the Hummer's windshield.

At the same time, Matt saw Al Hamar whirl around, brandishing a semiautomatic pistol.

Matt ducked down and rubbed his eyes. The scratch on his neck had absorbed some of the tranquilizer. Enough to blur his vision. He cursed silently and gave his head a quick shake.

The kidnapper yelled something that Matt didn't catch, then several bullets thunked into a tree to Matt's left. He was shooting at Al Hamar again.

So, they weren't working together.

Al Hamar yelped and toppled forward.

When Matt looked back at the kidnapper, the high-powered gun was aimed at his head. From that distance, the man couldn't miss. But before Matt could react and dive, he swung back toward the Hummer.

Why hadn't he shot him? He might not get as good a chance again.

Rising to a crouch, Matt took a precious split second to make sure his head was as clear as possible, then sprinted toward the Hummer, spraying bullets on the ground in front of the kidnapper. He couldn't kill the man. He needed him alive—at least long enough to find out where William was being held.

As he crouched behind a stand of bushes, he heard the hitch in the engine noise that signaled shifting gears.

Good, Aimee! Now turn around and get out of here!

But a Hummer didn't turn on a dime, or even a quarter. Still, she was trying.

Careful to stay hidden, he lifted his head just in time to see the kidnapper raise his weapon and aim at the Hummer's windshield.

Alarm ripped through him. The kidnapper was about to shoot Aimee. The high-powered blast would be enough to penetrate the tempered glass.

Matt raised his weapon, his breath catching as his finger sought the hair-trigger of the MAC-10.

Aimee would hate him if he shot the man who could lead them to her baby. But if he had to kill the kidnapper to save Aimee, then so be it. He'd find her baby some other way.

CHAPTER FOUR

FRIDAY 1600 HOURS

JUST AS MATT'S finger started to squeeze the trigger, the kidnapper lowered the barrel of his gun to the tires.

Matt's scalp tingled with relief. At least he was no longer aiming at Aimee. Still, he had to stop him from disabling their only means of getting down the mountain. He vaulted to his feet, brandishing the MAC.

"Hey!" he shouted. "You want your money? Then stop now! Or you'll never see it."

He swayed, but immediately caught himself. Blinking away the haze that threatened to obscure his vision, he yelled, "In fact, you'll never see tomorrow!"

He strafed the ground in front of the kidnapper. But the other man didn't take the bait. His rifle barrel didn't even waver. He fired.

A tire exploded with a loud crack.

A second shot. A second crack.

The Hummer rocked dizzily, then tilted to the passenger side. It was going over.

Aimee!

Matt loosed another volley of bullets, closer this time. He still hadn't ruled out killing the man.

The shooter dove for the ground. But in one smooth motion, he righted himself and fired again—this time at the Hummer's gas tank. Metallic thunks peppered the vehicle's frame.

Wincing each time the kidnapper shot, Matt tried to draw a bead on him, but the kidnapper's duck and roll had positioned the Hummer between them.

Matt sprinted toward the vehicle. He had to stop him. It was only a matter of seconds before a bullet hit the gas tank.

Suddenly, the man stopped shooting, slung his rifle over his shoulder and ran toward the disabled vehicle.

He was going after the money.

Matt had to stop him before he got to Aimee. He broke into a run. His legs pumped, his heart raced. The earth and the sky went topsy-turvy and he stumbled, but he recovered his footing and kept going.

The tranquilizer was doing more than turn Matt's world upside down, though. His legs were as heavy as lead weights. It was like a bad dream. As hard as he pushed, he couldn't beat the other man.

The kidnapper vaulted up the vehicle's undercarriage like a free climber and ripped open the driver's-side door.

Reaching in, he grabbed Aimee's parka and yanked her up and out through the door. She struggled, but she was no match for the big man. He shoved her over the side. Then he dove back down and popped out immediately with the briefcase.

By the time Matt rounded the rear of the Hummer, the kidnapper was back on the ground.

Finally, Matt had a clean shot. He stopped and took aim, blinking rapidly. He wanted to disable him without killing him.

But Aimee's crumpled form filled his wavering vision. She was lying near the Hummer. Too near. Her feet were mere inches from the widening puddle of gasoline.

The kidnapper seemed preoccupied with the briefcase, but Matt couldn't count on that. In one stride he'd be close enough to grab her. He could use her as a shield.

Or kill her.

Swallowing against dizziness brought on by the tranq, Matt carefully tightened his finger on the trigger.

Aimee stirred and moaned, distracting him for a split second. When he turned his full attention back to the kidnapper, the man had produced an old-fashioned silver cigarette lighter in his hand. He flipped open the lid.

Matt aimed at his right shoulder, concentrating on keeping the sights of the machine pistol steady.

Aimee sat up. The kidnapper's sharp gaze met Matt's as he stepped backward and sideways, putting her between himself and Matt. He crouched down, making himself too small a target to hit without endangering Aimee.

As Matt watched helplessly, he nodded at him, then struck the lighter and tossed it over Aimee's head and into the middle of the pool of gasoline.

The small flame looped through the air as if in slow motion. When it was a couple of inches above the puddle, the fumes caught and flared. By the time the lighter splashed into the liquid gasoline, the flames were two feet high and spreading.

The kidnapper turned and sprinted away to the east.

Matt couldn't worry about him. The fire was growing, and flames were rising only inches from Aimee's legs.

"Aimee, get back!" he yelled.

She scrambled backward, her eyes wide and bright with terror.

Pocketing his gun, Matt rushed toward her. A shot rang out—but not from the direction in which the kidnapper had run.

It came from the south. *Al Hamar.* Matt dove the last few feet. He landed next to Aimee as red flames licked at her hiking boots.

Scooping his hands under her arms, he lifted her and heaved her as far as he could and then dove on top of her, covering her body with his, shielding her head with his hands.

Behind them, the flames roared and spit like a massive beast. The ground trembled beneath them and a whistling sound filled the air.

The flares! He'd packed a dozen of them into the rear of the Hummer.

"What's that?" Aimee whispered.

"It's okay," he whispered. "You're okay. Just stay still." Matt hunched his shoulders and pressed his cheek against hers, doing his best to shield every inch of her body with his. He could feel her panicked breaths against his cheek, hear them sawing in and out through her throat. He could smell the lemon sweetness of her hair.

She stopped wriggling and turned her head a little more, which put her lips about an inch away from his. He closed his eyes and pretended they weren't there.

He couldn't tell how many of the flares fired because suddenly, with a deafening roar, the gasoline exploded.

For an instant, the air grew totally still and quiet, as the conflagration sucked in oxygen. Then a blast of heat strafed them, like the breath of a fire-breathing dragon.

Matt felt the sting of heat across the backs of his hands and the nape of his neck.

After several seconds, he lifted his head slightly and peeked at the Hummer. It was still engulfed in flames, but they were weakening.

Their supplies and equipment. He stiffened, and felt Aimee move beneath him.

"Matt?"

"Stay still," he commanded. He rose to a crouch with his weapon drawn and rapidly scanned the clearing, but they were alone. The kidnapper and Al Hamar gone.

He turned back to Aimee. "Why didn't you turn the Hummer around and get out of here like I told you to?"

"He shot you!" she hissed. "I saw you go down. I thought you were dead. I had to save my baby."

He held her gaze for a moment, wanting to berate her for endangering her life by not obeying him, but she lifted her chin and stared at him with defiance in her eyes.

It occurred to him that there was probably no emotion in humans stronger than the one radiating from her. The fierceness of the love of a woman for her child.

There was no way he could counter that.

Setting the machine pistol down, he shrugged his daypack off his shoulders.

"What are you doing?" she asked.

Ignoring her, he quickly assessed his clothing. Had he landed in gasoline when he dove for Aimee? He didn't see any stains, and didn't smell gas.

"Don't move," he said, pointing at the ground where she sat. "I'm going to see if I can salvage anything out of the Hummer."

"You can't go near that," Aimee said. "Wait until the fire dies down."

He shook his head. By the time the flames died down there would be nothing left. Hell, there was probably nothing left anyhow.

He approached the burning vehicle cautiously.

Everything inside was black and smoldering, or still burning. By the red-and-yellow flickering light, he saw what was left of the baby seat, melted down to a nearly unrecognizable lump of plastic. Behind it, in the back of the vehicle, he could see the damage caused by the flares that he'd packed to help Deke set his helicopter down in the dark.

Then he spotted his backpack. There was nothing left of his supplies and equipment. The nylon webbing that crisscrossed its lightweight frame had burned and melted.

Matt cursed silently. Everything he'd packed so carefully—planning for any contingency—was burned and useless. His double sleeping bag, the concentrated nutrient packs, rain gear, snowshoes, spare batteries for the GPS locator and phone, first aid kit, even the water canteens, were gone.

He sucked in a deep breath, and coughed as smoke scalded his throat. It was getting thicker and blacker as the flames died.

There was still plenty of heat, which would have come in handy if it weren't almost certainly toxic, judging by the smell. Between the upholstery, the gasoline, oil and other fluids, and the various plastics and dyes, there was no telling how contaminated the air was.

They couldn't stay near that fire.

He headed back to where Aimee was waiting.

She took a breath to speak, and coughed when she got a lungful of smoke. She took his hand and let him help her stand.

She looked over her shoulder. "I need to get my bag. William's baby food and diapers and—"

"They're gone. Burned up. My supplies are, too. We'll have to make do."

"But—"

"Come on. We need to get away from here. That smoke is toxic."

Aimee coughed again, proving his point. She looked up at him and gasped. "Oh! Matt, you're bleeding. It's all over your face and neck."

He touched his ear and winced, then looked at his hand. A fresh smear of blood stained his finger. "Don't worry. I'm okay," he said shortly, as a wave of dizziness reminded him just how handicapped he still was by the tranquilizer.

"Hell, another quarter inch and the bullet would have missed me completely."

Aimee pushed his hand away and stood on tiptoe, looking at the wound. "That's not funny," she snapped.

She touched the curve of his ear, near the raw scrape. "It looks like the bleeding has almost stopped."

He shrugged away her touch. It took concentration to ignore the gentle brush of her fingers.

"Stand behind me." He held the pistol waist high and swept the clearing with it and his gaze.

She grasped his sleeve and pointed toward the east. "He ran into the woods in that direction. We've got to go after him."

Matt twisted away from her grip and put a hand on

her shoulder. "He's long gone. The fire gave him a big head start."

"No! We've got to go. We have to catch up—"

"Aimee. He's twenty minutes ahead of us. It's getting dark. We'll never catch up to him tonight."

She turned and stared at him, the brightness of her green eyes fading as understanding dawned. Her hands covered her mouth. A stray flake of snow caught on her lashes.

"But—he got the money," she cried. "And he's still got William. He doesn't need my baby any longer. What if—"

A giant fist squeezed his heart at the utter desolation on her face—in her voice. He opened his mouth to lie, to feed her false hope. "We'll find him, Aimee. Don't worry—"

"Don't worry? Don't—?" She gulped in a desperate breath. "He's my *baby*. He's so little. He's only seven months old. He will *die* without me."

She doubled her hands into fists. "Don't tell me not to worry!" she screamed.

He steeled himself for her attack, figuring she had a perfect right. He hadn't kept his word. He'd let both men get the best of him. One had sneaked up on him because he'd let his guard down. The other had turned his own equipment into a weapon against him.

But she didn't. She pressed her fists to her eyes. "What do we do now?" she whispered.

Matt gently pulled her hands away from her face. Then he touched her chin. "Aimee. Look at me."

She raised her gaze to his, and he winced at the unbearable sorrow in her eyes.

"The kidnapper doesn't have the money," he said.

Aimee's eyes went round. "What?"

"We put a few thousand dollars in the briefcase, on top. But as soon as he digs down a few layers, all he'll find is scrap paper."

"He doesn't have—?" Aimee's pale cheeks flared with pink. She sent Matt an incredulous smile.

Matt shook his head. "I've got it here, in the day-pack. If he'd given William to you, I'd have given him the pack."

"He doesn't have the money," she said in awe.

Matt nodded. "That's right."

"So he *has* to take care of my baby until he gets it." *If the money is what he's after.*

For an instant he allowed himself to bask in the joy on her face. Then a flake of snow drifted past her cheek, followed by another, and another.

He looked toward the west. The sky was dark with thick, gray clouds. He grimaced and shivered as a fat snowflake slipped down the back of his neck.

Where was his parka? There, on the ground near the woods.

"We'd better get going," he said as he went over to get it. "The storm's heading this way. As soon as it's over I'll call Deke and we'll—" He bent over to pick up the parka, and suddenly the world turned upside down—several times. His knee hit the hard ground with a painful thud.

"Matt?"

He jerked his head up. Her blurry, wavering face filled his vision.

"Matt! What's wrong?"

He held up a hand. With more than a little effort he closed his fist around the down-filled jacket and pushed himself to his feet. "I'm okay. I got a little dose of a tranquilizer dart when the second guy grabbed me. It's almost worn off."

"Tranquilizer dart?" Aimee's smile faded. "I don't understand. Why did the kidnappers need a tranquilizer dart?"

He rubbed his eyes and shook his head.

But she wouldn't let it go. "I don't understand. These men, these kidnappers—why bring all those weapons—" She stopped, her eyes narrowing.

"Why did *you* need a machine gun?"

When he met her gaze, his throat spasmed, and that punishing fist tightened and twisted until his heart wanted to burst. But before he could answer, she lifted her chin.

"Okay. Let me make it easier on you. Just answer this one question for me. The question you never answered yesterday. How did you happen to show up back in Wyoming just in time to be available when William was kidnapped?" she asked.

"What?" Matt answered automatically.

"You. Heard. Me." A muscle ticked in her jaw and her nostrils flared. She took a step toward him, holding his gaze. "I woke up at six-thirty yesterday morning to find that my baby had been abducted from right under my nose. And then before noon you showed up." She pressed her fingertips to her mouth for a second. "You must have been here for days, or—or weeks for all I know."

Matt swallowed. "I flew in Tuesday night."

She nodded shakily. "Not even two days." She looked away, as if composing herself, and then looked at him again. "Why?"

"Why what?"

"Matt, stop it. Why did you fly back here on Tuesday, and my baby was kidnapped on Wednesday? Am I supposed to believe that was a *coincidence?*"

"Aimee, I don't know what you're thinking—" He was lying again. He knew exactly what she was thinking.

What was the connection?

"Answer me."

More snowflakes fell. The storm was almost upon them. By sheer force of will, he stopped himself from examining the sky. Aimee needed as much assurance as he could give her right now—which admittedly wasn't much.

"I came back to Wyoming because Irina called me back. She had to stop looking for Rook."

Aimee's mouth fell open. "Had to stop? Oh, no. I didn't think she would ever give up. She must be devastated."

He nodded. "She is. But she can't do it anymore. She's out of money."

A little frown appeared between her brows. "She called you last week?"

He nodded, wondering what she was thinking. She didn't have the information he and Deke had. She knew nothing about Rook's relationship with Novus Ordo, or the threat he'd posed to the mysterious terrorist as long as he was alive.

"These men—"

"Aimee, I don't know either of them."

She shook her head slowly. "They don't have William, do they? This isn't about my baby at all." Her hands pressed against her chest, as if trying to stop the pain.

"Oh, dear heavens," she gasped. "That other man—he wasn't speaking English."

"I don't know them—" he repeated, but she cut him off with a gesture.

"But you know who they are, don't you?" she snapped. "They have something to do with whatever you've been doing overseas. They followed you back here to Wyoming. Somehow, they knew they could get to you by kidnapping my baby."

"Aimee, don't—"

"They don't care about William. They want you," she whispered. "For all you know, my baby is dead."

CHAPTER FIVE

MATT CAUGHT AIMEE'S shoulders as she swayed. "Listen to me," he said firmly.

She steadied herself by closing her fingers around the sleeves of his sweater.

"William is still alive. I know he is." Dear God, he hoped she believed him. The reticence in his voice was painfully obvious to him.

She looked at him, her eyes filled with doubt and despair. Slowly, a little of the anguish faded from her expression. "Do you really think so?"

He forced his stiff lips to smile. "I know so. I swear, Aimee, I have no idea who these men are, but you saw the way the kidnapper grabbed the briefcase and ran. He couldn't wait to get to the money."

Dear God, he hoped his desperate explanation sounded plausible.

He took a deep breath. "But he's going to find out that we outsmarted him. And now we've seen him. We can identify him. He can't afford to let anything happen to William now."

He did his best not to wince. He wasn't sure if it was the tranquilizer circulating in his blood, or the desperation clouding his brain, but his reasoning had holes so big he could have driven the Hummer through them if it hadn't burned up.

He prayed that Aimee wasn't thinking rationally enough to dispute him. Right now what she needed was reassurance, not raw truth.

And she certainly didn't need to know that he echoed her suspicions. He wasn't sure who either of the men were, but he knew there was more going on than just the kidnapping of a baby for money.

He shook his head, trying to shake off the tranquilizer's effect, and another snowflake slid inside the neck of his sweater.

He looked up at the sky. The clouds were dark, feeding the dropping temperature. Within an hour, the sun would go down, and then the mercury would plummet. They were running out of time.

He had to make a decision. Several, if he could remember what they were. A lungful of icy air helped to clear his head.

He glanced at his watch and then stared at the tangle of briar bushes where he'd last seen the terrorist who'd followed him from Mahjidastan. He had to check on him.

He knew the man was wounded. He'd heard him shriek when the kidnapper's bullet had hit him. But after that the terrorist had fired a shot. Had that been the last brave effort of a dying man? Or a parting shot before he escaped to lick his wound? He had to find out.

Good. He rubbed his temples. At least he finally had come to a decision.

"Aimee, get over here and stay behind me. I need to check the area, in case Al Hamar is wounded or dead, and I don't want to let you out of my sight."

"Al Hamar?" Her eyes widened, then immediately

narrowed. "You know his name? I thought you said you didn't know either of them."

He sighed and spread his hands. "I don't. I got a text message from Deke, telling me—" He stopped. "It's complicated, Aimee. I just need you to trust me."

She shook her head slowly. "Do I have any choice?"

"No," he said grimly. "Have you ever shot a pistol before?"

"No. Rifles, shotguns, bows and arrows. But not a pistol." She sounded like she was about to cry.

"It's okay. This is a Glock." He pulled the small handgun out of his daypack and handed it to her. "It's loaded, and it doesn't have a safety, so it's ready to shoot. You pull the trigger the same way you do a rifle. And you hold it in both hands, like the cops on TV. Okay?"

"I think so."

"Trust me, you probably won't have to use it. But I need to know—can you shoot a man if you have to?"

She lifted her chin. "Will it help me get William back? Then, yes, I can."

"Okay. Stay directly behind me. By now the guy's either dead or long gone. But there's no way I'm leaving the area until I verify that he's not waiting to ambush us."

Aimee met his gaze. "I'm ready."

The determination in her expression told him she meant it. To his surprise, something welled up in his chest until it almost cut off his breath. Her bravery and trust awed and scared him.

"Good," he said roughly. "Let's go."

He held the MAC-10 at waist level, ready to shoot if necessary, as he moved cautiously toward the bushes. A couple of feet away, he held up his hand.

"Wait here. Remember what I told you in the car? Same goes here. If you hear anything—anything at all—hit the dirt. Copy?"

"Yes."

He crouched and crept forward to the edge of the patch. Peering through the tangle of bare briar-studded vines didn't work. They were too thick. He straightened, weapon at the ready, and moved close enough to see over the tops.

The briar bushes covered about four feet of ground. Beyond that he saw new scrapes and crushed twigs and leaves.

Glancing back at Aimee, he drew a circle in the air with his left hand. "I'm circling around," he mouthed, then held up his palm. "You stay there."

She nodded carefully.

He circled the bushes and bent to study the scrapes on the ground. In among the dried leaves and twigs, Matt saw a saucer-sized pool of blood. Beyond it, dark red drops drew a path toward the trees, like bread crumbs left by Hansel and Gretel.

"He's wounded, but not fatally. He got away." He followed the trail of blood toward the trees, dividing his attention between the ground and the wooded area ahead of him.

At the edge of the clearing, he stopped. For a few seconds, he stood still, listening for the sound of a motor, but all he heard was the wind rustling the bare branches. Carefully, he followed the blood trail for a few more steps, until the underbrush was too thick to penetrate, and the tree's roots met and intertwined on the ground.

He backed away, staying in his own footsteps until

he reached the stand of bushes. When he turned, he nearly ran into Aimee.

"When I tell you to stay put, you've got to stay put," he said sternly, wishing he felt like smiling at her determined stance.

She stood, legs apart, holding the Glock like every cop on *Law & Order,* although her expression more closely resembled that of a terrified witness.

"The kidnapper definitely wounded him. He's losing a good bit of blood. I don't think he'll try anything else. If he's got any sense, and if he's got a vehicle—which I'm sure he does—he's probably headed down the mountain by now."

"What do we do now?" she asked.

He frowned. "If I had the Hummer, I'd send you down to it. But without it we're not going anywhere, except to find a way to get you out of this storm."

Aimee shivered and hunched her shoulders against the wind. She was already feeling the cold, even in her down parka and balaclava.

His insulated underwear was keeping him warm. If he thought it would help her, he'd strip it off and give it to her. But the suit had been custom-fitted to his body for maximum insulation. It would be much too large for her, and therefore useless. Besides, if he were going to keep her safe, he had to keep himself warm and mobile.

Aimee still held the Glock. He put on his parka and lifted the daypack onto his shoulders. Then he took the Glock and stowed it in a side pocket.

After glancing up at the sky one more time, he pulled the satellite phone out of his pocket and looked at it. No signal.

Why was he not surprised?

He wasn't sure if the problem was the cloud cover or the cold, but it didn't matter. There would be no night-time rescue tonight. He couldn't contact Deke or anyone else until the storm passed.

He put the phone away and pulled out the GPS locator. *Again, no satellite reception.* He'd have to rely on old-fashioned methods of finding his way. He'd memorized the maps, so he knew where they were going. He just hoped they could make it before the storm caught up to them in full force.

It was almost 1900 hours. Seven o'clock. They had, at best, thirty minutes of daylight left. A stab of apprehension pierced his chest. He'd mapped out three shelters within reasonable distance of the ransom drop point. The one closest to his primary rendezvous point was 4.8 miles, heading 41 degrees, almost directly east. The next closest to rendezvous was 4.5 miles at 18 degrees.

The third shelter would be the easiest walk. It was two miles away, but the direction was 30 degrees, which put it farthest from the primary rendezvous point.

He could picture the grid in his head. If he were alone, he'd head directly for the primary shelter. A hike of 4.8 miles would be less than an hour at his usual pace, even in snow.

But he figured Aimee could cover about three miles per hour at best, and that didn't take the snowstorm into consideration. It would take her almost two hours. Which wouldn't be so much of a problem if they'd gotten started an hour earlier.

But they hadn't. And as he'd feared, the storm was moving in at least three hours ahead of predictions, just as he'd told Special Agent Schiff. So he had no choice but to head for the nearest shelter, even if it was farthest from the primary rendezvous point.

"How far do we have to go?" Aimee asked, as if she were reading his mind.

"With any luck we can make it in an hour or a little more," he said, knowing he was being optimistic. The longer it took, the harder it would be. He could smell the snow in the air and he figured the wind was already up to twelve miles per hour. His prediction was that it would reach fifty miles per hour or more before the storm played out. And Matt didn't want to be caught outside in it.

He sure as hell didn't want Aimee exposed. Once they made it to the shelter, they could get a good night's sleep and get an early start.

Plus, as soon as the storm moved out, he could contact Deke and arrange a new, closer rendezvous point. He could tell Deke to bring replacement gear and supplies, and pick up Aimee.

He shook his head. Getting Aimee to leave without her baby was going to be a trick. Surely two ex-Special Forces operatives could convince one small civilian female to get into a helicopter.

Matt's brain fed him a life-sized picture of that.

"We'd better get going," he said.

She looked up at him and a couple of snowflakes caught in her lashes. They looked like stars sparkling in her eyes. She blinked and scrunched up her nose, and desire lanced through his groin, surprising the hell out of him.

Damn. At least it chased the drowsy haze from his head.

AIMEE FLEXED HER right shoulder and suppressed a groan. It was already sore, and she had a feeling it would be black-and-blue by morning. She'd landed on it when the kidnapper tossed her out of the Hummer.

Matt glanced up as if he'd heard her. When she met his gaze, he gave her a little nod and then quickly looked back down at the small, handheld electronic device he held.

His effort to be reassuring wasn't very successful, though, mostly because he wasn't the kind of guy who could hide his feelings.

Throughout high school, college and the six years of Bill and Aimee's marriage, Bill and his three friends had been inseparable. They'd called themselves the Black Hills Brotherhood because of the near-death experience they'd shared as kids.

She knew all of them—Matt the best, because he'd been Bill's best friend.

It was interesting how alike the four were—and how different. Deke Cunningham and Rook Castle would have had no trouble winning at poker. Even Bill had always had a pretty good poker face.

Matt, on the other hand, was as easy to read as a first-grade storybook. Like right now. His brows drew down in a V across his forehead as he looked at the tiny screen of his device and then up at the cloudy sky.

He was worried about them reaching shelter before the storm hit. She was, too. It was getting dark, and the wind was picking up.

She wasn't sure why she'd asked about going back down the mountain. Maybe because it would have been nice to have a choice, even though she'd never leave without her child. Or maybe so she could understand exactly how bad things were, now that the Hummer had been destroyed.

They were on their own, with no transportation, a

snowstorm on its way, and not one but two men who wanted to harm them. And her baby was still missing.

She figured she had a pretty good handle on how bad things were.

Per Matt's instructions, she'd dressed for the trip as if they were going to picnic at the North Pole. Layers, layers and more layers, he'd told her.

Of course, she'd lived in Wyoming all her life, so she knew how quickly the weather could change in the mountains, especially this time of year. And she knew that the most important thing to remember was to keep one's body core warm. So she had put on a tank top, silk long underwear, a cotton pullover, a wool sweater and her down jacket. She was set for any temperature.

Aimee's fingers were beginning to tingle with cold. She pulled off a mitten and stuffed her hand inside the elastic sleeve that covered her other arm. The skin-to-skin contact warmed her fingers almost instantly. The chill seeped into the skin of her other wrist, but it would warm back up within seconds.

She pulled her mitten back on and then did the same thing with her other hand.

Meanwhile, Matt was still studying the weather.

"Is everything okay?" she asked.

He stuck the handheld device into a pocket of the small daypack he carried on his back, and then smiled at her. "Sure. We need to get a move on, though. As I told you, it's going to take us an hour or so to get to the nearest shelter. And that storm is catching up to us."

She clenched her fists inside the mittens, and bit her cheek in an effort to stop the tears that stung her eyelids.

She'd been congratulating herself for already figuring all that out. Hearing Matt say it, however, seemed to make their situation more dire, and less simple. It was one thing for her to wonder if she were overstating their predicament. It was quite another to hear Matt verify that things really were that bad.

"Remind me again how everything is going to be all right?" she begged.

Matt tugged off his glove with his teeth and took it in his other hand. He stepped closer to her and touched her cheek, then her chin, with his warm fingers.

"Hey," he said, coaxing her chin upward so he could look into her eyes. "Pull your cap down. You look like you're getting cold."

"I'm a little chilly," she admitted. "Matt? How sure are you that William is okay?"

A shadow of doubt flickered across his face as he curled his lips in a smile. "Very sure. I promise you, we'll find him and he'll be fine."

As he spoke, the weight of worry that was squeezing her chest let up a little. It occurred to her that whatever he told her, she believed without reservation.

It was strange that his thoughtful answer coupled with the uncertainty that had briefly touched his features, made him more believable than Bill, who had often stared at her expressionlessly, rather than giving her a straight answer.

She watched him closely. Was he more trustworthy than her husband had been? Or was Matt, too, trying to protect her from the truth?

His teeth scraped lightly across his lower lip as he checked his pack and got ready to go.

Aimee arched her shoulder again.

He'd said it would take about an hour to get to the shelter. She hoped he was being realistic, although she was afraid he was overestimating how fast she could move.

For the next half hour or so, Aimee kept up with Matt better than he would have expected. Not so much better that he revised his estimate of how long it would take them to get to the shelter, but fast enough to keep his body producing heat. From the sound of Aimee's breathing, she was keeping her heart rate up, too.

That was the good news. The bad news was that the storm was about to catch up to them. The wind was easterly, so it helped propel them forward, but the sun had gone down, the sky was cloudy and dark, and the air was heavy with moisture, making the wind bitingly cold.

They didn't talk much, just trudged along doggedly. Most of their conversation consisted of Matt asking if she was all right and Aimee replying that she was.

Then it started to snow, and Aimee started slowing down—way down.

He figured they were at least another half hour from the shelter. The temperature had dropped by at least ten degrees, he was sure, and the wind was probably up to thirty miles per hour, enough to make Aimee stumble when it gusted.

He wrapped an arm around her waist and half supported her, pushing her to walk a little faster. "Come on, Aimee. We're getting close. You've got to keep moving or you're going to get sick."

"I am a little chilly," she said, just as she had every time he'd asked.

Only this time, her words were slurred.

He reached back to a pocket of his daypack and retrieved a windup flashlight. He gave it about a minute's worth of winding. Then he shone it in her face.

"Wha—?" she said, her hand coming up to block the light.

"Stop for a second," he said. "I just want to take a look at your face."

"No. I'm fine." She kept going, one foot in front of the other, shuffling along. "I wanna get there."

"Aimee," he said more loudly. "Stop." He gripped her arm.

She tried to pull it out of his grasp, but it was a half-hearted effort. "No. Keep going," she muttered.

He shone the flashlight in her face, and saw how pale she was, and how translucent and gray her lips looked. He aimed the light at her eyes. How did the prettiest, plumpest snowflakes always manage to get caught in her lashes? They drifted away as she blinked against the flashlight's bright beam.

Her pupils were dilated, and barely reacted to the light.

It was what he'd been afraid would happen.

Aimee was hypothermic. If they didn't get to the shelter soon, she could die.

CHAPTER SIX

MATT KNEW HYPOTHERMIA didn't require freezing temperatures to affect someone. But he also knew they were being pummeled by winds that made the temperature that was already below freezing seem at least five degrees colder.

Plus the snow was wet, and dampness was seeping into their clothing.

He pulled off his down jacket, wrapped it around Aimee and snapped it closed. That gave her two layers of down, the best light insulation there was.

Then he dug the hood out of its pocket and tugged it down over her balaclava. He should have done that a long time ago, but he'd overestimated her endurance.

"Not a good idea," she muttered.

"What?"

"Now you'll be cold. We'll both be cold." She giggled faintly.

He was worried about her. "Come on, Aimee. We're not far from the shelter. Let's race."

"No," she drawled. "Don't wanna race. Tired."

"I know," he said, putting his arm around her again to support her and urge her on ahead.

"Sleepy, too. I need to get home. William's waiting for me."

"Aimee, do you know where we're going?"

For a moment, she didn't answer. Then, quietly, almost too quietly for him to hear, she spoke. "Home?"

He tightened his arm around her waist. "Listen, Aimee. We're up on Ragged Top Mountain. We're having an adventure. It's kind of like a treasure hunt." The wet snow was beginning to penetrate his wool sweater and underwear. He shivered, wishing he had the waterproof poncho that had burned up in his backpack.

"It's really important that we get to the shelter within the next twenty minutes. Can you walk really fast?"

She nodded. "I'm not sure. My feet aren't there." She laughed, a sound like ice cubes tinkling in a glass. "I mean, I know they're there. I just can't feel 'em."

"That's okay. They're there. I can see them." Matt smiled at her and looked up at the dark, cloud-filled sky. *God, help me get her to the shelter in time. Don't let me lose her. William needs her—I need her.*

MATT LIFTED THE blankets that hung over the door to the shelter and pushed Aimee inside.

He'd already made her wait while he reconnoitered to be sure no one else was there. He figured both the kidnapper and Al Hamar already had a destination. The kidnapper was headed for wherever he was keeping the baby. And if Al Hamar had any sense he'd get off the mountain and get his wound attended to.

The shelter was primitive, with a wide opening on the east side and blankets as the only coverings for the two windows that faced north and south. The inside was ice-cold, but this version of ice-cold was at least ten degrees warmer than the outside. He shuddered as his body took note of the small increase in warmth.

After shrugging off the daypack, he shone the flashlight's beam around. Two cots, a fireplace, a couple of chairs. He examined every inch of the space.

Firewood? Where was firewood? Then he saw it. A small pile of limbs and branches against the far wall.

Under a window. Coated with a sheen of snow. What idiot had stored the firewood there? He grimaced. The wood was wet.

"Matt?" Aimee's voice quivered.

He pulled her toward one of the cots. "I've got to get you out of those wet clothes," he said firmly. "And get you under the covers. Hurry."

She looked at him without moving.

He pushed his jacket off her shoulders and jerked the insulated hood and watch cap off her head. Her hair was wet and she was shivering so much her teeth chattered.

"Okay, Aimee. We're going to get you warm. Trust me?"

"I'm a little chilly," she whispered.

"I know, sweetie, I know." He unzipped her down parka and pushed it down her arms. "I'm just going to get these wet things off you, okay?"

She nodded shakily. "I'm sleepy."

"That's good," he lied. His second lie to her.

Drowsiness was a symptom of hypothermia, a severe one. It meant her body temperature was dropping to dangerous levels. He had to work fast.

By the time he got the parka and her hiking boots off, she'd almost quit shivering. That wasn't a good sign, either.

He talked to her while he undressed her. Nonsense things. Little reassurances, endearments, the kind of things one might use to soothe a frightened child.

Finally, she was down to a little tank top and her underpants. They weren't wet, but there wasn't enough to them to provide any warmth. All they were good for was preserving a little of her modesty and titillating him a lot.

Her skin was cool to the touch, and her fingers and toes were cold. He examined them closely, but they didn't appear to be frostbitten—yet.

He was tempted to rub them, but he knew better. Too much rubbing could damage freezing skin and nerves permanently.

He checked out the cots, which, thank God, weren't near the windows. The blanket he unfolded was slightly damp, but it was made of wool. Even wet, wool would still keep her warm—once he *got* her warm.

He lay her down on the cot and put the blanket over her.

"Stay there, okay? I need to get a fire going." He grabbed two blankets from the other cot and piled them over her, too.

Then he turned to the fireplace. The wood stacked inside it was wet, like all the other firewood. He brushed the snow away from the wood piled under the window and dug through it.

Toward the bottom, he found some sticks that weren't wet through. Grabbing an armful, he stacked them in the fireplace and took a couple of wet-weather fire-starter sticks out of his pack. He placed them under the branches and lit them with all-weather matches.

The starter sticks flared immediately. Now if the wood would just catch before they burned out. He adjusted a limb here, a branch there, until he was sure it was arranged for the best draft, and that was it. That was all he could do.

He watched for a few seconds, encouraged by the crackling and spitting as the hot flames generated by the starter sticks burned off the dampness.

He stripped down quickly, until he was covered in nothing but his boxers and goose bumps. All his clothes were wet, even his insulated underwear.

He was shivering, and he knew his body temp was

down, but he wasn't hypothermic, thank God. His core was still warm.

Working as quickly as he could, and keeping one eye on the struggling fire and one on Aimee, he spread their clothes on chairs that he sat in front of the fireplace. If he could get the fire going, maybe they'd dry by morning.

He found some hurricane candles on a shelf and lit them, then carefully poked at the fire, checking the draft. To his relief, a few of the small branches caught.

"Hey, Aimee, I think we're going to have a fire before too long." He rose and picked up one of the hurricane candles. Crossing the room to the cot, he held it so the light shone on her face.

"Aimee, are you awake?" Her eyes were closed and she was lying too still. He touched her cheek, then reached under the blanket and found her hand. Icy. Dammit. He looked at her fingers. They were still white and pinched.

"Okay," he said, hoping his voice sounded calmer than he felt. "I'll tell you what we're going to do. I'm going to move the other cot next to the fire and lay you there. I've got a mummy bag—that's a head-to-toe sleeping bag, made for subzero conditions. It's a single, but if I unzip it, we can both get under it, like a blanket. How does that sound?"

He didn't like that she was nonresponsive. He knew how to treat hypothermia, but most recommended treatments assumed that dry clothes and a heat source were available.

Until the fire caught enough to actually generate heat, Matt only had one source of warmth available—his own body.

He checked the other cot. At least it was no wetter than the one Aimee was on. He pulled it over in front of the hearth, grabbed two of the blankets from on top of Aimee, and spread them over the mattress. The wool would hold the heat in.

Then he bent over Aimee. "Aimee, sweetie, can you wake up? I need you to wake up for me."

She stirred and opened her eyes. They were glassy and not quite focused. "Is it William?" she whispered.

His heart twisted. She was dreaming, maybe even hallucinating. "Aimee, listen to me. Sit up for me. Can you tell me how you feel?"

"I'm tired," she said. "Sleepy."

"I know. And you can go to sleep, just as soon as we get you over closer to the fire and get you warm. Come on. Let's move over to the fireplace."

She pushed at the blankets covering her.

"That's good. Here. I'm going to pull the covers down so you can get up."

Her eyes met his briefly. "Matt," she said. "What a nice surprise. Bill will be so glad you're here."

He'd thought he couldn't carry any more guilt, but her slurred words cut him to his soul. She *was* hallucinating. She thought Bill was still alive, thought they were all still friends.

Don't worry, he told himself. *Tomorrow she'll remember, and hate you again.*

If she lived until tomorrow. Unless he got her warm, she wouldn't last that long.

"Let's go," he said and lifted her to her feet. She almost collapsed against him. He wrapped his arm around her waist and half carried her to the cot.

Her skin felt cool, pressed against his. He had to

get her body temp up—and fast. "Here we are," he said softly. "Just lie down there, and I'll get the sleeping bag."

She obeyed him without protest. She lay down and closed her eyes. "Cold," she murmured.

"I know, Aimee, but I'm going to fix that." He grabbed his daypack and retrieved the small bundle that was the compressed down sleeping bag. He pulled it out of its stuff-sack, unzipped it and shook it out to fluff the down.

"I'm just going to lay the sleeping bag over you, and then I'll put a couple of blankets on top."

He looked down at her. She lay on her side, facing the hearth, with her arms wrapped around her middle. The warm light from the fire made her pale skin look like the color of a ripe peach. Her bare legs and arms were silky and delicately muscled. The little top and panties emphasized her slender curves. Her dark hair was still damp and beginning to wave around her face.

She looked the way she had in high school. Fresh, beautiful, vibrant. No wonder Bill had fallen in love with her.

Matt swallowed against the lump that rose in his throat from just looking at her.

"All right, scumbag," he muttered to himself as he spread the down bag over her like a blanket. "Stop ogling and get started warming her up."

He fetched two more blankets. The down inside the sleeping bag was the ideal insulator. It was lightweight, held in heat and wicked out moisture. But Matt wanted some weight on top to seal in the heat his body produced, because he couldn't afford to lose even a couple of calories to the chilly room.

He carefully placed the blankets over the spread-out sleeping bag. Then, after a check of the fire to be sure it was lit and growing, he slid under the covers. Aimee's back was to him, so he cautiously moved closer. The scent of lemon assaulted his nostrils. How, after everything she'd been through, did she still smell so fresh and clean?

Her skin was cold, but apparently his body didn't care. When his groin came in contact with her backside, he swallowed a groan and grimaced. The feel of her supple body affected him—a *lot*.

He felt himself growing hard, felt his heart rate rise. Clenching his teeth and cursing himself for his weakness, he pulled away.

Aimee whimpered and scooted backward slightly.

Since her skin felt cool to him, his must feel hot to hers. "Okay, Aimee. I'm going to get as close to you as I can—" *and keep my sanity.* "It's just to warm you up. I promise I won't make you uncomfortable." Too bad he couldn't promise himself the same thing.

He scooted closer, wrapping his arm across her shoulders and pulling her close to his chest. He knew he had to concentrate on her core, rather than her chilled arms and legs. What made hypothermia deadly was that the body got chilled straight through. The most important thing was to warm up the vital organs. Once her core temperature rose, her arms and legs would start warming up.

He gritted his teeth and pressed his thighs against the backs of her legs.

Keep it professional, Parker.

After a while, Aimee's breathing grew more even, and she relaxed.

Matt lay there, listening to the wind and silently thanking whoever had built the shelter for taking the weather patterns up here into consideration. The shelter's solid back wall was turned against the predominant wind direction, which was easterly.

Aimee sighed in her sleep, and half turned, so that her cheek was no more than an inch from his nose. In the firelight he could see the faint dusting of freckles on her smooth skin. The scent of lemon and the delicate curve of her cheek made his mouth water.

He slid his hand down her arm, doing his best to avoid touching any other part of her. When he reached her wrist, he pressed his fingertips against the silky skin and counted her pulse. It was faint but steady. Then he took her hand in his.

At least her fingers weren't icy cold anymore. He sighed in relief. She was warming up. He was pretty sure she was out of danger. But he knew that if it had taken them any longer to get here, and if he hadn't been able to get a fire started, she could have died.

He breathed deeply and tried to relax. For the moment, they were safe. He needed to get as much rest as he could while he had the chance.

Because tomorrow wasn't going to be easy. Tomorrow, he was going to have to explain to her why they were pressed up against each other and practically naked, why it made sense that he'd brought her up the mountain instead of down, and why he hadn't kept his promise to her—his promise to place William Matthew safely into her arms before the day was out.

CHAPTER SEVEN

SATURDAY 0400 HOURS

AIMEE CAME AWAKE SLOWLY. She was hot. And thirsty. She stirred, trying to push the covers back, but they wouldn't move. Someone was lying very close to her—too close. Someone with a very large, very warm body.

Her eyes flew open, and she saw the crackling fire. *Fire?*

Where was she? Her pulse thrummed in her throat and she suddenly felt claustrophobic. She pushed herself up to a sitting position, kicking at the covers and gasping for breath.

"Aimee?"

"Who—?" She dug her heels in and propelled her body backward, away from whoever was pressing so close against her. She sucked in a huge breath, preparing to scream.

"Aimee, it's Matt."

A hand touched her shoulder.

She gasped and coughed.

"Shh. You're okay."

"Matt?" She blinked and looked at the figure that sat up next to her. "Matt? What are you doing—?"

She pushed at him.

"Aimee, whoa! You're going to fall off the cot."

He reached out toward her, but she recoiled instinctively. She was in bed—in bed! What kind of crazy dream was she having about Matt, of all people?

"I was just trying to warm you up. You were cold—too cold. I had to get your body temperature up. Do you remember?"

She stared at him, trying to process what he was saying. She couldn't, any more than she could figure out why she was here in this strange room next to him.

He was bare-chested, his skin glowing like gold in the firelight. His dark hair was tousled and wavy, as if he'd just toweled it dry.

She lifted the edge of the covers and looked down at herself. All she had on was a little tank top and panties.

"What's going on? Why—?" Had Matt undressed her? She raised her shocked gaze to his and absently registered a look of apology in his expression.

"I had to," he said. "You were freezing."

She stared at him as bits of memories flashed across her brain.

Matt wrapping an arm around her and telling her she was going to be okay.

Snow blowing in her face, her eyes and lips stinging with cold—the smell of gasoline—the sounds of gunfire—

And the awful, menacing words crackling down the phone wire. "If you want to see your baby again, *you* will deliver the money."

If you want to see your baby again—

"William!" she cried, his name ripping from her throat. Suddenly they were all there. All the memories. All the terror. All the anguish. "My baby! Where is he?"

"Aimee, shh. Try to stay calm."

She heard the words, but hardly registered where they came from. All she knew was that they cut like a razor through her heart.

"Calm? My baby is gone. They stole him, out of his bed." Her hands flew to her mouth. "I was asleep. I was asleep and they took him."

Her eyes burned, and her mouth was dry. So dry. She licked her lips.

"You're thirsty. I'll get you some water."

It was Matt, she realized. Bill's best friend.

Safe as houses.

But he wasn't. He'd taken Bill away from her and let him die. He'd shown up like a knight in shining armor at the very moment when she needed a hero, but he'd let William's kidnapper get away, and he didn't save her baby. Pain lanced through her and she clutched at her middle.

When Matt rose, she saw that his lower body was almost as bare as his upper. He was dressed in nothing but snug-fitting boxers.

They *both* were nearly naked. She rubbed her temple, wishing she could put all this information together and come up with a reasonable understanding of what was happening.

She knew who he was now. And she knew they hadn't rescued William. But where were they? And how had they gotten there?

"I melted some snow, once the fire got going," he said conversationally. He picked up a metal cup and filled it from a pan that sat near the fireplace.

"Here." He held out the cup.

She couldn't move. She still clutched the covers to her chest like a shield.

"Come on, Aimee. Take the cup. You need to drink some water." Slowly, carefully, he reached out a hand and took hers, gently prying her fingers loose from the blanket, and pressed the cup into her palm. It was cool.

He turned and went back to the fire, where he picked up pieces of clothing. For the first time she noticed two straight-backed chairs by the hearth.

He piled the clothes on the hearth and spread other pieces over the backs of the chairs.

She watched him as she lifted the cup to her lips. The flat, tepid water tasted wonderful. She drank the whole cupful.

"Our clothes will probably be dry by morning."

"Could I have some more?" she asked, and at once felt guilty because she was warm and safe and enjoying water while her baby was out there somewhere—alone. Maybe thirsty. Maybe cold. The pain hit her again, swift and sharp.

"Oh—" she gasped.

Matt took the cup from her hands. "What's wrong? Are you hurting?"

"I want—I need my baby." Tears stung her eyes, but she lifted her chin and swallowed them. "Do you—" She paused, terribly afraid she knew the answer to the question she was about to ask. "Do you know where he is?"

He filled the cup and handed it back to her, then filled another one and drank it himself. He went back to checking and rearranging the clothing. "No. I don't know where he is right now. But the storm is almost over and I'm hoping that by morning the clouds will have cleared away. We'll meet Deke at the rendezvous point and he can take you back with him. As soon as I find William, I'll—"

"What?" She was still having trouble sorting everything out, but her brain finally put his words together in the proper order.

He can take you back with him.

"No!" She slammed the cup down on the wooden floor with a clang. "I am not going back without my baby."

"Aimee, you have to. You can't stay up here. I don't have the supplies or shelter to take care of you."

"Why can't Deke bring supplies?"

"Because he's going to get you to safety while I rescue William." He picked up a pair of dark leggings, pulled them up and tugged a matching long-sleeved shirt over his head.

"But—"

"Listen to me, Aimee. I can't concentrate on rescuing William if I'm worried about you." He sorted through the clothes until he found her silk turtleneck and handed it to her.

"You need to put this on and get back under the covers. It's still a couple of hours until morning. After the snowstorm started, you got hypothermic. So from now on you're going to be susceptible to the cold. You need all the strength you can muster."

She took the shirt and pulled it on. "Don't ignore me, Matt. And don't treat me like I'm going to break. I was confused when I first woke up, but I'm not now." *Not completely.*

She smoothed the shirt down over her abdomen. "I can't sleep anymore. William is out there. I have to get ready. We have to go find him."

Matt sat on his haunches, tossed back the rest of his water and sat the cup on the hearth. He picked up a stick and poked the fire.

"You need to rest," he said again, not looking at her.

She wanted to be angry at him, needed to be. But his quiet, deliberate actions didn't invite attacks. In fact, his composure was calming.

For a moment she was mesmerized by the silhouette of his profile, outlined by the orange glow from the coals. It was classic and grim. She could believe he was an ancient warrior, staring into the flames as he prepared his mind for battle.

Suddenly, a memory from the night before flashed across her mind. He'd been lying next to her on the cot, his legs and chest pressed against her from behind. She remembered the thick warmth of his skin against hers, the rapid rise and fall of his chest and belly. The feel of his erection, hard and hot against her. He'd groaned, then whispered something.

I promise.

That was all she remembered. But she knew that, whatever that promise had been, he'd keep it.

It occurred to her that he was in his element here. Weather and survival had been his specialties in the Air Force. There were probably only a handful of people in the world as well trained as Matt to rescue her baby.

He hadn't been exaggerating when he said he couldn't take care of her and do his job. She was definitely a handicap. She knew that. He couldn't move as fast or as stealthily with her along. He couldn't focus all his concentration and energy on overpowering the kidnapper and rescuing William if he had to be concerned about her safety. But she was right, too. When he found William, she had to be there.

Matt might be the only person she could trust to find her child, but she was the only one who could protect him.

BY THE TIME they got away from the shelter, it was after 0700 hours. Matt had figured out hours earlier that they were going to miss the 0800 rendezvous point he'd arranged with Deke. To have any chance of making it, they'd have had to leave before daylight, while the wet snow was still falling. And he wasn't about to expose Aimee to the possibility of hypothermia again.

He'd ventured out of the shelter several times during the night to check the weather. The storm had done exactly what he'd figured it would do. It had moved in ahead of predictions. But what he hadn't expected was the second front that had moved in right behind it. He'd seen the low pressure system that had been building behind the first. It hadn't looked significant, and it had been hours behind the first, larger storm.

But then the first storm had stalled, hovering over the mountain for hours after its predicted movement eastward. The extra time gave the second storm plenty of time to catch up and gain strength.

Yesterday's weather forecast had the second storm not moving in for another twelve hours. However, by the time the first storm passed through, the second one was already rolling in.

The good news was that it was a weaker front, and hadn't dropped nearly as much snow. By 0630 the snow had stopped and the storm was beginning to dissipate.

Matt figured that within another hour the skies might be clear enough for him to use his satellite phone.

He'd found a pair of snowshoes in the shelter. He gave them to Aimee, despite her protests. He could survive, even if his feet got wet. She couldn't.

In the place of the snowshoes, the firewood, a liter-sized plastic bottle filled with melted snow, and two of the wool blankets, Matt had left four of his eight remaining fire-starter sticks and extra all-weather matches for the next traveler who sought refuge there.

He'd fashioned one of the blankets into a makeshift pack, tying the corners into knots and using duct tape from his daypack. So this morning he carried the makeshift pack containing his electronic devices, the water, the other blanket, several high-calorie protein bars, and the money, and Aimee carried the daypack with the sleeping bag and the lighter items. He had the heavy machine pistol and she had the Glock.

"Let's go, Aimee," he called. He'd told her to stay in the shelter until he was sure they were ready to go.

She appeared at the opening, stuffing strands of hair inside the balaclava she'd folded up and donned like a ski cap. Her face was rosy and fresh-looking. Thank God her pallor from the night before was gone.

"You walk in front."

"Are you sure?" she asked. "Wouldn't it be better if you set the pace?"

He looked at her in surprise. "That's a good question."

"You don't have to act like you're about to faint. I told you, I've done a little hiking in my time."

"Letting me set the pace would be a good idea, if we were evenly matched. But you wouldn't be able to keep up with me. If I lead, I'll be tempted to walk too fast, and then I'll have to slow down to let you catch up. That'll be extremely tiring for me. At the same time, you'll be trying to keep pace when I speed up, which will make *you* very tired. If you set the pace, you can adjust it to your level of conditioning, and I can find your rhythm. That way we'll both conserve our energy."

Aimee sent him a little smile. "All that *and* good-looking."

His brows rose. She'd surprised him again.

"Yeah," he replied. It was good to see her smile. He suspected it was unlikely that she was genuinely amused. She was probably just putting on a front, hoping he wouldn't figure out how scared she was.

As if he could miss it.

She moved in front of him, a little uncertain balancing on the snowshoes.

After the third time she almost stumbled, he called out, "I thought you'd done some hiking."

"I didn't say it was in snow."

He smiled again, and a warmth that had nothing to do with the temperature spread through him. "Now you tell me."

He looked at his watch. By his best calculations, they were about six miles away from where Deke would be circling, looking for them.

Judging by the time they'd made last night, allowing for the fact that they weren't battling a snowstorm and Aimee wasn't handicapped by hypothermia this morning, it would still take them at least two hours, maybe more, to get there, trudging through the wet, packed snow. He figured the temperature was about thirty degrees.

And it would rise as the sun rose. While that meant they'd spend the day peeling off layers of clothing so they wouldn't sweat, at least the heat would burn off the rest of the clouds.

Aimee said something that the wind picked up and blew away.

"What?" he called out.

She turned her head. "Do the clouds look like they're thinning? Can you get a signal on your phone?"

He looked up at the clouds that hung heavily above them. They were dissipating behind them, to the west. Pulling out the satellite phone, he checked the signal.

Nothing.

"Not yet."

He kept checking over the next hour. Finally, the phone responded with a weak signal. He dialed Irina.

"Matt!" she cried as soon as she picked up the phone. "What happened? Where are you? Do you have the baby?"

"No. But the kidnapper doesn't have the money, either. We're headed toward the first rendezvous point, but we're not going to make it in time. Tell Deke we can be there by 1000 hours for sure—"

"Matt, listen. The helicopter's been sabotaged."

Had he heard right? "Sabotaged? There at the ranch with all your security? That's impossible!"

"It happened. We don't know how. Someone drained all the oil. When Deke tried to take off, the motor burned up. It's going to take all day to put in a new motor."

"Deke would never take off without checking everything."

"Right. The oil gauge registered full. It had been tampered with."

"What can he do? I need to get Aimee out of here. She's not trained for this weather or this terrain, and most of my supplies burned up in the Hummer."

"Repeat. I missed that."

"My supplies burned up in the Hummer."

"The Hummer burned? You're on foot?"

"Yeah."

"—get Deke right on it. But listen. There's something—at least two more—"

"You're breaking up."

"More storms—this way."

"Okay. I'll check it out."

"There's one blowing in now. It'll probably reach—area—Ragged Top within the next two hours."

"Damn," Matt breathed. "Okay. I can deal with the weather. What else?"

"It's big, Matt. Schiff got an anonymous call early this morning. The caller said—Aimee's ba—the Vick cabin—get that?"

"Baby? Cabin?" Matt looked at Aimee. She'd been listening to his side of the conversation the whole time. She met his gaze. He knew shock and relief were plastered all over his face.

Her face lit up, tempered with hesitancy, as if she weren't quite sure she should actually dare to be excited yet.

He nodded at her and smiled. "Got it."

"—gave him the kidna—"

"Gave him what?"

"Name. It's Kinnard."

"Kinnard?"

"The police are familiar with him. He's a small-time hood—muscle for some local loan sharks, that sort of thing. And years ago—arently did work for Boss—"

"For who?"

"Boss Vick."

That shocked Matt. He turned away from Aimee's curious gaze. For the moment, it might be wise to keep that last tidbit of information to himself.

"Can you verify that?"

"Margo denies ever hearing—less knowing him—warrant for—papers. But—to take—"

"Irina, I can barely understand you. Can Deke make the Sunday rendezvous?"

"—get in—pick up—Sunday 0900."

"Got it, 0900. Out."

Matt disconnected, and then tried to access the weather reports via satellite. But the cloud cover was getting thicker, and reception was spotty.

He'd have to continue to rely on old-fashioned methods of reading the weather and predicting what would happen next.

"Matt?" Aimee had waited patiently while he talked to Irina, but he could see that she was bursting with curiosity. "Did she say *baby?* At the cabin?" she asked hesitantly.

"Someone called in an anonymous tip this morning, letting the FBI know that your baby, your William, is there."

"He's there? At the cabin? Oh—" Aimee capped a hand over her mouth. Her eyes glittered with unshed tears. "Oh, Matt. Do you think the caller was telling the truth? Do you really think he's all right?"

Matt nodded. "From what Irina said, it sounds like he's fine."

She pressed her fingertips to her lips for a few seconds, then ran toward him.

Before he realized what she was doing, she slammed into him, wrapping her arms around his neck and hugging him tighter than he'd ever been hugged in his life.

He stood there for a second, not knowing how to react. But her joy, her relief, her sheer happiness at knowing her child was safe, began to seep in past his reserve. He wrapped his arms around her and hugged her back.

She buried her face in the hollow between his neck and shoulder and hung on. After a few seconds, he realized that he felt tears against his neck.

"Hey," he said, gently pushing her away and peering at her. "Are you okay?"

She nodded as tears flowed down her cheeks and ran over the corner of her mouth. She sniffed. "I'm so—so relieved. I was so scared."

His heart was twisting again. He'd never known an internal organ could warp in so many different directions. "I know you were. I don't think I've ever seen you cry."

She swiped her fingers across her cheeks. "I don't. Ever."

"I guess this is a pretty special occasion then."

Her smile broadened and she laughed. "I guess it is." She blew air out between her lips, wiped her cheeks again, and then straightened and looked him in the eye.

"So how far are we from the cabin? How fast can we get there? Who's there with him?"

"Whoa," Matt said, holding up his hands. "I can't tell you who's there with him, but I can tell you that we're about ten miles from the cabin and we can get there in four or five hours. But only if you turn around and walk."

She grinned at him. "Which direction?"

The maps he'd memorized suddenly went completely out of his head, knocked out by the dazzle of her grin. He'd seen it before, of course, but not in a long time. And never directed solely at him.

"Hang on a minute," he croaked, holding up a hand. He pulled his glove off with his teeth and retrieved the printed maps from his pocket. After a little shuffling, he came up with the right one.

"Okay. Bear 18 degrees north of east."

"Bear what?"

He laughed ruefully, held up the compass and took the reading, then pointed. "Go thataway."

She turned and looked. "Thataway?"

He shook his head. "Walk!"

With a swish of her hips, the impact of which was mostly lost under the down parka, Aimee turned and started walking.

Matt stuffed his maps back into his pocket and tugged on his glove, all the while lecturing himself about how uncool it was to be lusting after his best friend's widow.

Especially here. Especially now. They were in a dangerous situation. His job was to take care of her, to protect her. Getting emotional led to screwups. He knew that from personal experience.

Twenty years ago, he, Deke, Rook and Bill had found themselves trapped on a mountain ledge when a storm blew in. He'd been the youngest of the four, and the most scared. Rook and Deke, and even Bill, only two months older than him, had stayed calm. But he'd sobbed as the reclusive Vietnam vet Arlis Hanks had pulled him up using a rope and a block and tackle. That was the last time he'd cried.

Shaking his head at the memory, Matt looked up.

Aimee was nowhere in sight.

CHAPTER EIGHT

SATURDAY 0900 HOURS

"Aimee!" Matt shouted. "Aimee!" His heart slammed against his chest wall, ripping the breath from his lungs.

He broke into a run. The terrain here was fairly even, and the trees were sparse. He could see for several yards. How could she have disappeared?

God, please don't let her have fallen over a ledge.

That thought stopped him in his tracks as alarm sheared his breath.

Stay calm. Cool. Rational.

The words echoed in his head with each cautious step he took. Combined with deep, even breaths, they helped to slow his pounding heart. He placed his feet into her snowshoe prints.

Within about ten paces he saw the indented ribbon of snow that marked a creek bed. She must have fallen in.

"Aimee!" he shouted.

"Matt! Here!" Her voice was shrill with fear.

"Stay still. I'll be right there." Within a few steps, he could see the hole in the snow. He approached carefully.

Several feet from the place where Aimee had fallen, he lowered himself to his hands and knees and crawled until he could peer over the edge.

Aimee was sitting in a pile of snow.

"Aimee? Don't move. Are you all right?"

She looked up. "Yes," she said disgustedly. "My butt hurts, but not as much as my pride." She moved to stand.

"Wait. Are you sure you're okay? Nothing's sprained? Wrists? Ankles?"

She shook her head. "I've checked everything. I didn't move because I didn't know how I was going to get back up there."

Matt laughed. "That's easy," he said, and proceeded to show her just how easy it was.

Back on high ground and standing beside Matt, Aimee brushed snow off her pants as she surveyed the place where she'd fallen. "What did I fall into?"

"A creek bed, and not even a very deep one." He pointed behind them and then in front, tracing the creek's meandering path to where it disappeared among the evergreen trees. "See that narrow ribbon of snow that's kind of sunken?"

"Oh. I should have seen that." It would have saved her a sore butt and sore pride. "So all that extra snow blew into the creek? It sort of collects it, I guess."

"That's exactly right. Spend much time hiking in the snow and you learn to notice things you might not otherwise. Little signs like that dip in the snow or a shadow that might indicate a rock. Things that can hurt you or even kill you if you don't pay attention."

"Okay, so tell me again why I'm leading, if you're the expert?" She grinned at him. Not even her fall could spoil her good mood. She felt like laughing and running and dancing.

In a little while, she would have her baby back in her arms, safe and sound. That was worth every minute of the past day. Every second.

Matt's brows drew down. "Good point," he said. "Okay. I'll take the lead, but you've got to keep up. Tell me if I go too fast."

"Okay, sir," she said. "You go in front, sir, and I'll follow. But please, keep showing me the secrets the snow is covering up. Never know when that kind of thing might come in handy."

Before they headed out again, Matt shed his parka and stuffed it inside his makeshift pack.

The snug-fitting wool sweater he wore over his insulated underwear glistened in the sunlight. Wool was too fuzzy to clearly outline the muscles in his arms and torso, but Aimee hadn't forgotten how he looked with the firelight glinting off the planes and angles of his naked torso last night. Nor had she forgotten how his warm, strong body felt pressed against her.

Bill had been good-looking, with his light brown hair, his hazel eyes and the dimples all the girls in high school had gone crazy over. He was always voted most handsome and most likely to succeed. He'd been big and tall, and captain of the football team.

Matt, on the other hand, had once been voted most shy. His dark hair, brown eyes and strong features weren't as classically handsome as Bill's had been. His nose was a little too long, and he'd never played football. He'd been on the swim team. His muscles had always been long and lean. In fact, some had considered him downright scrawny.

But after last night, Aimee had decided that Matt was a dangerously attractive and sexy man.

"Okay, let's go," he said, sending her a puzzled look. "You sure you're okay?"

She nodded and shrugged her shoulders to rearrange

the daypack into a comfortable position. As she moved into step behind him, she considered her thoughts.

She was sure she'd seen him in a bathing suit. She was positive she had. She and Bill and Matt had all gone down to Florida on spring break one year, and they'd all stayed in the same room. But she hardly remembered Matt at all. What she remembered about that trip was that she and Bill had had sex for the first time. In the hotel room—with Matt asleep on the other bed.

Her cheeks burned. Dear heavens, what had she been thinking? Granted, it was years ago, probably long forgotten by Matt, if he'd even woken up, but still—how embarrassing.

And now, after having spent the night pressed against his lean, hard body, thinking about that long-ago experience kind of turned her on. Guilt brought heat to her cold cheeks.

Stop it, she warned herself.

Matt held up a hand. "Shh."

She froze.

He sent her a quick look over his shoulder, and then cocked his head, listening.

Before she realized that he'd moved, Matt had grabbed her arm and pulled her toward him. He propelled her over to a stand of trees and followed her several feet in, until they were surrounded by trees on all sides.

Then he crouched down, and pulled her back between his knees.

"Stay quiet," he whispered in her ear.

"What is—"

He put his fingers across her mouth. She nodded

against them and after a couple of seconds, he removed them.

For a long time, they crouched there, spooned awkwardly. Even through layers of clothes, the sense of intimacy was as strong as it had been the night before.

Her insides stirred, tingling with sensations that she hadn't felt in a long time. She yearned to lean back, to press herself against Matt the way he'd pressed his body against hers last night. Her eyes drifted closed as the tingling centered itself in her core.

He put his hands on her shoulders. She wanted to cover them with hers, to take them and pull them around her, so she could feel the way she'd felt last night. As much as it scared her to admit that she wanted him, that was how much she longed for him to touch her, to kiss her and, yes, to make love with her.

She told herself it was because he made her feel safe.

His fingers squeezed her shoulders, massaging them. He leaned forward, his breath warming her cheek. Was he feeling the same thing she was?

Then she heard it. A buzzing sound. Very faint. She turned her head but she couldn't tell where it was coming from. What was it? An engine?

Her pulse sped up. An engine. A helicopter! Maybe it was Deke, coming to rescue them. He could take them to the Vicks' cabin and help them rescue William. Her breath caught in an excited sob.

But if it were Deke's helicopter, why were they hiding?

"Is that an engine?" she whispered.

Matt put his ear next to hers and nodded his head.

"Helicopter?" she asked hopefully.

He shook his head no. "Snowmobile."

Snowmobile? But that could be anybody.

Anybody.

"Oh."

He pressed his fingertips against her lips again, warning her to stay quiet.

Slowly, over what seemed to be an endless stretch of time, the noise of the engine grew louder. It kept growing louder, until it sounded like it was close enough to run them down.

Matt put his hand on the back of her head. "Put your head down. And don't move."

As she lowered her head, Matt pressed his forehead against her back. She could imagine what the two of them looked like. Two small, fragile humans dwarfed by the tall trees, crouched together, hoping and praying that they couldn't be seen by someone whizzing by on a snowmobile. Or someone searching for them—

Her heart pounded so loud she was afraid it could be heard over the motor's noise.

As the engine noise grew deafening, she felt Matt straighten. He left his hand resting gently on the back of her neck, so she didn't budge. He grew so still that if it weren't for the slow, steady rise and fall of his chest, she might have been able to forget he was there, pressed against her.

Okay, no. She wouldn't forget the feeling of his body molded to hers—not for a very long time.

Finally, the noise of the engine faded into the distance. Aimee waited until Matt took his hand away from the nape of her neck before she sat up.

"Ah," she moaned as her muscles relaxed from their cramped position. She looked at Matt. "Who was it? Could you see anything?"

He nodded grimly.

"Was it the kidnapper?"

"Nope. It was Al Hamar. There was a lot of blood on his pants. The kidnapper must have hit him in the side. He didn't look happy, but he didn't look like he was too handicapped by the wound, either."

"He didn't see us." She phrased it as a statement, but she watched Matt's face for confirmation. "Where do you think he's going?"

He rubbed his thumb across his lower lip, and averted his gaze. "I'm afraid he's probably headed for the cabin, just as we are."

And as quickly as that, all sense of safety, all confidence, all joy at the knowledge that William was only a few miles away and safe, dissolved, and Aimee was back in that awful place where she'd existed since six-thirty Wednesday morning.

"Why?" she moaned. "I thought you didn't think he was connected with the kidnapping. How would he know about the cabin?"

Matt's jaw clenched. After an instant of wavering, his gaze met hers. "All I can figure out is that both he and Kinnard are—"

"Kinnard?" Aimee didn't like how Matt was acting. He obviously didn't want to tell her something.

"That's the kidnapper's name."

"The man who took William? Who is he?"

"According to the FBI, he's a small-time hood who has operated around the Crook County area for the past twenty years or so."

"You said *apparently.*"

Matt straightened. "We should get going."

"No. *You* should tell me what's going on. Who do

you think Kinnard is, and what are you trying not to tell me?"

"I think both men are working for Novus Ordo."

"Novus Ordo? The terrorist?" She felt the blood drain from her face. She'd thought nothing could be as bad as having her baby kidnapped. But by *terrorists?*

"You're talking about Novus Ordo?" she asked. "The man whose face nobody has ever seen? The one they say is more dangerous than Bin Laden?"

Matt swallowed and reluctantly met her gaze. "We believe he had Rook Castle assassinated, because Rook saw him—he may be the only person outside Novus's inner circle who has ever seen the man's face."

"I don't—understand." What did Rook Castle and an infamous terrorist have to do with her? With her baby?

"I know. It's complicated. But the theory is that since Rook's body was never recovered, and since Irina has been searching for him all this time, Novus has been watching her, just in case."

"In case Rook is still alive." Aimee couldn't believe she was hearing—much less beginning to understand— what Matt was saying.

Matt nodded. "So since security is so tight around Castle Ranch that Irina and Deke are virtually untouchable, Novus is trying to capture me, to interrogate me about Rook."

"So a *terrorist* kidnapped *my baby* to get to you?"

"I'm not positive, but if Kinnard is working for Novus, and if the anonymous caller was telling the truth—"

"Then the cabin is a trap." Aimee's heart felt ripped to shreds. She put her gloved hands to her mouth and breathed into them, trying to stop the panic from rising in her throat. She spoke, her words muffled by the thick gloves.

"We can't go to the cabin." She swallowed panic and fear and breathed in courage. "They'll capture you."

Matt took her hands away from her mouth and held them. "I made you a promise. Nothing—*nothing*—is going to stop me from keeping it."

Her breath hitched.

"Everything we know points to William being at the cabin. We're going."

SATURDAY 1400 HOURS

"Remember what I told you," Matt said.

Aimee barely heard him. It had taken four hours, but they were finally looking down at the cabin from their vantage point on a rise to the west.

She stared at the primitive log structure. She knew a little about it from Bill. His father, Boss Vick, had spent an obscene amount of money to equip the simple dwelling.

He'd brought a crew up one summer who'd cleared trees, installed a generator and carted appliances and furniture up. He'd made it into a comfortable winter retreat, if one didn't mind skiing in or living with the prospect of being snowed in.

Aimee had always thought the idea of spending so much on a hunting shack was wasteful, but right now, the amenities sounded wonderful to her—the generator, the appliances, the comfortable furnishings—because they meant that her baby was warm and comfortable and well-fed.

And in the hands of terrorists.

"Aimee? Did you hear me?"

She nodded. "I don't make a move until you've gone down there and verified that nobody is waiting to shoot us when we step out into the open." She couldn't take her eyes off the house. She squinted, but couldn't see through any of the windows. But that was okay. Whether she could see him or not, her baby was in there. Her fingers itched—her arms ached—to hold him.

But Matt was right. They had to take precautions. There were at least two people on this mountain who meant them harm.

"You'll wave *all clear,* and motion me to come down. Or you'll hold up your hands, palms out, and press them down, meaning stay where I am." She demonstrated what he'd shown her earlier.

"Good. And if something happens to me?"

She pressed her lips together and squeezed her eyes shut. "I run for the cabin. Matt, maybe this is not a good idea. Maybe we ought to wait until Deke gets here. Spend the night up here, or—"

It nearly killed her to suggest waiting. She thought she was going to die if she had to wait one second longer to hold her baby, but the prospect of Matt being captured by terrorists—captured and interrogated—was nearly as horrible to contemplate as the possibility that she might never see William again.

"No." He shook his head, dislodging snowflakes from his hair. He held out his gloved hand and several more fell onto it. "See that? It's starting to snow again. The storms from last night are only the beginning. There are more stacked up, waiting for their shot at us. And we have no shelter." He craned his neck and examined the sky.

"There's a very good chance that we wouldn't survive the night. With just the mummy bag for the two of us, it's too risky. Getting to the cabin is our best chance."

"What if we both go down at the same time? We can watch each other's backs. You'll have that machine gun thing and I have the Glock. We can hold them off."

His face softened into an almost-smile. "Or...we could wait until nightfall. We could probably sit out a storm during the day without freezing to death. Even behind the clouds, the sun still provides a lot of heat. But after sundown is a different story."

"I like that idea—waiting until dark."

Matt kept his gaze on the cabin and the surrounding area. "We need to get to work if we're going to spend the rest of the day here. I want to build a snow shelter. It'll hide us and keep us warm after the clouds roll in. Plus it'll protect us from the snow and the wind." He peered through the trees at the cabin, then scanned the tree line above and below the clearing. He didn't see anyone.

That didn't surprise him. Kinnard was definitely right at home on the mountain, and Al Hamar was almost certainly from a mountainous country—Afghanistan or Pakistan—and trained in guerrilla tactics. Either one of them could be anywhere—in the cabin or hiding out, ready to ambush Matt and Aimee as they approached it.

"We don't want to be seen, so we have to work quickly and at the same time stay hidden. So be prepared to crawl around."

"What do you need me to do?"

"Right now, keep an eye on the cabin while I scout around for the best place to locate our shelter. I like that overhanging rock over there. We need to hurry, though. From the looks of the sky, by the time we get the shelter built, we're going to be very glad to have it."

SURE ENOUGH, BY the time the shelter was ready, the new storm had rolled in, bringing another sky full of heavy, snow-laden clouds and a nasty mix of freezing rain and snow.

Aimee sat inside the cramped space, waiting for Matt to come inside. He'd spread a space blanket on the ground and folded one of the blankets on top of it. He'd covered the downhill side of the lean-to with the other blanket, and that made a huge difference in the inside temperature.

Matt pushed aside the blanket and climbed inside, bringing freezing air and icy spray with him. He'd taken off his parka, which he draped over the makeshift backpack. "Not bad, if I do say so myself. What do you think?"

She tried to smile, but she knew she wasn't pulling it off. "Better than the Ritz."

"Hey," he said, his voice closer than she'd expected. It was nearly pitch-black with the blanket closed. And granted, the entire space of the shelter was about six feet by three feet. Still, she'd figured he'd hover near one side and she'd cling to the other.

"How're you doing? It'll be dark within about three hours. Then we can sneak down to the cabin and check things out. Meanwhile…" He paused and took a breath. "Meanwhile, you should take off your parka. Believe it or not, it'll be easier to adjust to the temperature without it on. Plus, when we get ready to go, you'll be glad you have another layer to put on."

Aimee carefully shrugged out of the down jacket. She held on to it and used it to cover her hands. She'd taken off her gloves, which were wet from piling and packing snow.

"Matt, can I ask you a question?"

"Sure. Anything."

"You said Irina and Deke were untouchable because of the security around the ranch."

"Right. Rook installed the best equipment money could buy. And all the employees are screened carefully."

"But when you were talking to Irina, you mentioned sabotage. At the ranch."

He stared at her for a moment. "I did. Somebody tampered with Deke's helicopter. Irina said it was definitely sabotage." He cursed. "I heard it but it didn't sink in. Irina could be in danger." He shook his head.

"You're awfully hard on yourself."

"What?"

Aimee sent him a small smile. "You're out here, protecting me, and doing your best to rescue my baby, but at the same time you're beating yourself up for not thinking about Irina's possible danger."

He shrugged. "I feel responsible."

"I know you do. It's the kind of man you are." She settled against the rock that formed the back of their lean-to. "From everything I know about Deke Cunningham, I'm guessing he can protect Irina."

"Yeah. He can."

For several minutes, they sat silently. Aimee could feel Matt's tension. Was he still kicking himself? She figured it was time to change the subject.

She looked around at the shelter he'd built. "I guess

this is how the first Americans lived for hundreds of years."

"Thousands. Yeah. We're soft these days."

"Not you," she said, poking his bicep with her finger.

He laughed, a soft rumbling sound. "Yeah, me."

She lay her hand on his arm. "Not you," she murmured.

His gaze snapped to hers. Even in the near blackness, his dark eyes picked up a reflection from somewhere. And in that reflection was the thing that had been born of their necessary closeness in the shelter the night before. The awareness that they were not just two people bound by their love for his friend and her husband.

Aimee cringed at what she'd done. One poke might have been just an innocent gesture. One teasing touch could be ascribed to friendship. But she'd touched him twice. She'd *lingered.*

That was no innocent gesture.

After the awkward silence had swelled to uncomfortable proportions, he uttered a small chuckle. "Oh? Well, what about you? You aren't looking so bad." He slid his hand along the line of her shoulder and upper arm. "A little on this side of skinny."

That was all. Yet her body burned as if he'd trailed hot fingers over its entire length.

"My guess is you've got some fair-sized biceps yourself."

Aimee moistened her lips.

Innocent teasing, she told herself. That's all it was. How long had it been since she'd felt like laughing, even a little bit? Other than when she played with William. Besides, she'd known Matt for most of her life. He was a friend.

There might be a smidgen of sexual tension between them, the natural attraction between a man and a woman forced together by circumstance. That's all this was.

Natural. Understandable. Easily ignored.

What could a little teasing hurt? It was better than sitting here in gloomy silence for hours. A little humor would help pass the time.

She squeezed her fist and flexed her arm muscles. "Fair-sized biceps? I beg your pardon. Check this out."

His fingers closed around her biceps—it felt like they completely circled her upper arm.

"Yeah," he said softly. "You're a regular American Gladiator."

His breath fanned her cheek. He was that close.

Aimee had no idea what to do next. However, apparently he did. He let go of her arm and slid his hand around her shoulders.

"Here." His voice rumbled through her like the purr of a lion. "We can keep each other warm."

His arm was firm and big and comforting, and his body radiated heat. Aimee was tempted to tuck herself into the warm, safe nook created by his torso and arm.

He pulled her closer.

She sighed and gave in to temptation, relaxing against him.

His breaths ruffled her hair. She raised her head, wanting to feel him breathing on her skin. When she did, her nose brushed his chin, and she breathed in his scent. He smelled of snow and evergreen, with a hint of smokiness. It plummeted her back to the night before and his warm embrace.

Her breath caught.

He uttered a small moan, deep in his throat, and then pressed his forehead against hers and slid his fingers up her shoulder to cradle the back of her head.

"Aimee—"

Her heart fluttered—with fear or desire, she wasn't sure. She had no idea what he was going to do or say. She had no idea what she *wanted* him to do or say. As far as she was concerned, they could sit like this for the next three hours.

She was pretty sure that three hours of Matt's full attention would bolster not only her courage, but her energy and her resolve, as well.

"Aimee, I need to tell you something."

She rolled her forehead from side to side against his. "No, you don't." *Don't ruin this moment with reality. Don't make it anything more than it is. A stolen instant out of time.*

"I do. I need to expl—"

She kissed him. Just grabbed his face between her hands and—smack. No hesitation, no nips or teases or nibbles. Just a full-on, openmouthed kiss.

And she did it because sitting here in this dangerous, tense situation, pursued by men who could be working for the most ruthless terrorist on the planet, waiting for nightfall so they could rescue her seven-month-old baby, she still felt safer than she had in years.

She didn't want him to jerk her back to reality with guilt-ridden explanations about why he didn't go to Bill's funeral, or come back for William's christening.

She *knew* how guilty and responsible he felt. She knew because he was that kind of guy. He took the heat, the hits, the blame. Not in some arrogant, look-how-responsible-I-am way, either. When he succeeded, he did so quietly, without fanfare.

When he failed, he handled that quietly, as well.

By the time all that had flitted through Aimee's head, Matt's initial shock had faded.

He leaned forward and kissed her back. As fully and enthusiastically as she'd kissed him. He didn't waste any time hesitating or testing her reaction.

He *kissed* her.

And she discovered that beneath Matt's ordinary-guy veneer ran an undercurrent of passion, need and sexual hunger far greater than she'd imagined. His heart beat strongly, rapidly, vibrating through her as his mouth moved over hers with authority and exquisite gentleness. A thrill of unexpected desire pulsed through her all the way to her core. She leaned closer, yielding to the promise of his kiss.

But then he stopped. He lifted his head and hovered there, his lips so close to hers that their warmth still lingered on her mouth.

"Matt?"

He was frowning, his eyes as black as coals. "What are we doing?" he whispered.

CHAPTER NINE

A TWINGE OF uncertainty embedded itself beneath Aimee's breastbone at Matt's question.

Don't ask what we're doing, she wanted to say. *Don't make it more than it is—or less.*

But she didn't have the courage to say that, so she tried to make light of it.

"Staying warm?" Her eyes had adjusted to the darkness, so that she saw the uncertainty there.

He smiled, but the worry didn't leave his eyes. His gaze roamed over her face, as if he were searching for something. "I'd really like to talk to you about—"

Aimee put her fingers over his mouth. "Please don't. Not now. I need to concentrate on William."

"Sure. Of course." He pulled away. "Sorry."

"Don't do that. Don't get all honorable and responsible on me."

"I'm confused," he said. "I'm not sure what you want from me."

She took a deep breath. "I'm tired and cold and scared, and I'm feeling very alone." She nibbled on her lower lip for a second. "Is it possible I want the same thing from you that you want from me?"

Matt's eyes widened, and then narrowed. He sat unmoving for a moment, and then touched her chin with his forefinger. "I never meant to come on to you. I didn't intend to let this happen."

"I know that. Me, either. But it's happening." She looked down. "At least it is for me."

"Aimee—"

She looked at him from under her lashes, hearing his unspoken plea. "Just hold me for a little while. Hold me and keep me warm."

"No problem," he said with a sigh. "No problem at all." He settled back against the rock and cradled her against his side. His other hand held her head against his chest, and she felt him press a kiss against her hair.

She could hear his heartbeat, steady and fast. After a few moments, Aimee felt his thumb sliding across her cheek in a rhythmic, sweet caress. She sighed and curled her fingers against his chest. When she did, his heart sped up and his breaths turned ragged.

He stiffened, and she knew he was aroused. If she stirred, or if he did, she'd find out for sure just how turned on he was.

It surprised her just how much she wanted to find out.

She knew Matt almost as well as she'd known her own husband. Probably better than any other man she'd ever met. He wanted her. His body told her that. But he would never act on those feelings.

He valued honor and loyalty above all else. In his mind, acting on sexual feelings for his best friend's widow was a betrayal of her trust in him.

If she left it up to him, the stolen kiss and this warm embrace were as far as he would go. But even if she regretted it later, right now she wasn't willing to stop.

Heaven help her, she wanted more. Much more. The thought of touching him sent a thrill of desire humming through her. Her breath caught and her pulse raced.

She turned her head and pressed a soft kiss to the sensitive underside of his chin, feeling a triumphant satisfaction when he gasped quietly. Then she shifted, to gain easier access to his mouth.

For an instant, he sat still and unyielding, but she persisted, kissing his mouth and cheek, wrapping her arms around his neck.

Finally, he dragged her across his lap and gave her back kiss for kiss, caress for caress, until both of them were out of breath.

Matt lifted her again, and somehow she ended up lying on her back with him hovering over her. After a searching look, he lowered his head and kissed her again.

She'd never experienced anything like the feeling of his mouth on hers, of his body pressed against hers. He was aggressive and gentle at the same time. Demanding and giving. He rested his weight on his elbows so he could look at her. His erection pulsed against her thigh.

She slid her hand down his ridged abdomen until her palm found his hardness. The feel of his erection, firm and vibrant against her fingers, even through the barrier of his clothes, sent desire thrumming through her like a drumbeat.

He shuddered, and she knew he was almost to the edge. He felt for the buttons on her pants while at the same time his tongue slid over the sensitive skin of her neck. When his teeth scraped her earlobe and his breath warmed her ear, her whole body contracted in erotic reaction.

By the time she realized her pants were gone, his fingers were sliding inside the waistband of her underwear. Before he even touched her, she was gasping for breath.

Then his fingers reached their goal. She cried out.

He stopped, but she moaned in protest. "Matt, please. I need to feel you, too."

His dark eyes searched her face. Then he sat up, disposed of his pants, and stretched his length against her again.

Her backside was cold, pressed against the poor insulation of a thin blanket, but Matt's legs, his torso, his groin, radiated heat. His erection, hard against her, burned her skin with a delicious heat that turned her insides to liquid fire.

She closed her fingers around him, feeling his velvety hardness jump in her hand. At the same time his fingers slid through her nether hair and raked gently along the folds that hid her center.

She arched, the pleasure almost painful in its intensity. Pleasure she hadn't felt for far too long.

He teased her there, circling and coaxing, dipping and withdrawing, again and again, as his mouth traveled from her neck to her collarbone and on, to find the tip of her breast and nip at it through the thin silk of her long-sleeved pullover.

Then he lifted himself and settled between her thighs. His rigid shaft rubbed against her, driving her desire. She opened to him, oblivious of the chilled air and the icy cold ground.

Bending his head, he nibbled at her lips, then pulled back and looked into her eyes.

"You okay?" he whispered.

In answer, she arched her neck and reached for his

mouth with hers. "I'm ready," she whispered against his lips, knowing what he would know within seconds. Her core was liquifying, flowing, preparing to receive him.

He looked deeply into her eyes as if searching for something, then with deliberate, torturous slowness, he sank into her.

She moaned as his full length filled her and spread exquisite longing like golden, fluid light through her body. Enveloped in a haze of erotic sensation, all she could do was feel.

He stayed there, buried in her, his face tucked into the hollow between her neck and shoulder, for an interminable time. The feel of his breath on her neck was, if possible, more intimate than the sensation of his hardness filling her. It was a gesture of surrender, of trust, she realized.

He was blind with his eyes tucked into the darkness. He was vulnerable with his neck exposed to possible enemies. He was open, undefended.

Her eyes filled with tears. She slid her hand around the nape of his neck, and turned her face toward his.

Then he moved, and her body spasmed, sending electric shocks of pleasure tumbling through her. He slid out, out, until he hovered at her opening, then in to fill her again. The slow friction increased her wetness and made each successive thrust easier.

Each time he pushed into her, he sped up slightly, his body coaxing hers to keep pace with him. He stayed suspended above her, watching her. She realized that he was gauging her response and tailoring his movements to hers.

When she thought she would burst with anticipation, when her breasts were puckered and tight and her entire body felt electrified, he sat back on his haunches and pulled her legs atop his thighs. Then he held on to her waist and thrust again and again, filling her more completely and more deeply than she'd ever imagined possible.

Faster, deeper.

At last, he wrapped his arms around her and lifted her upright. He held here there, suspended, until she whimpered with need, then lowered her onto him. His powerful thighs flexed as he thrust upward.

Aimee gasped and cried out as a place inside her that had never been touched shattered. Matt kissed her, swallowing her breathless cries. Then he came, too, violently and thoroughly, his jaw clenched and his eyes squeezed shut as he poured everything into her.

With one last powerful thrust, he rocked with her and against her, continuing the dance as their climax faded.

After a few seconds of sitting there, draped against each other in the afterglow of sexual fulfillment, he splayed his fingers over her back again and gently lowered her to the ground, following her and settling beside her.

She lay her head on his shoulder as tears filled her eyes and ran over the bridge of her nose.

He touched one with his thumb and smeared it across her cheek. "What's happening here?" he said tenderly. "Is something wrong?"

She shook her head slightly. "No. Nothing."

He kissed her forehead while his thumb swirled over her skin, spreading and drying the dampness.

"Then why are you crying?"

She shrugged and bit her lip to keep from saying *because this is a special occasion.*

MATT WOKE UP cold and stiff. Something sharp was poking him in the back. Something soft and sweet-smelling was pressed against his chest and side. He'd been dreaming about Aimee.

Aimee. He opened his eyes and discovered that his dream had come true. She was asleep with her head on his chest. Her brown hair was wavy and soft, and it tickled his nose. He'd kissed that hair, that brow, those lips.

Carefully, he lifted his arm and glanced at his watch. Almost seven. They'd slept for over two hours. The realization disturbed him. He'd left himself—and, more importantly, Aimee—vulnerable and exposed. The makeshift shelter was a pathetic cover. Had anyone happened by, they'd have been caught or killed.

He lay still for a moment and listened. He heard nothing but the wind whistling through the naked tree branches, and the muffled silence of falling snow. Occasionally, he heard a branch crack and fall, weighted down by snow and ice.

Aimee stirred and murmured something in her sleep. Matt ran his palm lightly down her silk-covered arm as his heart squeezed in regret.

He'd done worse than leave her vulnerable by falling asleep on watch. He'd taken advantage of her by making love with her. She was completely dependent on him to keep her safe. She was frightened for her baby. And he'd promised to take care of her.

Instead, he'd let his feelings get involved. He'd acted on his personal desire, rather than in her and her baby's best interest. He'd relaxed his vigilance and put her in danger.

Despite his self-recrimination, his brain replayed the highlights of those few stolen moments—the supple firmness of her skin, her heavy breasts with their swollen nipples, the way she opened to him as he sank hilt-deep inside her.

To his dismay, his erection grew and strained, the physical symbol of his betrayal of her. He'd never allowed himself to be close to her, afraid that she or Bill or someone who knew them would see the truth in his face—how smitten he'd always been with her. He'd never even admitted to himself how much he'd wanted her.

Until now. He closed his eyes and clenched his jaw, forcing his brain back to his mission. Carefully, he slid his arm from around her and sat up.

She stirred, so he pulled the corner of the mummy bag over his lap to hide his erection, disgusted with himself.

She opened her eyes and looked at him in sleepy confusion. Then her eyes widened. He stared, mesmerized by the myriad emotions that flitted across her features.

To his surprise, she didn't turn away in disgust, or scream for help. Finally, she scraped her lower lip with her teeth and dropped her gaze.

Embarrassed? Humiliated? *Afraid?*

"Aimee, I'm sorry."

Her eyes snapped back up to lock with his. "Sorry?"

He nodded miserably. "We need to dress. It's almost dark, and I want to watch the cabin for a while before we make our move."

She shivered, and then ducked her head, searching around the cramped space for her clothes.

Matt turned the other way and dressed. Then he checked his MAC-10 to be sure it hadn't gotten wet, and loaded it. He did the same with the Glock and handed it to Aimee, handle first.

"Remember. From this point on, there's a chance you'll have to shoot someone to save your life or William's. You have to decide now whether you can do it. Don't aim if you're not prepared to shoot. And don't shoot if you're not prepared to kill."

She nodded, accepting the gun and sliding it into the paddle holster she'd already put on. As soon as she'd finished dressing, she started rolling up the blankets.

Matt stuffed them into his homemade pack and then took the mummy bag's stuff-sack from Aimee and packed it.

The sound of a motor starting up echoed across the canyon. He froze, listening. The motor revved once, twice. He touched Aimee's arm.

"Stay right here."

"Matt—"

"Stay here, and don't make a sound."

He carefully pushed the blanket aside and slipped out. When he'd sneaked as close to the edge of the overhang as he dared go, he used his eyes like an eagle or a hawk would to strafe the ground and search for prey.

Down below, Kinnard was on the snowmobile. As he watched, Kinnard revved it again, then turned off the engine. He cursed as he climbed off the vehicle and stomped back toward the cabin.

Had he forgotten something?

Without moving a muscle he didn't need to, Matt groped in his backpack until his hand closed around his binoculars. He pulled them out and watched Kinnard mount the snow-covered steps.

As the kidnapper reached for the door handle, a loud crack rang out, practically over Matt's head.

Kinnard whirled and looked in their direction. Matt

didn't move. A huge branch crashed noisily as it fell through lower branches. It hit the ground not ten feet away from him with a deafening thud.

Kinnard stood perfectly still, watching and listening. His head was raised and his gaze was on the trees that were still swaying as they rebounded from being hit by the falling branch.

Matt knew that where he sat was partially obscured by tangled underbrush. He also knew that if he moved, Kinnard's brain would separate his gray-and-green-and-white camo from the surrounding natural foliage.

Behind him, he heard Aimee stirring.

It took every ounce of willpower he possessed not to move or speak.

Stay still, Aimee.

Matt didn't take his eyes off Kinnard as the man squinted up at the place where the branch had fallen. Behind him, Aimee continued to move. If she decided to push the blanket aside, they'd be sitting ducks.

Finally, the kidnapper's rigid stance relaxed. He glanced around, then went inside the cabin. Matt didn't dare move. If Kinnard was just retrieving something he'd forgotten, he'd be out within seconds. Sure enough, Kinnard appeared again almost immediately, climbed on the snowmobile, started it up and headed northeast. Matt got a glimpse of the rifle in its scabbard, attached to the right side of the vehicle.

His breath hissed out between his teeth. He lifted the binoculars again and examined every inch of the cabin. As he was studying the layout and trying to remember anything he could about the couple of trips he and Bill had made up here when they were kids, a dim light came on in one of the windows.

His pulse sped up as a young woman appeared, holding a baby. She was rocking from one foot to another and bouncing the boy in her arms. As he watched, she bent her head and kissed him on his forehead.

A frisson of relief slithered down his spine. The woman's stance and demeanor were that of a caregiver. A nanny, maybe. Or a mother. She was obviously caring for William.

Aimee's baby was in safe hands—for the moment.

He sent up a brief *Thank You* prayer as he turned his gaze back to the northeast. The hum of the snowmobile's motor was waning. Kinnard was gone, at least for a while.

They needed to make their move now.

He detached the blanket from over the shelter opening and rolled it up. Aimee had searched the inside of the shelter to make sure they weren't leaving anything.

"Got everything?" he asked, looking around.

"I think so. What was that motor?"

"It was Kinnard on his snowmobile. He just took off on it." Matt took her arm. "Aimee, as far as I can tell, right now William is in there alone with a young woman who appears to be taking *very* good care of him."

"Really?" Her gaze zeroed in on the cabin. "You saw him? He's all right? Can I see? Oh, Matt. Can we go now?"

"Listen to me. We've got to act fast. Kinnard headed north. He may be planning to hide up there and watch for us."

Matt rubbed his thumb across his lower lip and looked up at the sky. "The snow is coming down harder, so that's on our side. If we circle around to the south side of the cabin, and the snow keeps up, we should be able to sneak into the cabin without him seeing us."

"What about the girl?"

"When I saw her, she didn't act as if she were being watched. There didn't appear to be anyone else there, either. She was totally concentrated on the baby. But we have to go in as if there were armed guards in every room." He set his jaw and looked Aimee straight in the eye.

"That means you can't go rushing to William. You have to stay with me and do exactly as I say." He gripped her arms. "Can you do that?"

Her eyes glittered with dampness. She opened her mouth but nothing came out.

"Can you?" he growled. "Because if you can't, you're going to have to stay up here, hidden, until I can get him. I can't take care of both of you at once."

CHAPTER TEN

SATURDAY 1900 HOURS

AIMEE CLOSED HER eyes and took a deep breath. Then she lifted her chin. "I can do it."

He pushed away his need to touch her, to pull her close and kiss her and promise her that everything was going to be all right. This was a mission—he needed to act like a commander. And somewhere inside him he had to find the detachment and focus that made him good at his job.

And Aimee had to act like a soldier.

"This is a covert operation, Aimee. I'm the commander and you're my team. You follow my orders. If I say *abort*—then we abort the mission and retreat. Is that understood?"

Her lower lip trembled visibly, and her eyes glittered with unshed tears. But she nodded.

"Are you sure? Because if I give the order, you have to leave William and do what I tell you. Can you do that?"

Her chin lifted. "Yes, sir."

Fierce longing and aching compassion took his breath away. For one instant, he abandoned his Special Forces training and allowed himself to be just a man. He cupped her cheek and leaned in to kiss her trembling lips.

When their lips touched, a thrill swirled through him that nearly buckled his knees. "I swear to God, Aimee, if you can trust me, I will save your baby."

She pulled away and gave him a solemn look. "I trust you," she whispered.

IT TOOK THEM forty minutes to trudge down the hill and around to the south side of the cabin. Despite what Matt had told Aimee, he was hampered by her. If he'd thought for a minute he could have safely left her in the shelter while he rescued William, he'd have done it.

If he'd thought he could wait until he could get a message through to Deke to fly a man in to help him, he'd have done that. But he had no time, and more importantly, no intention of leaving Aimee to fend for herself for even a short while.

He had to rescue them both.

So he clenched his jaw and moved at a pace far slower than he wanted to. As they approached the south, downhill side of the cabin, he quickly repeated his instructions to Aimee.

"I'll go in first. You wait for my hand signal. I'll wave you on as soon as I can verify that the room is clear. If you don't see me, you stay right where you are until you do." He looked at her evenly.

"What do you do if I don't come back out?"

She swallowed. "After ten minutes, I head for the door and—and give myself up." She paused. "Matt—?"

"No. No questions. You give yourself up."

She nodded reluctantly.

"Okay, once we're inside—do you remember what

I told you about the layout?" He was going by what he remembered from his early teens. He hoped to hell he was at least partly right.

"The big room is in front. The right-hand door goes to a bedroom, the left-hand door goes to the kitchen."

"Right, and the kitchen is where I saw the girl holding William."

"You're going through the bedroom and around to the kitchen from the north side. You'll wait until I go in through the south door and surprise her. When you hear me speak, you'll come through the north door."

"Good. After that, just listen to me. I'll tell you what to do."

She nodded.

He looked at her and sent her what he hoped was an encouraging smile. "Ready?"

Aimee's throat closed up, but she nodded. A week ago, if anyone had told her she'd be part of a mountain rescue mission to save her own son, she'd have called that person insane.

Now, here she was, ready to stage a dangerous rescue at the side of a Special Ops soldier who was one of the best search-and-rescue specialists in the country.

They were about to rescue her seven-month-old son from kidnappers.

A trembling started deep within her and quickly spread out to her hands, arms and knees. She held on to the Glock with both hands, hoping it would give her strength and courage.

In front of her, Matt stole forward, his entire body tense with expectation. He was ready for anything. His broad shoulders looked strong enough to support the world. His body, even in the bulky coat and camo pants, moved with the powerful grace of a big cat—a leopard maybe, or a cougar.

He was so strong yet he could be so gentle. She knew if anyone in the world could save her baby, Matt could.

Dear heavens, she trusted him. And she believed him—believed every word he said. She hadn't wanted to. She certainly didn't want to believe that he couldn't have prevented Bill's death. It was so easy to blame someone.

He turned his head and glanced at her over his shoulder, his profile strong and assured as a warrior. Then he gestured, waving her forward and pointing to an evergreen.

She rose to an uncomfortable crouch and eased forward, staying in the shadow of the tree. Her pulse sped up and her mouth went dry. She reached behind her and seated the paddle holster, making sure it was secure.

Matt shifted his weight to the balls of his feet, then held up his hand, thumb and first finger forming an O for OK.

She sent him the same gesture back.

He pointed to his own head and then forward.

He'd given her the five-minute crash course in signals, so she knew he was telling her that he was about to move forward. He didn't look back at her, so her responding nod was wasted.

As he half crawled, half crept toward the two steps that led to the cabin's door, she waited. Her limbs twitched with the need to move, and her pulse sped up.

She fought to keep her breathing even as she watched him unlock the door and slip inside. He'd warned her that once he'd disappeared into the house, she'd feel an almost uncontrollable urge to follow him.

It's the hardest thing to learn about stealth recon-naissance, he'd explained. *When your commander gives you an order, his life and yours rest on him being able to trust you to carry out that order, even if all it means is that you stay still.*

She'd thought she understood. But he was right. She burned to move a few steps forward, enough to be able to see through a window.

She set her teeth and clenched her fists. She would not move. As much as it was killing her not to be able to see what he saw, not to be able to lay eyes on her baby. Her scalp burned, and despite the cold air, a drop of sweat ran down her back.

"Come on," she muttered. "Hurry up."

MATT STOOD IN the front room of the cabin, listening. He heard water running, and a feminine voice talking in low, soothing tones. Then he heard a giggle and a splash.

The girl was giving William a bath. The excruciat-ing tension in his shoulders and neck relaxed, sending a rush of relief through him all the way from his head to his feet.

William was safe and happy.

He needed to take a look at the kitchen before he gestured Aimee in. He didn't want to leave her outside any longer than he had to, but he'd ordered her to treat this like a mission, and he had to do the same thing.

It was dangerous to leave her out there undefended, but that's how he would handle it if she were a BHSAR specialist. Except that if she were a specialist, she'd know how long to wait and when to move, even if she didn't get a signal.

Matt glided forward a few steps and peered in past the door hinges. Although the light given off by the oil lantern was dim and flickering, his narrow view caught the edge of the sink. He saw William's arms waving, and the girl's hand gliding a soapy washcloth over his pink, new skin. She laughed. She sounded young, maybe not far out of her teens.

Hopefully that was a good sign. If she were young and enchanted by William, chances were she'd be easily manipulated into talking about Kinnard.

He angled his head enough to get a view of the rear door to the kitchen. In the dimness it was impossible to tell if it was unlocked, but at least he'd remembered the cabin's layout correctly. There *were* two doors to the kitchen.

He retraced his steps across the room, thankful that the floorboards were solid, not creaky. He slipped through the front door and closed it. Then he gestured for Aimee.

She rose and moved stealthily forward and up the steps. He let out the breath he'd been holding. Thank God she was all right. He'd only taken a few seconds to reconnoiter, but he knew all too well that it took only a few seconds to kill.

"They're in the kitchen," he whispered in her ear. "She's bathing William and he's happy. He's splashing water everywhere."

She swallowed and then nodded. "Bath time is his favorite time of day. He thinks it's funny to splash water on me—" Her voice cracked.

"It's okay, Aimee. He's right there and he's safe. Now—I'm going around through the bedroom. Give me sixty seconds and then step through the left door—

that's the door to the kitchen—get the drop on the girl. And be careful."

She hadn't taken her eyes off the door. He understood why. Her baby was on the other side of it. "Don't take your eyes off her for an instant and—" he touched her chin, forcing her to look at him "—don't let yourself get distracted by William. It's important, Aimee. Your life and his depend on it. Our mission is to rescue him. Right now you've got to be a soldier, not a mother. Do you understand?"

Pain lit her eyes, but she nodded.

"By the time you get the drop on her, I'll be coming in the rear door and we'll have her in a cross fire. Okay?"

"How will I know sixty seconds?"

He counted for her. "Count like that. Don't let your anxiety let you speed up the count."

She nodded. "Okay."

"One final thing. Get her to sit down. Keep away from the window. I saw her. That means Kinnard might be able to see you. Let's go." He peered around the door and then pushed it open. He gestured for her to go to the left door and he'd go to the right.

He pointed at his watch, indicating that she should start counting.

She nodded.

He slipped through the door and took a couple of precious seconds to study the bedroom. He'd give just about anything to find something that identified Kinnard's first name or any information about him or the girl. But the most remarkable thing about the room was the pile of pillows on the bed.

He crossed to the bathroom, which led from the bedroom onto the enclosed back porch.

Good. He'd remembered the layout.

The porch had a half-paned door and two windows. Directly in front of the back door was the door to the kitchen. Through it he could hear the girl talking to William, but he couldn't make out what she said.

Come on, Aimee. He looked at his watch and saw that she had twenty more seconds. He itched to get in, grab the baby and handcuff the girl before she knew what hit her. But he needed Aimee there to take her baby.

So he waited and watched the second hand crawl around.

FIFTY-NINE, SIXTY. Aimee took a deep breath, trying to control her anxiety. She adjusted her two-handed grip on the Glock, laid her shoulder against the door and took a deep breath.

"Here we go, pretty boy," the girl said. William gurgled happily.

Aimee's throat spasmed and her heart squeezed so tightly it hurt. *Her baby.* She almost cried out loud. Closing her eyes, she drew in another deep breath, and shouldered the door open, leading with her weapon.

"Don't move!" she snapped.

The girl shrieked and clasped William to her chest. "What? Who—?" She stepped backward.

"I said—don't move." Aimee's nervousness was completely overshadowed by the horror of what she was doing. She swallowed against the bile that rose in the back of her throat. She'd never aimed a weapon at anyone in her life. Yet here she was, threatening a pretty young woman who was holding *her* baby.

She was aiming a loaded gun at William—her own son. The thought and the action made her physically ill. She looked at the door behind them, absently noticing a pair of snowshoes hanging on a hook.

Where was Matt?

The woman shifted William to her other arm. "Who are you? Where—where did you come from?"

"I'm asking the questions," Aimee snapped. "What's your name?"

In the flickering lantern light, Aimee could see that the young woman's hair was a flat beige color, and her shocked dark eyes were rimmed with pale lashes, which made her look younger than she probably was. She opened her mouth but nothing came out.

"I asked you what your name is."

"Shellie," she said, her voice rising in pitch. She hugged William tighter. "It's Sh-Shollie. What's going on? Who are you?"

Aimee gestured with the barrel of the pistol. "Sit down."

Shellie started around the table.

"No. Sit here." Aimee glanced at the window over the sink, where tie-back curtains hung. She needed them closed.

"Hold it," she snapped.

Shellie froze.

"First, close the curtains." She gestured with the gun.

Watching her warily, Shellie tucked William into the crook of one arm and reached for the curtain ties with the other.

As soon as the fabric fell into place, obscuring the window, Aimee gestured again.

"Now sit."

Shellie obeyed. She bounced William on her lap.

Aimee's sore heart filled to bursting with equal amounts of joy and pain. Joy because her baby was obviously safe and happy. But her arms ached to wrap around his soft, plump little body.

She shivered. The kitchen was much warmer than outside, but she could feel a chilly breeze. "Why aren't you using that generator?"

Shellie looked from the baby to her and back again. "I had it on earlier. We're low on fuel."

Aimee glanced at the door to the porch. What was Matt doing? More than anything, Aimee wanted to lay her weapon down and take William away from Shellie, but she'd promised Matt she'd act like a soldier.

He'd given her an order, and he expected her to carry it out. She had to hold Shellie at gunpoint until he came in.

She quickly glanced around the kitchen, squinting in the dimness. Near the cabinets on the other side of the stove was a step stool. She lowered her head and crept across in front of the window, then nudged the stool closer to the kitchen table and sat on it. Her hands were getting tired, so she set the gun on her lap and rested one hand on the grip. The barrel was still aimed at Shellie.

Matt hadn't told her to talk to the girl, but he hadn't told her not to, either. "Who hired you?" she demanded, her gaze still hungrily assessing every inch of her son's body, to make sure he was all right.

Every time she spoke, his blue eyes turned her way. It was the hardest thing she'd ever done not to look at him. If he started crying, she didn't know if she could stop herself from picking him up.

"Hired me? I don't—"

"Don't lie to me." She picked up the Glock and aimed it at the girl's head. "Who brought you up here and left you to take care of—" Aimee paused. "What's the baby's name?"

She didn't want Shellie to know the baby was hers. If the woman knew that, it would give her a weapon that Aimee couldn't counter.

Shellie licked her lips nervously and lifted William to her shoulder. She patted his back. "I don't know his name. My boyfriend brought me up here. Listen, please don't hurt the baby."

Aimee uttered a short, ironic laugh. "Don't hurt the baby? Oh, don't worry, Shellie, I'm not going to hurt the baby. But if you don't give me some straight answers, I am definitely going to hurt you."

"Okay, okay." Shellie licked her lips again. "My— my boyfriend told me he needed me to watch his—his niece's little boy for a few days. She's sick, and—"

"I said, the truth!"

"But that *is*—"

"You really believe you're up here on the top of a mountain in a snowstorm because your *boyfriend's niece* has a cold?"

William's big bright eyes widened. He turned his head to look at her and frowned and began to whine.

Shellie's eyes grew wide and filled with tears. She sniffed. "You don't understand. When Roy tells you to do something, you don't get in his face about it, you know? I mean, he's been real good to me, but when he says do something, you just gotta do it." She shrugged and took her hand off William's back to wipe her nose on the sleeve of her sweater.

"Who's Roy?"

"He's my boyfriend. I told you."

"Roy who?"

Shellie's eyes narrowed, as if she were weighing the advisability of telling a stranger Roy's full name. Then her gaze dropped to the Glock and she swallowed. "Roy Kinnard. Look, did he do something wrong? 'Cause I didn't know nothing about it if he did. I just watch the baby."

Aimee lowered the gun again. It sounded like Shellie was completely in the dark about Roy's activities. But slim as it was, there was a chance that she was acting. Aimee's instincts told her to believe Shellie was telling the truth. But she couldn't trust her instincts. Not with her baby's life literally in the woman's hands.

"Oh, he's asleep," Shellie said softly.

Fierce longing arrowed through Aimee. She tamped it down. "Where does he sleep?" She kept her voice as hard as she could make it.

"In—in the bedroom. I pile pillows around him so he won't fall off the bed."

"You have children?"

Shellie laughed. "No, but I practically raised my two little brothers. I know all about babies."

Aimee wanted to call out to Matt, but she knew there must be a reason he was keeping quiet. What if something had happened? He'd told her to give herself up if he didn't show.

Apprehension stole her breath. She couldn't do that. She was here, in a warm, safe house with no one but a skinny girl standing between her and her baby. Right now she was in charge. She had the advantage, and she had to keep it.

"Put him to bed." Aimee aimed the gun at Shellie again.

Shellie stood carefully, still patting William on the back. She started toward Aimee, toward the closed door where Matt was supposed to be.

"No!" Aimee snapped. "The other way." She stood and blocked the door.

Shellie looked surprised, but she turned and stepped through the doorway into the big front room and across to the bedroom door.

Aimee was right behind her.

Shellie shifted William and reached for an oil lamp.

"No light." Aimee took a deep breath. "You do what I tell you to—nothing more," she ordered the girl. "I don't want any lights turned on. Just put Wi—the baby—to bed."

Shellie obeyed.

It broke Aimee's heart to watch another woman do the things she always did for William. Her heart twisted in agony to have him so close, and yet too far, in every sense of the word, for her to touch.

"There you go, darlin'," Shellie cooed. "Sleep tight." She leaned over and kissed William's round pink cheek.

Aimee nearly lost it. She bit her lip—hard—to stop herself from moaning aloud. "Sit down, on the foot of the bed, and keep your hands in your lap, so I can see them."

She didn't want Matt to come into the kitchen and find nobody there, but she wasn't sure how concealing the kitchen windows were. Besides, she didn't think she could leave William alone, not even for a moment, now that she'd found him.

Aimee sat at the head of the bed, near William. She

leaned back against the headboard and rested her gun hand on her lap.

"Now, how about telling me who Roy is and who he works for."

MATT PRESSED HIS back against the wall next to the half-paned door, his MAC-10 in his hand. He'd been about to burst in on Aimee and the girl when the clouds had parted, allowing the moon to light the snow-covered landscape.

Aware that Kinnard was still out there, probably waiting for a chance to ambush him, he'd flattened himself against the wall, and carefully surveyed the clearing around the cabin.

He wasn't worried about Aimee. As he'd listened to her barking orders and questioning William's caregiver, he'd smiled and his chest had swelled with pride. She was handling the girl like a pro.

He was relieved when Aimee directed the girl to take the baby into the bedroom. He would have much more freedom to handle Kinnard knowing that Aimee and William were out of the way.

Just as he'd decided it was safe to move across the porch to the kitchen door, he detected movement out of the corner of his eye.

He angled slightly, just enough to check the area close to the house. Nothing. Maybe he'd seen a rabbit or a deer, or even a wolf, but he didn't think so. His instincts, honed by four years in Air Force Special Forces, told him it was a human predator.

Crouching down, he crept across the porch to the door. He was taking a chance. If Kinnard saw the lantern's light, he'd know someone had opened the door.

But Matt would rather lure Kinnard to the kitchen than take a chance on him circling around to the front door. He wasn't about to get himself in a position where Aimee and William were between Kinnard and him.

Matt slipped into the kitchen. The lantern was still lit, although it looked low on oil. The curtains were closed but he knew his silhouette would be visible if he stood. So he slinked across the wooden floor to the table and extinguished the lamp.

He pulled his infrared glasses down from his forehead. He figured Kinnard was likely to have infrared glasses, too, so he stayed hidden as much as possible while he slipped back over to the porch door and opened it. Staying in the shadow of the open door, he rose enough to look out. The moon was still bright.

Then he spotted a figure sneaking down toward the house from the north. Matt recognized Kinnard's burly silhouette. His weapon was slung over his shoulder as he carefully picked his way across the snow from tree to tree.

Matt waited, watching. Once Kinnard got to the clearing, he'd have to step into the open to come any closer. Matt's fingers tightened on the MAC-10. He could take Kinnard out at any time. He'd used deadly force a few times as an Air Force Special Op, but always as a last resort. A *dead* last resort.

No, he wanted Kinnard alive. He wanted to find out who had hired him, and why. He knew he was capable of extracting every bit of information Kinnard had, if he were willing to apply the necessary impetus.

Still, to be safe, he kept a bead on the man as he paused at the edge of the trees. As Matt watched, the kidnapper pulled on a pair of infrared glasses, swung his rifle off his shoulder and held it ready as he stepped into the clearing.

As if on cue, clouds covered the moon. Without the glasses, Matt would be blind in the cloudy darkness. Yet he could see Kinnard's heat silhouette, and he tracked him across the snow-covered ground through his gun's scope.

Kinnard swung the rifle slowly across the windows and doors of the cabin. Matt ducked back into the shadow of the doorway as Kinnard swiveled the barrel his way.

He waited, counting the seconds, considering what he would do if he were the other man. After enough time had passed that the man should have moved on to survey the next window, Matt took a chance and peered out.

Sure enough, Kinnard was aiming at the far west window as he eased forward, his shadow crawling across the moonlit snow.

Matt took a deep breath and rapidly crossed the door's opening, flattening his back against the left facing. Now he was in a better position to shoot, if he had to.

He angled around the facing to get a better look at Kinnard's position.

A shot rang out—cracking the cold, silent air.

Kinnard went down.

CHAPTER ELEVEN

SATURDAY 2000 HOURS

AIMEE SHOT STRAIGHT up off the bed at the sound of the gunshot. Before her brain could process the meaning of what she'd heard, several other shots followed—each one quieter than the last. *Echoes,* she realized.

But echoes of what? Matt's gun? Or Kinnard's rifle? Matt's gun was fully automatic, but she'd only heard the one shot and some echoes. That scared her—a lot.

Had Matt been shot?

William started to whimper. Shellie jumped up, reaching for him.

"Stop!" Aimee barked, pointing the barrel of the Glock at Shellie's head.

Shellie froze, her hands out, fingers spread.

"Don't move a muscle," Aimee whispered.

"That was a gunshot. It scared him," Shellie protested.

"Hush!" Aimee dared a quick glance at her baby. He hiccoughed and stirred, probably as much disturbed by the tension in the room as by the gunfire, then settled back to sleep. She held her breath and listened.

She didn't hear another shot, but a low deep rumbling rose from somewhere.

Shellie raised her head.

"What's that?" Aimee asked.

When Shellie didn't answer, she took a step toward her. "I asked you a question."

"It sounds like snow moving." Shellie licked her lips. Her fingers twitched, and her eyes darted back and forth from the gun in Aimee's hand to the baby.

Aimee moved away from her, toward the door that led into the living room. She didn't want to take a chance that Shellie would try to rush her and take her gun away. "You mean an avalanche?"

Shellie's dark eyes met hers. She nodded. "A small one. That gunshot may have dislodged the wet snow."

Panic fluttered in Aimee's throat. "Is it coming this way? What happens if it hits the cabin?"

Shellie shrugged. "This late in the year, when the weather's getting warmer, slides happen a lot. Can I pick up the baby? He's going to be scared."

Aimee looked at her son, then back at Shellie. *No,* she wanted to say. *He's my baby. I'll pick him up.* But the only thing she knew about this woman was that she cared for William. She wouldn't hurt him. What she would do to Aimee if she let down her guard, Aimee didn't know.

Doing her best to keep her face expressionless, Aimee nodded. "Have you got a safety seat?"

Shellie nodded. "Right there in the corner."

"Don't move. I'll get it." Aimee backed toward the corner and grabbed the child safety seat. She sat it on the foot of the bed near Shellie then backed away.

"Put him in it."

"Uh, ma'am? You're his mother, aren't you?"

Aimee froze. Was she that transparent? "Why would you say that?"

Shellie smiled as she strapped William safely into his seat. "I can see how he reacts to your voice. And you can't keep your eyes off him. I don't exactly know what Roy's doing, but I do know this baby needs his mama." She pushed the seat toward Aimee. "Take him. I know you're dying to."

Aimee forced herself to keep her eyes on Shellie. "No. I can't." She'd promised Matt that she could be a good soldier. William was safe. She didn't have to hold him to know that. Her hands tightened on the Glock's handle and she shook her head.

"He knows I'm here. And I know you've taken good care of him."

"I've been waiting for someone to get here. I called the police this morning, before Roy got here." Tears formed in Shellie's eyes and slipped down her face. "I know you don't trust me, but I did take care of him."

"You made the anonymous call?"

"Please don't tell Roy. He gets mad. But I was afraid something would happen to the baby."

"Thank you, Shellie," Aimee said, just as another deep rumble filled the air and she felt a shudder—she had no idea if it were the cabin floor or her own legs shaking, until she saw the lantern's flame waver.

Her fingers tightened on the Glock. First the gunshot and now an avalanche. Her head spun with panic and worry. Matt was out there. What if he'd been shot?

Had she found her baby only to lose Matt?

KINNARD HADN'T MOVED. Matt kept the MAC and his eye trained on the kidnapper's torso. Even with the infrared glasses, he couldn't tell if any of the shadows he saw were blood. And he couldn't risk going out to check.

Because the gunshot hadn't been from a Glock semi-automatic, or any other kind of handgun. That shot had come from a rifle at least as powerful as the one Kinnard carried. A gun he'd heard firing before.

It had to be Al Hamar, Novus's man who'd followed Matt back from Mahjidastan.

Kinnard had shot him back at the ransom drop point. Matt had seen the blood. But obviously Al Hamar's injury wasn't serious. It certainly hadn't kept him from following them.

Now he was trying to kill Kinnard. Matt had to assume it was because Kinnard was trying to kill Matt.

He'd be happy if Kinnard and Al Hamar got into a cross fire with each other, leaving Matt free to get Aimee and William to safety. But he knew it would be dangerous to let down his guard, so he crept back through the kitchen and into the front room. He wanted to check out the downhill side of the cabin and try to pinpoint Al Hamar's location.

Just as he started across the floor, he heard Aimee's voice, ordering the girl to precede her out of the bedroom.

As soon as he saw her, he spoke quietly. "Aimee."

Both women jumped.

"Matt! Are you okay?"

"Yeah. Shh. Get down, both of you."

"Where did that shot come from?"

"South. Below the cabin. I think Kinnard took a bullet."

"Roy?" the girl cried. "Roy's shot? Oh my God!" She set the baby seat down on the floor. One hand went to her mouth and the other pressed against her tummy.

"Calm down, Shellie," Aimee snapped at her. "Don't move."

Matt pushed his infrared glasses up onto his forehead and watched the two women's silhouettes.

"Is William okay?" he asked.

"He's fine. Shellie took very good care of him. Matt, she's the one who called in the tip."

"What? She called the police—?"

"Where is he? Where's Roy?" Shellie sobbed. "Is he in the kitchen?"

"He's outside," Matt said. "Settle down. We'll check on him as soon as I can be sure Al—the shooter—is gone."

"No! No!" Shellie ran for the front door.

"Shellie, wait!" Aimee cried.

"Hold it!" Matt said. "I need to ask you some questions about the kidnapping."

"No! I have to get to Roy! How could you shoot him?" Shellie broke for the door.

Matt dove for her but she got to the door first and slipped through, shoving it wide enough to block Matt and slow him down.

"Matt, stop her! She'll get killed." Aimee headed for the door.

"Aimee, no!" He stepped in front of her and caught her against his chest. "Get down! Get William."

Aimee immediately dropped to her knees and crawled back to the baby.

"Stay here. That's an order." Matt slid through the open door and onto the front porch. Falling to his stomach, he held the MAC-10 ready to fire. He couldn't see anything.

He crept to the side of the porch, watching every direction. He didn't want to end up shot or captured. He still had work to do. He had to get Aimee and her baby off the mountain.

Shellie's voice sounded muffled and far away as she screamed for Roy. Matt needed to see around the side of the cabin, but the porch didn't extend to the corner.

He pulled down his infrared glasses again and

scanned the area to the south. Nothing stood out that looked like a human. Sliding off the porch, he crawled westward along the cabin's wall, staying as much in the shadows as he could, keeping an eye out to the south for the shooter.

By the time he reached the southwest corner of the cabin, he could hear Shellie crying. Flattening himself against the cabin's wall, he peered around the corner and saw her crouched beside Kinnard, who was stirring.

He breathed a sigh of relief. Shellie was okay, and Kinnard was still alive. He needed to question them both.

While he watched, Kinnard sat up with Shellie's help. Matt saw a patch of black on the front of his winter camos. Blood. He must have taken a bullet in his shoulder, because he was moving pretty well. If he'd been hit in the chest, he wouldn't be upright.

Shellie rose to her knees, still holding on to Roy.

A tiny red dot appeared on the side of her head.

"Look out!" Matt yelled, breaking into a run. He risked a glance behind him, but didn't see anything.

He pushed his legs to pump as fast as possible through the wet snow. "Get down!"

He was about four feet away from the two of them when Shellie turned her head in his direction. The red dot was centered on her forehead.

"Down!" Matt shouted. "Look out!"

Kinnard reached for her to try to pull her to the ground.

A loud crack drowned out all other sound. Shellie's head jerked, then slowly she toppled over.

"Shellie! Oh God!" Kinnard yelled, trying to get to his feet.

Matt saw the red dot slithering up Kinnard's chest and neck.

"Kinnard, duck!"

The kidnapper hit the ground and rolled sideways.

A second crack. Snow puffed as the bullet plowed into the ground barely two inches away from Kinnard's shoulder.

Matt dove into the snow and immediately raised up to shoot, but he knew his MAC wasn't powerful enough to reach the terrorist. So he hurled himself across the snow-covered ground and grabbed for Kinnard's rifle, but the sling was twisted around the other man's arm.

A third shot zinged past Matt's head. At the same time, Kinnard rolled again and sat up, trying to untangle the rifle sling. After a couple of seconds, he got it loose and raised the weapon to his uninjured shoulder.

"You SOB, your man shot Shellie!" Kinnard yelled.

"Not my man," Matt said. "You don't know him?"

"Hell, no. Who the bloody hell is he?" Kinnard bellowed.

"Tell me who hired you, and I'll get you to the cabin."

"Go to hell." Kinnard brandished the rifle in Matt's direction, but Matt grabbed the barrel and twisted it sideways, then shoved the end of it into the snow.

"Listen to me. Do you know who hired you?" Matt growled, aiming the MAC-10 at him. "Was it Margo Vick?"

Kinnard let go of the rife with a groan. "All I know is I was told where to go, when to get there, and how long I had to grab the kid before the alarm went off."

Another shot rang out and Matt and Kinnard both dove for the ground.

"You had to know who you were dealing with. You made the ransom call."

"I didn't do nothing but grab the kid and bring him

and Shellie up here. The same guy who hired me told me to meet you for the ransom. He told me to kill the woman and the baby once I'd captured you. But Shellie wanted the baby—" He stopped. "Shellie!"

Just then a low rumbling that Matt hadn't noticed grew louder. He felt the ground beneath them tremble.

"Snowslide!" he shouted, scrambling to get his feet under him. He had to get to the cabin.

Kinnard cursed and began crawling toward the trees.

The rumbling grew in volume. Matt looked to the north, toward the peak of the mountain, and saw the white cloud foaming upward toward the heavens, obscuring the moon's light.

He was at least forty feet from the cabin. But about eight feet uphill was a sturdy-looking evergreen. Its trunk looked just about right for him to be able to hook his arms around.

He lunged forward, scrambling to get a foothold in the wet snow. He managed to shove his way through the branches and wrap his arms around the trunk as the first billowing drifts of snow reached him.

He ducked his head and locked his hands around the barrel of the MAC-10, praying that the steel and his fingers would hold.

But he was pretty sure he was going to be buried anyway.

Dear God, he prayed. *Let Deke find Aimee and her baby. Keep her safe.*

AIMEE HEARD THE roar and felt the ground shake.

Avalanche.

Muffled thuds jarred the walls and windows, rattling the glass. It was snow slamming into the cabin's walls.

"William!" she cried, throwing herself across the remaining foot or so of hardwood floor and grabbing his seat in her arms.

A vague memory from childhood tickled the edge of her brain. A children's education piece on what to do in a snowslide. The most important thing, she recalled, was to keep a pocket of air in front of one's face, and of course, not to panic.

She and William were inside, and probably safe, even if the cabin was buried, but what about Matt?

Dear heavens, he was out there with no protection.

She heard his voice as clearly as if he were next to her. *Take care of William. I'll take care of myself.*

You'd better, she answered silently. Holding on to William's safety seat, she crawled across the floor to the central wall that divided the kitchen from the bedroom. It seemed like it would be the strongest place to wait out the slide.

Provided the snow was heavy enough to crush the cabin, they might survive.

She lay down against the wall and cradled William's seat against the curve of her body.

"Hi, William Matthew Vick," she whispered, touching his cheek for the first time since he'd been kidnapped. "Smile for me," she coaxed. He waved his arms and cooed.

She leaned forward to kiss his little face. "That's right. I've been waiting a long time to see you, too." Her eyes filled with tears. She blinked and one fell on William's forehead. She wiped it away.

"Hang in there with me," she said softly. "I've got someone I want you to meet. He's a brave man. He took care of your daddy and he took care of me."

As she spoke the words, she realized that she meant them. Matt would have done everything in his power to save Bill—even sacrificed himself if it meant Bill could have lived to see his son. That was the kind of man Matt was.

She smiled sadly and blinked away her tears. "A very brave man," she whispered as the rumbling of the cascading snow grew louder and the cabin's timbers creaked and groaned.

Behind her, glass shattered. She pulled William closer and covered his seat with her torso and arms.

As THE SNOW piled up around Matt, he pondered whether the latest theory of surviving a snowslide made sense. It was called the Brazil nut effect. The theory was that, when shaken, larger and less dense objects rose to the top of water, snow or, in the case of Brazil nuts, the contents of a can of mixed nuts.

The idea was to let the moving snow shake you to the top as more dense rocks and limbs were plowed under. Many experts felt it made more sense than the theory of trying to swim by flailing one's arms.

The snow was piling up over his head, and his arms and legs were trembling, they were so tired. The tree's trunk was bent almost double and its roots were coming loose from the ground.

Matt figured that if the Brazil nut theory were wrong, he had two chances—slim and none. But he opted for optimism.

With a deep breath, and gripping the MAC-10 as tightly as he could with his exhausted, frozen right hand, he let go of the tree and let the snow carry him down the mountain.

Take care of William, he whispered silently to Aimee. *Don't worry about me.* As the snow billowed around him and he covered his nose and mouth with his left arm, warm tears mixed with the freezing crystals on his cheeks.

SUNDAY 0700 HOURS

MATT WAS FREEZING. He was afraid to move, afraid of finding out that he couldn't. For a few minutes, he lay doubled in on himself like a fetus, figuring that eventually he'd get up the courage to move. And he'd count himself lucky if his fingers and toes didn't break off when he wiggled them.

The sun was up. That surprised him. The last thing he remembered was floating on snow in the darkness. Now the sun felt warm on his shoulder and back. But strangely, there was also warmth below him. Warmth and sticky wetness.

Don't let it be blood.

Not yet brave enough to move, he assessed his position. His head, covered by his parka's hood, was tucked between his shoulders, and its hem was pulled down as far as it would go over his butt. He didn't remember doing any of that.

All he remembered was letting go of the tree and floating downhill on a wave of snow.

And praying that Aimee and her baby were all right. *Aimee!*

He straightened—or he tried to. He couldn't move, and it wasn't just because his muscles were ice-cold.

Something was on top of him, weighing him down. *Snow?* He took a deep breath, preparing to push against the weight, and his nostrils filled with the unmistakable spicy smell of evergreen needles.

When he tried to move, pain shrieked along his nerve endings.

Nausea engulfed him. Sternly, he forced his brain to rise above the pain and think rationally.

One part of his body hurt more than all the rest, but for the life of him he couldn't figure out which part it was. The pain seemed to be everywhere at once. And the nausea was making it worse. He stuck out his tongue and lapped at a few snowflakes that were caught on his lips.

Then, carefully, he flexed his ankles, relieved that his brain still had that much control over his limbs, and waited. They weren't causing the nauseating pain.

After a few agonizing seconds, his cold calf muscles responded and relaxed. Matt blew out a breath. One by one, he tested each muscle without actually moving. Each time, he cringed and braced himself for the shrieking pain. It was a slow, excruciating process.

Finally, he concluded that his feet and legs weren't the problem.

Then he realized he hadn't opened his eyes. When he did, he saw the crisscrossed shadows of evergreen branches. Inhaling carefully, he smelled wood, evergreen—and blood.

Oh, hell. The sticky stuff was blood. Trying not to move his head, he looked down at himself, and saw where the blood was coming from.

A small branch was embedded in the meaty part of his left forearm.

He gagged and his mouth filled with acrid saliva as his stomach heaved. Icy sweat beaded on his face and trickled down the side of his neck. What if that wasn't the only branch that had impaled his body?

What if he couldn't get to Aimee and William?

Lying still, Matt racked his brain for a way to free himself from the tree.

He had a small handsaw in his backpack. He groaned in frustration. The backpack had burned up in the Hummer. What did he have on him?

A knife. In a scabbard attached to his belt. Now if he could just get to it.

In between several bouts of nausea and a couple of periods of unconsciousness, he finally worked the knife out of its scabbard with his right hand without ripping the stick out of his arm.

Once he had the knife in his hand, it was only a matter of about a half hour of excruciatingly slow and careful sawing to cut the thin stick loose from the branch. And then another thirty or forty minutes to extricate himself from underneath the branch. Afterward, he barely remembered anything about it, except for the awareness that he was taking much too long and bleeding a lot.

All in all, it was a miracle that he lived through it. And a miracle that the thin branch hadn't broken a bone. He shuddered, hoping the miracles didn't run out too soon, because he was pretty sure he was going to need a few more of them.

And as hard as he tried to pretend that it wasn't a problem having his forearm skewered on a stick, he knew better.

So much for miracles. With only one arm, he wasn't sure even a miracle could help him save Aimee and William. But he had to try.

As he put his right glove back on, he heard something.

It was a baby—crying.

William!

He was close. At least he was close to them. His eyes filled with tears. Now all he had to do was figure out exactly where he was in relation to Aimee and the baby.

Looking around, he noted that whatever he was sitting on, it was a few feet above the surrounding snow. He blinked, trying to get his bearings. Maybe if he stood…

He tried to tuck his left arm against his chest, but the stick was in the way.

With a sick desolation, he faced the truth. He couldn't do anything until he got rid of the piece of wood. The good news was that it was barely more than a twig— maybe a half inch in diameter and around four inches long. The bad news was that four inches was hardly enough to grip.

With his right hand, he picked up a twig lying nearby and put it between his teeth, then tried to view his impaled arm detachedly, as if it were someone else's.

For a few minutes, he bathed his forearm in snow, numbing it with cold.

Then, biting on the twig, he carefully wrapped his right hand around the two inches of bloody wood protruding from the inside of his arm. He took deep breaths until he was drunk on oxygen. Then with a roar, he slowly and deliberately pulled the stick out of his arm.

And passed out.

CHAPTER TWELVE

MATT'S ARM HURT like hell. He opened his eyes and looked at the matching holes on either side of his forearm, where the stick had been.

He frowned. *Stick?*

Eventually, he remembered that his arm had been impaled on a small sharp branch, and that he'd pulled it out himself. Maybe it was a good thing that he didn't recall the specifics.

The two holes on either side of his arm were oozing blood. Another miracle. The stick hadn't shredded an artery.

He licked his dry, chapped lips and tried to sit up. Reflected sunlight nearly blinded him.

He looked down. He was sitting on something metallic. He brushed snow away to reveal a slab of tin.

A tin roof. He was on top of the cabin!

His whole body trembled in relief. That's why he'd heard William crying. Aimee and her baby were directly below him. All he had to do was get to a door or window. Then he could get them out and get them to the next rendezvous point and they'd be safe.

Rendezvous point. Deke.

Matt shook his head as trepidation churned in his stomach. How was he going to get them to the rendezvous point? He wasn't even sure he could stand up.

He'd arranged for Deke to put down near the peak at 0900 hours. But since the last storm and the avalanche, he had no idea what conditions were like there.

He needed to talk to Deke.

Awkwardly digging into the inside pocket of his parka with his right hand, he pulled out the satellite phone. At least the sky was clear this morning. He pressed the call button on the phone. The light came on. Thank God the battery wasn't frozen.

He read the time on the phone's display. After 0800 hours.

He punched in Deke's number.

"Matt!" Deke's voice was distorted by static. "Son of a gun! What the hell's going on?"

"Deke." His voice was hoarse and shaky. He cleared his throat. "Are we on for 0900?"

Static filled his ear. He turned his head, trying to get a better signal.

"—don't know if I can—put down—"

"Deke," Matt shouted. "0900. 0900. Be there."

"—firmative—"

Deke was worried that the new snow would make it impossible for him to set the helicopter down near the peak, but he would be there.

It was up to Matt to make sure Aimee and William got there. Between them, he and Deke would figure out how to get them into the helicopter.

Matt checked the battery life of his phone. Not good. It was down to one bar. He pocketed it and awkwardly pushed himself to his feet, holding his throbbing left arm close against his chest. The first thing he saw was the barrel of the MAC-10, sticking out from under a dusting of snow and partially hidden by the tree.

He grabbed it, wondering if the cold had rendered it useless. Then he scanned the landscape, assessing the slide's wreckage.

The slide had deposited what looked like about two feet of powder over the snow that had already fallen.

About twenty feet away, something stuck up at an odd angle from the snow. Matt shaded his eyes and squinted. It was a body, clothed in winter camo.

Kinnard. Damn. Based on the angle and rigidity of his body, he had to be dead and either frozen or in rigor.

Turning toward the south, he searched for any sign of Al Hamar, with no luck. His best estimate of when Al Hamar's rifle shots had come from put the terrorist beyond the worst of the piled-up snow. If he'd stayed put, he was probably unhurt.

Matt couldn't afford to assume that Al Hamar was no longer a threat.

Matt had to proceed as though the terrorist had survived the storm. He surveyed the whole visible landscape, but didn't see any new footprints, any disturbance of the new snow. He saw no sign that suggested anyone had been there.

Kinnard was dead. But Matt had to assume that Al Hamar was still out there somewhere. That meant Aimee was still in danger. Because although Novus needed Matt alive so he could be questioned, he had no use for Aimee or her baby.

Matt looked back at Kinnard's frozen body. This time he spotted the assault rifle, half buried in the snow. He needed that rifle. So he used a few precious minutes to trudge through the snow. He confirmed that Kinnard was dead. Then he dug the rifle out of the snow with his good hand.

Turning back toward the cabin, he examined the tree that had fallen onto the cabin's roof, and onto him. Its roots were still partially embedded in the ground. And that meant that only part of the tree's weight was resting on the cabin.

At that instant, the tree creaked and settled, shaking the cabin. Its movement drew his attention to a branch that had penetrated the roof in the same way the stick had penetrated his arm.

Dear God, don't let Aimee or William be hurt.

Matt cautiously approached the downhill side of the cabin. As he got closer, he saw the damage the big tree had caused. The sides of the cabin had been crushed.

The slight bump he saw in the roofline told him the central portion of the structure had withstood the weight of the tree better than the sides. But the way the tree was creaking and moving, its roots might give way at any minute, and its full weight would flatten the cabin.

He had to get Aimee and her baby out of there.

Cradling his hand, he climbed over the snowdrifts and landed on the porch with a thud, jarring the hell out of his arm.

The pain was like a punch to his gut. For a few seconds he couldn't get his breath as dizzying nausea racked him.

Then he heard William crying again. He couldn't tell exactly where the sound was coming from, and ice crystals had formed on the panes of the door. He rubbed them away, trying to see inside.

"Aimee!" he called. "Aimee! Are you okay?" He couldn't see anything through the glass panes. The inside of the cabin was pitch-black.

"Aimee! Answer me!"

SUNDAY 0900 HOURS

THE HEAVY TREE that lay on top of the cabin shifted as the snow melted around it, and the roof creaked and groaned. Aimee shook her head as she stared at the huge branch that had speared through the cabin's roof right in front of the wall where she'd huddled with William. It had missed them by several feet, but somehow that wasn't comforting.

She jumped and cringed as a thud reverberated through the cabin. Another tree falling? She wasn't sure. All she knew was that the loud bang was the latest in a long night full of very scary sounds. Many of them from the cabin itself. The center wall where she'd huddled with William had turned out to be a very good choice.

When the tree had hit the cabin, glass had popped out of the windows and studs and logs had cracked loudly. Nails screeching against wood, and logs crunching under the weight of the tree, had continued all through the night.

Every screech, every crunch, had Aimee cringing and hovering over William to protect him, terrified that the cabin's structure wouldn't hold for another second.

She clutched William closer and whispered to him. "I know, William, I know. You're so uncomfortable. Your mommy isn't taking very good care of you." She took a shaky breath. "You're wet and hungry, and all I've got is this cold bottle of formula."

Earlier, she'd dared to leave William long enough to weave her way into the kitchen around the debris. She'd found a bottle turned upside down on the drain board, with its top beside it. Further searching had yielded two cans of baby formula.

William had taken a little formula, but he scrunched up his face, making sure his mommy knew he didn't like it. That, plus his reaction to her fear, made him fussy.

She'd held him through the rest of the night, singing lullabies and trying to pretend for his sake that she didn't believe they were the only survivors of the snowslide. Trying to believe that Matt was out there somewhere, trying to get to them.

"Aimee!"

She stopped murmuring to William and listened. She'd dozed a few times during the night, only to wake up thinking she heard Matt calling her. But it always turned out to be the wind howling or the timbers of the house rubbing together.

"Matt?" It was foolish, she knew, to answer the wind, but there was nobody to hear her except William.

"Aimee? Are you all right?"

That sounded real. She held her breath, listening. Hoping with every fiber of her being that it really was Matt. At the same time fearing she was hallucinating. She was desperately afraid that he hadn't survived.

Then she heard a pounding on the door. She looked up, squinting against the glare of sunlight on snow. Pushing herself to her feet, still clutching William to her chest, she forced her stiff muscles to move.

She had to thread her way around the limb that had impaled the roof, and between fallen beams and broken glass, but she finally got to the door. She rubbed frost off the glass. "Oh, dear heavens, Matt! It's really you."

"Aimee."

Standing in front of the door with the sun and bright snow behind him, he looked like an angel. The parka's hood was pushed back. His ears were bright red, his cheeks were chapped, and his mouth was compressed into a thin line, but he was there. And he was beautiful.

He grabbed the doorknob and pushed. It didn't move. "Matt, the cabin's crushed—"

"Get away from the door." He put his right shoulder against it and shoved.

Something cracked, and a broken board fell, barely missing his arm.

"Matt, stop! You're going to get hurt." Aimee had never seen him so desperate.

He kicked away the board and pulled his MAC-10. "Get as far back as you can. I'm going to break the window."

"Wait!" Aimee yelled.

He stopped, surprised.

"Matt, the door's stuck, and the cabin is collapsing. Slow down. We need to figure out what to do."

He pressed a gloved hand against the glass. "Listen to me. We don't have time. Deke is going to be at the peak in less than ten minutes. I've got to get you and William up there."

Her first reaction was excitement. "Deke's coming?" They were safe.

But Matt's face told a different story. He looked exhausted, desperate, defeated.

Shifting William's weight to her right arm, she laid her left hand against his right on the other side of the cold glass.

"What's wrong?" she asked softly.

He laid his forehead against the glass. The corners of his mouth were white and pinched. "My phone is almost dead. I won't be able to contact Deke again."

Aimee heard what he didn't say. This was their last chance. "Break the windows," she said, and backed away.

He met her gaze. She wasn't sure what he was looking for in her eyes, but she knew by looking at him that his goal was the same as hers.

Get William to safety.

He swung the handle of the MAC-10 at the panes of glass.

She wanted to cry at the weakness of his swing. He was exhausted. He'd spent the night out in the freezing cold. He'd fought to get to them. She was terribly afraid that he was using up the last dregs of his strength to save her baby.

And she was going to let him do it.

Several blows later, there was a fair-sized hole in the door. Not large enough for her to get through, but plenty of room for William's safety seat.

"Matt, stop! That's enough." Without waiting to hear his response, she ran back to the wall and secured William into his safety seat. Then she took one of the blankets she'd used for warmth, and wrapped it around the seat.

When she looked up, Matt was bracing himself to swing again. "Get back," he shouted.

His hoarse voice and his pinched face attested to his exhaustion. He was hovering at the end of his strength.

Would he make it to the peak? She had to believe he would.

"Matt. There's no time. Here."

"What are you doing?" Matt cried. "Another couple of minutes and I'll have enough room to get you out."

"No. There's no time."

He stared at her as if he didn't understand what she was saying. After a second, he nodded.

She kissed William and took a precious few seconds to whisper to him. "I swore once I got you back in my arms I'd never ever let you go. You're the most important thing in my life. You *are* my life. But I can't keep you safe here."

She touched his chin and he giggled, which brought tears to her eyes. "That's right. It's too cold here. So Matt's going to take you someplace where you'll be safe, and I'll see you soon, okay? You can trust him. I do."

She kissed him one last time, then covered the seat with the blanket, and handed it through the broken panes to Matt.

When he reached out his right hand to take the baby seat's handles, Aimee saw the blood that stained the left sleeve of his parka.

"Matt, you're bleeding."

He shook his head. "Not so much anymore."

"You can't make it to the peak like this. What happened?"

His grim mouth flattened. The only color in his face came from the bright spots on his cheeks. "I'll make it. Stay inside. Stay warm. I'll be back for you," he rasped.

She blinked away tears. She touched his hand. "I know you will."

Gripping William's seat, he turned away.

"Matt," Aimee called.

He looked over his shoulder at her.

"I trust you."

For an instant, his gaze held hers, then he nodded and turned. He carefully maneuvered the sloping hill of snow in front of the cabin, holding tightly to the baby seat with his right hand.

Aimee watched him as long as she could. Finally, she had to accept that no matter how hard she strained, she wouldn't get another glimpse.

The man she'd once thought she could never count on now held her baby's fate in his hands. And she'd told him the truth.

She trusted him to keep William safe.

She moved back to the center wall, wrapped herself in the remaining blanket, and sat down to wait for Matt to return.

She didn't allow herself to consider that he might not make it back.

Above her, the snow-laden boards creaked ominously.

MATT HEARD THE helicopter long before he saw it. The rhythmic drone of the propellers was strangely soothing. He matched his pace to the engine's cadence.

At least he was warming up. Probably the combined efforts of climbing and maintaining his balance with only one arm. Setting the baby seat on a downed tree trunk, he lifted the blanket slightly to check on William. It was the third time he'd peeked.

But no matter how much he lectured himself that he needed to keep the blanket in place so William didn't get cold, he found it impossible to go more than a few minutes without checking on him.

William was fussy and unhappy, but he'd stopped crying. That worried Matt.

Like he knew anything about kids.

He figured the baby was wet or hungry or both. He

hoped that was all that was wrong. But as fussy as William was, whenever Matt checked him, his blue eyes latched on to Matt's and widened.

"Do you have any idea who I am?" Matt whispered. "I'm your godfather. Not that I deserve to be. I haven't done a very good job of taking care of you so far, but I'm hoping I can fix that in just a couple of minutes."

William waved his arms and whined.

"I know. It's cold. But you're about to have an adventure that possibly no man your age has experienced."

His mouth twitched. "That's right," he said. "You *are* a man. A little man right now, but a man. A brave, good man, just like your daddy."

At that moment, Matt noticed that the sound of the helicopter had gotten louder. The propellers appeared from the other side of the mountain, rising up like the cavalry coming over the hill in a B Western movie.

Matt sat the baby seat down and waved with his right hand.

Deke, in his supercool sunglasses and his helmet and earpiece, waved back. He maneuvered the bird so that he was hovering almost directly over Matt's head. The downdraft created by the propellers whipped around, lofting the blanket that protected William.

Matt knelt and tucked the corners of the blanket securely around the baby.

When he glanced up, Deke was holding up his satellite phone. Matt reached for his, hoping the battery hadn't died.

To his relief, he saw that its light was on.

"I'm glad to see you're still upright. The weather service reported an avalanche, and I could see the results when I flew in." Deke's voice was cut by static.

"I rode it. Kinnard and his girl didn't make it."

"Damn. Aimee and the baby okay?"

Matt nodded. "Drop a basket," he yelled into the phone. "You're taking the baby."

A surprised expletive slipped from Deke's lips. Then he recovered. "You got it. Be right back." The helicopter rose and angled away from the mountain peak.

Matt knew what he was doing. He needed room to hover on autopilot while he secured a rescue basket to a rope.

While he waited, Matt made sure that William was snugly strapped into his safety seat. Then he tucked the blanket in tightly. "Okay, William Matthew Vick. You ready for your great adventure?"

To his utter shock, William giggled. Matt couldn't stop himself from smiling. He pulled off his glove and traced the baby's plump cheek with his forefinger.

"You're as beautiful as your mother," he whispered, surprised when his voice broke.

Above him Deke was back, maneuvering until he hovered directly over them, blasting them with downdraft. Then he lowered the heavy metal basket. Matt grabbed the cold steel.

Even the slightest movement made his arm shriek with pain. But the only way he could hang on to the basket was to embrace the line with his left arm.

He picked up William's baby seat and lifted it over and in, then grabbed the bungee cord that was attached to one side and ran it through the handles of the baby seat and secured it to the other side. By the time he completed those maneuvers, he was dizzy and sick with pain.

He looked up, still holding on to the cage, and waved at Deke, who gave him a thumbs-up.

Matt watched, not breathing, as Deke activated the crank that raised the basket. When it was close enough, Deke leaned out and grabbed it, lifting it in through the open door. Once the basket was safely inside, Deke sent Matt another thumbs-up, then held up his satellite phone.

Matt retrieved his phone.

"—the hell's wrong with your arm?"

"Forget it," Matt growled. "Get the baby out of here."

"What about you and Aimee—?"

"You'll have to put down."

Deke nodded. "Six hours?"

Matt had racked his brain about where Deke could safely set the helicopter down. The original secondary rendezvous place was a clearing two miles southwest from the cabin. It was probably the best choice.

"Secondary rendezvous," he yelled into the phone.

Deke shook his head and shrugged. "Wha—?"

The static was growing. Matt knew his phone was about to go dead. "Secon—dary ren—dez—vous," he enunciated slowly.

Deke ducked his head, listening. Then nodded. "—dary—"

Relief nearly buckled Matt's knees. Deke had heard him.

"Deke," he yelled. "Anything on the sabotage?"

Deke shook his head and spoke, but all Matt got was static. He looked at his phone's display in time to see the battery light go out. It was dead. That was it. This would be the last communication until they were rescued.

If they were rescued. He waved the phone and shook his head.

Deke frowned and then held up six fingers.

He wanted confirmation of the time. *Six hours.* Enough time for as much snow as possible to melt.

Matt nodded and gave Deke the thumbs-up.

Deke returned the gesture, grinning. Then he held up his forefinger, followed by five fingers, then his closed fist, and his closed fist again.

1500 hours. Three p.m.

Matt repeated the signs with his right hand.

Deke mimed a salute, turned the helicopter and flew off.

Matt watched until it disappeared over the edge of the peak. Then he fell to his knees, his stomach heaving and clenching, although he had nothing in it. Then he raked up a small handful of snow and let it dissolve on his tongue, hoping the chill would chase away the queasy dizziness.

The pain in his forearm had become a constant agony, made worse by the numbness in his fingers. He unzipped his parka and tucked his hand inside, hoping to warm his fingers without having to move them. He felt warm blood trickling down his cold arm. He shivered.

Then he staggered to his feet. He had to get back to Aimee. She'd be happy to know that William was safe.

He'd be happy if he could get her safely to the rendezvous point before he collapsed from blood loss.

CHAPTER THIRTEEN

SUNDAY 1100 HOURS

IT HAD BEEN almost twenty-four hours with no communication from Kinnard. He hoped to hell the jerk hadn't run off with the money. He trusted him, but only so far.

He tried Kinnard again. No response. It wasn't the storm this time. The skies were clear. He tried Kinnard's girlfriend, too, but no luck there.

Maybe Parker had killed them.

He drummed his fingers on the computer table. Parker could certainly have killed Kinnard. From what he'd seen in the years he'd worked for Black Hills Search and Rescue, it was pretty obvious that Parker would do anything for one of his oath brothers—or for Aimee Vick.

But killing the girl who'd been brought in to take care of the Vick baby—that was another matter. Parker wouldn't have the stomach for that.

He stood, kicking his desk chair backward. Looking out the window at the Black Hills, he doubled his hands into fists and forced himself to stay calm. Hopefully, Kinnard and the girl were dead. If they'd turned tail and run, all his careful plans could be in jeopardy.

He picked up his prepaid cell phone and looked at it. He did not want to make this report, but he had to.

AIMEE SQUINTED AGAINST the glare of the sun on the brilliant white snow outside the cabin door, and swung the stick of firewood at it one more time. To her relief, the pane of glass finally broke.

The stick of firewood she wielded in her gloved hands was heavy, but the cabin's door was solid wood and the frames that held the six panes of glass were solid. Even the glass seemed to be reinforced.

She'd been working ever since Matt had left. She didn't have a watch, but she knew it had been a long time—maybe too long.

No. She wouldn't—couldn't—worry about William. Matt would die to save him.

She swung again, letting the reverberation of the blow shake that thought from her mind.

"Matt—won't—die," she muttered as she swung again and again. He'd promised her he'd be back. She believed him.

"He—won't—die." She dropped the log from her aching hands and blew out a breath.

She eyed the hole where the glass panes had been. It was big enough for her to crawl through—probably. But if she climbed out now, she'd have nothing to do but sit in the snow and wait for Matt to show up.

The roof creaked again, and Aimee cringed. The fear that had dogged her ever since the sun had begun beating down on the snow sent her pulse skyrocketing. What if the roof collapsed?

Maybe it was a good idea to go ahead and climb out.

She could wait for Matt outside in the sunshine, away from the possibility of being crushed when the tree's last clinging roots let go and dumped its full weight on the cabin roof.

She grabbed the daypack, and then remembered the food and drinks she'd seen in the kitchen. Running into the kitchen, she chose a few things to put in the daypack. Too much and it would be too heavy to carry. Then she went through the kitchen drawers, checking to see if she saw anything that might come in handy. She found a couple of odd-shaped pieces of metal that she assumed were key rings, a small can opener with no handles. She had no idea if it was broken or if it was made that way, but she stuck it in the bag anyway.

One of the drawers seemed to be dedicated to first aid supplies. She grabbed antibiotic ointment, gauze, tape and a small bottle of alcohol. Then she saw a pair of scissors and stuck them in the pack, as well.

Lifting the pack, she grimaced at its weight. "I'll ask Matt," she told herself, "He can dump whatever he thinks we don't need."

Back in the front room she examined the hole in the door and brushed away all the glass shards and splinters of wood she could see. Folding the blanket several times, she lay it over the bottom of the jagged opening.

Outside, drifts of snow glistened with water where the sun hit them.

She went back to the kitchen and grabbed a chair to drag over to the door, but stopped when she heard something. She glanced up, cringing. Had the tree's roots finally let go?

"Aimee?"

A thrill lanced through her. "Matt?" She whirled. There he was, on the other side of the broken door. Spots of color stained his cheeks, standing out against his pale skin and pinched mouth. His left hand was tucked inside his unzipped parka, and blood stained the sleeve—more than before.

"Matt!" She was stunned at his appearance. His face was set, with lines of pain etching it. His eyes were too bright, and appeared sunken. And his face was horribly pale. She pasted a smile on her face, trying not to show how worried she was about him. "Is William—?"

He nodded and a tight smile lightened his drawn features. "He's safe. Deke's got him." His voice was hoarse, and he was obviously trying to sound upbeat.

"You put him in the helicopter?"

"Actually, he rode up in a basket."

"A basket?" she repeated, horrified at the picture his words evoked.

"These are specially designed for rescuing people. Like the ones they used down in New Orleans during Katrina."

"Oh." She wasn't convinced about the safety, but if William was fine, then that's all that mattered.

He coughed. "I see you found something to do. You finished breaking in the windows."

"I figured it was about time for me to chip in."

"Let's get you out of there."

"You just stay back. I can do this myself."

He lowered his gaze and complied. That sent an arrow of hurt through her. Not because she needed his help, but because he knew he was too weak to offer it.

She grabbed the daypack and lifted it through the broken window. Lowering it by one strap, she let it fall to the ground. Then she pulled the chair over.

Standing on it, she climbed through the broken panes and hopped to the ground. Then she picked up the blanket, shook it out and rolled it up.

"Leave it," he said.

"Are you sure? Because I can carry it—"

"Leave it."

She tossed the blanket back inside. "How far are we going?"

"About two miles."

"Two miles? That's not bad. Deke's going to meet us?"

He nodded. "At 1500 hours. Three o'clock."

She frowned. "Isn't that a long time?"

"Not really. About five hours from now. He needs time for the—sun to melt the snow," he said raggedly. "And we need time to get there. Let's go."

"No." Aimee crouched and unzipped the daypack. She dug in it for the first aid items. "We're not going anywhere until I take care of your arm. You're still bleeding. What did you do?"

He caught her arm. "No."

"Matt, yes! You're about to collapse. You can't go any farther until we stop that bleeding."

"Not here. The tree—"

As if on cue, the branches creaked and scraped across the tin roof.

Of course. The tree. They had to get out of the way, in case it fell. "Come on, then. Let's get away from here."

"Go on," Matt said tightly. "I'll follow."

"Oh, no, you don't. You took care of me when I was hypothermic. It's my turn."

She zipped up the daypack and slung it onto her back, sticking her arms through the straps. "Will it help you to lean on me?"

Matt's mouth turned up in a wry smile. "I already am," he muttered. "More than I should."

After a couple of seconds, he shook his head. "No. Please go on. I'm going to be slower than—than you."

Aimee could tell his voice was getting weaker. *Don't quit on me,* she wanted to say. But that wasn't fair. He'd pushed himself further than she ever would have been able to. He wasn't quitting.

His wounded body was betraying him.

So she headed south for about fifty feet, stopping at a fallen tree trunk that was about the right height for sitting. She brushed snow off and sat to wait for him to catch up.

He walked slowly, doggedly, as if all that was keeping him on his feet was sheer determination. It broke her heart to watch his struggle. It took all her self-control not to run to help him.

Her eyes burned and her throat closed, but she busied herself with unloading the first aid supplies.

When he got to her she looked up, masking her feelings with a smile. "Sit down and let me see your arm."

He didn't even try to argue. He propped the rifle against the tree trunk and slid his parka off his right arm. Then he carefully peeled the sleeve off his left arm, doing his best not to move his arm.

His sweater was soaked with blood. Aimee swallowed against the nausea that rose in her throat. "Sit," she said as evenly as she could.

She took the scissors and cut the sleeves off his arm. "Oh, Matt. What happened? Is that a gunshot wound?"

His back was straight but his eyes were closed. "No," he muttered. "A branch."

"It went—" She twisted his arm slightly so she could

see the underside, grimacing when he moaned. "It went all the way through?"

Dear heavens, don't let me hurt him. She knew that was a wasted prayer. She had to clean and wrap his arm. Everything she did was going to hurt him.

"I've got to get your watch off." His hand was swollen and discolored, and the watchband looked unbearably tight. "Please, believe me. I don't want to hurt you, but it's got to come off."

It wasn't easy, and Matt was wheezing in pain by the time she was done, but she got the watch unfastened. She put it on her wrist and buckled it in the last hole.

"Aimee—" he gasped. "Before you—get started, hand me the rifle."

"It's right next to you—" She stopped as understanding dawned. He knew where it was. He just couldn't lean over to get it. Every bit of strength he had was devoted to keeping himself upright. She couldn't imagine what it had cost him to ask her to pick up the rifle and put it in his hand.

She grabbed it and held it so he could get his right arm around it and his finger on the trigger. "Thanks," he breathed.

"I don't have anything to give you for pain," she said as she sat back down and gently touched his arm.

"Just hurry."

As quickly and as gently as she could, she poured alcohol over the top of his arm and caught it with gauze pads underneath. She cleaned both awful, gaping holes as well as she could, doing her best to ignore Matt's harsh breathing and frequent grunts of pain. By the time she was done, sweat was beading on her forehead and Matt had gone quiet.

"I don't know how doctors stand it," she muttered as she squeezed antibiotic ointment onto a clean gauze pad, applied it to the upper wound and did the same with the wound on the underside of his arm. Then she took a roll of gauze and wrapped it around his arm.

"Is that too tight?" she asked.

Matt raised his head a bit and he carefully moved his fingers. "Okay," he said shortly.

She secured the ends of the gauze with adhesive tape.

When she finished, she straightened and examined his face. His skin looked tight and drawn across his cheekbones. His mouth was compressed into a thin line, his nostrils and the corners of his lips were white and pinched. And sweat glistened on his forehead and neck.

"I'm done," she said. "Are you okay?"

"I will be."

She took a last gauze pad and wiped his face and neck, noticing that he was trembling.

"Okay, I've got something for you." She pulled out a self-heating container of hot chocolate. "I figured if I asked, you'd tell me to leave it because it was too heavy. But I think you're going to be glad I have it. I found it in one of the cupboards."

Pressing a button on the bottom of the container, she activated the chemical reaction in the container's sleeve that heated the chocolate drink inside.

"In about ten seconds, this is going to be hot chocolate. You need to drink it."

"We need to go."

"No. You're not going anywhere until you drink this." She waited until the container felt hot in her hands. Then she popped the tab and firmly pressed it into his right hand. "Drink."

"You need—"

"Listen, Matthew Parker. I haven't been out in the snow all night, and I didn't just single-handedly save a helpless infant. And I haven't lost pints and pints of blood. That chocolate's all yours. Besides, I had some already. I'm full."

She didn't miss his sidelong glance. She was lying, and he knew it.

Even though nothing but the nylon shell of her parka was touching the shoulder of his sweater, she felt the shudder that racked him as he swallowed the hot, sweet liquid.

Something shook loose inside her, and tears filled her eyes. Strangely, that had been happening a lot the past few days. She knew what Matt would say—probably what most people would say.

Your child's been kidnapped. It's natural to cry.

But that wasn't true—not for her. She'd decided a long time ago that for her, crying equaled losing control. For her entire adult life she'd prided herself on never crying.

All those times when control had slipped through her fingers, leaving her feeling helpless and impotent—her parents' deaths, Bill's illness and tragic death, even William's kidnapping—at least she could say she didn't cry.

Ever since she and Matt had joined together to rescue William, she'd begun to look at tears differently. They had more to do with relief and joy and even sadness than with failure on her part.

Right now her tears reflected a poignant concern for Matt and a deep-seated satisfaction that, finally, she was able to give him back a fraction of the help he'd given her. She only hoped the energy in the chocolate drink would be enough to carry him to the rendezvous point. She watched him to make sure he drank every drop.

Matt's first swallow of hot chocolate spread through him like a flame of desire. As soon as it hit his stomach, however, a deep, bone-rattling shudder had racked his body. Partly a result of the hot liquid flowing through his chilled body, warming his insides. But also the clenching response of his empty stomach suddenly being hit with the sugary substance.

Once the initial queasiness passed, he actually felt a little better. The unrelenting pain in his arm was the same, but each throb didn't plaster black-edged stars before his eyes or trigger his gag reflex.

"Why don't you eat an energy bar?" Aimee said. "I've got several."

He squeezed his eyes shut and moved his head a fraction in a negative direction. He knew his gut wouldn't accept the chewy, fiber-rich bar.

"We need to get going." He stood. For a second, the black-edged stars blinded him again, so he stood still, waiting for them to fade. He wasn't going to get far if the pain in his arm kept up. Just standing jarred it.

"I need you to do something else for me," he said.

Aimee looked up at him. "Anything," she said.

"Do you have any more tape or gauze?"

She looked into the bag. "Both, why? Are you hurt somewhere else?"

"I need you to immobilize my arm against my middle. If it starts bleeding again, I'll probably pass out, so I need to keep it as still as possible."

Aimee cut the left arm of his sweater and his long underwear, all the way up to the neck. Then she wrapped gauze around his wrist and back until his forearm was sealed against his torso. "I don't know how we're going to get your sweater or your undershirt back on."

He shook his head. "Just hand me the parka."

Finally, once he had his parka up over his right shoulder and draped over his left, he cautiously lifted his head, steeling himself against nausea and dizziness.

A flicker of light caught the edge of his vision. He squinted in that direction, but didn't see anything except snowdrifts and fallen trees. Was it his weakness, playing visual tricks on him?

He moved his head back and forth, trying to catch the reflection again. It could have been a piece of ice that caught the sun just right, or a tiny scrap of metal turned up by the snow.

Or it could have been something more ominous, like sunlight glinting off binoculars—or the barrel of a gun.

"Do you need to rest for a little while longer?"

"No," he said, rubbing his temple with his right hand. If someone—Al Hamar—was watching them, he didn't want him to think he'd spotted him.

And he didn't want Aimee to know his suspicion. She wouldn't be able to keep from looking behind them, and that could be fatal. He was still counting on Al Hamar needing him alive. All he had to do was make sure the terrorist couldn't get a clear shot at Aimee.

The only way he could do that was to stay so close to her that Al Hamar couldn't shoot her without running the risk of hitting him.

"I need something else," Matt said.

Aimee looked at him in surprise. "Sure. What do you need?"

"I need to lean on you." He held up Kinnard's rifle. "Hook the rifle over my right shoulder. Then I'm going to put my arm around your shoulders, just to keep me steady."

Aimee bit the inside of her cheek, doing her best not to cry. She saw in his face that he wasn't used to asking for help. "No problem," she said, putting a false brightness into her voice. "I might even get the chance to cop a feel."

She stepped in close enough to him so he could put his arm around her shoulders. "Can I put my arm around your waist without hurting you too much?"

Matt's breathing was fast and short. "I'd be—insulted if you—didn't."

Gingerly, she slid her hand under his parka and wrapped it around his middle, feeling the hard muscles of his back. Even covered by layers of clothes, they felt like long straps of steel.

It terrified her how frail and breakable the human body was. Not many hours ago, his lean, rock-hard body had covered hers, strong, demanding and unbearably sexy as they'd made love.

A thrill tightened her stomach at the memory. It seemed unreal now, like a fantasy, or a dream. It was a moment stolen out of time.

This was reality. Matt injured, needing her support.

Although the arm clutching her shoulders was corded with muscles, he leaned on her heavily, at this moment needing her more than she needed him.

It took a long time to figure out how to walk with Matt so close to her. Finally, once they found a rhythm, it seemed as if he were hardly leaning on her at all.

AIMEE LOOKED AT Matt's watch on her wrist. It was two o'clock. She'd been denying the truth for over an hour.

But the fact was that Matt was getting weaker—much weaker.

After he'd drunk the chocolate, he'd started out walking strongly, barely even resting his arm on her shoulder.

But the farther they went, the heavier he got. He was losing strength fast. She'd tried to get him to stop and eat something, but he'd refused. She'd forced him to drink a few of sips of water, but the last two times she'd held the bottle for him, he'd shaken his head doggedly and refused.

She was pretty sure her makeshift bandage had stemmed the flow of blood, but not in time. She knew he'd lost too much already. She knew nothing about blood loss or first aid, but it made sense that if he was losing blood he should be drinking water.

"Matt, here. Have some more water."

He shook his head. "Not now," he whispered.

It was the same answer he'd given the last three times she'd asked.

He turned his head to look behind them, as he'd done a number of times. Even though he hadn't said anything, she knew what he was doing. He was worried that someone was behind them, following them.

"I know there's someone following us," she said.

He didn't comment, but she felt a deep breath shudder through him.

"It's the terrorist, isn't it? You told me you found Kinnard dead, so it's got to be Al—Al—?"

"Al Hamar."

"So how do you want to handle him? Just keep ignoring him? It's after one o'clock. We should be getting close to the rendezvous point."

He nodded. "Half a mile—maybe." His voice was nothing more than a raspy whisper.

Half a mile. They'd only come three-fourths of the way? It felt like they'd been walking for hours.

And Matt sounded so weak it made her want to cry. But crying wouldn't accomplish anything. He'd been so strong for her. It was her turn to be strong for him.

"Matt. I'm not taking another step until you drink some water. You of all people should know that if you're losing blood, you should be drinking water." She uncapped the bottle and held it out.

"Drink," she commanded.

He took the plastic bottle, but all he did was fill his mouth. He acted like it was agony to swallow.

"Are you nauseated? Do you want another hot chocolate?" She tried to give him a smile. "It'll do you good."

He shook his head and swallowed the mouthful of water with difficulty. Then he blew out a hard breath, as if the mere act of swallowing had exhausted him.

His face had turned from merely pale to a very scary gray color. And she knew gray-tinged skin was not a good sign.

He wasn't going to make it.

As soon as that thought crossed her mind, her brain screamed in protest.

No. Matt couldn't be dying.

Oh, yes, he could, her rational brain answered her back.

The water bottle fell from his hands.

"Oh, no. That's all we've got!" Aimee let go of Matt and reached for the bottle, which had rolled away. The water represented life to her. If she could get him to drink the water, he'd be okay.

"Aimee!" Matt rasped.

She grabbed the bottle. "We only lost a little bit. It's still half-full."

She turned, holding the bottle up.

But Matt had gone down on one knee. His head was bent and as she watched, the rifle slipped from his shoulder.

"Matt! Oh, I am so sorry." She stood.

He lifted his head. "Get down!" he yelled hoarsely. "Now!"

She dove for the ground, her hands plowing snow in front of her.

Then she heard the gunshot.

CHAPTER FOURTEEN

SUNDAY 1500 HOURS

MATT HEARD THE bullet whiz by his ear. His entire body clenched at the sound of the shot.

Ignoring the pain that throbbed through his injured arm, he grabbed the strap of Kinnard's rifle and crawled toward the pile of snow that marked where Aimee had fallen.

"Aimee," he whispered desperately. "Are you okay?"

He saw the top of her head.

"Keep down," he snapped, expecting another shot at any second.

He slithered like a snake across the melting snow until he was close to her. Then he flipped over, so he was facing the shooter.

He was going to have a hell of a time shooting with only one arm, but he could do it if he had to.

Aimee was in danger. He had to take a shot.

Lifting his head up over the top of the snow, he scanned the clearing, but didn't see anything.

"Matt?"

"Don't move." He knew he could outwait the other man. It would be hell to lie in wet snow with the pain in his arm stealing his breath and his fingers going numb again, but he was only minutes from getting Aimee to safety. He wasn't about to give up now.

Clammy sweat stung his eyes and rolled down his neck. His empty stomach cramped, sending nausea crawling up his throat.

There. A flash of sun on metal. He lifted the rifle with his right hand and looked through the scope, but he couldn't focus.

His eyes were blurry. He lowered the rifle and bent his head to wipe his eyes on his sleeve, but his sleeve was wet.

"Here," Aimee said. From somewhere, she pulled a dry piece of cloth and handed it to him.

He wiped his eyes and face. She took the cloth back. "Can I do something to help you hold the rifle? I could lie down and you could prop it on my back."

Matt barely heard her. Something else had grabbed his attention. He cocked his head and listened. He wasn't sure if he could trust his ears. He'd already found out he couldn't completely trust his eyes.

He rolled onto his right shoulder and looked up. He had heard the rhythmic whup-whup of helicopter blades.

Aimee followed his gaze. She gasped. "Matt! Is it Deke?"

Without waiting for him to answer, she waved her arms. "He's here! Deke!" she cried.

"Aimee, don't!" His left arm jerked, an instinctive move to try and grab her. He couldn't stop an involuntary cry. He sucked in a breath.

"He sees us."

Just as she pulled her arms down, another shot rang out.

"Ow!" she cried, grabbing her hand.

Matt pushed himself up onto his right elbow. "Aimee! Are you hit?"

She looked at her hand. "I felt something hot—but I don't see anything."

"Give me your hand."

He examined it closely. There was a tiny red scrape along the flesh of her palm below her little finger. "Looks like the bullet barely missed you."

He closed his eyes for a second, willing away the dizziness and blurred vision. Then he glared at her. "Could you please stay still, and do what I tell you?"

She bit her lip and her cheeks turned pink. "Yes, sir," she whispered.

"Bastard's desperate. He knows once Deke lands he's got no chance to kill you or capture me." He raised his head again, scanning the area for the shooter. "We've got to stay down until Deke lands," he told Aimee. "If Al Hamar starts shooting at the helicopter, Deke will have to abort."

"Abort?"

Matt nodded grimly. "We can't afford to lose the helicopter, or Deke. But don't worry. He's got a high-powered rifle on board. Maybe even a machine gun. He'll be back, loaded for bear."

She nodded, but her eyes were wide with fear.

"Our job is to stay down until he can put down. If I can, I'm going to take out Al Hamar when he tries to shoot the helicopter again. I'd like to take the SOB alive, but that may not be possible. The most important thing is to get you out of here."

"No," she snapped. "The most important thing is to get *you* on that helicopter and to a hospital. I'll take my chances."

Matt felt his chapped, cracked lips widen in a smile. It hurt but he didn't care. He raised his brows. "You'll take your chances…"

Her cheeks got pinker, but she lifted her chin. "That's right. In fact, why don't you give me that rifle and I'll take care of Al Hamar, or whatever his name is."

The terrorist was shooting again, this time at the helicopter. Over the sound of the rotors, Matt heard the zing of a bullet ricocheting off metal.

Deke took the bird up a few dozen feet, but he didn't turn away.

Matt squinted up at him. "Come on, Cunningham. That's just stupid."

"What? What's the matter?"

"Deke's drawing his fire." Matt swiped his forehead on the sleeve of his parka again and flipped over onto his stomach, suppressing a groan.

"Why?"

Matt swallowed the bile that was threatening to erupt from his throat. He felt like he was about to puke his guts up. The good news was that his arm had quit hurting. It was just numb.

Or was that the bad news?

Pushing away those thoughts, he lifted the rifle and sighted through the scope. "He knows our terrorist friend's got to come out from his cover to get a shot at him. He's drawing him out so I can shoot him." He blew out a harsh breath. "I hope I can."

Aimee scooted over closer to him.

"I told you—"

"Matt, lean on me. Use me to brace the gun."

Matt's right arm was shaking with fatigue and weakness from loss of blood. He shook his head. "I can't even figure out what you're talking about."

"Here. Move over." She crawled around until her body was perpendicular to his. "Now let me lie down in front of you and you can brace the gun on my back. Won't that work?"

He didn't want to tell her that most of what she'd just said sounded like gibberish to his buzzing ears. He just watched as she lay flat on her stomach in front of him. "Now, can you brace the barrel of the rifle on me?"

Slowly, his brain processed her words. "Maybe so," he whispered. "I can try."

"Listen," Aimee said. "Deke's coming lower. Al Hamar will probably shoot at him." She took a long breath. "Get ready."

Matt set the barrel of the rifle across her shoulders and pushed himself forward until he could see through the scope. "Aimee?"

"Yeah?"

He blinked sweat out of his eyes, and swept the scope back and forth, looking for the terrorist. "I love you."

Her body stiffened, making the scope wobble. "Hey. Stay still. I almost had him."

"Are you okay?" she asked, a worried tone in her voice. "You sound like you've been drinking."

"Hold still." He concentrated all the energy he had left in him on watching through the scope. Then he saw him. Al Hamar. He'd slipped out from behind a tree to get a shot at Deke. He'd braced himself and was aiming at the helicopter that loomed over their heads.

"Don't move," Matt whispered. "I've got him." His vision wavered, but hell, it was a short shot. And the guy was presenting a perfect target, the way he stood with his feet apart. It was a sucker shot.

Slowly, carefully, Matt squeezed the trigger. He saw the man jerk, saw blood blossom on the leg of his pants. As he watched, the terrorist dropped to his knees.

Then the man turned the rifle on Matt. For an instant they were scope to scope, then Al Hamar shifted his barrel downward. He was going to shoot Aimee.

Matt pulled the trigger again and again and again.

The last thing he remembered was a burst of bright stars before his eyes.

SUNDAY 2000 HOURS

THE CLEAN WHITE SHEETS and pillow felt like heaven to Aimee's exhausted muscles and chapped skin. Even the cotton hospital gown couldn't have felt better if it were the finest silk.

But what felt better than all that, even better than the warm bathwater or the delicious hot soup they'd given her, was the tiny bundle that was nestled into the crook of her arm.

She looked down at William. He was asleep. He'd seemed singularly unconcerned that she'd been gone. As soon as she'd stopped kissing him all over his face and touching every tiny perfect finger and toe, he'd fallen right to sleep.

"Must be nice," she murmured drowsily, "to be so sure that everything's fine in your world." She chuckled softly. "Know what, William? I think they gave me something to make me sleepy." She reached for the cup of water on the bedside table and took a small sip, letting the cool wetness slide down her throat. "I'm just going to take a little nap while you're sleeping. Then when I wake up, we'll go find Matt."

Matt. Her heart gave a slight jump. Deke had told her he was going to be fine. Hadn't he? Her eyes drifted closed.

Or had she dreamed it?

She didn't remember much after Deke got them into the helicopter. Just his deep, reassuring voice, saying everything was going to be all right.

But what else was he going to say in that situation? *Sorry, guys, looks like you're not going to make it?*

Then he'd put the helicopter down on the roof of the hospital and all kinds of mayhem had broken out.

Men and women dressed in blue with rolling tables had rushed out into the wind and grabbed Matt.

Aimee remembered trying to see where they took him, but more people ran out and grabbed her. Somebody leaned over her and said something, and that was all she remembered until she woke up while a nurse's aide was bathing her.

Nurse. The nurses could tell her about Matt. She reached for the call button. Her movement disturbed William and he whimpered.

"Sorry, baby. I'm just going to call the nurse." But her arm was tired, and her eyelids were heavy. "In a minute," she whispered and tucked her arm closer around her baby.

THEY WERE BACK. Parker and Aimee Vick. According to a brief message from Irina, Parker was in surgery and expected to be okay, Aimee was fine, and she and her child had been reunited.

He couldn't deny that he was relieved that the child hadn't been harmed.

But how the hell had Parker managed to outsmart Kinnard at every turn? Kinnard knew these hills and conditions better than anyone he'd ever known. Parker was supposed to be a weather specialist and something of a survival expert, but Kinnard had at least three inches and fifty pounds on him, plus all the time Parker had been overseas in the military, Kinnard had been roaming the mountains, learning how to survive. Having been a Marine, he already knew how to fight.

He had to find out what had happened out there.

His cell phone rang. He glanced at the display. It was Irina's administrative assistant, Pam Jamieson.

"There's a briefing in the conference room in twenty," she said, all business as usual.

"Got it," he responded.

Good. He'd have information to pass on tonight. He glanced at his watch. He had just enough time to check on the next phase of the plan. With any luck, by this time tomorrow, Deke Cunningham would no longer be protected by the security surrounding Castle Ranch.

MATT JERKED. THE TERRORIST! He was shooting at Aimee! Matt tried to pull the trigger, but he couldn't. Something was wrong with his hand.

He opened his eyes. All he saw was blue and white. Blue walls, low blue light. White sheets.

Sheets?

He looked down at himself. He was covered up to his chest by a white sheet. His left arm was wrapped up like a mummy and his right arm was strapped down, with tubes running in several different directions.

What the hell? He felt drugged. The way he'd felt years ago when he'd woken up from an emergency appendectomy. His eyes burned and his mouth was dry, but not as dry as it had been. His arm hurt, but not as badly as it had before.

Before what?

Closing his eyes, he tried to wipe his mind free of all the confusing and disturbing images that were clicking through it like a slide show gone out of control.

—Aimee, lying so close to the spreading pool of gasoline.

—Kinnard pointing that assault rifle at her.

—His own arm impaled by a sharp piece of wood.

—Kinnard's girl jerking as the bullet hit her head.

—Deke hauling up the basket carrying its precious cargo.

Matt growled and opened his eyes. Closing them had only sped up the slide show. He stared at the ceiling, counting off the pictures as they flashed across his inner vision, trying to pick out the latest ones and shuffle them into some sort of order.

He remembered Aimee waving at Deke, and the horrifying sight of the red dot wavering on the front of her parka.

He remembered her lying down in front of him so he could use her as a prop for the rifle barrel. He remembered pulling the trigger again and again and again.

But for the life of him he couldn't remember anything after that. What a weakling he was. Some rescuer he was. It was pretty bad when the rescuer himself had to be rescued.

It was a good thing Deke was there, because if it had been left up to him, Aimee would probably be dead now.

Aimee. He had to find her—check on her. He looked around for the nurse call button, and discovered that someone had had the foresight to put it next to his right hand. With more effort than he'd have thought he'd need, he lifted his hand enough to get his finger on the button and pressed it.

"—help you?"

"Get me a nurse now!" What he heard in his ears was nothing like what he'd intended. He'd barked a command, but a raspy whisper was all that had come out of his mouth. Plus the very act of punching the button and speaking had started his heart hammering and his head pounding.

He closed his eyes and pretended that the dampness that leaked out from under his lids wasn't tears.

"Mr. Parker, are you all right?"

He turned his head enough to see the pretty young

woman dressed in some kind of smock with dogs and cats on it.

"Get me unhooked from all this stuff. I've got to check on Aimee."

The young woman smiled as she stepped over to the bed and patted his hand. "I'm glad to see you're awake and feeling better, but you're not going to be able to get up for a while. You've only been out of the recovery room for an hour or so."

"Recovery room?"

"The surgery on your arm." She punched some buttons on the monitor that was beeping behind his head, and checked the bag of fluid that hung on a pole beside him.

"Everything looks good. You have some visitors who have been waiting for you to wake up. They're down in the coffee shop. I'll call them, and in a few minutes, I'll bring you a sleeping pill."

"Visitors? Is it Aimee?"

"Aimee? The young woman who was brought in with you? No." She pulled off gloves he hadn't noticed she had on and pumped a bit of antiseptic gel on her hands from a dispenser hanging on the wall.

"Wait a minute. Where am I?"

She pointed at a whiteboard, hanging on the wall directly across from his bed, where the name of the hospital, the date and the names of his nurses and aides were written. "You're in Crook County Hospital. Today is Sunday and my name is Jean. I'll be back soon."

Matt studied the tubes and needles that were sticking out of his right hand, trying to decide how much it would hurt to pull them out. He wanted to look more closely at them but for some reason he found it very hard to lift his arm. So he turned his attention to his other arm. He still had his hand. It was sticking out from the huge roll of bandages. It looked swollen and discolored, but at least it was there.

Before he had a chance to wonder what the surgeons had done to it, the room door opened and Irina Castle came in, followed by Brock O'Neill and FBI Special Agent Schiff.

"Matt! Oh my goodness, you look awful!" She laughed self-consciously as she stepped around to the far side of the bed and patted his hand. "I mean, you look wonderful, given all that you've been through. How are you feeling?"

Brock nodded and scowled as if he were irritated to see Matt alive. But that was his usual expression, so Matt merely nodded back.

"Where's Aimee?" he asked Irina.

"She and William are doing fine. Aimee's been admitted overnight, but they should be able to go home tomorrow." Irina looked at Schiff.

He stepped forward. "Sorry, but we need to talk to you."

Matt ignored him. "Irina, Aimee can't go home by herself. She's been through too much. Can you do something? I don't think it's a good idea for her to have to depend on Margo."

"Don't worry. We're going to take good care of her." She picked up the cup of water and held the straw to his lips. He took a couple of swallows and coughed.

"Margo Vick won't be going anywhere near Aimee," Schiff said. "Not anytime soon. I can promise you that."

"What are you talking about?"

"Once we found out that the baby was being held at the Vicks' hunting cabin, we got a warrant for Mrs. Vick's financial and telephone records, and her home. We found that a million dollars had been liquidated within the past week. Mrs. Vick and her accountant claim to know nothing about it. There were also two calls to Margo Vick's home telephone from a survivalist group of which Kinnard is a member."

"*Was* a member," Matt said.

Schiff's eyebrows rose.

"Kinnard's dead. I'll give you a statement, and I can pinpoint the location of the body within a few yards." Matt didn't mention Shellie. He'd give a formal, complete statement later.

The FBI special agent pulled a PDA from his pocket and made a quick note, then continued. "The telephone calls from the survivalist group were short, less than a minute. Mrs. Vick stated that she received a couple of calls in the past week, and she was asked to hold. She said she held for a short while, and then hung up."

Matt cut his eyes over to the FBI special agent, "It's possible she was framed."

"I know. It's beginning to look that way."

That surprised Matt. He lifted his head and immediately regretted it. The movement hurt his arm and he felt queasy. "What do you mean?" he asked softly.

"We picked up the body of the second man who was following you. Cunningham gave us the coordinates. He was carrying a cell phone, with a message from an unidentified number. The message was in Arabic. We got it translated. Basically, it said— " Schiff looked back at his PDA "—KILL KIDNAPPERS. NO SURVIVORS TO ID US."

Matt's pulse jumped. "The kidnapper *was* hired by Novus."

"Novus?" Schiff frowned. "The terrorist Novus?" He turned to glare at Irina.

When he did, Brock took a step closer to her.

"I figured the dead guy might be somehow involved with your search for your husband, but *Novus Ordo?*"

Irina gazed at him evenly.

"Well, that explains a lot. Not everything, but a lot. We had the voice of the caller who set up the ransom drop analyzed. There were certain inflections and idiomatic inconsistencies that indicated that English may not have been his first language."

"May not?" Irina repeated.

Schiff nodded. "The results were inconclusive. My expert said it was possible that the caller was trying to alter his phrasing to make us think he might not be American."

Matt closed his eyes and sighed. "So we can't prove whether the whole thing was engineered by Novus or not."

"It would help if all the people involved in the kidnapping weren't dead. Couldn't you have left one of them alive?"

"Agent Schiff," Irina broke in. "Matt needs to sleep. He's still under the effects of the anesthesia from his surgery."

Schiff sent her a sharp glance. "Fine. I'll get his statement tomorrow, when he's feeling better. Mrs. Castle, may I speak to you after we're done here?"

She put her hand on Matt's forehead and brushed his hair back. "We'll see."

"Irina, what about—what about the sabotage?" Matt whispered.

Irina leaned over. "We'll talk about that later," she said softly.

Just then the nurse came in. "It's time for Mr. Parker's medication."

Irina kissed him on the forehead. "Don't worry about Aimee," she whispered. "I'll see you tomorrow."

Brock hadn't said a word the entire time. In fact, he'd hardly moved, except when he'd intercepted Schiff. He'd just listened intently to everything that was said.

As Irina and Schiff left the room, Brock met Matt's gaze and nodded, the scowl still on his face.

The nurse injected something into the IV tubing that ran from the bag of fluid down into his hand. "There you go, Mr. Parker." She peeled off her exam gloves, then turned and looked at him.

"Who was that man?" she asked, her eyes wide and her cheeks flushed.

"The guy in the suit?"

"No. The one with the eye patch. The dangerous-looking one. Who was he?"

Matt's eyelids were getting heavy. "You mean Brock O'Neill?" he muttered. "That's a real good question. I'm not sure any of us know who he is." He peered at her. "You want me to introduce you?"

She laughed and shook her head. "Oh, no. I was married to a dangerous man once. I'll never make that mistake again. You get some sleep and I'll be back later to check your vital signs."

MONDAY 1100 HOURS

THE DOOR TO MATT'S hospital room was closed. It had taken Aimee much longer than she'd anticipated to be discharged, although the doctor had promised her yesterday that he was only admitting her overnight for observation. The nurses on her floor had brought her a set of scrubs to wear and had outfitted William with clothes from the pediatric floor.

But now, finally, she was here. She was supposed to

be waiting downstairs for a taxi that the floor clerk had called, and she felt slightly guilty for leaving the driver sitting there, but she had to see Matt.

She shifted William's baby seat to her left hand and started to knock. But she hesitated. What if he were asleep? Or being given a bath? Or what if he didn't want to see her?

She took a deep breath. No matter what he wanted, she *was* going to see him, if only for a few minutes. She wasn't about to leave the hospital without making sure he was okay.

"If he's asleep, we'll go," she whispered to William. Instead of knocking, she gently pushed the door open.

The room was dark. The curtains were closed. The only light came from the weak, recessed fixture above the bed. He was asleep.

She knew she should turn around and leave, but she couldn't take her eyes off him. She'd been so afraid he wouldn't make it. They'd taken him away so fast once the helicopter had landed.

She moved carefully over to the bed, hoping that William would stay quiet. The shadows cast by the dim light emphasized the pain lines etched between his brows and around his mouth.

His hair was a little bit tousled, enough that she wanted to reach out and brush it back from his forehead. And his mouth was as straight and grim as it had been the last time she'd seen him, right before the emergency doctors had taken him off the helicopter and rolled him away.

"I'm so sorry," she mouthed, not really sure why she was apologizing. Mostly that he'd been hurt so badly for trying to help her, she supposed.

"You've got nothing to be sorry for," he whispered.

She jumped, jostling the baby seat. William made a tiny whimper of protest, but Aimee couldn't take her eyes off Matt.

He opened his eyes, those deep, dark eyes, and looked at her.

"Matt," she breathed, her pulse hammering in her throat. "You're—okay?"

His mouth curved up slightly. "Depends on what you mean by *okay.* I'm here, and essentially in one piece." He lifted his right hand, which was attached to what looked like a tangle of tubing, and pressed a button on the bed. The head of the bed raised up.

He winced slightly, and Aimee's gaze went to his left arm, which was covered by a fat bandage. "What—what did they say about your arm?"

His long, dark lashes swept downward. "The doctor came in earlier. He said all I needed to know was that they cleaned the wound, sewed some muscles and tendons back together, and stitched it all up." He looked down at the bandage. "He said it wouldn't be pretty, but with a little luck and a lot of physical therapy, it would probably work okay, thanks to whoever cleaned and bandaged it."

Aimee took a long breath. "I'm so glad."

"Me, too, although I have a feeling he really meant a *lot* of luck." He raised his gaze to hers. "How are you? You look good."

"I'm good," she said, nodding. "I'm fine. I brought someone to see you."

"William—?" Matt's voice broke, and Aimee's heart felt like it was cracking in two.

She smiled. "He wants to say thank you." She swallowed the lump that had risen in her throat.

"Let me see him."

She set the baby seat down and took William into her arms. "Can I sit down?" She nodded toward the side of his bed.

"Sure. Bring him over here."

She bounced the baby in her arms as she walked around and sat gingerly on the edge of the bed. She propped William on her lap.

Matt lifted his right hand, then checked his gesture. "Think the tubes will scare him?"

As if in answer, William cooed and waved his arms.

"I don't think anything about you could possibly scare him. He's happy to see you."

"Yeah?"

"William? You know who this is? Remember Matt? He's your godfather. He saved you."

"Aimee, don't—" Matt's hand fell back to the bed.

"Don't what? Tell my son the truth? You did save him. You saved him and me."

Matt leaned his head back and closed his eyes. "If you're going to tell him the truth, tell him the whole truth. Tell him what happened to his father. Tell him that I didn't have the sense or the courage to refuse to take Bill skydiving. I didn't have the good sense to make him take some practice runs or do a buddy-dive."

"Bill had skydived before. His carelessness wasn't your responsibility."

Matt blinked. "Why have you suddenly changed your mind?"

"Changed my mind? What are you talking about?"

"Are you feeling sorry for me? Is that it? What happened to blaming me for letting him die?"

"I never blamed you."

"Hah." He squeezed his eyes shut and shook his

head. "I saw how you looked at me when I brought his—when I brought him home."

"Matt, I can't remember what I did or said or even thought that night. What I do remember is what Bill always told me. 'You can count on Matt.' He said that the day before you and he left on your trip. 'Matt's safe as houses.'"

Matt lifted his head and looked at her. "I don't know why he thought that."

"I do, now."

He stared at her, his dark eyes glittering with unshed tears.

"It took me a while to understand what he meant. He knew you, maybe better than anyone. He knew you'd die, if by dying you could save an innocent life."

He shrugged and winced. "For some reason, Bill always believed in me."

William was getting restless. He began to fret. "I guess I'd better put this little guy back in his seat."

"Can I—?"

Aimee knew what Matt was trying to ask. She held William close enough that Matt could press a kiss to his fat little cheek. "Hey there, William," he whispered. "Are you glad to see your mom?"

She turned to fasten William back into his seat.

"Aimee?" She didn't look up. She was busy blinking away the tears that she couldn't stop. Seeing Matt kissing her little boy had shattered the last fragile pieces of her heart.

"Aimee—"

She lifted her head without really looking at him. "I'm listening. I just need to get William Matthew settled."

"Could you—maybe one day—give me a chance?"

She froze for an instant, wondering if she'd heard what she thought she had. Then she tested the last strap, to be sure William was safe in his seat.

Slowly, she raised her gaze to his. "Give you a chance?"

The muscles of his jaw worked. "I—" He swallowed. "I love you."

She gasped softly. "You said that before. I thought you were hallucinating."

He shook his head. "I wasn't hallucinating." Then his gaze wavered.

She'd seen him face killer snowstorms, assault rifles, gasoline fires, a horrible injury, but this was the first time she'd seen him nearly paralyzed with fear.

Her mouth stretched into a grin, even as fat tears slipped from her eyes and plopped onto her hands. "I am—so glad," she said, her voice shaking with sobs. "Because I wasn't sure how I was going to—tell you that I fell in—love with you the minute you bullied me into letting you go to the ransom drop with me."

"You did?" he said, his brows shooting up.

"Well, it didn't hurt that you made the supreme sacrifice of warming me with your own naked body."

"Anytime," he said, smiling at her.

"Promise?"

"You—" He paused. "You're okay with me being William's stepfather? I mean—are you saying you'll—you know?"

"I have something to tell you. When Bill found out he had cancer, he made me promise him something."

"Yeah? What?" Matt still looked scared.

"He made me promise that when I was ready, I'd think about you first."

She'd done pretty well so far, but remembering Bill's words and thinking about how prophetic they were, she looked at the man she knew would keep her and her son safe. Love and desire welled up inside her, and pushed away the last bits of the rigid control she'd always clung to like a lifeline. For the first time in her life, she broke down and sobbed.

Matt lifted his hand. "Aimee, are you okay?"

"Sure." She sniffed.

"You're crying."

"I know," she wailed.

Matt's mouth curved into a smile. "Does that mean this qualifies as a special occasion?"

She leaned over and kissed him on the mouth as tears streamed down her face. "I think it qualifies as the first in a lifetime of special occasions."

* * * * *

THE SHARPSHOOTER'S
SECRET SON

For Debbie and Lorraine

CHAPTER ONE

THEY CALLED THEM ghost towns for a reason.

Black Hills Search and Rescue Specialist Deke Cunningham wasn't afraid of anything. Not anymore. But the late afternoon shadows spooked him. They moved with him, reaching out like gnarled fingers across the empty, dusty main street of Cleancutt, Wyoming. He tried to shake off the feeling, but it wouldn't shake. Probably because today he wasn't working a routine assignment to rescue a deserving but nameless innocent.

Today he was searching for his ex-wife.

He glanced at the GPS locator built into his phone, then at the two-story building with the letters *H E L* barely readable above the door. The *O* and the *T* had long since faded.

This was it. The location where BHSAR computer expert Aaron Gold had finally managed to triangulate Mindy's last cell phone transmission.

Mindy. She didn't deserve this. She hadn't deserved anything she'd gotten for loving him.

And he'd never deserved her.

Deke approached the two-story building, doing his damnedest not to swipe his palm across the nape of his neck, where prickles of awareness tingled. He was being watched.

No surprise there.

He even knew who was watching him. The same person who'd kidnapped his ex-wife. Well—who'd *ordered* her kidnapped, anyhow.

Novus Ordo. The infamous international terrorist who'd already targeted another member of the BHSAR team, Matt Parker.

We've got your wife, the obviously disguised voice on the cell phone had said.

Alarm bells had clanged in his head and his gut had clenched with worry. Still, he'd had to smile a little. Whoever the kidnapper was, he had no idea what he'd gotten hold of when he'd grabbed Mindy Cunningham.

"Ex-wife," he'd muttered, working to sound bored and uninterested. "And be my guest. You can have her."

"This is no joke, Cunningham. We've got her and we'll kill her if you don't do what we say."

"The only thing I think you've got is her cell phone and a death wish."

The kidnapper had taken the bait. He'd put Mindy on the phone.

Deke Cunningham, don't pay them one red cent! It's a trap—

Tough words. Exactly what he'd expected from her. But beneath her brave words he heard fear—a soul-deep terror he'd never heard in her voice before. And that, more than anything the kidnapper said, scared him to death.

Something was wrong with her. Something beyond being kidnapped. While that alone would be enough to terrify any woman, his Mindy was made of stronger stuff.

In the twenty years since he'd first spotted her hanging by her heels from the top rung of the elementary school jungle gym, he'd never seen anything she couldn't handle.

Except him.

Her tight, strained voice, cut by static, still echoed in his head as he paused at the bottom of the dilapidated wooden steps of the only hotel in Cleancutt, Wyoming.

He'd heard about the ghost towns of Wyoming all his life. Eighty years ago, Cleancutt and other coal-mining camps had been booming towns. But by the 1950s, underground coal mining had given way to strip-mining, so today Cleancutt was a ghost, a dying piece of history located near the city of Casper.

A vibration started in his breast pocket. *Damn it.* His phone.

As he retrieved it, he glanced around him, in case he could catch someone watching him, waiting for him to answer. But the display read Irina Castle, his boss, not Mindy. He pressed the talk button without saying anything.

"Deke, where are you?" Irina asked.

"I'm busy," he said quietly.

"You did it, didn't you? You went after Mindy alone. I told you to wait until I could arrange a meeting with Aaron Schiff."

"Irina, do *not* get the FBI involved in this. It's too dangerous for Mindy. I'll handle it. Besides, you know the drill. They threatened to hurt her if I brought backup."

"And *you* know the drill. My specialists never take unnecessary risks."

"This one was necessary."

Irina blew out a sigh of frustration. "You told Aaron not to tell me where you are." Her voice was accusatory.

"It's for your own good, and Mindy's. You can't know. It's too dangerous for you. Besides, there's nobody alive who's better trained to run a covert rescue mission than me." He'd meant the comment to be reassuring, but it hung in the sudden silence between them.

Irina's husband, Rook Castle, had been the best until he'd been assassinated by Novus Ordo two years ago.

"Aaron and Rafe have my projected timeline," he continued. "They know what to do. You've got to trust me, Irina."

"I don't like it."

"You think I do? I should have known what was going to happen as soon as Matt told me he'd been followed back here from Mahjidastan. I should have anticipated that Novus would go after Mindy."

Novus Ordo was desperate to find out why Irina had suddenly called Matt Parker back from assignment in Mahjidastan and announced to her employees that she was ending her two-year-long search for her husband—or his body.

"It's not your fault, Deke."

"The hell it's not. I should have taken care of her, put her in protective custody." He shook off the feeling of failure. He'd let Mindy get captured. Now he had to rescue her.

"Don't worry, Irina. I know more about Novus than anyone alive. You listen to Rafe and Aaron and Brock. They each have their instructions. Their primary mission is to keep you safe." He paused. "And, Irina, don't leave the ranch without one of them with you. Make sure all three of them know where you're going and who you're going with."

Irina sighed in frustration. "You sound like you don't trust your own team."

"My helicopter was sabotaged. I don't trust anybody but you and me."

"You mentioned your timeline. What is it?"

"I plan to be out of there with Mindy in less than twenty-four hours."

"What's your drop-dead time?"

"Seventy-two." He had his timeline. He wished he knew what Novus's was.

"Be careful, Deke."

He hung up and started to pocket his phone, then hesitated, looking at the display.

Two days ago, the BHSAR recovery team, along with the FBI, had found the body of the man who had tried to get his hands on Matt Parker.

Papers and a prepaid cell phone found on the dead man proved his involvement in terrorist activities, with ties to Novus Ordo. It was bad enough that it took only a couple of hours for Novus to find out that Irina had recalled Matt. What made it so much worse was the ruined helicopter rotor on the floor of Deke's hangar that proved his bird had been sabotaged. The grounded helicopter had caused Deke to miss a critical rendez-vous point and had almost cost Matt Parker and Aimee Vick their lives.

There was only one explanation for those security breaches.

Both the sabotage and Novus's intel had to have been engineered by someone who had unrestricted access to Castle Ranch. They had a traitor in BHSAR. Someone who was working for Novus.

Deke had put his most trusted specialists to guarding Irina. He just wished he could trust them without reservation.

But there was only one man in the world, other than himself, whom he could trust with Irina's life.

Trying to ignore the fact that his fingers were shaking, Deke dialed a number he'd thought he'd never call.

Irina's innocent action had negated everything Rook Castle had done to keep her safe.

Deke listened to the electronic message, hoping he was doing the right thing. He spoke quickly, quietly, then hung up.

It was done. Two years ago he'd made a promise to his best friend, Rook Castle. Today he'd broken it. But he'd had no choice. It was time to raise the dead.

DEKE CAREFULLY CLIMBED the crumbling steps and put his shoulder against the weathered front door of the abandoned hotel. He stopped dead in his tracks when it creaked loudly. Clutching his weapon in both hands, he listened.

Nothing. Not a scurrying rat or the buzz of a disturbed insect.

He'd expected Novus to come after him. He'd hoped the terrorist wouldn't be savvy enough to go after his ex-wife. Hell, they'd been divorced over two years.

It disturbed him that Novus knew that much about him. Mindy was his weakness.

His only weakness.

The air force had done what nothing else ever had—it had made a man out of him. He could fly a helicopter. He could shoot a housefly off a general's lapel at two hundred yards—hell, he could take that shot *while* flying a bird.

Being a Special Forces Op had taught him there was nothing he couldn't face and conquer.

But with one disappointed look, and the sparkle of a tear, Mindy could reduce him to his pathetic, arrogant high-school self, trying to bully his way through school and drink his way through life.

He stood outside the hotel's door and wondered what kind of traps Novus had set for him. He'd have preferred a face-to-face confrontation, but he already knew the publicity-shy Novus wouldn't do that.

There was a reason the terrorist wore a surgical mask in every known photo. An excellent reason. And only a few people knew what that reason was.

Yeah, he was walking into a trap. But Novus had baited it with the only lure he couldn't resist.

His ex-wife.

All those thoughts swirled through his mind in the two seconds it took for him to flex his fingers, retighten them around the grip of his Sig Sauer, and take a deep breath.

Here goes.

He nudged the door another inch and slipped through.

The hotel lobby could have been lifted out of one of the Western movies his old man had watched when he wasn't passed out from cheap vodka.

When Deke stepped inside, eyeing the ornate desk and curved staircase, glass crunched under his boot. Shattered prisms from a broken chandelier.

Then something moved at the edge of his vision.

Startled, he swung around. His finger tightened on the trigger.

A raccoon. It scurried across the room, claws clicking on the worn hardwood floor like faraway machine-gun fire.

Deke's breath whooshed out and his trigger finger relaxed. He took another step, eyeing the dark room beyond the arched doorway. He figured it was the dining room.

What was the raccoon running from? He crossed the lobby and angled around the arch so his back stayed to the wall.

Heavy curtains revealed only slivers of the late afternoon sun. The smell of mildew and rotting wood tickled his nostrils. He held his breath, resisting the urge to sneeze as he moved silently across to the shrouded windows and reached up to push the drapes apart. Too late, he saw the flash and heard the report.

Something stung the curve of his cheek. He whirled, ready to shoot, but whirling turned out not to be such a good idea.

Things got real hazy real fast. A fuzzy shadow loomed in front of him. He aimed, but as hard as he tried, he couldn't make his fingers hold on to the gun, and he couldn't make his legs hold him up.

As the room tilted sideways, the haze before his eyes turned to black.

DAMN, HE HATED the waiting. He liked to be the one making the phone calls. When he had to wait to be called, he couldn't control who might be listening.

He paced back and forth in front of the big picture window, with its panoramic view of the Black Hills, until he couldn't stand it any longer. He yanked the blinds shut. He despised those desolate looming mountains.

He'd seen enough of them to last him the rest of his life and beyond.

The prepaid cell phone hidden in his shaving kit rang.

Finally.

"Everything's in place here."

"No change here."

"There better be a change soon."

"I'm working on it. Do you have any idea of the level of security around this place? It's tripled since—"

"Do you have any idea of the time constraints we're facing?"

"I think I'm close—"

"You think? You'd better know! We've only got one chance. I'm guessing you remember what'll happen if you fail me."

"Why all the mind games? It'd be a hell of a lot easier to just go in and get it over with."

"Are you questioning my methods? Because you're not indispensable. Nobody is."

SOMETHING SOFT ROCKED against his side, rousing him. His mouth felt stuffed with cotton and his stomach clenched. Beneath the nauseating smell of mildew and rotten wood, he noticed a sweet, familiar scent.

He tried to push through the drowsiness, but whoever had filled his mouth with cotton had put lead weights on his eyelids. He wanted to turn over, but he was too tired.

The unmistakable supple firmness of a female body rocked against him again. "Eee!"

"Mindy, sugar," Deke mumbled. "Move over."

Whoa. A sharp blade of reality sliced through his mental fog. That wasn't right—on so many levels. For one thing, his tongue wasn't working, so all he'd managed to do was grunt unintelligibly.

"Eee, ake uk," she retorted.

What was she saying? Maybe she was dreaming. Maybe *he* was.

"Okay," he whispered, smiling drowsily to himself. "You know what happens when you don't move over." Anticipating her giggles and kisses, he turned—or tried to.

He couldn't move.

He wasn't in bed. He *sure* wasn't in bed with Mindy. That hadn't happened in a long, long time.

So where the hell was he?

More shards of reality ripped through his brain. The flash of gunpowder. The biting sting in his cheek.

He forced his eyes open. It was dark. Totally dark.

Danger! His heart rate skyrocketed and his Special Forces training kicked in.

Judging by the way his head wobbled like a bobble-head doll, he figured he'd been drugged. He clenched his jaw and worked to gather his thoughts.

The gunpowder. The sting. He'd been shot with a tranquilizer gun. Ah, hell.

He bit down on his tongue, using the pain to clear his brain. Giving in to drugs—or fatigue, or torture—in combat rescue missions could be fatal. Not only to the rescuer, but also to the innocents depending on him for their safety, their protection, their very lives.

Before he could help anyone else, he had to assess his own condition. He needed to take inventory.

Blood? No stickiness or wet warmth.

Broken bones? He shifted enough that his arms ached and his legs cramped. No.

Other injuries? Nope. Just the sting from the tranq dart. That and the drug it had delivered.

Location? Somewhere dark and damp.

Position? Tied up—arms behind his back, and gagged. He pushed his dry tongue against the cloth in his mouth. Gagged tight. Then, gingerly, he moved his legs—and nearly fell off the crate.

That explained the cramps. His ankles were tied.

Mission? Not quite as easy. What was he doing here, tied up and drugged?

"Eee!"

Mindy. Her voice ripped the haze from his brain. That was it. He'd come here to rescue her. Novus Ordo had kidnapped her to get to him.

Her soft warmth was close—way too close for comfort. Her shoulder was touching his. Judging by her restricted movements and incoherent mutterings, she was tied up and gagged, too.

He wanted to reassure her, but that would be a waste of breath with the gag in his mouth. So he spent his energy getting rid of it. He rubbed his mouth and chin against his shoulder, not easy with his hands tethered behind his back.

His neck and jaw ached like a sonofabitch, and the skin on his chin was raw by the time the cloth peeled away from his tongue and lips.

His throat was too dry to swallow. "Mindy? You all right?" he croaked.

Her answer was a frustrated growl.

"Okay, okay, just a second." He scooted closer and twisted until he was leaning heavily against her shoulder.

Another not-so-good idea. But this time it was because he got a whiff of that tangerine bath stuff she always used. He bent his head and nuzzled her cheek, feeling for her gag with his mouth.

Soft, warm, tangerine sweetness. That solved the dry-mouth issue. Her familiar scent made his mouth water and his body tighten in immediate, familiar response. He clenched his jaw and swallowed a groan of frustration. Sex had never been the problem between them.

It sure as hell hadn't been the solution.

Mindy stiffened at his frustrated moan, slamming his brain with a harsh reminder that this wasn't old times, it was deadly serious.

But she didn't lash out at him or try to move away. In fact, she angled her head to give him better access to the cloth that gagged her.

He bit and tugged at it with his teeth until it began to loosen. He tried to hold his breath, tried to ignore the soft, sensual tickle of her hair against his nose and cheek.

After a lot of tugging and nibbling and some extremely uncomfortable brushing of his mouth against her lips, cheeks and chin, he finally got her gag loose.

When he straightened, his head felt clearer, although wherever they were was dark as the cargo hold of a C-17 transport plane at midnight. The only light was pitifully dim and came from a window high above their heads.

The smell of mildew and dirt chased away Mindy's familiar, evocative scent.

"Basement," he muttered. They had to be in a basement.

Mindy groaned and wriggled against him.

"Min? Are you okay?" he asked, squinting in the

darkness. He could barely make out the silhouette of her face. Her dark clothes blended into a pool of shadows just below her shoulders. "Did they hurt you?"

She shook her head. "Just practically broke my arms when he tied me up." Her normally husky voice was soft and raspy.

And sexy as hell.

Deke cursed to himself. What a chump he was. After all this time, his ex-wife could still turn him on just by talking.

She coughed. "By the way, thanks for involving me in your little adventure."

And she could still tick him off.

He took a deep breath and winced when the blast of air sent a piercing ache through his temples. "Here we go again," he muttered.

"Don't even try to tell me this doesn't involve one of your rescues," she rasped.

"You think I'd put you in danger if I could help it?"

"What I think is that you've gotten yourself in over your head again. You're never going to learn that you can't save everybody. And even if you could, it wouldn't fill up that hole inside you."

Deke grimaced. It was an old argument, and he'd be damned if he let her lead him down that road again.

He raised his gaze to hers and curved his lips in a confident smile, prepared to give her back a smart retort. But even in the dimness he could see the fear that darkened her olive-green eyes. The same fear he'd heard in her voice. It knocked the confidence right out of him.

"Min, are you sure you're okay? You don't sound too good."

She focused on a point somewhere behind him and

to his left. Then she arched her neck, and sonofagun if she didn't stick the tip of her pink tongue out to moisten her lips.

Do not go there, he ordered his brain. But it went there anyhow—to all the amazing things Mindy could do with her tongue. Not the least of which was cut him down to size with a well-chosen word.

"I'm—okay," she rasped, then coughed again.

He knew how she felt. Her throat sounded as dry and sore as his. "What the hell happened? How'd they kidnap you?"

"I got a call about some—something addressed to me that had been delivered to the wrong place." Her voice gained a bit of strength as she talked. "When I went to pick it up, they grabbed me."

"Damn it, how many times have I told you—don't go to strange places alone. You know how dangerous it can be."

"Right," she croaked. "Because of your dangerous profession. Well, silly me. Since we've been divorced for two years I was kind of hoping your danger wouldn't rub off on me anymore." Her hand went to her throat.

"Besides, this was a young woman. She told me she was also pr—" She stopped.

"Also what?"

After a split-second pause and a brief shake of her head, she continued: "She said a store had delivered some things to her by mistake. They were addressed to me. She asked if I could pick them up because she was—ill."

"Damn it, Min. That's an obvious scam. I can't believe you fell for it."

"Would you listen to me?" she snapped. "She said the sender's name was Irina."

Deke's scalp prickled. More proof that Novus had deliberately targeted Mindy. He'd expected it, but that didn't mean he liked it.

"The girl said that?"

She nodded. "I should have been suspicious, because Irina wouldn't know— I mean, there's no reason she'd send me a b— a gift out of the blue."

"What's the matter with you? Did they drug you, too? You sound strange."

"As soon as the door opened, somebody dragged me inside and stuck something in my neck. The next thing I knew, I woke up here."

"Did you get a look at them?"

"No. I was blindfolded until they brought you in this morning. He took my blindfold off right before he left. I never saw him."

"But it *was* a man? What did he tell you? Anything? What made you think it had anything to do with me?"

Mindy made a small, impatient noise. He knew the look she was wearing, as well as if she were standing in a spotlight. He'd seen it too many times before. It was her *do not treat me like an idiot* scowl.

"What made me—? Maybe because I've never done anything that would cause anyone to kidnap me. You, on the other hand—"

"Me what?" His evasion was automatic. He'd practiced evading the truth from the time he could talk. It was ingrained in him—part of his survival tactic.

But he knew she was right. He'd done plenty in his lifetime that might make him the target of revenge. Not the least of which had been just two years ago.

A lot of people, including Mindy, would want his head on a pike if they knew what he'd done—for and *to* his best friend. His only friend.

However, what *a lot of people* thought meant nothing. He'd do it again. That and more, for the one man who'd always believed in him—who'd trusted his life to him.

His life *and* his death.

I just hope your sacrifice wasn't in vain, Rook. Because here they were battling Novus Ordo again. And this time he wasn't going to give up.

"Okay, fine," he snapped at Mindy. "Supposing for the moment that I've screwed up your life yet again. I can't change that. But I can do my best to get us out of here. I promise, as soon as I can manage it, I'll get you back to the normal, safe life you like so much."

CHAPTER TWO

IF HER MOUTH didn't hurt so much, she'd smile at Deke's words, Mindy thought. *The normal, safe life you like so much.*

She'd give anything for normal and safe right now.

But as usual when Deke was around, normal and safe had left the building.

His words were on target. She'd loved him most of her life, and loving Deke wasn't exactly a recipe for normal. Certainly not for safe.

Loving Deke was a recipe for disaster. Not that her heart cared. Nor her body. He'd always been the sexiest thing on the planet. From his sun-streaked brown hair to his startling sea-blue eyes. From the hard line of his jaw to his broad, leanly muscled shoulders. Even his battered shearling jacket couldn't hide the power and grace of his six-feet-plus body.

A wave of nausea reminded her that this was no time to be ogling her ex-husband. She swallowed against the queasiness that was fast overtaking her. It had plagued her ever since the moment yesterday morning when she'd rapped on the apartment door. Even before the door opened, she knew she'd made a mistake.

Deke had warned her often enough not to wander around strange places by herself. But the message had been so simple, so innocent sounding.

Hi. Mindy Cunningham? I just received a delivery from Babies First that belongs to you. It's from an Irene or Irina Castle. I'd bring it to you, but I'm on bed rest for the last month of my pregnancy. Can you pick it up?

When she got to the address, the person who opened the door wasn't a pregnant woman. Wasn't even a woman. It was a man. Something about him—the expression on his face or the gleam in his eyes—confirmed that she'd screwed up.

Before she could react, he'd grabbed her arm and pulled her inside, slamming the door behind her. Then he'd shoved her up against a wall and stuck something into the back of her neck.

He'd drugged her.

She was terrified that whatever he'd given her might hurt the baby. It was her worst fear—that something might happen to her little Sprout.

As if he knew what she was thinking, Sprout kicked. She rubbed her tummy and smiled sadly.

Until she'd acquired this tiny passenger that depended on her for his very life, she'd have said her worst fear was that she'd never be able to get over the man sitting next to her.

Deke Cunningham, air force veteran, sharpshooter, alcoholic, adventurer and ex-husband.

Once their divorce was final, her plan had been to never see him again. But the best-laid plans…

Just over eight months ago, he'd come to her mother's funeral. One of about three times in his life she'd seen him in a suit. He'd been handsome as a *GQ* model, and more gentle, sweet and protective than he'd ever been before.

For that one night, he was the man she'd always known he could be.

At the end of the evening he was still there, at her house. Just to make sure she was okay, he'd said.

When he got up to leave, somehow she'd asked him to stay. They'd somehow ended up in the bed, and she'd somehow ended up pregnant.

So much for getting over him.

"Mindy, you're not okay. They hurt you, didn't they?"

His voice was controlled—barely, but that was all about him that was. His intensity and anger washed over her like scalding hot water. Anger, not at her, but on her behalf.

"No, I'm not injured. Just tired and hurting."

He'd never understood why she hadn't wanted him to be angry for her. He'd never realized that his anger— even when it wasn't directed at her—still scared her.

And that was why, although he needed to know what he was up against—deserved to—she couldn't tell him. Not until she absolutely had to.

Like the coward she was, she planned to put off that revelation as long as she possibly could, because scalding water didn't begin to describe what Deke would throw at her when he found out she was pregnant— with *his* child.

"Deke, we've got to get out of here. The guy told me he'd be watching me. He'll be back anytime."

"Yeah, we do. Can you move? Turn around. Let me see your hands."

Could she move? Hah. *Not too well,* she wanted to answer. Like an overloaded supply plane, she was carrying heavy on the front end.

She twisted until her back was to him, working to

suppress the grunts and groans that went with everything she did these days.

By the time he said "That's good," she was breathing hard.

"Min, are you sure you're okay?"

She squeezed her eyes shut and nodded. "It's the drug," she said as evenly as she could. "It's making me light-headed. And I'm hungry."

He chuckled. "No surprise there."

Mindy bit her lip against the poignant memories that bombarded her. The sweet teasing, the tickling matches, the kisses. Dear heavens, she'd missed him. It didn't matter how many times her head reminded her heart that they were as compatible as jet fuel and an ignition source.

He twisted on the wooden crate until he was facing her back. Then he bent double to look at the ropes binding her hands.

He uttered a short burst of colorful curses. "Damn it, I can't see anything."

"Can you bite them like you did the gag?"

He sniffed in disdain. "My teeth aren't that good. Stay still."

Mindy waited. It soon became obvious that Deke was scooting around until his back was to hers. Then he shifted closer and twisted some more, until they were pressed together like bookends.

She felt his hands on hers, big, warm, protective, as they explored the ropes.

He let go a string of colorful curses. "…Those sons of bitches," he finished.

Mindy's pulse skittered. "What is it Deke? What's wrong?"

"Nobody's this stupid. Everything about this, from the moment you called, has been too easy," he muttered. "Too pat."

"Too easy? How is this easy?"

"They used your phone. Didn't even bother to keep the call short. Like they were telegraphing their location. And now, these knots are just strong enough to be frustrating. If he'd wanted to, he could have used knots I'd never be able to untie."

"That makes sense," she rasped. "I tried to warn you that it was a trap to lure you here."

"Trust me. I'd already figured that out."

Deke's hands moved over hers, touching and manipulating as he worked to loosen the knots.

"Ow!"

"Sorry."

"No, I'm sorry. My thumb got a little twisted."

"I'm almost done."

She listened to his labored breathing as he worked. "Deke, why do they want you? You know who they are, don't you?"

She winced as the knots began to loosen and the circulation increased in her fingers. "This is connected to a case, isn't it?"

He shook his head. She had her back to him and she knew he'd done it. Was it a movement of the air, a rustle of his clothing? Or was it the connection they'd always shared? Even when they couldn't share their dreams or their heartbreaks.

"I'm not on a case right now. I'm trying to stick close to the ranch. Irina's not doing well. She's stopped searching for Rook."

"What? Oh, Deke. I can't believe she'd ever— Did she find out something?"

"Ran out of money." He pushed air out between his clenched teeth, a sure sign he was frustrated about something.

"She stopped because of *money?*"

"She either had to stop the search or fire at least two specialists and cut back on voluntary cases."

His fingers strained against hers as he picked at one of the knots. His breath hitched and he grunted quietly.

Mindy knew what he was feeling. His arms were tied behind his back, just like hers were, and she couldn't even imagine the pain in his wrists from working against the stiff ropes. She wanted to say something, to at least acknowledge the pain he was going through. But Deke Cunningham would never admit pain. Not pain. Not hurt. Not heartache.

"But Rook's her *husband.* I can't believe she'd quit for *any* reason. I'd never—" she stopped, biting her tongue—literally. *Never give up* was what she'd been about to say.

But she had. She'd given up on them.

"Well, she did." Deke's curt answer told her that he hadn't missed what she'd almost said. His breath hissed out between his teeth again. A sure sign that he was hurting.

Not knowing what else to say, she kept talking about Irina Castle. Maybe if he got irritated enough with her, it would distract him from the pain in his wrists.

"She must be devastated. It would be bad enough to give up if she knew it was useless. But not to know, and to have to stop because of money. When did she makc that decision?"

He didn't respond, just kept working silently.

He didn't want to tell her. Dear Lord, she knew him so well. "When, Deke?"

At that moment she felt the ropes give, releasing the strain on her shoulders, arms and wrists. Pain shot through her muscles as they relaxed. She bit her lip and tried to suppress a groan.

"Easy," Deke muttered. "Don't move too fast. You'll regret it, trust me."

It was one of the cryptic remarks that reminded her how little she knew about this man she'd loved as long as she could remember. She slowly flexed her arms and shoulders, clamping her jaw against the pain, as her brain filed that tidbit of information away with the others she'd collected over the years.

He knew how it felt to be tied up for hours—or days.

He twisted around. "Turn around this way. I need you to get my knife," he said. "It's in my left boot, *if* they didn't strip-search me while I was out. They took my gun. Thank God I ditched my cell phone."

She twisted awkwardly around until her shoulder bumped his. "They didn't search you after they brought you down here. They didn't have time. One of them got a phone call, but he obviously didn't want to talk in front of me, so they left." She looked down, but the tiny window didn't provide enough light for her to see that close to the ground. Still, she knew she couldn't bend over far enough to reach his boot.

"Good. See if you can grab my knife."

"No," she said flatly. "I can't."

"Come on, Min. It's sticking down in the side of my left boot. You remember where I keep it."

"I *can't*."

"Why not?"

She bit her lip. She'd put off the *big reveal* as long as she could.

"Are you injured? Too stiff? What?"

She almost cried. He assumed she was hurting. And she let him think that. Dear heavens, she'd never realized what a coward she was.

"These knots are so slippery, I'll bet I can loosen them." He kicked his feet back and forth, working the ropes. "There." He inched around.

Mindy could see his head and shoulders in the dim light. She'd already felt the comforting softness and smelled the old-leather smell of his jacket. So it was no surprise that even with the darkness leaching the color out of everything, she could see the way it bunched across his constrained shoulders. She could even see the shadow of his too-long hair on the sheepskin collar.

He straightened his leg and barely missed brushing her tummy with the side of his boot. She flexed her cramped fingers and rubbed the indentations on her wrists. Then quickly, she wrapped her right arm around his calf and got her hands behind the boot heel and tugged.

"Pull your foot backward against my hands."

"You got it, sugar."

Her heart twisted until she wanted to cry out. "And don't call me sugar," she hissed.

He pulled backward, inadvertently pushing his heel into her tummy. "Hey—" he said.

Mindy cringed. "What?" she snapped.

"Have you gained weight?"

"Deke, this is serious."

He didn't say anything for a couple of seconds. "I know it is."

Tugging harder, she finally got a purchase on the boot heel and jerked it off his foot. His knife fell into her lap as something clattered against the crate and onto the floor.

"There," she said, breathing hard as she pushed his foot off her lap and picked up the knife. She pressed the button that sprung the blade. It snicked into place.

Deke jumped at the sound. "Hey, careful. It's sharp."

"I remember that, too." She slid the knife blade between his wrists. The blade sliced through the thick rope as if it were warm butter.

Deke carefully relaxed his shoulders and moved his arms. He grunted a couple of times.

She knew what he was going through. He hadn't been tied up as long as she had, but she figured the kidnappers hadn't been as careful with him as they had with her. His hands had to be on fire as the blood rushed back to them.

She handed him the knife, her heart pounding. When he leaned over to cut the ropes binding her feet, would he see why he'd gotten the impression she'd gained weight?

She held her breath while he cut the ropes. "I had a cigarette lighter in my boot with the knife. I think I heard it fall."

Mindy felt around with her foot until she touched a small cylinder. "Here it is." She kicked it toward him.

He grabbed it and sat up, grunting. "Whoa! I can understand why you didn't want to bend over. I'm still kind of woozy." He reached a hand out to the wall beside him and stood. His shadow loomed over her. "Can you stand up? We need to get out of here."

Mindy crouched there, her shoulders hunched. Right now, he couldn't see anything. But as soon as she stood—

Dear God, please help me. When Deke sees me, I'm going to need all the courage you can spare.

He was about to find out that she was pregnant. She had no idea what he'd do.

She *did* remember what he'd said he'd do.

Years ago, when they were seventeen, she'd had a scare. She was late, and the pregnancy test had read positive. When she'd told Deke, his reaction had been immediate. Shock and abject terror had darkened his features.

You're pregnant? No. No way. You gotta do something. There's enough screwed-up Cunninghams in the world already.

She'd been stunned and frightened. But she'd understood. If she'd had the baby, Deke would be gone. But the issue was moot, because a few days later she'd started her period. They'd never spoken about it again.

Now here she was, six weeks away from bringing a Cunningham into the world. And six seconds away from Deke finding out.

"Stand up." He held out his hand. "You'll be woozy, but I won't let you fall."

Mindy sucked in a deep breath and took his hand. Struggling, bracing herself against the wall, and with a lot of grunting and groaning, she managed to push herself upright.

When their gazes met, his expression softened and

his fingers tightened on her hand. "Hey, Min. It's been a long time." His mouth quirked.

She swallowed hard. "Long time," she replied, with a nervous nod.

"I'm so sorry they hurt you," he whispered. He leaned in closer, a gentle smile on his face.

Then he stopped—dead still. His gaze flickered downward.

Her mouth went dry. She couldn't move. All she could do was stand there.

She knew what he saw. A dark wool peacoat, navy blue pants and low-heeled boots. Pretty standard wear for this weather.

But the peacoat stuck out to *there,* and he'd just bumped into her tummy.

Her hands moved to cradle the baby. She couldn't stop them. It was an innate reaction, a protective instinct. Shielding her baby from what was to come.

Trembling with trepidation, she braced herself.

Deke stood frozen, his face lit by the fading beam of light from the tiny window. As wan and dim as the light was, she still saw the color drain from his face. His blue eyes widened and his mouth dropped open.

Mindy cradled her belly tighter.

"Min—?" His voice broke.

She bit her lip as her heart broke.

He shook his head as if to clear it— or to deny the truth before his eyes.

Then it hit—the storm of Deke's anger. His brows lowered until his eyes were dark and hooded. "Mindy, what the hell have you done?"

She tried to hold her own against Deke's fiery gaze, but she couldn't. She had to look away.

"Deke, that kidnapper is coming back anytime. It's been hours since he checked on me."

"I'll deal with him when he gets here." His voice was tight with what? Confusion? Shock? Fury? She couldn't sort out all the emotions. For the first time since she'd known him she wasn't sure what was behind his clipped words.

"How did you—?"

The baby kicked, probably feeling her distress. She rubbed the spot and he calmed down. "How? The usual way."

"So who's the lucky guy?"

And there it was. Deke Cunningham's patented defense system. More efficient than any antimissile missile the government had ever dreamed up. It was as effective and high-tech as the Starship *Enterprise*'s shields, and as quick to rise to protect his heart.

Although she understood why he did it, his words still hurt. She braced herself. "You are."

CHAPTER THREE

MINDY SUCKED IN a deep breath as she watched her ex-husband and waited for the explosion.

His face was still lit by that small rectangle of light. If he realized it, he'd move—cover his reaction with darkness. But right this second she had a unique opportunity to watch his face as he processed what she'd said.

His eyes widened in panic for a split second, then narrowed. His brows knit in a frown and he blew air out between his clenched teeth. "That's impossible. We haven't even seen each other in almost a year."

"Eight months plus a week, to be exact," she murmured.

"Eight—oh. Your mom's funeral." He shot her a look before he turned away, out of the wan spotlight. Then tightly, "Why didn't you tell me?"

"You know why. Look at your reaction. Now can we focus on the kidnapper, who's going to show up any minute?"

"Fine," he snapped. He wiped a hand down his face and around to rub the nape of his neck.

When he turned back around, his features were carefully neutral and his voice was all business. "What do you know about this place? Where's the door?"

She ignored his curt tone and pointed behind them. "There's a staircase back there. I hear the door open. I see light until he closes it. Then he comes down the stairs. Twelve. Twelve steps."

Deke tried to concentrate on her words. She was absolutely right. They needed to get out of there before their captors came back.

But all he could think about was her...condition. And she was right about his reaction. Years ago she'd come to him, worried that she might be pregnant, and he'd lost it. Yelled at her.

Scared her. His heart twisted with regret for an instant, then leapt again in renewed panic.

The idea of having a kid scared him. More than anything he'd ever come up against—before or since. And he'd faced a lot.

But a baby. His mouth went dry and his chest tightened.

Damn it, he didn't have time to be distracted by emotion. He had to focus. He squeezed his eyes shut and forced himself to concentrate on the danger. To forget that his ex-wife was carrying his child.

He growled under his breath and looked in the direction she'd indicated. He recognized the stairs. Their shape stood out as a darker shadow ascending into blackness.

The basement was so damn dark, and the light from the window above was waning. He was pretty sure, based on his instinctive sense of direction, that the window faced east.

He'd driven in from the east, from nearby Casper. He wasn't sure what good that information did him, but at least he was oriented now.

"It's getting dark out. What else have you seen? Did the man bring a light with him?"

Mindy's hands were cradling her belly and her head was inclined. A serene expression made her face as beautiful as a Madonna. Amazingly, even in the darkness of the basement, she glowed. She was lush and beautiful. He wanted her so bad he ached.

Stop it!

She looked up, frowning. He could see her processing his words. "No. The last time, he and another guy were dragging you. I couldn't figure out what I was hearing until you grunted." She smiled. "No mistaking that growl. Anyhow, when they took off my blindfold I tried to take in as much as I could before they left and closed that door. I saw something over there, beyond that stack of wood. Maybe a door, or an opening of some kind."

"Stay right there," Deke ordered, pointing at her feet. He moved carefully toward the place she'd indicated. The entire floor was dirt, and littered with boards and logs along with pieces of broken furniture.

Within minutes it would be too dark to see, but his senses took in the shapes of the shadows and the musty smells. He figured that there was very little down here newer than fifty years old.

Finally, his outstretched hands touched the wall. Mindy was right. Complete darkness had already encroached on this end of the basement. He ran his hands over the rough-hewn boards. If there was a door, he couldn't find it.

He rapped on the wood, listening for a hollow echo. No luck. Every place he knocked sounded solid as a rock.

Finally, as a last resort, he reached in his pocket and pulled out the disposable cigarette lighter. He shook it. Fairly full. Striking it with his thumb, he used its light to quickly examine the wall.

"Deke?"

Mindy's scared voice, harsh with the strain of holding herself together, tore through him.

"Just a minute, sugar," he said, studying the crevices between the boards. If there was an opening in this alcove, he couldn't find it.

The lighter was beginning to burn his thumb, so he let go, then turned around and made his way back to her.

"Okay. I'm going upstairs and check things out. You stay here. You were right about the alcove, but I can't find a door anywhere, and we're almost out of light."

"Deke, you can't go up there. You said they wanted you to get out of the knots. That means they'll be waiting up there to ambush you."

"I'd be surprised if they weren't. But I'll deal with them. When I call you, we'll make a run for it."

Mindy shook her head. "No. It won't work. You can't—"

"Have you got a better idea? Because I don't. Our only other choice is to wait until they come back, and I'm not going to fight them down here so close to you. You could get hurt. Now give me my knife and stop arguing. You're wasting time. Nothing's going to happen to me."

"You don't know that—"

"Nothing ever has."

"We both know that's not true."

Deke clenched his jaw. The arguing had always come so easily. Just like the sex. Two things they'd always gotten right.

They'd learned early how to push each other's buttons.

"My knife, Mindy."

She handed it to him.

He closed it and stuck it in his pocket. Then he dropped the disposable lighter down inside his boot.

"Grab those ropes and sit back down. I'll wrap them loosely around your hands and feet, so you'll look like you're still tied up if they—" he paused "—get past me."

"Wait. I don't understand."

"If they come down here, I want you to look like you're still tied up. That way they can't blame you for trying to escape. Just me."

Mindy slowly bent down, reaching a hand out to steady herself against the wall.

Deke grimaced. This was going to be harder than he could have imagined. She was so handicapped by her pregnancy that she couldn't even bend down. He cupped her elbow.

"Okay, never mind." He led her over to sit on the wooden crate and fetched the ropes.

"Put your hands behind your back."

He took her hands and carefully looped the rope around them. Then, bending in front of her, he wrapped the second rope around her feet.

He straightened. "Good. In the dark, it'll look like you're really tied up."

"I *feel* like I'm really tied up. Are you sure about this?" Her voice was edged with panic.

"Trust me, sugar." His mouth flattened in a grimace, just like it did every time he said those words to her. She couldn't trust him. He knew it, and she knew it. He'd let her down too many times.

"But how—"

He placed into her palm one end of the rope that was wrapped around her hands. "Hang on to that end of the rope. When you pull it the ropes will fall off. The ropes around your feet aren't secured at all. Just kick them."

"Deke, I don't like this."

He glanced at the lone window, high above their heads. Then, closing his eyes, he formed a mental blueprint of the main floor of the hotel in his brain. "If the desk is there, and the stairs are there—" he muttered, tracing the most likely route out of the building.

"Listen to me, Min. That window faces east. My car is out there. Whatever you do, keep yourself oriented. The front of the building faces south." He pointed in that direction. "Which means these stairs are on the north side. That door probably opens into the kitchen."

He laid his palms against her shoulders. "Relax," he said, massaging the muscles there. "You can let your hands rest against the ropes. They won't give unless you jerk the end you have in your fingers.

"The dining room is through an arched doorway to the right—east—of the desk. I want you to wait down here until I call you. If you don't hear anything within a half hour, undo the ropes and run up the stairs. If you see a clear shot to a back door, take it. Otherwise run through the dining room into the lobby and hightail it out the front door."

"Hightailing is not so easy these days."

Deke grabbed her arm. "Listen to me, Min. Your life and the life of—" He couldn't say the words. "Whatever happens, you *have* to save yourself. Got it?"

She bit her lip and looked up at him. "Deke, I—"

"Got—it?" he bit out.

"G-got it."

"When you get to my car, you'll find a spare key and a cell phone under the driver's seat."

"Who's supposed to be there to help—?"

"Drive like hell due east. Call Irina. Her number is first on the call list."

Mindy stared at him, wide-eyed. On her face was a mixture of trust, fear, doubt and a shadow that didn't come from the dim light in the room. It came from inside her. Slowly, she nodded.

He turned toward the stairs and stopped.

He was leaving Mindy undefended. Mindy and his unborn child. A strange mixture of pride and abject terror weakened his knees.

He'd saved a lot of innocent lives, and while he understood that underestimating his enemy could be fatal, he'd never once doubted his own ability.

Okay—once. Right now, he felt like a rookie who'd been handed two equally deadly choices.

For the first time in his life, he hesitated over which course to take. For the *second* time ever, the awful consequences of failure slammed him in the face.

There was a reason Deke Cunningham never thought about losing. Because to consider the results was unbearable.

If he went out there armed with a four-inch switchblade, he had a very good chance of succeeding—against one or two, maybe even three opponents. But if he failed—

If he failed, he left Mindy and his child vulnerable. That was unthinkable.

He turned around. "Here's what I'm going to do," he said, stepping over to her and bending down until his lips were next to her ear. "Keep the knife."

She looked shocked. "But—"

"Shh."

"But, Deke," she whispered. "That's your— No. I mean, no, you can't go out there with nothing."

He held out his hands in front of her face. "I've got these. Now, where do you want me to put the knife? In the pocket of your coat?"

She shook her head. "Everything I put in those slanted pockets falls out. Put it in my bra."

"Your—?"

"Shh." She smiled wryly. "It's not like you don't know where it is. Do you want me to do it? And then you can retie the ropes around my hands?"

He shook his head, rubbing his face against her silky, tangerine-scented skin. "I'll do it." He opened her coat and unbuttoned the three buttons at the neckline of her sweater, then he pulled the knife out of his pocket.

"Okay," he whispered, feeling like a kid about to cop his first feel. He felt that awkward, that shy, that excited.

Quickly he slid his hand down through the neckline of her sweater. When his fingers slid over the rising mounds of her breasts, he almost gasped. They were so full and round and firm.

Her body was preparing for her child. Awed and speechless, and working as fast as he could, he slid the knife between her breast and the cup of the bra.

"Does that feel okay?"

Her head inclined slightly. "It's good," she murmured, sounding a little breathless.

He extracted his hand and rebuttoned her sweater. Then he pulled the lapels of her coat together. When he lifted his gaze, she was looking up at him.

He wanted to kiss her so badly he ached. Not a lover's kiss. Just a gesture of caring, a promise that he'd do anything to protect her and the child that she sheltered inside her.

But he'd made her so many promises, and he'd broken them all.

So instead, he made a vow to himself. A simple vow.

Yet one more difficult to keep than any promise he'd made to her, kept or not.

He vowed that when she was safe, he'd get out of her life and stay out. He grinned as pain stabbed his heart. Leaving her meant leaving his child. Still, she and the baby would be better off if he was out of their lives. And she knew it.

She deserved a chance to make a new life with her baby. The kind of life she'd always wanted but never had with him.

A normal, safe life.

"Ready, Min?" he whispered.

She lifted her chin and her eyes drifted shut. After a second, she opened them again. "I'm ready."

After one more tug on the lapels of her coat, he left her there and climbed the stairs. At the top, he turned around to check on her. He couldn't see her. Everything below him was a lake of darkness.

That was good.

He nodded in her direction, knowing she could see him, then reached out toward the doorknob. His hand stilled just millimeters from the knob as qualms assailed him.

"Here we go, Min," he whispered. "Be ready for anything." He turned the doorknob carefully, repeating the warning to himself. Then he pushed open the door.

The room in front of him was nearly as shrouded in darkness as the basement below. He took a careful step forward as his eyes sought the source of the faint light he'd seen under the threshold. It seemed to be coming from behind the open door. Probably daylight from the dining room and lobby.

Without moving, he listened. *Nothing.* Still the uneasy feeling that had prickled his nape—the feeling that someone was watching—wouldn't leave him.

He took a step forward so he could pull the door shut behind him. A blinding bright light flared in front of his face.

He squeezed his eyes shut and whirled toward the light, swinging his clasped fists like a sledgehammer, hoping to take down whoever was holding it.

Fireworks exploded inside his head, snapping it backward. He grabbed at the doorknob, but his hand barely brushed it.

He managed to get his feet under him, even though the blow still rang in his head and his eyes were still blinded. He swung his fists, seeking a target, but just as he connected sidelong with what felt like an arm, something heavy and forceful hit him in the middle of his chest.

He fell backward through the open door. He managed to grab the stair rail, but it didn't hold. Nails screeched as the wood gave way. He heard a scream. *Mindy?*

His butt bumped down a couple of stairs before he managed to stop himself.

He still couldn't see, but over the years he'd honed all his senses. Now they came to his aid as he reacted instinctively, like an animal.

He heard a heavy step on the hollow stairs, felt the swish of air that indicated movement close to him.

He scrabbled to get his feet under him and prepared to launch himself at his attacker. Before he could do more than tense his thighs to spring, a dark figure loomed in his blurry vision and swung something shiny at his head.

MINDY KNEW SCALP wounds bled a lot. That was Nursing 101, but she'd been an administrator for so long she'd forgotten a lot of the everyday side of nursing, like how bad a little bit of blood could appear.

The cut on Deke's forehead wasn't little. An inch-long diagonal slice was laid open above his right eyebrow, and he looked like he'd lost a fistfight with a heavyweight.

The guy standing over him wouldn't have made middleweight soaking wet. He was medium height and skinny, and dressed as if he'd stepped out of a B Western, down to the curled-brim black hat and the red bandanna tied over his nose and mouth. He still clutched the big six-gun he'd used to coldcock Deke.

As she watched, he cautiously nudged Deke's ribs with a silver-toed cowboy boot.

Deke stirred and groaned.

The man jerked his foot away.

Mindy held her breath, trying her best to stay still. She'd almost given herself away by jumping up when Deke tumbled down the stairs. She *had* screamed at him.

He'd rounded on her and warned her in a gruff, fake Texas drawl that if she didn't shut up he'd stuff a rag in her mouth and blindfold her. She'd nodded meekly and stayed as still as her worry and agitation would let her.

"Get up, Cunningham," the gunman growled. He stood over Deke, watching him warily, one hand pointing his gun and the other resting on what looked like a stubby billy club. "You think you're pretty smart, don't you? Getting yourself untied. How come you didn't untie your girlfriend? Oh, wait. She's your wife, ain't she? Or is that your ex-wife?"

Deke pushed himself up to his hands and knees and shook his head, slinging droplets of blood in a semicircle around him.

"Min?" he rasped.

At that instant the cowboy reared back and kicked him in the gut. He dropped with a pained grunt.

Despite her resolve, Mindy gasped aloud.

Deke's grunt stretched out into a growl. He bowed his back and dropped his head.

She watched in stunned awe as he got his feet under him and sprang up like a big cat. He hurled himself at the gunman.

The gunman barely sidestepped in time to avoid being bowled over. Deke checked his lunge, twisting and falling on his shoulder.

The man turned toward Mindy, pressing the barrel of the gun into her temple. "Don't make another move," he yelled. "I'll kill her. She's disposable now that I've got you."

"Stop!" Deke shouted, as he rolled and shot to his feet. His hands spread in a gesture of surrender. "What do you want? Just tell me what you want."

Don't, Mindy wanted to cry. *Don't give in to his scare tactics.* But even if she could have spoken, she was too terrified to put up a brave front. She was terrified—for herself, yes, but more for the baby.

She closed her fist around the piece of rope in her hand, wishing she could figure out a way to surprise the gunman.

Something of what she was thinking must have shown in her face, because Deke shook his head, a subtle movement worthy of a major league pitcher refusing his catcher's signal.

Meanwhile, the gunman thumbed his ridiculous hat up onto his forehead. His little beady eyes crinkled. The red bandanna tied around his nose and mouth stretched, suggesting a grin.

"Whadda I want?" he growled in his silly Texas accent. "I want answers—"

"Fine," Deke broke in, spreading his hands wider. "Let Mindy go, and I'll give you all the answers you could possibly want. Fire away."

The man shook his head slowly from side to side. "Not yet. If I ask you now, you'll just lie to me. I figure it'll take a couple days to wear you down," he drawled. "By then you'll have tried everything you can think of to escape or get the drop on me, and you'll fail every time. You'll be hungry and thirsty and tired. Even better, your gal there'll be pretty darn sick from hunger and exhaustion, seeing as how she's *that* close to whelpin' that pup. It yours?"

"That's none of your damn business. Who the hell are you anyhow?"

"So it ain't yours." He chuckled nasally. "She been sleeping around on you, ain't she?"

Deke went still. Mindy knew he was about two seconds from a firestorm.

"Deke—" she said quietly.

He shushed her with a wave of his hand and lowered his head. His dark eyes glowed dangerously. "Who are you?" he growled.

Mindy watched his fingers curl—not into fists. They curved like claws, ready to sink into the soft flesh of the man's neck. His knees bent slightly, like a cat about to spring.

The gunman took a half step closer to Mindy's side

and pressed the gun barrel into her flesh. "I'm asking the questions here, Cunningham. You'll find out who I am soon enough. Meanwhile, you can call me Frank James." He chuckled. "Now it's time for you to get a taste of what's to come."

"You come near me again, you'll regret it for a long time."

The bandanna stretched again, and the black eyes crinkled. "Don't worry, Cunningham. I'm not planning to come near you. Not right now."

He cocked his weapon slowly, drawing out the *snick-snick* of metal against metal. Mindy felt the end of the barrel scrape against her skin.

Deke's head jerked slightly and his face drained of color. "Wait!" he snapped.

She closed her eyes involuntarily, and her shoulders tensed.

"Wanna play a game? How about Russian roulette? How about you, Mrs. Ex-Cunningham?"

"Put the gun down," Deke warned. He stepped forward, his hands still out, and still curved like claws.

Mindy pulled the end of the rope Deke had left in her hand. Just as he'd promised her, the ropes immediately loosened and dropped silently to the floor. She had no idea what having her hands loose would do for her chances. But if an opportunity presented itself, she planned to be ready.

"Don't move!" Frank James shouted. Coward that he was, he moved behind Mindy, and put one hand against the side of her head while he pressed the barrel into her temple with the other.

Deke hadn't taken his eyes off James since the instant he'd cocked his gun. His expression was a mask of fear and nausea. He believed Frank James would shoot her.

The realization of how afraid Deke was sent panic fluttering into her throat.

Right now they were in a standoff. Deke couldn't rush James without fear that he'd pull the trigger. James couldn't easily lower his gun without the fear that Deke might jump him. And she couldn't do anything.

Or could she?

Her hands were free, and James didn't know that. Considering his position, if she interlaced her fingers to form a double fist, she might be able to slam him in the groin and get away.

Okay, maybe not get away—not constrained by her bulk as she was. But at least she could give Deke a chance to jump him while he was doubled over with pain. Maybe Deke could even grab his gun.

Of course she could also get herself shot in the head. But at least she'd be shot trying to do something. Frank James didn't sound like the most stable kidnapper on the planet. He could accidentally pull the trigger at any second.

Here goes. She looked up at Deke and slowly winked at him. His brows drew down slightly. He gave her another of his World Series-caliber head shakes.

But she couldn't obey him. She had to try something. With excruciating slowness she pushed her fingers together, moving her shoulders as little as possible.

She moaned loud enough for James to hear her as she drew up carefully, until every muscle and tendon in her arms and shoulders were tense and poised, preparing for one ultimate purpose—driving her fists into Frank James's groin.

"Shut up," he snapped.

"But I'm hurting." She made her voice small and hesitant. "I need to move my legs. Please?"

James made a growling sound in his throat, but he eased off the pressure of the barrel at her temple.

Mindy shifted position, using the movement to brace her feet on the floor. Then she took a long, slow breath, and sighed, as if in relief.

Deke's body tensed expectantly. At that instant, she rammed her fists backward, putting all her weight and all her determination behind the blow.

She connected.

James squealed and dropped his gun.

Deke dove forward.

Mindy froze, staying as still as possible. She felt Deke's hands sliding under her arms. He lifted her up off the crate and out of the way.

But by the time he'd turned back to James, the man had retrieved the short baton from his belt. He flicked his wrist and it telescoped.

Deke stopped in midlunge and backpedaled. He held up his hands, palms out, and glanced back her way.

James flicked his thumb and a faint crackling hum filled the air.

Mindy stiffened. What *was* that thing?

Then he lunged, as if with a fencing sword, right for Deke's solar plexus. Deke tried to pull back, but she was too close behind him, so he took the full brunt of the attack. His spine arched sharply and he growled between clenched teeth. Then he flopped to the ground like a discarded rag doll.

CHAPTER FOUR

"DEKE!" MINDY SCREAMED, as he collapsed to the dirt floor of the basement. "What did you do to him?"

"Shut up, honey, or I'll give you a dose of the same."

She cradled her belly and glared at Frank James, or whatever the heck his name was. She was so damn helpless.

I love you, Sprout, but you're crippling me.

Deke heard Mindy's scream, but he couldn't make sense of what she'd said. He had to get to her

Cold dirt scraped against his cheek.

What the hell was the ground doing there?

He tried to lift a hand, but his hand wasn't paying attention to his brain. Nor were his feet. Even his eyelids seemed stuck open.

He saw a movement in front of his eyes. Something glittery—silver? James's damn cowboy boots. Fake and all show, just like the lowlife who was wearing them.

Kick me again, bastard, and I'll make you regret it. At least that was what he wanted to say, but his mouth wasn't cooperating, either.

From somewhere he smelled the aroma of tangerines, mingled with dirt, mildew and the faint odor of burnt hair.

Then, more static filled his ears, his muscles spasmed in unbelievable pain and lightning struck his head.

* * *

WHEN HE GOT back to his room it was almost midnight. The strategy meeting Irina had called had lasted a lot longer than planned, mostly because they couldn't agree on a course of action.

He'd tried to sound helpful but neutral. Trouble was, everybody else was doing the same thing. Ultimately the only decision that was agreed upon was that Irina would not leave Castle Ranch until the threat from Novus Ordo was over.

He could see in the other guys' eyes that they were as skeptical as he was that she'd be able to stay put that long.

He bolted his door and put the chain on, made sure the blinds were closed, then went into the bathroom and dug in his shaving kit for the miniature cell phone.

Sure enough—a missed call. Reluctantly, he pressed the callback button, wishing he had good news to report.

THE INSIDE OF Deke's eyelids screamed with pain.

It was that damn sand. It got into everything. Slowly, he opened his eyes to a narrow slit. The tent was dark, so he had a few hours before Novus's man came to torture him again.

He came every day. Every damn day. With that laugh. That gun.

That sound.

An icy shudder of helpless terror crawled up his spine as he relived those awful few seconds. They never varied.

First, the pressure of cold steel against his temple. Then the split second of screaming panic and soul-wrenching sorrow before the hammer clicked against the empty chamber.

The sound triggered a cold sweat of relief, and the casually curious question of whether he would hear that same clicking sound if the hammer impacted a live round.

Finally came the regret that he'd lived through one more day. Because that meant tomorrow he'd have to face the same fate again. The inside of his mouth turned to sand-blown desert.

Taking a deep breath and cringing against the anticipated agony of his dislocated shoulders, he moved. Pain shrieked through him, but not the pain he'd expected.

What the hell? He hurt everywhere—not just his shoulders. His hands weren't even bound behind his back.

Something had changed. But why? He'd been in this hell called Mahjidastan so long he'd lost count of the days. The predictability, the inevitability, had become as torturous as the pain and fear.

He carefully lifted his head, which hurt like a son-of-a-bitch. Taking a cautious breath, he coughed.

Dirt, mildew, old wood—completely different from the stink of urine and camel dung he'd expected. This wasn't Mahjidastan, the tiny disputed province in the region where Afghanistan, Pakistan and China joined.

He opened his eyes. Not easy. They were matted with dried blood and caked with dust. Blinking and wincing as he stretched his sore neck tendons, he lifted his head again, even more cautiously this time, and looked around.

Slowly, his brain gathered up his scattered, disorganized memories.

He was in a ghost town, in the basement of an abandoned hotel. He'd come here to rescue Mindy. *Mindy and their unborn baby.*

He stiffened at that thought, causing his muscles to seize in bone-cracking pain, bending him double. With a superhuman effort, he unclenched his fists. Holding his breath, he stretched his legs. As long as he moved with unbearable slowness, the spasms stayed away—for the most part.

Frank James had slugged him, kicked him and then Tasered him.

"Mindy!" he croaked. The last thing he'd seen was James holding that damn gun at her head. The sight had come closer to breaking him than anything he'd ever faced in his life. Because he knew the dread, the fear—the sound of that hollow click. He would give his life if it meant that Mindy never had to experience that.

Immediately, that image was replaced by another one. The image of shock and agony on James's face when Mindy hit him in the groin.

Deke chuckled, which knotted his neck muscles and sent a painful spasm through them. That was his Mindy. She'd acted with the ingenuity and determination that had made him love her from the moment he'd first laid eyes on her when they were ten years old.

Then reality sheared his breath. Where was she? Had that weaselly coward Tasered her? Had he hurt their baby?

He'd kill him with his bare hands if he had.

By moving slowly and stopping when a twinge foreshadowed a muscle spasm, he got his feet under him. Damn, but everything hurt.

He'd been Tasered before, in training. But that was

nothing compared to this. He spread his fingers carefully. The amount of voltage Frank James had used could do serious damage. Hell, it could kill. The spasms caused by the electric shock could stop the heart.

He had to find Mindy, make sure she was all right.

He leaned against the wall as his knees threatened to buckle and his head spun dizzily. Bile burned in his throat, and nausea sent acrid saliva flowing into his mouth.

He forced himself to think rationally. Chronologically. First things first. How long had he been unconscious?

He looked at the shadows on the floor. Light was coming in from somewhere above and behind him. He turned his head, squinting through his aching eyes.

That window. He recognized it. He was still in the hotel's basement. The way the light streamed in, and its bright yellow color, told him it was daylight —morning. At least he could see better than he'd been able to last night.

There were the crates they'd been sitting on, and in a tangle on the dirt floor were the ropes that had bound them.

"Mindy!" he croaked, then stopped and listened.

Nothing. A knot of fear tightened in his gut. "Mindy, sugar? You've got to answer me. Where are you?"

If that ridiculous cowboy had hurt her—

Frank James had to be working for Novus Ordo. It was the only thing that made sense, given everything that had led up to this point.

"Damn you, Novus!" he growled. "This is your doing. I know it."

He knew Novus and Novus knew him. It was Novus

who'd had his helicopter shot down during a covert rescue mission over northern Mahjidastan. Who'd had him tortured, made him reveal how he had found his camp, and how he knew Novus was holding Travis Ronson, the only son of Wyoming senator Frederick Ronson. The senator had been a great friend of Rook's dad, and Travis, who was a journalist with the Associated Press, had disappeared while embedded with American troops in Afghanistan.

Rook had come after Deke in the middle of a windstorm. That's when he'd gotten a look at Novus's bare face without the famous surgical mask he always wore.

Novus knew him—knew that no matter what he did to him, Deke would never break. He also knew the lengths Rook and Deke would go to in order to rescue each other.

So all this, the cleverly tied ropes, the near escape, were Novus's revenge on Deke for escaping and his proof that he was stronger and smarter than Deke.

He was toying with him, like a cat with a mouse. Waiting for him to break.

It didn't make sense to Deke that a man with a goal of destroying the United States would spend time toying with a man just for revenge. Didn't he have better things to do? Like achieve world domination?

Now, he'd taken Mindy away again and left Deke to find her. It was a deadly game of hide-and-seek—with life or death hanging in the balance.

He knew Novus Ordo was a smart guy. He hadn't gotten to be the most feared terrorist on the planet by being sloppy. He'd worked fast and smart to get this complex plan in place in the week since Irina had stopped the search for Rook.

He'd lured Deke here by using Mindy as bait. It was exactly what Deke should have expected. He'd said as much to Irina two days ago.

"You surprised Novus when you suddenly called Matt back from Mahjidastan. He knew he had no chance of getting to you through all your security, so he targeted Matt first, figuring the reason you stopped was because Matt had found him. But Matt outsmarted his man."

Irina had nodded as Deke went on. "So Novus goes after the next obvious target. Me." He'd ground his fist into his other palm in frustration.

"He knows if anybody has information about whether Rook is still alive, I do. So he approaches it the easiest and most logical way, just like he did with Matt. He goes for the most bang for his buck. With Matt, it was his best friend's baby. With me, it's Mindy."

"Your Achilles' heel," Irina said matter-of-factly.

The three words echoed in his brain. She'd hit the nail square on the head. Mindy was his weakness.

His only weakness.

He'd promised Mindy he'd save her. And he would. He may have broken promises before, but he couldn't break this one. If he did, Mindy would die.

He licked dry lips as his gaze roamed around the basement, studying the layout. He hadn't gotten a chance to search the whole thing last night. There might be other alcoves or secret doors.

Before he'd headed out alone for Cleancutt, he'd spent as much time as he dared studying maps and satellite photos of the area.

His heart had sunk when he realized the call had come from an abandoned coal-mining town. A big one.

It was one of the few that had actually grown rather than died around 1950 when underground coal mining had given way to strip-mining.

So it made sense that some of the newer buildings, like the hotel, had been built over old mining tunnels. It was highly likely that this basement connected to at least one of them.

Pushing away from the wall, he took a step, relieved that his muscles were no longer spasming, although they still trembled. So he concentrated on putting one foot in front of the other, taking it easy until he could be sure his knees wouldn't collapse.

He started his search of the basement under the window. It was the best-lit area and therefore the easiest to search.

He examined every wall, every nook and cranny, holding to his grid pattern. Finally he ended up on the far west side, where he'd looked for a door the night before.

In the dim daylight, he saw that the timbers lining the wall of the alcove looked different from the wood on the other walls. In fact, they looked like a door, except there was no handle.

He rapped on the wood with his knuckles. Yep. Solid as a rock. Cursing to himself, he moved his hand a few inches and rapped again.

His instincts had always been excellent, and combining that with the maps he'd studied and the local history of the area, he figured this was the most likely place for a door into the mine.

The mine he wasn't even sure was there.

Just as he moved his fist another few inches, preparing to rap again, he heard something. He froze, his knuckles millimeters from the rough wood. Closing his eyes, he listened.

There it was again. A faint rapping—muffled, barely audible.

He rapped again. And again heard the muffled answering rap.

"Mindy?" he called softly.

Nothing.

He drew a breath to yell, then paused. What if Frank James heard him? Yeah? So what? He'd bet money this was part of Novus's cat-and-mouse game, anyhow.

As he prepared to knock, the muffled rapping began again.

"I'm here, Min. Where are you?"

Was he projecting or, worse, hallucinating? He had to believe he'd really heard her. If she was on the other side of the wall, then there was a way through it. And he'd find it.

He rapped on every square inch of the alcove wall, starting at the top. The sound remained flat and solid.

He stopped again and listened.

There it was again. The answering rap. It didn't sound like she was knocking on the same wall he was.

"Mindy! Can you hear me? Is there a door?" He kept on, testing every inch of the wall. When he got down to knee level, he sat on his heels, wincing as his knees trembled and his leg muscles protested.

He knocked again. And got a different sound. A hollow sound.

Yes! His pulse pounded, sending pain arcing behind his eyes. *Damn Taser.*

"Mindy?" he called.

He heard something! A faint low murmur. It was her. He knew it.

Immediately, doubt sliced through him. What if it wasn't Mindy? What if it was another trap designed to wear him down?

Then he'd crawl right into it. He wasn't about to ignore even the smallest chance that Mindy was on the other side of the wall, counting on him to save her.

He examined the boards with his eyes and fingers. If he had to, he'd break it down with his bare hands to get to her.

He couldn't see anything unusual, but he sure as hell felt something. A slight difference in temperature—a slight movement of the air. Digging the lighter out of his pocket, he thumbed it.

Sure enough, the flame wavered. There was air behind the rough planks.

After a few frustrating seconds of digging at the corners of the boards, he thought of his knife. He reached toward his boot and then remembered. He didn't have it.

It was inside Mindy's bra. A thrill slid through him as he thought about how warm it would be from the heat of her body. He shook his head.

"Get out of my head," he muttered under his breath, and focused on digging out all that wood putty with his fingernails.

A long time later, with his fingertips scraped and sore, he called out to Mindy again.

"Mindy, if you can hear me, move back. I'm going to kick these boards in." He banged on the wall with his fist. "Right here. Okay?"

A faint tap answered him.

He sat back and drew his knees up to his chest.

"Okay," he hollered. "On three. One—two—"

He braced himself with his hands behind him. "Three!" He slammed the heels of his boots into the planks as hard as he could. The thud echoed through the basement.

Propelling himself forward, he examined the damage. *Not much.* "Min, stay back."

He rocked backward and stomped the wood again, and again. The fourth time it gave, with nails screeching as they separated from wood. Although his legs quivered with fatigue and reaction to the Taser, he kicked at the splintered wood until he'd opened a hole big enough to crawl through.

For a few seconds he sat quietly, listening. Had the deafening noise alerted Frank James? He waited, but nobody came.

If the fake cowboy wasn't sitting back watching his efforts through a hidden camera, Deke was certain he was listening and waiting, and probably laughing at Deke's efforts.

Lying down on the dirt floor, he peered through the opening, which was barely wide enough for his shoulders. "Mindy?" he whispered.

No answer.

He eased a bit farther in, holding his breath.

It could still be a trap.

A movement at the corner of his vision drew his eye. He tensed.

"Deke—?"

He clamped his jaw against the flood of relief that closed his throat and stung his eyelids.

She was there. And her voice sounded strong. But it was still undercut by that same terrified, desperate tone he'd noticed on the telephone. At the time he'd known something was horribly wrong, but he hadn't known what. Now he did.

She was afraid for her baby.

"Everything okay in there?"

"Yes," she answered.

"You alone?"

"Yes."

She sounded terrified. He hoped she was telling the truth. Once, he'd been able to tell by the timbre of her voice. Could he still?

What would he do if Frank James had her?

Nothing different. He was making himself vulnerable to attack by crawling through the small trapdoor, but he didn't have a choice. If he were alone, he'd reconnoiter, figure out the best place to defend his back and ambush his enemy.

But he wasn't alone. He had to get to Mindy.

"Stay back. I'm coming through." He ducked his head and slithered through the hole, then stood. It was damn dark in here. Darker than the basement with its tiny window. He wished he had something more than a disposable lighter.

Deke could barely make out her silhouette. "Min, honey? Are you okay? Are you alone? Did he hurt—"

Suddenly a firm, round tummy collided with him, and slender but strong arms wrapped around his waist. "Deke, I was so scared. I was afraid he'd killed you."

Deke's throat seized. He swallowed hard against the lump that suddenly grew there. Carefully, feeling as if he might break her if he squeezed too hard, he wrapped his arms around her shoulders.

She laid her head in the hollow between his neck

and shoulder—her favorite place to sleep, she'd always told him.

"Nah," he croaked, then had to stop and clear his throat. "You know me. Nothing can break me. I'm fine. What about you? He didn't Taser you, did he?"

Mindy clung to Deke for dear life. If she could crawl inside him she would. Body to body, especially through clothes, wasn't enough. No matter how many times she'd feared for Deke's safety, even his sanity, she'd always known he would never hurt her. She'd always felt safe with him.

Almost always.

She hugged him tighter. His strong arms tightened around her—a little. He was holding back. Partly because he was still stunned and angry about her pregnancy, she was sure.

But that wasn't the whole reason. In all the time she'd known him, he'd never opened up to her—not completely.

She knew him so well—probably better than anybody alive. So she knew there was a deep core to Deke Cunningham that she'd never been able to penetrate.

She would bet a lot of money that nobody ever had. Or would. It broke her heart. It was the one thing she'd wanted from him that he'd never been able to give her—his complete trust. It was one of the reasons she'd finally given up and gotten a divorce.

"Min?"

She shook her head against the soft cotton of his shirt. "He didn't hurt me."

"How'd you get here? Can you find your way back?"

"I'm not sure. He blindfolded me again and we walked—it felt like hours. When he left me here it was so dark. I don't know how long I've stood here. I was afraid to sit down." She shuddered.

"That's right. You're pretty paranoid about creepy-crawlies, aren't you?" She felt his chest rumble with soft laughter.

"Don't laugh at me. And no. Not this time. I was so tired I'd have gladly sat in a nest of cockroaches. But I was afraid I wouldn't be able to get back up."

"Sorry." The amusement was gone. "Tell me every-thing you remember. Did you have to crawl through anything? Bend over to get through a door?"

"No. We went upstairs and then down again—twice. I think he was trying to confuse me. But once we went outside, I think into a different building. Then down a different set of stairs. Did you come from where we were tied up?"

"Yep. The old hotel. How'd you keep up with which building you were in?"

"Mostly by smell. The building we were in smells like mildew. The other one—wherever it was—had more of a smoky odor to it."

"Good! We might be able to find our way out by following our noses." Deke bent his head and kissed her forehead.

His lips moving against her skin took her back to those innocent high school days, when they'd been good together. Before they were old enough to understand that love alone couldn't always conquer fear or fill the hollow places left inside by an uncaring parent.

"You've got dried blood all over your face." She brushed at his temple and cheek, then ran the pad of her thumb gently across his closed eyelid. "And that cut needs to be washed and bandaged." She touched the skin around the cut and he winced. "Plus, you're going to have a bruise on your forehead."

"Yeah? Well, it'll match the rest of them."

Tears stung her eyes and she squeezed the lids shut.

"You getting hurt is not funny to me." She pushed away from him.

He let go immediately.

When he did, she swayed. She knew what was wrong. She was tired. She was hungry. The *baby* was hungry. He got so restless when she didn't eat. "I need food."

"So what's new?"

"I mean for the baby."

He stiffened. "Oh. Yeah." He straightened and looked around. "Got any idea which way you came in?"

"I think we came from somewhere back there." She gestured toward a heavy wooden door on the north wall. "But I could be totally turned around."

"Okay." He wrapped his fingers around her upper arms and set her gently away from him. "Do you still have my knife? He didn't search you, did he?"

"No." She unbuttoned her sweater, retrieved the knife from her bra and handed it to him.

He closed his fist around it, soaking up her warmth. "You stay right there. I want to explore a little."

"Don't leave me," she breathed. She clutched at his white shirt. "If I lose you in the dark, I'll go crazy."

"You'll be fine. I'm not going far."

"Deke, what if he's waiting for you again?"

"I'll be ready for him. You stay right there."

Holding his knife in his right hand, he fished out the cigarette lighter with his left and struck it, then took a second to get his bearings. The trapdoor he'd come through was on the west wall of the basement. So he turned south, following the dirt wall until it curved around to the west. From the hollow sound of his footsteps and the whisper of air in his ears, he figured he was in a tunnel.

He walked a few feet farther, but nothing changed. The tunnel looked totally abandoned beyond the tiny circle of light cast by his lighter.

After extinguishing the lighter and pocketing it, he blindly examined the walls, but all he felt were thick, rough boards, like railroad ties, and dirt walls. In a few places his fingers brushed across some sort of mesh screening, probably designed to hold the dirt in place.

He felt along the ground with his feet, from wall to wall, but found nothing. No rails for the coal cars. This tunnel had probably never been finished. It was a dead end.

He retrieved the lighter and struck it again as he turned to retrace his steps. He'd felt steel rails under his boots in the alcove where Mindy was waiting. The rails led into the tunnel on the north side of the alcove. That was their only hope of getting out.

Just as he rounded the curve, back to the area where he'd left Mindy, light flared, revealing two dark silhouettes. Deke smelled the phosphorus smell of a match and the unmistakable odor of lantern oil. Alarm pierced his chest.

James. He had Mindy.

"Mindy?" He cautiously pressed his right arm against his side, hoping to conceal his knife. He didn't want to take a chance that James would catch a glint from the steel blade.

"Howdy, Cunningham," Frank James drawled. "Nice of you to join us. I've been waiting for you."

He hung an oil lantern on a nail above their heads with one hand, while his other aimed a Colt .45 revolver directly at Mindy's head. The red bandanna across his face stretched as he grinned.

Terror sheared Deke's breath for a second time. Previously, when he'd seen the steel barrel pressed against her temple, he'd sworn that if it killed him, James would never again get her into that life-or-death situation.

But here they were. And just like before, his consciousness was split in two. Half saw her precious head, once again threatened by the 9 mm barrel with its lethal cargo. The other half spun through a whirlwind of memories—the hot metal cylinder pressed against his own skull, the distinctive *snick-snick* of the hammer cocking, the slow grind of the barrel turning, and finally, the hollow click as it hit the empty chamber.

He knew the horror of waiting to hear those sounds. A shudder rocked his whole body.

He shook his head and stared at her. He had to stay here, in the present, on alert.

Her wide green eyes sparkled with tears as her hands cradled her tummy. "Deke, I didn't know—"

"Shut up!" James yelled.

Deke wanted to reassure her with his gaze, but he didn't think he could pull it off. So he turned his attention to James so she wouldn't see how scared he was that the man might be dumb enough to actually shoot her.

His only chance was to distract James and turn his anger toward him and away from Mindy.

"You're a coward," Deke growled. "Hiding behind a woman—a *pregnant* woman."

"You better watch yourself, pardner. You're not the one in charge here."

"In charge? Are you saying you are? Give me a break. You don't even have the guts to use your real name. You're named after an outlaw—hell! Not even a real outlaw. You're named after the *brother* of an outlaw."

Frank's eyes narrowed and his gun hand shook. "You shut up. Frank James was a great outlaw. As great as his brother."

Deke felt triumphant and apprehensive at the same time. He'd gotten to him. He'd struck a vein with the remark about the cowboy's moniker.

The guy was obviously under somebody's thumb. Most likely Novus. Frank was exactly what he looked like. A hired gun.

"Yeah, not so much. The only thing I remember about Frank James is that when people talk about Jesse they sometimes say, 'and Frank, too.' I know something else, too. I know you're ashamed of something or else you wouldn't be wearing that ridiculous bandanna over your face like a bad TV cowboy."

"You don't know anything about me." A red spot appeared in the center of James's forehead. And his gun hand shook.

That scared Deke. Nobody could trust a nervous gun hand. Still, he had no choice. Somehow, he had to catch the guy off guard. All he needed was two seconds.

"I know enough to know you couldn't pull this off alone. You're working for Novus Ordo, aren't you?"

The gun barrel shook even more at the mention of the terrorist. "Shut up! You think you know so much.

You don't know nothing." Dark spots dotted the bandanna where sweat rolled down James's pinched face.

Deke shifted to the balls of his feet and curled his fingers, ready to attack. *One second.* He only needed one second.

The cowboy was breathing hard, practically gasping, and the bandanna was fast becoming soaked. He looked like he was on the verge of panic.

Deke concentrated on keeping his own breathing even as he studied the other man. He'd bet money— hell, he was betting his life and Mindy's and her unborn baby's—that the coward had never killed anybody.

At least not face-to-face.

He could do this. He was bigger, stronger and faster. He *could* stop James before he got off a shot.

He had to.

As if he sensed Deke's resolve, James looked him dead in the eye. His beady pupils gleamed with malice as he cocked the hammer. He turned his head toward Mindy, still holding Deke's gaze.

Then his finger squeezed the trigger.

CHAPTER FIVE

HORROR CLOSED DEKE'S throat as he watched James's finger tighten on the trigger.

The sound of metal sliding against metal made him cringe. The chamber slowly turned.

Knowing he could never beat the bullet, and propelled by terror, Deke slung his knife underhanded at the cowboy's arm, then lunged at him with full-body force.

All hell broke loose.

Mindy screamed.

James squealed as Deke slammed into his skinny torso, pushing him against the timbers that lined the mine shaft. Gravel and dirt rained on their heads and peppered the dusty floor.

Deke shouldered James in the solar plexus as hard as he could. They crashed against the wall, and James's breath whooshed out. Deke closed his left hand around James's right wrist and beat it against the timbers, again and again.

Finally, the gun thudded to the dirt floor.

"Grab the gun, Min, or kick it away." He drove his forearm into James's face, trying to crush his nose and slam it up into his brain. James grunted and tried to shove Deke off him, but Deke wasn't about to let go.

He fisted his hands in James's shirt and dragged him forward, then body-slammed him against the wall again.

"Mindy!" he yelled.

She didn't answer.

Terrified that she was hurt, he threw the cowboy down to the ground, slamming his face into one of the steel rails, and whirled.

"Mindy!"

The oil lantern's flickering light sent shadows chasing around the tunnel. But none of them looked like her. Deke blinked as he scanned the small space.

"Deke—"

A wave of relief washed over him, so sharp, so spine-tingling, that it almost drove him to his knees. He turned toward her voice and saw a shadow move.

"Min," he breathed. She was on the ground. "Are you hurt?" He reached for her.

"I don't think so." She wrapped her arms around his neck as he lifted her.

"Stay back," he whispered, and set her gently against the far wall.

Her eyes slid past him and widened in the flickering lantern light. "Look out!"

When he whirled, Frank James was diving for the gun.

Deke dove, too, landing on top of the smaller man. He shoved him out of the way and reached out to grab the gun.

When he did, a searing pain slashed up his arm. Shocked, he fell backward.

Behind him, Mindy cried out.

He rolled and dove for the gun again, but it wasn't there. James had it.

Deke was on the ground and James was standing, so he wrapped his arms around the silver-toed boots and jerked, hoping to knock James off his feet. Deke got his right foot under him for momentum and stability, but when he threw himself forward to unbalance James, his foot slipped.

He tried again and managed to head-butt James in the stomach. The man's breath whooshed out as he tumbled backward.

A thrill of triumph filled Deke's chest. He spotted the gleam of the knife blade at James's feet. He lunged for it.

At the very instant his fingers closed around its hilt, the heavy wooden door behind James opened and a big shadow loomed in the doorway.

Deke tried to check his momentum, but his feet slipped again. As if in slow motion, he saw the blue-white arc of the Taser coming at him.

MINDY WATCHED IN horror as a large, dark man appeared from nowhere. The light was behind him, so he was barely more than a silhouette, but she saw the blue light and heard the static.

The Taser.

Helpless to do anything, she merely stared as Deke's spine arched and the fine muscles hidden under his smooth, golden skin trembled. Then he dropped where he stood, his legs collapsing as if they'd turned into rags.

Then the big man kicked him out of the way. "Where's the woman?"

Deke had set her against the far wall, in the shadows. But she knew they'd spot her any second. There was no way she could defend herself, so instinctively, she closed her eyes and pretended to be unconscious.

"I don't know," James gasped, struggling to breathe. He coughed. "Forget her."

"Here she is."

Mindy's muscles tensed, and it was all she could do to keep from cringing.

"Leave her!" James yelled breathlessly.

She heard the bigger man's footsteps, felt him standing over her. She didn't know why she thought it was so important to keep up the pretense that she'd passed out, but she did.

"She's out cold. I can grab her."

"No! What did I just say?"

"But they could get away."

James's breathing was almost back to normal. "Get over here," he ordered.

Mindy heard the man's heavy footsteps recede.

"Now pay attention," James whispered.

She held her breath, listening.

"They're not going to get away. This isn't about capturing them. They're already captured. It's about—" James lowered his voice even more, too low for Mindy to understand.

She opened her eyes to narrow slits. The two men had their heads together. She could hear the hiss of James's whisper, but couldn't understand a thing.

The big man nodded. "I'll get the knife."

"Leave it. It'll make him think he's smarter than us." James coughed again and took a deep breath. "Let's get out of here."

He opened the door on the north wall, and the two men disappeared through it.

Blinded by the bright light from the open door, Mindy scooted blindly across the dirt floor toward Deke. Several times, her bottom bumped against the raised metal rails.

As her night vision came back and she made out his silhouette, she noticed the blacker-than-black pool that was spreading under him. It wasn't just a trick of the shadows.

It was blood.

Deke's blood. That's why he'd kept slipping as he'd fought James. She'd seen James jerk Deke's knife out of his side with a roar and brandish it as Deke dove for the gun.

The lantern's light had reflected off the blade as it sliced an arc through the air. Behind the blade, red droplets had scattered in a fine spray that caught the light like tiny rubies.

Then Deke had gone down.

"Deke," she whispered, touching his forehead with her fingertips. She knew it would be foolish to assume that their kidnappers were gone for good. So she kept an eye out for the least hint of light.

"Deke, wake up. Are you okay?"

He groaned and stirred.

"Deke? Answer me."

He made a low growling noise in his throat and tried to push himself to his hands and knees, but his right arm wouldn't hold his weight. He collapsed again.

She didn't know what to do. Watching him struggle helplessly sent fear burrowing into her—soul-deep fear. She'd never seen him weak or injured. The sight was like a slap to her face.

Deke Cunningham was flesh and bone, just like everyone else. Just like her. He was breakable.

She pressed her palm against his forehead. "Wake up," she pleaded. "I'm going to need your help. I don't think I can stand up by myself."

He made a noise. It could have been a groan or a brief snort of laughter. Carefully, holding his right arm against his side, he rolled up into a sitting position, got his legs under him, and pushed himself to his feet.

Mindy looked up. His face, distorted by the wavering lantern light, was a grimacing mask of pain. She had no idea what being Tasered felt like, but if it could do this to her ex-husband, it had to be bad.

But what really worried her was the knife wound in his arm.

In typical Deke fashion, he composed his face, then looked down at her and crooked his mouth into a half smile. He held out his hand.

"You can't just give me a hand up," she said wryly. "I'm way beyond that. This is not going to be pretty." She rolled over to all-fours, and slowly, using the wall for support, she carefully pushed herself to her knees.

"Can you come around and get your left hand under my arm and lift?" She was embarrassed by her helplessness in front of him, and he picked up on that.

"What's the matter, Min? I've seen you in more interesting positions than this." He moved to her right side and hooked his elbow under her arm.

"This is different."

He lifted her with a grunt. "Yeah. You weigh more."

"Not funny," she grunted, as she managed to stand with a whole lot of help from him. "I'm sorry. I know that hurt you."

"No problem," he muttered.

She stepped to one side so the lantern light shone fully on him, and gasped when she saw the amount of blood that soaked the arm of his jacket.

"Oh, no, Deke. All that blood."

"It's okay," he muttered. "What about you? Did that bastard hurt you?"

She shook her head. "You took care of me. Now I need to take care of you. Take off your jacket."

Once he'd managed to peel the jacket off, she lifted the slashed cotton fabric away from the wound and hissed through her teeth.

"It's nothing," Deke protested, pulling back.

"Oh, no, trust me. It's *something,*" she retorted. "You've got at least a six-inch gash. You need stitches."

"How do you suggest I get 'em?"

She winced at his gruff tone. He didn't like to show weakness—any kind of weakness. Not physical, and certainly not emotional. He never had. He'd learned early that weakness drew predators like a shark to blood. So he'd long ago decided that the best defense was an impenetrable shield and a strong offense.

Over the years she'd watched him learn those lessons, from his alcoholic father, from the other kids in school, from life. She'd been there for every brick he'd laid to fortify his heart.

She understood that his anger wasn't aimed at her. She just happened to be in the way. Just as she'd been many times before.

With the ease of long practice, she ignored his words and his attitude. "I can't sew up the wound, but I can wrap it."

"Min, we don't have time—"

"Just shut up and take off your shirt."

With a frustrated sigh, he complied. He kept his right arm still as he undid the buttons with his left hand. When his shirt was hanging open over his bare chest, she took his left hand. "I'll get this button," she murmured.

He let her undo the sleeve, then he shrugged the shirt off with a groan, and carefully slid it down his right arm.

"Oh, Deke. Look what he did to you." Dark bruises covered his side, where James had kicked him with those silver-toed boots. His right forearm was coated with blood, and in taking off his shirt he'd smeared the blood all over his abdomen and chest.

He shrugged, sending ripples along the muscles of his shoulders and arms.

Mindy couldn't take her eyes off him. They'd been married for nine years and lovers for two years before that. She knew every inch of his body. Every curve of muscle. Every scar.

He seemed leaner, harder, and yet at the same time less harsh. Every bit as handsome, though. And every bit as sexy.

Memories washed over her—the feel of his hot, naked body against hers. That silk-over-steel strength and the unimaginable thrill of being filled by him.

As she'd told him many times, their problem was never the sex. She was just as turned on by him as she'd always been. Maybe more.

She still wanted him. She was eight months pregnant, cold, hungry and terrified, and yet the desire was still there, humming, vibrating, singing, inside her.

Stop it. The stirrings she felt were just hormones. Hormones and habit.

Even as she lectured herself, she knew she was lying. Deke's golden-tanned skin, his sleekly defined muscles, the slope of his broad shoulders and the harshly beautiful planes of his abs, hips and flanks, were as familiar to her as her own body.

Actually, more familiar right now. Considering that for the past eight months her body had been in a constant state of change and still was.

She rubbed her tummy where his son was wiggling around. Her little Sprout was proof of that. Even on the day she'd buried her mother, the one thing that had succeeded in drawing her out of the poignant sadness was Deke, with the sweet gentleness that he revealed only to her.

Dear heavens, she loved him.

No, I don't, her rational brain responded immediately.

But arguing with herself was useless. She might not be able to live with him. But she would always love him.

"Well?" he grumbled. "Are you just going to stand there while I bleed to death?"

His voice sounded irritated, but his eyes held a spark of amusement, and his mouth a ghost of a smirk.

Her face burned with embarrassment. Damn him, he knew what she was thinking. *Great.* Something else that hadn't changed. A splinter of irritation stung away some of her desire.

"Sorry," she muttered. She yanked the shirt out of his hands and ripped it into strips.

"Min, I didn't mean—"

"I need something to wash out the wound." She spoke briskly, not giving him time to apologize. She glanced around, her gaze stopping on the lantern. "The oil."

"No. No way."

"Why not? It's hot, and it's a good disinfectant."

Deke shook his head. "It's a better fuel source. As soon as you're done playing nurse I'm putting that sucker out and taking it with us. We'll need it."

"I don't want to wrap your arm without washing it."

"Wash it later. Wrap it now. That sonofoabitch is going to come back, once he licks his wounds. I don't plan for us to be here."

"Did you hear James and the other man talking?" she asked as she quickly and efficiently wrapped his arm, doing her best to keep the edges of the wound together without tying the bandage too tight.

"Talking? When?"

"After he Tasered you."

"Seems like I heard something, but it didn't make sense. It's hard to think when electricity's frying your brain. I think I passed out for a few seconds." He rubbed his temple with his left hand. "Why?"

"They had a perfectly good chance to capture us both again. You were paralyzed by the Taser and I was on the ground, helpless. But James told the other guy not to. He said 'it's not about capturing them.' Then he said to leave you the knife. He said, 'It'll make him think he's smarter.'" She looked up. "What's going on?"

Deke shook his head. "He's playing cat and mouse with me. He wants me to believe I can get us out of here."

"*I* believe you can."

He gave her a ghost of a smile. "Thanks. But I have a feeling I'm a little outnumbered. I'm pretty sure there are more than two of them. I'd bet money that every exit is guarded."

"So—we're mice in a maze? And if we run the maze correctly our reward is death?"

"Something like that."

Those three flat words frightened her more than his anger or even his fear ever could. He was the bravest man she'd ever known. So why was he accepting the inevitable now, after all the things he'd endured?

Endured. That was it! He knew they were outnumbered and outflanked. His only choice, given the handicap of having to worry about her, was to conserve his strength and hers—to outwait and outwit the enemy.

Something he'd said earlier, when he was trying to stop James from shooting her in the head, niggled at the edge of her brain. But she'd been so scared that her brain had been incapable of processing what he said. She tried to replay his words in her head, but they flitted away, leaving her with nothing but a question.

"Who is the enemy?"

"What?"

She jumped. "What?"

"You said something."

"No, I didn't." Had she spoken aloud? She savagely ripped the ends of her makeshift bandage, berating herself for not watching what she said.

"Ouch. Where's the knife? Cutting the fabric would be easier—and less painful than tearing it."

"It fell over there." She gestured in the direction of the door.

"Hurry up. I need to get it. And by the way, yes, you did say something. You said, 'who's the enemy?'"

She tied the torn ends of the bandage to keep it in place.

"Did I? Well, it's a good question. You never did tell me what you did that made Frank James kidnap me, and why he's playing cat and mouse with you. He obviously knows who you are."

He looked at his fingers and flexed them, as if the most important thing in the world to him was making sure the bandage wasn't too tight.

"Deke, look at me. Who's behind all this?"

His head ducked a fraction lower, then he raised his gaze to hers. "I've never seen Frank James before."

Mindy studied his face. This was her childhood sweetheart, her lover, her former husband. The man she knew better than anyone in the world. The set of his jaw, the tiny wrinkles at the corners of his eyes, the flat line of his mouth, told her he was holding something back.

She almost laughed. *So what's new?*

He swiveled and headed toward the wooden door.

"Deke, what are you—?"

Then he held up the lighter and kicked around in the dirt. He was looking for his knife.

She watched him and tried to remember what he'd said back there when Frank James was holding her with a gun to her head. He'd tried to bluff James out of pulling the trigger by distracting him with insults and playing on his obvious cowardice.

He'd said something that hadn't fit with the rest of his verbal jabs. Something that sounded real—and disturbing. She could almost hear it in her brain. Almost, but not quite.

Suddenly, the memory hit her. His voice echoed in her head.

You couldn't pull this off alone. You're working for Novus Ordo.

Novus Ordo. "Oh, dear heavens," she choked out through the hand that had flown to her mouth. The realization stole her breath. The man who'd captured and tortured Deke. "It's Novus Ordo."

"What?" He looked at her suspiciously.

"Don't even try that 'I don't know what you're talking about' innocent tone with me, Deke Cunningham." She took a step backward, as if distance could protect her from the knowledge that was swirling around in her brain.

After Deke had come back from Mahjidastan, he'd been a different man. He'd never told her what had happened to him over there, but his best friend had.

Rook had told her how Novus Ordo, the infamous terrorist, had captured Deke when his helicopter went down. He'd described some of the torture Deke had endured at his hands.

Rook had begged her to stick with him, to help him heal.

And she'd tried. But Deke had refused her help—or anyone else's. Refused vehemently. Then he'd gone away and left her alone.

The empty shell of his body had still been there, but the man she'd loved all her life had disappeared—into drink, into depression, into self-loathing. The man she'd believed was unbreakable had been broken.

So in self-defense, before he sucked her into the abyss with him, she'd filed for divorce.

Then Rook had been assassinated, and the speculation had started—on a national scale. Novus Ordo, the most feared terrorist since Bin Laden, was rumored to have ordered the death of the highly decorated former Air Force colonel Robert Kenneth Castle because of a personal grievance.

Mindy had feared that Rook's death would send Deke over the edge, but through Irina she knew that he had moved to Castle Ranch and had taken over BHSAR operations, while Irina handled the business aspects and searched for proof that Rook was still alive.

It seemed that Rook's death had brought Deke back to life.

"That terrorist is behind this, isn't he?"

"Come on, Mindy."

Mindy lifted her chin pugnaciously. "No. You come on. Don't treat me like an idiot. Irina stops searching for Rook and a week later here we are, being held captive because you know something that you're not telling me. I heard what you said to Frank James. I can put the pieces together. Novus Ordo thinks you know where Rook is, doesn't he?"

Deke's eyes narrowed and the tiny wrinkles between his brows deepened. He scowled at her.

"Oh my God, you do!"

For an instant, Deke stared at her as if she were a ghost. Then his mouth and jaw relaxed. He shook his head. "No. I don't know where he is."

Mindy frowned at him. "Why are you—?" One look in his eyes and her question died on her lips. Without moving his head, he shifted his gaze above her, then to his right and his left then back to stare at her.

She understood immediately. He suspected that they were being watched or listened to. She gave him a small nod and took a deep breath.

"You really don't know?" she asked, doing her best to sound like she believed what she was saying. "But what about all those rumors that he's still alive?"

"They've stuck around because Irina wouldn't give up. But now she has. Rook Castle is dead."

"So what about Frank James? Do you think he's working for Novus?"

"He could be. I'd have thought Novus was smarter than that, but maybe not. He may have ordered Rook assassinated, but the body was never recovered. If I were Novus, and I thought my nemesis was still alive, I'd probably panic if his wife suddenly quit searching for him." He made an impatient sound. "Are you done playing nurse yet?"

She gave the bandage on his forearm a final inspection. "Fine. I'm done. But if it doesn't stop bleeding. I'll have to put spiderwebs on it."

"Hell, no, you won't." Deke stared at her. "What are you talking about—spiderwebs?"

"They can promote clotting. They work by—"

"Min." Deke held up his hand. "I don't care how they work. I won't bleed anymore."

She shot him an ironic glance. "You'll control it with your steely resolve?"

He nodded. "Damn straight I will."

Mindy chuckled. "That's my hero."

Deke winced at her words. She'd said them unintentionally, he was sure. She'd called him her hero ever since high school. Ever since the first time they'd made love, when she was seventeen.

He'd been careful and slow, determined to show her what sex was all about. Afterward, she'd lain in his arms, panting and spent, and awed by what had happened to her.

Eventually, she'd turned toward him. She'd touched his cheek and murmured, "You're my hero, and I will always love you."

He blinked and shook his head slightly, pushing the memories back—way back—to the place where he kept them locked up. That was a long time ago, when she'd loved him.

He was no hero now. *Hah.* Never had been. He'd never brought her anything but heartbreak. No wonder she hadn't wanted him to know about her baby. She'd tried to protect herself and her child from more pain.

And what had he done? He'd left her alone and vulnerable against attack. He was the one who'd gotten her into this, and now he had to get her out.

Without a scratch.

"Let's get out of here. I'm sure James already knows where we'll end up. But hell, there's nothing I can do about that." He carefully shrugged into his shearling jacket and grabbed the oil lantern off the nail.

The first thing he did was examine the slatted wooden door on the north wall. There was no knob, just a keyhole. "This is where they disappeared?"

Mindy nodded.

He pushed against it, but it didn't budge. Then he transferred the lantern to his right hand and tried to get a grip on it by inserting his fingers into the slats. "It's locked."

"What did you find in the other direction?" Mindy asked.

"Pretty much what I expected. I'm guessing this hotel was built here so they could use this tunnel junction as its basement." He pointed toward the south tunnel. "No coal car rails in that tunnel. So I'm thinking it's either closed or it's a dead end. I didn't go very far. I didn't want to leave you." He grimaced. "I left you too long as it was."

"You didn't know—"

"I should have." He gestured at the floor. Unlike the south tunnel, this branch had two sets of rails on its dirt-and-rock-covered floor. They extended down the corridor as far as he could see. "See? These rails have been used. You can see where they're worn. Obviously this tunnel has seen a lot of people come through it."

"But why would they need rails here? This looks like the end of the line—or the beginning."

"Look at that." He pointed at the planks and boards surrounding the trapdoor where he'd crawled in. "That was a door into the hotel basement. This other door may be to the mine foreman's office, or some other administrative type. They probably used a man car to travel from here down into the belly of the mine."

"Man car?"

"Traveled on the rails like the coal cars, but held passengers—the miners, of course—to carry them down to the deeper parts of the mine. But the inspectors, the bosses, the foreman, would travel down there, too."

"How do you know all this?"

Deke sent her a wry smile. "I read up on it as soon as I figured out where your phone call came from."

He bent over and picked up his knife, and then pointed to the trapdoor that led into the hotel basement.

"Can't go that way," he said, conjuring up a picture of Mindy getting on hands and knees to crawl through to the hotel's basement.

Not happening.

He pressed his bandaged arm against his side and clenched his teeth against the stinging pain as he looked at the two tunnels. His instincts had always been excellent. They'd gotten him out of dangerous situations many times.

But right now he had no idea which tunnel to take. What would Novus expect him to do? Take the south tunnel, which appeared to be abandoned and might lead to a dead end, trapping them? Or follow the coal-car rails, which careered down a steep incline to a tippling station, where they'd dump the coal into the larger railroad cars?

He cursed under his breath.

"What is it?" Mindy asked. "What's wrong?"

He pointed to one of the tunnels. "What do you think, Min? The lady? Or the tiger?"

CHAPTER SIX

"I DON'T THINK I can go any farther," Mindy said. She hated to tell Deke that. Hated to let him down. Her fingers were cramping from holding on to his belt and trying to stay directly behind him.

He'd been guiding her in the darkness, warning her of rough patches or a curve. They were walking on a steep downward incline—going deeper underground.

When he'd chosen the abandoned south tunnel over the north one that appeared to be open, she'd been surprised. But she'd kept her mouth shut, trusting him.

Twice already, he'd stumbled over broken boards and piles of dirt and rocks. Once he'd hit his head on a sagging roof beam.

She'd never been afraid of the dark until now.

This darkness was *total*. The sensation was claustrophobic, dizzying, terrifying. She couldn't see anything, not even her own hand. Even holding on to Deke's belt, she found herself drifting off to the right or left. And sometimes she felt like she was leaning—not standing up straight.

When that happened, she'd suddenly jerk upright. That earned her a bout of vertigo.

The vertigo would trigger panic, which would disturb Sprout, and that increased her nervousness. Especially when she thought about how deep underground they were.

Not even having Deke with her helped.

"Hang in there a little longer, Min." His voice sounded strained.

If Deke was worried, then it was seriously time to panic. "Deke—I can't!"

"Just a little more, Min. I think I hear something."

Her heart pounded. "What?"

He reached behind him and touched her hand. "Water running. Listen."

He stopped, and she stepped up closer to him. "I don't hear anything."

"I've got specially trained ears."

She heard the smile in his voice. And appreciated it. He was trying to keep it light. For her. Trying to help her through the blackness.

She sucked in a deep breath that hitched at the top like a sob. "You do—have nice ears."

"Nice? They're superb." He gently extricated her fingers from his belt and pulled her close, wrapping his strong arm around her waist.

"Listen," he whispered in her ear.

She started to tell him that as long as he was breathing that close to her ear, it didn't matter what was out there. She wouldn't be able to hear Niagara Falls.

As if she'd spoken aloud, he held his breath. She held hers, too.

And heard a faint ripple.

"There it is," she whispered in awe.

"Told you." His arm tightened around her waist. For the first time he seemed, if not comfortable, at least not especially uncomfortable with her rounded, unfamiliar shape.

Then, to her surprise, his head dipped and he nuzzled her hair.

"Let's go find that water," he said, straightening. "If we're real lucky, there will be another lantern there. Or some torches."

"Can you—" Mindy paused and took a breath. "I'm sorry, Deke, but can you light the lantern?"

"As soon as we get to the water, okay? I don't want to waste the oil."

Mindy felt like crying. She was so tired, so hungry, and so afraid that she'd never see light again. Her skin was clammy and cold. The air had been growing a little warmer as they went deeper, but suddenly, her neck felt cool—cooler than normal. She shivered as Deke took her hand and tucked it into his belt at the small of his back.

"Deke? I think I feel something."

Deke froze in midstride. "Something with the baby? Are you okay?"

"No. I mean, yes. I'm fine. It's not the baby. It's like air. I feel air on my neck."

He stayed still. Yet she knew from the change in the tension of his back muscles and from her familiarity with his body that he had his hand up and was testing the air.

"Come on," he said, and moved forward.

As they got closer to the running water and the sound increased, Mindy started thinking she saw something. Which was impossible, since there was no light anywhere.

She blinked, making sure her eyes were open.

Sure enough, there was something not quite hellhole-black in front of her. All at once she got her balance back, and the vertigo went anyway.

"Deke, do you—?"

"Shh!" His hand reached back and connected with

her tummy. She felt him flinch, but he didn't jerk away. "I need to check this out," he whispered. "Stay here."

Terror gripped her, causing her little Sprout to stir restlessly. She grabbed Deke's hand and squeezed it. "Deke, please. Don't leave me. Not in the dark."

"Stay here!" Deke's voice brooked no argument.

Mindy stayed. She trembled and hugged her tummy. Her eyes devoured the faint hint of less-than-total blackness in front of her. Her ears strained to hear the smallest sound that would tell her that Deke was all right. And her pulse drummed so hard and fast that she thought she might pass out. But she stayed.

Suddenly, a shadow moved directly in her line of sight. At first she wasn't sure she saw it. She attributed it to the darkness and her fear and anticipation. But it kept coming closer.

Looming, menacing, like a spectre out of a dark lagoon, it stalked toward her.

Her pounding heart sped up even more, until she could feel the throbbing in her temples, in her wrists, even in the restless movements of her baby inside her. Then Sprout kicked her—hard.

She gasped.

"Mindy?"

Deke. His precious voice was right there. In front of her. It was Deke.

"Deke?" she breathed.

"Yeah. I was counting my footsteps. I didn't mean to scare you."

"What did you find?"

His hand touched her upper arm and slid down until he found her fingers. He clutched them.

"Wait and see." He couldn't disguise the excitement in his voice.

Mindy's pounding heart calmed down immediately. Right now, here in this menacing, dark place, she caught a glimpse of the handsome, cocky teenager she'd fallen in love with so many years ago.

He'd been supremely arrogant—certain that there was no obstacle he couldn't conquer, no mountain he couldn't climb. Happy and teasing and gentle, excited to show her a new discovery. From the moment she first laid eyes on him, he'd been her hero.

She hadn't seen him in eight long months, although she'd come close to calling him a dozen times to tell him he was going to be a father. Then she'd thought better of it, decided that she and her child would be better off if she never got sucked into his self-destructive life.

Seeing him now, she wasn't sure she'd made the right decision.

She squeezed his fingers back. "Take me." She heard the tremor in her voice.

He put his arm around her waist and led her forward and around a curve. As soon as they rounded the corner, Mindy saw a silvery-blue light shining down from above like a spotlight. In the light's circle was the spring they'd heard. It warbled and bubbled, its shimmering water reflecting the light like something magical as it flowed over pale rocks.

"Oh—" She was speechless.

Deke's hand tightened on her waist and he nuzzled the delicate skin right in front of her ear. "Welcome to your fantasy forest glen, my lady," he whispered, a smile in his voice.

"This is so beautiful. How—?"

She felt him shrug. "Best I can figure, this is a major artery of the old mine. They put it here, where the underground spring carved out this natural cavern." He started forward, guiding her at his side as he talked.

"The light comes from what looks like a wooden chimney way above us. Look." He pulled her close to the stream and pointed above their heads.

Almost too distracted by the sheer incredible relief of seeing light before her eyes, Mindy finally assimilated what he'd said and looked upward.

"I think it's a ventilation shaft. They sometimes had problems with the air quality in these mines. So they'd build shafts to let in fresh air."

"And light!" she exclaimed.

Deke's finger touched her chin and his thumb urged her to raise her head.

She did. When she met his dark gaze lit by blue fire, her knees grew weak.

"And light," he murmured. Then he bent his head and kissed her.

His kiss was like coming home. Like heaven. Like life. She melted into the warmth and sensuality of his mouth on hers, and responded. He kissed her more intimately, and a thrill slid through her entire body, settling in her sexual core.

Then Sprout kicked her. She drew in a small, sharp breath and instinctively pressed her palms against her side.

Deke backed away instantly. "What was that?" he asked. "Are you all right?"

Mindy smiled sadly. "It's our son kicking. He likes to get me right here, in the side."

"Our—" Deke looked down at her tummy, then back up. His eyes glittered in the pale blue light that barely managed to chase the shadows away from the circle under the ventilation shaft.

"Our son," he whispered, an expression of awe lighting his face.

His words, his voice cut through to her heart. She heard fear, but along with the fear was a note of wonder.

And there he was—the man she'd never seen, the man she'd always known he could be. If he'd ever learn to trust her, or himself, enough.

She nodded and lifted her hand to touch his cheek.

But he took another step back, straightened and turned away. He walked over to the edge of the stream.

"You need some water," he stated matter-of-factly without turning around. "I found an old candle bucket in the corner. I cleaned it with sand and anchored it between some rocks so the flowing water would rinse it out."

Mindy felt like he'd ripped her heart right out of her chest. She'd always wondered what it would take to break through the wall he raised whenever someone got too close. Her love had never been enough. She'd hoped little Sprout would be.

But his damn pride and fear had overpowered him. So he'd forced his feelings—what he considered his weakness—back behind the wall that shielded his heart.

He kneeled and picked up the bucket and brought it to her, half-filled with water. His face was expressionless, his voice remote. "Here. I'll hold it while you drink."

She held the sides of the bucket between her palms and guided it to her lips. The galvanized metal rim was icy-cold, and she had trouble swallowing the water past the lump in her throat, but the few swallows she managed to get down tasted heavenly.

It was sweet and cold and thoroughly refreshing. It ran over the edge of the bucket and dripped down her chin onto her breasts and tummy.

Deke held the bucket patiently. As soon as she'd finished drinking, he turned on his heel and with his back to her, he drank his fill.

"Come over here," he said without turning around. As she followed him over to the wall, she took in what was around her. There was a small stack of railroad-ties against the wall that was obviously intended as a crude bench. Buckets were scattered around, sitting up or overturned. On the ground to the side of the railroad tie bench sat a large metal tray covered with a piece of steel screen. Several feet beyond the bench stood an old vehicle that looked like a wagon with a cover over it.

"What is all this?" she asked Deke.

"I think this was probably a popular lunch spot with the coal miners. Somebody took the trouble to build the bench and the stove. And check that out." He pointed to the vehicle.

"That's a man car. Covered with a blanket. Look at the lanterns attached to the sides. They look like they still have oil in them."

Mindy turned her head to look, but she must have moved too fast, because dizziness overwhelmed her.

Deke caught her arm. "Whoa. Sit down over here. You're exhausted, and I am *not* about to try and get you back on your feet if you faint."

She made a face at him as he tugged on her arm until she followed him over to the bench. He gently pushed her down.

"Now stay there. The miners who worked down here had a pretty clever setup. We'll have some dinner in a few minutes."

"Dinner?" she said weakly. As if on cue, her stomach growled and Sprout wiggled and pounded against her side.

"Yeah. Do you see the silver flashes in the stream?"

"No." She squinted. "Maybe."

"They're fish."

"Fish? There are fish down here?"

"I haven't figured out what kind they are, but I'm about to."

"What are you going to do?"

He picked up one of the buckets and brought it over for her to see. "Somebody punched holes in the bottom of this bucket."

"A lot of holes," Mindy agreed.

"I'm thinking they used it to fish—like a net. With any luck, I can anchor it in the water and come up with a few fish."

"Fish," Mindy breathed. "I'm so hungry I could manage to eat them raw. But—?"

Deke grinned at her and pointed at the pile of ashes and twigs. "Don't worry. We'll cook them the old-fashioned way."

WITHIN TWENTY MINUTES, Deke had a bucketful of fish, and the legs of his jeans were soaked through. He climbed out of the stream, shivering when his bare feet hit the air. The spring was quite a few degrees colder than the surrounding atmosphere.

He brought the dripping bucket over to the campfire site and set it on a piece of railroad tie.

Raising his head, he started to speak to Mindy, but her eyes were closed and her lips were barely parted. She was asleep.

Compressing his mouth into a thin line, Deke sat on his haunches and watched her for a few minutes. Her soft mouth, her delicate brows and the eyelashes that lay on her cheeks like big fuzzy caterpillars, all the little parts of her that were tattooed on his heart.

His gaze slid down her neck and breasts to her

tummy. Pregnant, she looked and acted so different. She had a contentment about her that she'd never had when they were together.

Just the sight of her soft, serene expression made his heart hurt. Why was she serene and happy now? Was it because he was out of her life? Why hadn't he been able to bring that look to her face?

As soon as the question rose in his mind, he knew the answer. It was simple. He could never give her ease and contentment, because he was a breaker. He broke promises, broke vows, broke hearts.

He sighed. Even if he couldn't give her contentment, he could give her his protection. He owed her that much. He'd brought her into this mess.

He resolved to let her sleep until he got the fish cooked, then once she ate, he'd make sure she slept some more.

For several minutes, he explored the cavern. It wasn't huge, but it was like a vast, empty auditorium compared to the dark, narrow tunnels that fed into and out of it.

The main tunnel had eight sets of rails that ran downhill, parallel to the stream. Four of the sets came from the tunnel behind him. Its incline wasn't nearly as steep as the north one. The other four came from the east—the tunnel from the anteroom in the hotel basement—and joined the first four just above the sharp downhill incline.

He continued northward, examining the walls for other tunnels. In a pocket close to the rail intersection, he found a pile of branches and twigs. Beside the pile was a bucket of kindling and one about half-filled with candles.

Deke propped his fists on his hips and looked back

toward the ventilation shaft, thinking about luck and coincidence.

A cozy campsite with readily available fuel, a water source and a light source. *It was too good to be true.* It could easily be the latest in a series of traps set by Novus Ordo. Force them to take this tunnel, bring them to a veritable underground paradise complete with everything they needed to fill their stomachs and calm their minds. Then attack them while they were asleep.

He had to hand it to Novus. It was amazing what he'd managed to put together on a moment's notice. Amazing and frightening. Deke wondered how many men Novus had in the U.S. who were available and willing to drop everything on an hour's notice to carry out a focused and unrelenting attack.

Oddly enough, he no longer felt that prickle on the back of his neck. Maybe Novus's men hadn't managed to wire this section of the mine.

He thought about what Frank James had said to him. *You'll be hungry and thirsty and tired. Your gal there'll be pretty darn sick from hunger and exhaustion.*

It made perfect sense, knowing Novus. He was wearing Deke down, as he'd done before. After his capture in Mahjidastan, Deke had been trussed so tightly his shoulders had been dislocated, then he'd been thrown into a filthy, stinking tent. Each day at the same time, a robed man brought him a bowl of foul-tasting mush and one of dirty water. Then hours later, another robed and masked man would come in, order Deke to rise to his knees, spin the cylinder of a revolver, and fire it at Deke's head.

Those two visits took about six to eight minutes out of his day. The other twenty-three hours and fifty-odd minutes, he was left alone to think about the next day, when they would come again.

Deke pushed his fingers through his hair and rubbed the back of his neck as a deep shudder racked him. He wanted to give Novus and his ridiculous toy cowboy something to think about. He wanted to leave this lovely, compelling little cavern behind and spend the night poised for ambush, waiting for them to come looking for him.

But Mindy was already dog-tired; her face was drawn and pale. Right now, the most important thing was to make sure she got nourishment and rest. For herself and her baby.

He brought a pile of branches back to the campfire and, using a candle stub for a starter, soon got a nice fire going. He washed a small piece of screening to put the filleted fish on, then set it on the stove to cook.

By the time the fish were cooked, Mindy was stirring. Deke took the makeshift plate over and set it beside her on the railroad-tie bench.

"What's this?" she murmured sleepily.

"Dinner. Unfortunately, this is the entire menu. I don't even have any salt—or utensils."

"This is perfect."

The fish was tender and fell apart easily. Deke held back and let Mindy have as much as she wanted. She downed at least six of the small filets. When she sat back and sighed with contentment, Deke, who had been busying himself with the fire, finished them off.

Then he brought her a bucket of water. "Drink first," he said, "then wash up."

She obeyed, then glared at him. "Now, you bring some fresh water up here and some sand or gravel."

He frowned at her.

"I'm going to wash your arm. *And* I want some of that lantern oil to disinfect it."

"I told you, Min—"

"I don't care!" She held up a hand. "You said yourself the lanterns on that car had oil in them. Now bring me some. And get those bandages off and use the bucket with the holes in it to wash them in the stream."

It was Deke's turn to obey. By the time she'd scrubbed the gash in his arm with sand and water, and poured lantern oil into it—which burned like a son-ofabitch—he was cold and strangely tired.

"Long before we had modern ways of cleaning and disinfecting wounds, people used kerosene, gasoline, even gunpowder, to clean wounds."

Deke uttered a short laugh. "I guess I'm lucky we don't have a gun. I can hear you now, telling me that fire is the best disinfectant."

"Don't make fun. If it gets any worse, I may have to burn it. See the inflamed areas at the edges of the wound?" she asked.

Deke didn't want to look. He felt like his arm was on fire, and yet the rest of him was shivering with cold.

"That's cellulitis. It means your wound is infected. I'll bet you have fever. Damn it, Deke. If you'd let me clean it when I wanted to, this wouldn't have happened."

"It's not a problem."

"Yes, it is. I've got to keep an eye on this. If we see red streaks starting up your arm, that'll mean the infection is serious."

"I'll be fine."

"You're already not fine. Now bring me those bandages."

It took only a few minutes for Mindy to wrap his arm. Afterward, he quickly cleaned up the campsite, doing his best to make it look as if it hadn't been disturbed. Then he helped Mindy cross the shallow spring. During his exploration earlier, he'd found a pocketlike alcove in the wall on that side of the spring. It was deep enough that they could sit in the shadows and see into the tunnels without exposing themselves.

"I'm going to have to sit you on the ground," he told Mindy. "But I promise there aren't any bugs."

She chuckled quietly. "Don't worry. Bugs are the least of my worries right now."

Deke looked at her, wondering how he was going to get her to the ground. If it weren't for his arm, he'd pick her up and lay her down, but she was right about his wound. It seemed to be getting hotter and more tender. He shivered.

If her efforts didn't stop the infection, he was terribly afraid he might not make it much further under his own steam.

But he didn't tell her that.

"How do you want to do this?" he asked.

"If you can hold my hands, I can lower myself to the ground. Getting up will be a different story, though."

He helped her to the ground. "Are you cold?"

She shook her head. "Not too bad. It's a lot warmer over here than on the other side of the creek. Wonder why?"

"There could be a fire smoldering on the other side of this wall. I don't smell anything, so I'm not sure."

"A fire?"

"Sometimes the coal in these underground passages catches fire. They can burn slowly for years before anything happens." He put his hand on the dirt wall behind them. The wall did feel several degrees warmer than the wall on the other side.

"Years? And what kind of anything?"

"Yep, years. Like fifty or so in some cases. Eventually the fire will use up all the air in the mine and can burst through the surface."

Mindy turned her head to stare at him. "It won't happen today, will it?"

He couldn't help but smile. "Not if we're lucky."

"Why couldn't you have just said 'Who knows?' when I asked you why the wall was warm."

"Ask me again."

She laughed quietly and Deke felt her shoulders move. He lifted his left arm and slid it around her.

"Why don't you try to sleep," he said. "I'll keep an eye out for predators."

Mindy's shoulders stiffened. "Predators? You mean Frank James? Or are there bears and things around?"

He tightened his arm around her and bent to whisper in her ear. "You let me worry about bears and things. You just worry about getting some sleep. You're exhausted, and you've got to rest so your baby can rest."

"*Your* baby," she murmured.

The two words ripped through him like a bullet. *His baby.*

He still couldn't make those two words work together. *He* didn't have a baby. He couldn't.

Not with his legacy. Not if he was anything at all like his father. *If?* Hell. There was no if about it. He *was* like his father.

His dad had been a mean, abusive drunk. Deke knew that his own battle had taken a different turn.

He'd drunk a lot and tried drugs a little. But early on he'd discovered that he was a surly drunk rather than a violent one, like good old Dad. He didn't lash out physically, but he definitely lashed out verbally, with hurtful, cutting jabs at anybody who happened to be in his way.

No. Fatherhood was not for him. No innocent child should ever be subjected to what he could dish out when he was under the influence. A very good reason why he never drank anymore. Not even beer.

"Deke?"

His thoughts slammed back into the present, and he realized he was squeezing Mindy's shoulders. He relaxed his hand. "Yeah, sugar?"

"You don't have to be afraid of him."

The image of his father, eyes black as night and deep lines in his scowling face, rose before his vision for a few seconds before he realized she was referring to the baby.

"This little Sprout is a lot like you already. And he's only just getting ready to be born."

"Sprout?"

She laughed. "I call him that. It just came out one day when I was talking to him." She rubbed her tummy with both hands. "Do you want to feel him move? It seems like he moves almost all the time now. I don't know when he sleeps."

"I, uh—"

"Come on. Give me your hands."

Mindy took his hands and placed them on her rounded tummy, which was much firmer than he'd expected it to be. He'd always figured a pregnant tummy would be sort of springy and mushy. But hers felt like a basketball, round and hard.

"Is that how it's supposed to be? All hard like that?"

Mindy laughed, and her laugh slid through him like old times.

Then something moved. Deke jerked his hands away.

"Okay, you big scaredy-cat, it's just your son."

Just?

She pressed his hands down again and slid them over to her side. "Here. Here's his foot. *Mmh*. Feel that? He just kicked me. It's his favorite pastime."

"He kicked," Deke whispered in awe. "That was his foot."

"See? You can tell he's very healthy. He's pretty big, too. The doctor thinks he'll probably weigh at least seven pounds."

"Seven pounds."

Mindy inclined her head and gently bumped Deke's chin. "You're funny. All you're doing is repeating what I say. Is Sprout here that intimidating?"

Slowly, he nodded.

Mindy yawned, so he extracted his hands from hers and put his arm around her again. "Lean against me and sleep. I'll keep watch."

Mindy tucked her head under his chin and settled against him, with her tummy pressed against his side. "Then you have to wake me up to stand guard while *you* sleep."

Deke settled gently back against the warm wall and watched the tunnel in front of them, wondering how long it would take for Frank James to find them.

CHAPTER SEVEN

HE DROVE THE SUV along the fence line, using only the moon's light to examine the chain links for tears or breaks. Headlights would ruin his night vision. Besides, although everyone knew it was his shift to guard the remote perimeter of Castle Ranch, at least without headlights they couldn't see exactly where he was or what he was doing.

Everyone at the ranch was getting cabin fever, so Matt Parker had suggested that the specialists patrol the perimeter. All of them had jumped at the idea. It wasn't their nature to sit idle while one of their own was in trouble.

He drove over a ridge—and there it was. Exactly what he'd been looking for. On a spread the size of Castle Ranch, there had to be sections that were totally hidden. And this one was perfect for his purposes. The top of the ridge had a clear view of the front of the ranch. Its other side was completely hidden from all directions by scrub brush. A sniper could hide out here for hours—days, if necessary.

His hands shook on the steering wheel. At least, the vengeance he'd longed for all these years was within his reach.

MINDY SLEPT LIGHTLY. It had been weeks since she'd slept well, thanks to her little Sprout. Now her bed consisted of hard-packed dirt in an underground cave in early April. Which meant the nights were still quite cold. If she didn't have Deke to lean on and snuggle up against, she'd be half or maybe three-quarters frozen by now.

But she did have Deke. At some time while she was asleep, he'd managed to maneuver so that her head was on his chest and her tummy rested in the cradle created by his thighs.

She closed her eyes and relaxed against him. Her right ear was pressed to his chest and his strong, steady heartbeat set a rhythm for hers.

And her Sprout's. She could feel the baby. He felt like he was gently rocking himself to the comforting drumbeat of Deke's heart.

The spring provided a lilting melody to the bass beat of Deke's heart, and water dripping somewhere close by added a sweet accompaniment. Above her head the pale light of the moon lent an idyllic glow to the underground cavern.

Right here, right now, Mindy could believe that she and Deke had escaped the tethers of the real world and traveled to a fantastical alternate universe.

Mindy took a long breath, and the scent hit her. Her heart skipped a beat and a thrill rolled through her. Leather, soap and heat. *Deke.*

Dear heavens, how could she face losing him again?

Sprout kicked her in the side. She grunted, and Deke stirred.

Mindy straightened, preparing to move away, but his arm tightened around her shoulders.

"Where are you going?" he asked sleepily.

She lifted her head. "I'm sprawled all over you. I figured you might want to change positions."

"Um, not right this minute. In fact, you may not want to move, either. You might be embarrassed."

"Why? What are you—" She stopped, because she knew what he was talking about. He was erect. The sensations her stretched-out tummy were sending her were different from her normal nonpregnant self, and so until she'd moved, she hadn't noticed.

Now that she had, the strangest feelings roiled through her. Feelings that she hadn't had for a long time. Okay, maybe she'd had them, but she hadn't acknowledged them. From the moment she'd accepted the fact that she couldn't live with Deke and his self-destructive ways, she'd done her best to curtail all of her feelings—bad and good.

She'd felt as if to admit that she was sexually frustrated was to admit that she was still in love with Deke.

So now, lying in his arms with his erection rubbing against her tummy, the feelings that had started with warmth and comfort and safety morphed into desire.

And that was ridiculous. She was over eight months pregnant. She shouldn't be feeling like this. In fact, according to all the books, she should be working up a good-size dose of resentment and irritation toward him right about now.

"What are you thinking about?" Deke asked.

Mindy's throat seized. Did she dare tell him that she was fantasizing ways they could make love on this dirt floor?

"Min? Everything okay?" He touched her chin with his fingertips and tilted her head so he could see into her eyes. When he did, his blue eyes widened slightly and his mouth quirked up.

He knew. Damn him. He always knew. Once, it had fascinated her that he could tell with a glance when she was turned on.

Now, it embarrassed her and left her feeling vulnerable. She lowered her gaze, but not in time. He made a soft growling sound deep in his throat that rumbled against her ear.

"Min, I didn't mean to get you involved in this." He spoke against her hair, his breaths warming her skin.

She nodded. "I know."

His fingers under her chin pressed harder, urging her head up again. "I'm so afraid I'll hurt you."

She opened her mouth to offer up the standard protest, but he dipped his head and stopped her words with his lips.

Dear God, she loved to kiss him. His kiss was a perfect reflection of who he was. Hard, determined, yet with an undertone of such gentleness that it made her want to cry with joy because he'd shared it with her.

She needed to stop—for her own sanity. Needed to pull back, physically and emotionally, from the precipice of sublime insanity that making love with him always plummeted her over.

He bent forward, pulling her closer, holding her mesmerized with just the touch of his mouth on hers.

She'd gotten used to the vagaries of her hormone-suffused body, but in the entire eight months she'd been pregnant she hadn't once had a lascivious thought. In fact some days she'd felt so uncomfortable and lonesome that she figured she'd never have sex again. And she'd been okay with that.

But right now—

Deke's mouth moved over hers with the confidence and strength she'd learned to depend on, until he'd proved to her that he wasn't dependable.

She kissed him back. She couldn't help herself.

He ran his thumb across the underside of her chin and then cradled her cheek in his palm. His kiss grew deeper, more intimate, more demanding. Her heart pounded and her insides thrilled as she tasted his tongue and the inside of his mouth for the first time in way too long.

Trailing his fingers down her cheekbone, he traced the line of her jaw. At the same time his lips slid across her cheek, caressing the tender skin in front of her ear. Deep within her core, a rhythmic throbbing began and grew, swelling like a symphony.

Inside her, Sprout wiggled and kicked. Her deepening arousal was disturbing him. She cradled her tummy and glanced down.

When she did, Deke pulled away. "Sorry," he muttered.

"Deke, don't."

Don't what? She couldn't answer her own question. Don't apologize? Don't stop kissing her? Don't make her remember how it felt to love him?

Ignoring the voice in her head that told her how foolish it was to go down that road, she slid her fingers around the nape of his neck and pulled him closer.

"Don't apologize," she said. "I need—" She couldn't verbalize what she needed, but he seemed to know. With a pensive, solemn expression, he sat up and shrugged out of his shearling jacket.

"Sit up for a minute," he said. When she did, he placed the jacket behind her back, then leaned over her and kissed her again.

He was so strong. She ran her hands along the corded muscles of his forearms, shivering when she encountered the damp bandage. Then her palms slid up to trace the shape of his biceps and triceps. She lifted her head and pressed her lips against his throat, feeling the pulse thrumming there.

Balancing his weight on his arms, he lowered himself until he could nip at the curve of her jaw, at her earlobe, at the sensitive skin just beneath her ear. His breaths sawed in and out in a deep, steady rhythm that called to something visceral inside her.

"Min?" he whispered into the curve joining her neck and shoulder. "I can stop."

She shook her head. "Not yet," she murmured. "Not now."

He took in a deep breath that hitched at the top. "Then you'll have to stop me before I—before I hurt you."

She swallowed an ironic laugh. *Too late,* she thought. That ship sailed a long time ago.

Deke wanted to push away. He wanted to be the stronger one. The one who kept his head.

But he knew he was doomed to failure. He'd never been able to resist Mindy's soft, full mouth or her sexy, made-for-loving body. Or the sweet way she always made him feel like a hero, even though they both knew he was anything but.

They'd been together since junior year in high school. They'd been lovers since graduation night. She knew everything about him.

She knew where he liked to be kissed, to be touched. She knew how to bring him to the point of no return with nothing more than a brief caress of her fingers. She knew that although he'd never admit it to any of his buddies, he loved for her to touch his nipples. The sharp, erotic sensation of her fingertips and nails on them nearly sent him over the edge.

As if she knew what he was thinking, she slid her palms down his biceps and over his pectorals. Then she rubbed his nipples until they stood erect. He gasped, and she chuckled.

Okay, then. He knew everything about her, too. This would be tit for tat.

Like right now. He buried his nose in the little curve between her neck and her shoulder. If he ran his tongue along the apex of her shoulder, right over the little bump covered by golden skin, she'd moan and squirm.

He did.

And she did.

His throat closed with laughter—and sweet, aching nostalgia. Her hands tightened around his muscled wrists. Absently, he remembered that her fingers didn't reach all the way around.

He shifted his weight to his left arm and began unbuttoning the buttons at the top of her sweater. He didn't dare look up. He was afraid of what he'd see in her eyes.

Excitement, anticipation or apprehension?

When she pushed his hands away, his heart sank all the way to his boots. His logical brain, however, reminded his heart that they were in this place because she was in danger, and it was all because of him.

He had no right to take advantage of her. She was at his mercy. Dependent on him for safety, for comfort, for strength—for her very life.

Which made her vulnerable. And he was exploiting that vulnerability by letting his body overrule his brain. What he needed to be doing right now was figuring out their next move.

He knew perfectly well what this idyllic refuge was that they had found. It was bait—to lure them into a false sense of security.

Novus Ordo was still out there and still plotting to wear him down, still playing cat and mouse. For the moment he'd lifted his paw, giving them a taste of freedom—a false belief that they had a chance to escape. As soon as they tried, he'd clamp down on them again.

Her fingers brushed across his again, reminding him that his hand was resting near her breasts. He pulled away, but she stopped him. He watched with bated breath as she guided his palm to her waist, and then slid it up until his fingers curved around the bulge of her tummy. Against his palm, her satin-smooth skin seemed to vibrate with life—hers and the life of the tiny child inside her.

He closed his eyes, and for a moment he existed only in the sensations that flowed through the nerve endings on his fingertips and palms. He didn't think he'd ever felt anything so alive, so vibrant, so awesome.

To his surprise, tears stung his eyes, so he lowered his head, unwilling to let her see his weakness. He'd never even dreamed of being a father, never once considered that a precious, innocent child could spring from these loins of his. From the same DNA that had produced his cruel dad, and himself.

He pressed his forehead against the warm bulge of her tummy and silently prayed that one day he might be worthy of her and her baby.

He felt the tears leaking out from beneath his lids. He couldn't let her feel the salty drops on her skin. He hadn't cried since he was in junior high school and his dad had showed him what happened to crybabies.

So, under the pretense of nuzzling her tummy, he managed to wipe his eyes on the tail of her sweater.

Her abdomen moved as she sighed. Her fingers tightened around his, and she slid his hand across the slope of her tummy and farther up, toward her breasts.

His breath hitched and he raised his gaze. "Mindy—"

"Hush, Deke," she whispered. "Please don't spoil this with logic and reason. It's nothing more than a moment stolen out of time. It's not like we've never done it before." She made a quick head gesture toward her tummy.

"But you're—"

She put her fingers to his lips. "Shh. Don't even go there. Please don't *think*. For once in your life, just feel. I need you to take me somewhere outside of here. Outside of myself, because if I keep worrying about what's going to happen, I'll go insane."

As she talked, she continued to slide his hand upward, to the underside of her breast. Then she gripped his wrist and guided him over the fullest part to the peak, pressing his fingers to her nipple. She gasped.

And sighed again.

Deke's first instinct was to jerk his hand away. She was pregnant. These weren't the small delicate breasts he'd teased and nuzzled so many times. These were big breasts, pregnant breasts. They were firm and full, and the nipple was large and erect, waiting for the hungry little mouth of her son.

Their son.

His body instantly hardened—muscles, tendons, bones—all stiffened in sharp, aching hunger. His mouth watered to taste the distended tip.

He caressed the nipple with the gentle touch of his fingers. As he did it hardened and puckered in reaction, and Mindy's breathing ratcheted up a notch. She blew air softly in and out, and her body writhed and arched the tiniest bit, revealing her yearning for more of what he offered.

So he cradled her full round globe in his hand, kneading and squeezing, then running his thumb across and around her ever-tightening nipple. His erection grew harder, longer, as his body throbbed in familiar reaction to her obvious need and desire. Turning her on had always fed his own desire.

But this—what he felt right now—was a level of longing he'd never before experienced. Not even when they were horny teenagers, searching for a place where they could be alone together.

"How—how does it feel?" he asked with trepidation. "To be pregnant?"

Mindy put her hand on top of his. It had always awed her how much bigger his hand was than hers. "It's really strange. Different every day."

She looked at the man who'd created this baby with her. He was so scared. She could read the fear in his face. Over the years she'd known him, she'd watched him forge himself into a warrior. He'd taught himself not to be afraid of anything. Yet this small, helpless life within her terrified him.

"He feels like you," she whispered, her voice catching. "It's like I have a part of you inside me all the time."

She'd known that, deep inside, but she'd never said the words, not even to herself. Now she understood the erotic dreams that woke her deep in the night. Now the indescribable longings she'd never acknowledged in daylight had a source. And the source was Deke.

He made a deep, throaty sound, and a shudder rumbled through him. His erection pulsed against her thigh.

Instantly, her body tightened in desire and in the deepest, most intimate part of her, a sweet familiar throbbing began.

Deke continued caressing the tip of her breast as

he lifted his head. He leaned forward until his mouth brushed hers.

Then he kissed her. A desperate, deep, soul-searching kiss. As his mouth took hers, she whimpered in uncontrollable response.

He froze.

She moaned in frustration as he pulled away.

"What's wrong?" she whispered.

"I'm hurting you."

"Deke, believe me, you're not." Mindy's breasts, her center, burned with frustration. "Please." She wrapped her hand around the nape of his neck and pulled his head toward her. "Don't stop."

And he didn't. He kissed her over and over, tasting her as if it were the first time. She was as sexy to him as she'd always been. Maybe more so. Something, whether it was her pregnancy or just the fact that it had been so long, had him so turned on that he was afraid he might explode like a horny kid. He pulled back, trying to control himself, but Mindy moaned in protest. She caught his hand and brought it to the apex of her thighs.

He felt her heat, even beneath the wool pants she wore. And when he pressed his palm against her, her already labored breathing sped up.

"Deke," she whispered, then gasped again. "Oh!" Her hand covered his, and she pressed down against his palm.

He listened to her shallow, rhythmic breaths, her small cries. And clenched his teeth to keep from following her climax with his own.

"Deke," she finally breathed. "Don't run away. Let me—" She reached for his pants zipper.

"No. This isn't a good idea."

"Why?" She clasped his hand in hers and brought his palm to her lips. She chuckled, still feeling the small aftershocks of her climax. "It's not like you can get me *more* pregnant."

As soon as the words were out of her mouth, she knew she'd screwed up. Royally.

Deke pushed away and sat up. "Nope," he rasped, as he pushed his fingers through his shaggy hair. "Apparently that was one time I managed to deliver maximum damage on the first try."

"Deke, wait. I'm sorry."

"For what? Getting pregnant? That wasn't your fault." He rubbed his eyes, then swiped a hand across his face. "It was your mother's funeral. I took advantage of your grief."

"You did not! It just happened. In fact, if I hadn't kissed you, you'd have been out of there like a cat with its tail on fire." She smiled briefly. "Trust me, Deke. I do not regret being pregnant."

"I do."

She flinched and her eyes pricked with tears at his quick, simple declaration. But she had known this was how he would feel. From the first moment she'd realized that she was pregnant, there had been no question in her mind.

She'd wanted the baby, whether Deke did or not.

Gingerly, as if he were a skittish colt, she took his hand and pressed it against her tummy.

"Can you regret this? He's your son, Deke. A part of you and me. If we're lucky, the best parts."

"And if we're not lucky?" He was thinking of his father.

"Trust me. In this we're lucky."

"Good to know," he muttered. "When we get out of here, remind me to buy a lottery ticket." He stared at his hand where it rested on her stomach. He still seemed awestruck—and terrified—by her pregnancy.

"Don't make fun of me. You have no idea how beautiful, how sexy you make me feel. I haven't felt either for months. Come back and lie down with me," she said. "I'm cold."

He scooted back over and reclined against the warm dirt wall, positioning himself so that she leaned against his left side.

She pressed her hand against his chest and tucked her head into the snug, sweet place between his neck and shoulder.

"This feels good," she whispered. "Like home."

Deke grimaced at her sleepy words and tightened his arm around her shoulders.

"Deke?" she whispered.

"Yeah, sugar?"

"What time do you think it is? And what day?"

It was a good question. He'd tried his best to keep up with the time. "It's dark. I'd guess it might be around midnight. Best I can figure, it's Thursday night. Or Friday morning."

He bent his head and pressed a kiss against her hair.

"Sleep, Min. I'll keep you safe." He leaned his head back against the hard dirt wall and stared at the starlit sky through the opening high above their heads. He felt her breasts rise and fall with her breaths, heard them slow and even out as she dozed.

The immediacy and strength of Mindy's response to him awed him—and terrified him.

He hadn't meant to lose control of himself, or get caught up in her growing reaction to his caresses.

All he'd wanted to do was taste, just for a moment, the sweetness of her kisses, feel the lovely soft firmness of her skin.

He hadn't meant to turn her on.

The thought sent a shudder of erotic thrill through him. He grimaced and shifted uncomfortably. He could easily and quickly take care of his discomfort, but he'd promised Mindy he'd keep her safe. He wasn't going to take the slightest risk of being distracted, not even for a moment.

Besides, from the very first time he'd touched her, when they'd both been innocent teens, he'd never known anything that fueled his own desire as much as stoking the fires of hers did.

She'd thanked him, but in truth she'd turned herself on. In doing so she'd turned him on, too. He'd gotten as much—well, almost as much—satisfaction as she had.

His eyes slowly closed, and his thoughts began to wander. He clamped his jaw. He couldn't sleep. He needed to keep lookout.

He couldn't do anything about the signs they'd left at the campfire. Probably didn't matter, anyway. Novus knew they were here. He'd probably arranged for the kindling and candles.

Deke snorted. If there hadn't been any fish in the spring, he'd have probably arranged for them, too.

He looked down at the top of Mindy's head. She was asleep in his arms, trusting him to keep her safe.

Anger, hot as a flash fire, whooshed through him. It took every ounce of his strength to stay still.

Why don't you just come and get me? he wanted to

stand up and shout. *Come on, Novus. Show your face. Fight it out, fair and square, like a man.*

He doubted they'd managed to wire the entire mine, so he'd probably be yelling to deaf ears, but it would sure make him feel better.

I know why you won't face me, you scumbag. You're no man. You're a coward. Just like your wormy outlaw brother. Frank James. Give me a break! Covering up your weaselly face with a mask! Just like your boss Novus.

"I'll be damned—!" *Just like Novus.* The significance of his comparison slammed him in the gut. He clamped his jaw and took long, even breaths, trying to slow his suddenly racing heart. Trying not to disturb Mindy.

Could that be it? Could this guy, obviously American, actually be the brother of Novus Ordo? Deke knew from Rook's description and the forensic artist's rendering he'd seen that the terrorist was medium height and skinny with a narrow face and beady eyes. And Rook had sworn that Novus, whose messages were always delivered on CD in a heavy, Middle Eastern accent, was actually American.

It would explain everything. Novus's obsessive need to hide his face. Frank James affecting that ridiculous bandanna. It might be a leap, but it made sense.

Why else would James hide his face? Deke knew the weasel didn't intend to let either Mindy or himself get out of there alive.

Deke cursed silently. He had information that could bring Novus down, and he had no way to get a message out.

Rook, you sonofabitch! I need you, man. More than

*I ever have before. Between us, we'd figure out who
Novus is and bring him and his brother down.*

"Deke?" Mindy lifted her head. "What's the matter?"

Damn it, he'd woken her. "Nothing, sugar. Go to
sleep."

She shifted. "Did you hear something?"

He shook his head and cradled the back of her head
in his palm. "Nope. Just thinking."

She laid her hand on his chest. "Must have been
some kind of thinking, to send your heart racing like
that. What were you thinking about?"

"Novus," he said reluctantly. He didn't want her to
know his fears. On the other hand, he owed her the
truth. He'd gotten her into this. He probably should tell
her exactly what and who they were battling.

"How we ended up here. It started out innocently
enough. Irina's accountant gave her final warning. He'd
apparently talked with her a few times before about her
depleted funds. But this time he warned her that if she
continued the same level of spending for another three
to four months, she'd be bankrupt. Irina had to make
a decision. Shut down BHSAR or stop spending a fortune searching for Rook. She made the only decision
she could."

"I still don't understand why she gave up. They were
more in love than any two people I've ever met. If I were
Irina, the only way I'd ever give up is if I saw the body."

Deke tried to suppress the thought that sprang to the
front of his mind.

*So your definition of giving up doesn't include di-
vorce?*

He bit his tongue until the urge to lash out at her for
leaving him went away. Hell, he knew he'd been an ass

and had hurt her in too many ways to count, but it still hurt that she'd done the very thing he'd expected her—that he'd pushed her—to do.

He clenched his jaw and continued his explanation. "When Rook left the air force, he still had his burning desire to rescue the innocent. Black Hills Search and Rescue was his baby. Irina knew that Rook would never want to give up his dream. So she made the choice he'd have wanted her to make."

He felt Mindy's shoulder quiver and heard her swallow a sob. "Min? You okay?"

She nodded against his shoulder. "It's just so sad."

"Yeah. Apparently, as soon as Irina stopped searching, rumors started circulating that she'd found him. The first indication we got was from Homeland Security, reporting on the increased international chatter. Especially in the regions around the corridor that joins Pakistan, China and Afghanistan. A small province called Mahjidastan."

"Where you were shot down."

He nodded. "Novus Ordo's headquarters."

Mindy pushed herself up to a sitting position, groaning with the effort. Deke moved to help her. "So Novus found out that Irina had stopped the search."

"Matt left Mahjidastan within six hours after Irina called him—on the first flight he could get. He was followed. Then as soon as he got back, Aimee Vick's baby was kidnapped. That means that Novus knew what Irina had done *before* the chatter started."

"But how—"

"Only one way. We've got a traitor inside BHSAR."

"Oh my God, Deke. Who? Don't you know everyone?"

"I know the BHSAR team. I've met the rest of the

staff. Don't know much about them. But the traitor has to be someone who knows everything that goes on. The specialists, Irina's personal assistant, her lawyer—"

"That's—what? Five people."

"Six, if I don't count Matt. Aaron Gold, Brock O'Neill, Rafe Jackson, Pam Jameison, Richards the lawyer, and maybe her accountant."

"I forgot about Rafe Jackson. I've never met him. Which one could do something like this?"

Deke shook his head. "Before all this started, I'd have said none of them. But now—everybody on the team, especially Irina, is in danger because I didn't identify a traitor in our midst. Think about it. They've already sabotaged my bird. Almost cost Matt and Aimee and her baby their lives."

Mindy considered the few times she'd met the other members of the team. "Brock's awfully secretive."

"Yeah, but can you see him betraying his country?"

"Maybe he doesn't consider it his country. He's Sioux, right? We destroyed *his* country."

Deke frowned at her.

"Or Aaron Gold? I only met him a couple of times."

"His dad was in the air force with Rook. He died a hero. Aaron was thrilled to be asked to join the BHSAR team."

"And Rafe Jackson?"

Deke didn't speak for a moment. "Rafe was born in England, but he went to a lot of trouble to become an American citizen."

"He's British?"

"Actually, his mother is from Saudi Arabia. His name is Rafiq."

"Wow. Any one of them could be the traitor."

Deke shook his head. "I guess you're right."

"What did you tell them about coming here to rescue me? I mean, if one of them is working with Novus, they know what's going on here."

"Let's just say I took precautions."

"What kind of precautions? What could you do to be sure the terrorist didn't find out vital information?"

"I'd rather not say."

"Really? Here, too?" Mindy craned her neck to look around.

"I have no idea. I just don't want to take any chances."

"So all this—it's because Novus is trying to find Rook, when he doesn't even know if he's alive? I guess whoever shot Rook didn't have the luxury of hanging around to make sure he died."

Deke sighed. "Guess not."

"Why don't they just go after you? Or Irina?"

"He can't get to us directly, and he knows that. There's too much security at the ranch. And it's the same reason he didn't just grab Matt. One of *us* disappearing would create an international incident, just like Rook's disappearance did. Since we're still connected with the military."

"So instead, he's grabbing those close to you."

Deke squeezed his eyes shut and rubbed his temple. "Something like that."

"Why? What's he after?"

"He's doing everything he can to be sure Rook can't identify him. You've seen the mask that Novus Ordo always wears?"

"Sure. I've seen the pictures they've shown on the news shows. It looks like those green and white dis-

posable surgical masks you can buy in any drugstore."
She uttered a short laugh. "He looks pretty ridiculous."

"Yeah, well, they've been effective. For several
years, he's been the most famous and most dangerous
terrorist on the planet. The mask fascinates people. It
makes him look mysterious."

"And nobody's ever seen his face?"

"That's the word. No one except his most trusted
inner circle. And Rook." Deke's gut twisted at his
friend's name. Rook had taken Deke under his wing
on the first day of first grade. He was only a few months
older, but he'd always been the stronger one, the more
courageous one, the leader. Rook had been born to lead,
and Deke had been perfectly happy to be his sidekick.

"He saw him when he rescued you."

He looked at her, surprised.

"Rook told me. He said you saved Travis Ronson's
life."

He'd never wanted her to know about that. Per-
versely, he would rather have her believe he didn't love
her anymore.

The truth, that his helicopter had been shot down,
which provided the means for Rook's team to find
Novus, painted him in a sympathetic light that he didn't
deserve.

"I only found out all that afterwards. The way Rook
tells it, he and his team hit their camp at night while
most of Novus's men were sleeping. He found the camp
by using the GPS locator in my shoulder."

"In your shoulder? Is it still there?"

"No." He reached with his right hand to touch the
little bump where the small chip was located, but
the movement made his inflamed wound sting so he

stopped. "The battery only lasts about a year. Still itches, though."

"So Rook rescued you."

"The team did. While they were transporting me to the helicopter, Rook took out a couple of guards with a silenced handgun, and found himself face-to-face with Novus, mask and all. Then a gust of wind ripped the mask right off him. Rook said he got an extreme close-up view before Novus covered his face with his arm."

"Oh my God! He saw Novus Ordo's face."

"Then two more guards tackled him. He almost didn't get away. One of them grabbed his dog tags and tried to choke him. About that time Brock O'Neill took out the other one with a machine gun. They got to the helicopter just as it was lifting off. Another few seconds and one of Novus's machine guns or flamethrowers could have grounded it. Then everybody would be dead." He wiped a hand down his face. "Truth is, it's my fault Novus targeted Rook."

Mindy shuddered. "What did Rook say about Novus? What did he look like?"

Deke laid his head back against the dirt wall. His mouth lifted at one corner. "That's classified."

"Right. Classified. Does Irina know?"

He frowned. "Probably."

"Do you think she's more trustworthy than me?"

"No. But—"

"Then tell me. You've always said how important it is to know your enemy. Well, I need to know my enemy, too."

He sent her a pensive look. "Okay. The latest, greatest, most infamous terrorist on the planet is American."

CHAPTER EIGHT

"Novus Ordo is American? No way!" Mindy stared at Deke, stunned. His head still rested against the wall behind him. He swallowed, and his Adam's apple moved up and down. The tendons in his neck and the muscles that joined his neck and shoulder stood out as sharp shadows. Dear heavens, there was nothing about him that wasn't sexy. Even his neck. Even his Adam's apple.

Deke smiled and her heart gave a little leap at the curve of his lips. "Way."

"Is— Was Rook sure? What did he tell you he looked like?"

"Rook said he was kind of ordinary looking, maybe of Irish or Scottish or British ancestry. But get this. He heard him curse, in a very American accent."

"Deke, this is unbelievable. Why would an American—?" She stopped. It was a silly and useless question. There had been other Americans who'd turned against their country. "But the audio recordings he's sent to the media have all been heavily accented English."

"Right. You notice he's never sent a video. Homeland Security's theory is that one of his inner circle makes the recordings for him. Plus Rook worked with a computer facial recognition analyst for the CIA. For the past two years the CIA and Homeland Security have been trying to find a match to fit his description."

"Have you seen it? The sketch?"

Deke nodded. "Average-looking guy. Medium height. Bordering on skinny. Long nose, close-set eyes, sharp chin."

Disturbingly similar to Frank James. The cowboy outfit and bandanna mask couldn't hide James's slender build, his beady eyes or his narrow face. With every passing minute, Deke was more convinced that James was Novus's brother, since, based on the sketch, he was too old to be his son.

Deke wasn't naive enough to think that Novus would be here carrying out this witch hunt himself, but he could easily believe that Novus's brother would do it. Hell, the sketch could be of Frank James himself.

He wondered what their real names were, and if they were born and reared in this part of the country or had located here because of Rook.

At least he had information that Novus didn't know he had, and he would guard that information with his life. It might be a way to bring Novus down.

"Deke?"

Mindy had asked him a question. "What?"

"What did Rook say about Novus's hair color? Was he dark or fair?"

"Rook couldn't see his hair because of his shemagh, but he said the CGI expert did a great job on the face."

"Shemagh?"

"That's the traditional Arabian headdress. Novus wears it on his head, but doesn't use it to cover his face. He uses the surgical mask for that."

"So none of you recognized the sketch? You'd never seen him before?"

"Nope."

"And the CIA has no idea who he is?"

He shook his head. "They've been going over all reports of missing Caucasian males from the past ten or so years, starting with the first known reports of Novus Ordo's involvement in terrorism."

Mindy felt like she'd woken up in the middle of a movie—a thriller. She couldn't keep up with everything Deke was telling her. She was still processing his astonishing statement: *Novus Ordo is American.*

More specifically, she was processing the realization that Deke knew so much about international terrorist activities, Novus Ordo and what sounded like classified government secrets.

He hadn't been kidding when he'd said *it's classified.* He had just told her a secret of global importance.

A sudden sense of overwhelming responsibility weighed on her shoulders. It was crushing. Suffocating. She put a hand to her breastbone as her pulse hammered in her ears. "Oh."

"Mindy? Is it the baby?"

She shook her head. "It's just—I almost wish you hadn't told me."

"I know what you mean. But after everything I've put you through, I figured you deserved to know. I can trust you not to tell anyone, can't I?"

"Of course you can. Deke, is *this* what you do? What you've been doing since you got back from Mahjidastan? You're a—a secret government agent? Some kind of covert operative?"

He laughed, but he sounded more ironic than amused. "No. BHSAR isn't a secret government agency. It's what Rook wanted it to be. A private search-and-rescue company that does as many volunteer rescues as paid jobs, if not more."

"A private company. So, what were you doing over there spying on Novus Ordo?"

"That was supposed to be a one-time thing. A personal favor asked of him by—" he paused and drew in a long breath "—by a friend."

A very high-placed, influential friend. Mindy had no doubt those were the words Deke hadn't said.

"If I hadn't gotten shot down…if Rook hadn't seen Novus's face…" He shrugged. "Once all this is over, we should be able to do what we thought we'd done years ago. Be private citizens who just happen to run a local search-and-rescue operation."

"With an occasional favor for a special friend or two."

Deke just shrugged and quirked up the corner of his mouth.

"I don't know how you've managed to stay sane."

Another harsh laugh. "Maybe I haven't."

"Oh, I think you're much stronger than you realize." Mindy lay back against the softness of Deke's shearling jacket.

"Yeah? Have you decided I'm not broken?"

The question sounded ironic, but Mindy heard an undertone that she'd never heard in his voice before—an anxiousness, as if the answer she gave to that question was very important to him.

"Hmm. I think most of your life you've looked at strength in the wrong way. You equate strength with rigidity. And that's dangerous. You don't need to be too strong to break. If you're rigid, then you can't bend.

And if you can't bend, you're doomed to break." She yawned. "Or something like that…"

"And bending. How is that a good thing? Isn't it like bowing down?"

She opened one eye and squinted at him. "No. It means you're resilient. You can take punishment without breaking. You'll be beaten down, but you'll spring back again."

A deep laugh rumbled through his chest. "You're exhausted. You need to get some sleep," Deke murmured.

"I'm not sure if I'll ever sleep again…" Her words faded.

"Oh, I think you will." He leaned over and pressed a kiss against her forehead. "I'm going to get up and take a look around, okay?"

"You need to sleep, too." She was already drifting off. *Sprout, don't you dare decide to be born until we get out of here. You can hold off another day or so, right?*

"I'll wait. I've gone without sleep for longer than this and survived. If you need me, call me."

"My hero," she whispered.

Deke slid carefully away from Mindy just as a deep rumble echoed through the cavern.

Mindy jerked and Deke stiffened.

That was an explosion. What the hell?

"What was that?" Mindy asked, worry lacing her voice.

"Thunder." Deke winced at his lie. "Go back to sleep. Even if it rains, we're protected here."

He rose to his feet and looked down at her. She'd already drifted back to sleep. She was so pretty, so young, so trusting, looking with her eyes closed and her face relaxed in sleep. Her silky-smooth hair fell across her cheek like chocolate-colored velvet.

God, I know I don't deserve to have a prayer answered, but don't make her suffer for my screwups. Please don't let her die.

What had gone so wrong? How had he let her get caught up in the train wreck that was his life? She didn't deserve this. She deserved a safe, stable home with all the special things that came with it: a husband who loved her and put her safety above everything else; beautiful, smart children she could be proud of; a life free of fear and danger.

The kind of life he could never give her.

His fists clenched as he turned away. It hurt his heart too much to look at her for very long. Especially like she was now. Innocent, vulnerable, trusting enough to sleep peacefully. It didn't seem to bother her that she had no one but him to protect her.

He should have brought backup. Rafe had been available, as had Aaron. But even if he'd trusted them enough, it would have been a fatal mistake. Novus had demanded that he come alone. He'd given him no choice. Out here on this lonely stretch of prairie, a second car or a second body would have been immediately noticeable. They could have been killed.

He fingered the bump on his shoulder. He hadn't told Mindy a complete lie. His scar did itch, partly because of the previous transmitter, but partly because of the new one. Who knew if it would prove useful, especially if they stayed underground. But he was glad he had it. He only wished he had some sort of two-way communication device.

If he stood directly under the ventilation shaft at exactly the right time, there might be a chance that one of the specialists would pick up on the chip's location. He needed to let someone know that Mindy was eight months pregnant. But he had no way to get the information out.

He should have hidden a two-way transmitter somewhere on him. But hell, they'd searched him. He was damn lucky they didn't get around to checking his boots.

Why hadn't he taken steps to protect Mindy from Novus like he had Irina?

Because he'd been clinging to the hope that after two years she was no longer close enough to him to be in danger. It was a stupid assumption.

Deke stood under the ventilation shaft as he argued with himself. And then argued with himself about the futility of arguing with himself. Finally, he stopped at the far end of the lagoon and stared at the coal-car rails that plummeted down the steep incline.

They couldn't go that way. He could make it on foot if he were alone, but Mindy would never be able to stay on her feet. The incline was about twenty degrees, which didn't sound like much, but in her condition she had enough trouble walking on level ground.

It amazed him that the heavily loaded coal cars had managed to stay on the tracks, especially if the tracks curved.

He did an about-face, just as another rumble shook the ground. Again, he held his breath. But nothing else happened. After another few seconds, the rumble faded.

He swallowed heavily. Those were explosions, not thunder. And he'd bet money he knew what was being blown up.

The mine tunnels. James was trapping them in here. And there were only two reasons he would do that. Either he was ensuring that the only way out was back through the hotel, or— Deke did not want to think about the second reason. But he had to.

Or James was sealing them inside the mine before he killed them.

But why do that when he could just man the exits?

Good question. Maybe Novus didn't have as many men at his disposal as Deke had assumed he had. Maybe James was blowing up the tunnels because he couldn't guard them all at once.

If that was the case, then maybe Deke could get the upper hand after all. He figured he could handle two-to-one odds—maybe even three to one.

He turned to stare at the other end of the tracks, wondering if one of the explosions had caved in that tunnel. With a shrug, he continued his analysis of the best way to proceed. It was something to do at least.

The upper incline was much shallower—nearly level. If he were Novus, he'd discard that incline and the branch tunnel that led back to the hotel. Those were the easy choices.

But then, if Deke was thinking about taking the most difficult tunnel, even with a pregnant woman in tow, then Novus would also think about it.

He sighed and rubbed his temples. His thoughts were whirling out of control. Probably the result of too little food and sleep, and too many zaps with James's fancy Taser. At least the racing thoughts had distracted him from his other problem—his frustrated libido. He dropped to his haunches and winced at the pressure of the denim on his not-quite-deflated erection. Okay, he wasn't totally distracted.

He dipped his hands into the cold spring and splashed water on his face. Then, sitting back on his heels, he let his gaze wander around the large room. The only sounds that reached his ears were the soft trilling of the spring and an almost inaudible whistle of wind from the ventilation shaft high above.

He massaged the back of his neck. Much as he would have liked to catch a few winks of sleep, he needed to search the area for anything he could use as a weapon.

With a tired groan, he rose to his feet and went searching. The first thing he wanted to do was check out that blanket on the man car. If it wasn't too filthy, Mindy could cover up with it. He was sure that she was going to get cold before the night was over.

He crossed the shallow spring and approached the vehicle. A quick inspection told him that not only was the wool blanket filthy and moth-eaten, it was mildewed, as well. It wouldn't be healthy for Mindy to wrap up in it.

Gingerly, he pulled the thing off the car and peered over the sides, holding the lantern high in the air.

He froze.

Dynamite. Old dynamite. Several bundles of it. And from the little he knew about it, old meant dangerous. Carefully, holding his breath, he lowered the lantern enough to get a good look at the sticks without letting the lantern's heat come close to it.

The first thing he noticed once the vehicle's floor was illuminated was a tangle of blasting caps. Dozens of them. The second thing he noticed was the bright spots on the surface of the sticks.

Crystals. Ah, hell. Those crystals were pure nitroglycerine. A bump—even a slight movement, could cause them to explode.

Hardly daring to breathe, he backed away from the car. Was that dynamite set to explode? He held the lantern up, searching to see if there was a fuse running from the car. But he didn't see anything.

So he crouched down, checking underneath, and walked all the way around, but he didn't see a fuse there, either. He did, however, find a crowbar leaning against the wall behind the car. Grabbing it, he straightened, blowing his breath out in a sigh. Maybe the dynamite hadn't been rigged by James. Maybe it had just been stored there for the past fifty or so years.

Still, the question remained. Did James know it was here?

It hardly mattered. They couldn't go near that car. They couldn't even breathe on it, or the nitroglycerine might blow. He headed back toward the alcove, testing the crowbar in his hands.

He crouched at the spring and scooped another couple of handfuls of water into his mouth, then sat back under the shaft and took his first deep breath since discovering the dynamite. He knew one thing for certain. They had to get out of here as soon as possible. In the meantime, on the minuscule chance that a satellite was in range and anyone might be monitoring transmissions, he'd stay under the opening as long as he could.

DEKE WOKE UP. He'd heard something besides the quiet sound of burbling water.

There it was again. A quiet moan.

Mindy!

He vaulted to his feet, swaying a little as the blood rushed away from his head, and ran to the alcove.

She was sitting up, her hands pressed against her stomach.

"Min? What is it?"

"I don't kn—" Her whole body stiffened, and a sharp gasp cut off her words. "There's something—wrong."

Deke sat and took her hands in his. "What can I do?"

She shook her head. Even in the dim light of dawn seeping in through the ventilation shaft, he could see how pale her face was.

"Hey," he said, keeping his voice as calm as he could. He squeezed her fingers gently. "I'm pretty sure you're supposed to breathe."

She looked up at him. "So now you know all about pregnancy?" Her voice was strained, belying the lightness of her words.

"I took a course."

"Nice to know."

She pushed a breath out through pursed lips. Then drew in another. Taking them long and slow.

"That's good. Good, Min." He brought her hands to his mouth and kissed her knuckles, buying some time as he racked his brain. He *had* taken a course years ago, during his air force training. It had included an overview of delivering a baby. A *brief* overview.

Dear God, please don't let this baby come now. There was no way he could keep a newborn infant safe. No way he could take care of Mindy.

Focus. What were the signs of labor? *Contractions,* he answered himself.

"Are you hurting?" he asked.

She shook her head. "Not now."

He nodded. "So that wasn't a contraction?"

Mindy closed her eyes and flattened her lips. "No. It was a contraction, all right. And I don't think it was the first one."

Deke's training was coming back to him. Beads of sweat prickled his forehead and the nape of his neck. "How—how far apart are they?"

"I don't know. They started in my sleep. I was having a little back pain. And once or twice I felt a cramp. I palpated my abdomen. The uterus is definitely contracting."

"I didn't understand most of that, but you're the nurse, so I'll take your word for it."

She sent him a wan smile. "Thanks."

"Is this—" he made a vague gesture toward her tummy "—is this it? Are you having the baby?"

"No." Mindy lifted her chin. "No. It's too early. And—look where we are. No. My baby will *not* be born here." She cradled her tummy. "Did you hear me, Sprout? Stay in there. We'll be home soon."

My baby. Those two words echoed in his ears. She'd told him that the baby was his. She'd even referred to him as *our baby* a few times. He was surprised how much it hurt to hear her say *my* instead of *our* right now.

He cleared his throat. "What can I do to help?"

Her olive-green eyes met his gaze. "Go find a way out of here, get help and come back and rescue me."

"Forget that. I'm not leaving you here. Especially if you're having the baby." And especially since he knew they were practically sitting on enough dynamite to blow the entire mine.

She glared at him. "I am not having the baby."

Despite the seriousness of their situation, her determination made him smile. "What? You're going to stop him from being born with your steely resolve?"

"Damn straight I will." She stuck her chin out pugnaciously.

"And you call me stubborn," he muttered under his breath.

"I heard tha— Oh!"

"Min?" He took her hand and squeezed it reassuringly. Her fingers tightened around his with surprising strength. "Breathe, sugar."

She kept a stranglehold on his fingers until the contraction was over. He spent the time watching her, and estimating how long it had been between contractions.

"I think it's been ten minutes since the first contraction," he said, as she pushed herself back against the dirt wall.

She nodded. "That's what I thought. Ten minutes apart. I'm in premature labor."

"Is that some kind of labor that comes before real labor?" he asked hopefully. He had a sinking feeling that the answer to that question was no.

Sure enough, she shook her head. His heart sank and his pulse sped up.

"It's real labor, but it'll go away. Like I told you, it's too early. He's not due to make his appearance for six more weeks." She pushed herself up a little more. "Can you bring me some water?"

Deke fetched her a bucket of water. She drank several swallows.

"I've got to lie down," she told him. "The recommendation for slowing or stopping premature contractions is to lie still for a couple of hours and drink lots of water. That's the best chance I have to stop them."

"Okay, so we'll wait for two hours, then we'll both get out of here."

Mindy shook her head. "I don't think I'll be able to walk. Not in two hours. I'd just go back into labor." She put her hand on his. "Deke, you've got to find the way out."

"No. I'm not leaving you."

She maneuvered herself into a reclining position and turned onto her left side.

"This is no time to start being sentimental," she said. "I need you to do what you do best. What would you do if I were an injured man? Or a female innocent you were sent in to rescue?"

He scowled at her. "You're not."

She scowled right back at him.

He relented. "I'd leave the man with a weapon to defend himself while I scouted the best way out. I'd probably carry the female out with me."

"You can't. You're injured, and I'm not only too heavy, I can't walk."

"I can't leave you here, alone and helpless."

"It's the only way. Now give me the knife and go find us a way out."

He silently handed the knife over to her.

"I know you've already figured out what Novus is doing," she said.

He nodded. "He's got all the exits manned, and he's figured out what he thinks I'm going to do. I'm telling you, he's got a time frame he's working within. As soon as he can figure out a way to get to Irina—" He stopped. He didn't want to tell her that Novus's timeline included killing the two of them as soon as he got his hands on Irina Castle.

"He's having fun trying to anticipate my next move. His favorite thing to do is toy with people."

"Like a cat with a mouse."

"And like that cat, he knows exactly when and how he's going to go in for the kill."

EVERYTHING WAS ABOUT CHOICE.

Deke had to give Novus credit. James had said Novus's goal was to wear him down. And as bad as he hated to admit it, Novus was accomplishing his goal. Because right now, Deke was just about at the end of his rope.

He was tired. He was weak and nauseated from loss of blood and the fever brought on by his wound. And he hadn't slept more than an hour in the last twenty-four.

Now, he'd literally come to the end of the line. He sat on his haunches and stared at the pile of rock and broken timbers in front of him. Dark shadows danced in the lantern's light, and the burbling of the spring mocked him. Every few seconds, a silvery reflection in the water caught his eye. The little fish, battling their way through the rocks to swim downstream.

Toward Mindy.

He thought about her, back in that alcove alone where he'd left her over an hour ago. That had been a bad choice. The fact that it was the only choice didn't make it good.

And now he was staring at the result of the rumbling he'd heard, the rumbling he'd told her was thunder. He knew the cave-in he was staring at had been caused by the explosion, because here and there, wisps of smoke still rose from the debris, and the hot smell of explosive and ozone permeated the air.

He'd tried to dig through the debris in a couple of places using the crowbar, but he hadn't gotten very far. All he'd managed to do was start a couple of small rock slides and stir up a fog of hot, choking smoke and dust. He couldn't take the chance of tumbling the whole wall of rocks and timbers down on his head.

So he had no choice here, either. He had to go back.

But what was he going back to? Another dead end and the choice of lying to Mindy or telling her the truth, that they were trapped in the mine?

Because if James had blown this tunnel then he'd blown the downhill one, too. It confirmed his suspicion that James didn't have enough men to guard every exit.

One thing in their favor. Maybe.

He cupped his left hand and scooped up water to drink, then bent down and splashed some on his face. After swiping the water from his eyes, he picked up the lantern and the crowbar and turned on his heel.

MINDY JERKED AWAKE. She'd heard something.

Dear God, let it be Deke.

She winced as her little Sprout kicked her, reminding her that he'd been asleep, too.

Holding her breath, she listened. There it was again. The noise that had woken her. And this time she knew what it was.

The crunch of footsteps on dirt and gravel.

Not Deke. Her pulse skittered, stealing her breath. Deke would have already called out to her.

As quietly as she could, she scooted farther back against the farthest wall of the alcove, pulling the knife from her bra.

She stared at the dim glow that outlined the alcove's

opening, doing her best to keep her breathing steady. The knife's handle was warm from her body heat, and although she'd seen the damage it could do, right now it felt pitifully small.

Then the light at the entrance changed, brightened.

Her breath hitched. Whoever it was had a flashlight. The beam was too concentrated to be a lantern.

Just then a contraction hit her. She gasped and bit her lip, working to stay quiet.

Deke? Where are you?

The footsteps grew louder and the flashlight's beam flitted across the alcove's entrance.

Her breath caught. Had they missed it?

It snapped back.

Her mouth went dry. She drew her feet up, trying to make herself as small as possible while the flashlight penetrated the darkness in front of her.

Then the pale blue moonlight was blocked by shadows—two shadows, and the beam swept back and forth, back and forth, as it crawled toward her along the dirt floor.

It touched the toes of her shoes. The sensation was almost physical.

She couldn't get a breath. Her left hand instinctively cradled her tummy as the circle of light climbed up her leg.

It was almost a relief when the beam finally blinded her.

"Hello, Mrs. Cunningham." The voice was unmistakable. Frank James. "Shame on your husband for leaving you alone."

AN HOUR LATER, he felt cool air on his heated face. In the next instant, his eyes detected a difference in the total blackness before him.

It was the end of the tunnel. He slowed, using his instincts and his honed senses to assess any danger, before he burst out into the open.

What if Novus had blown those tunnels, not because he didn't have enough men, but to separate Deke and Mindy? If he guessed that Deke would leave Mindy to investigate the explosions, this would be the perfect time to have James capture her.

Flattening himself against the tunnel opening, he scanned the open area.

Nothing.

As much as he wanted to believe that nothing was a good thing, his natural caution told him otherwise. He longed to rush over to the alcove and take Mindy into his arms, but he had to proceed as if he were infiltrating enemy lines.

Sweat trickled down the side of his face. He wiped it away, and felt the heat radiating from his skin.

He had a fever. That meant his damn arm was infected. He laid his palm on the bandage covering his wound. Sure enough, it was hot, too. And the pressure of his hand was excruciating.

Judging by the way his head kept threatening to spin and by the blackness encroaching on his vision, he was close to passing out. He swallowed.

Damn close.

He took a deep breath and eased out into the open. Hugging the wall, he slid around to the edge of the alcove, scanning the room the whole time, alert to any slight movement or sound.

He set the lantern down and lit it awkwardly. He held it in his right hand and brandished the crowbar in his left.

His pulse drummed in his ears and his heartbeat shot sky-high. He wished it was merely the anticipation of seeing Mindy safe and sound, but he knew it was an adrenaline response, readying him to attack.

Rocking to the balls of his feet, he angled around the alcove opening.

No Mindy. Even though he'd expected it, his heart sank. She wasn't where he'd left her.

At that moment, a movement in the shadows at the back caught his eye.

"Mindy?" Even as the word formed on his lips, the shadow lunged toward him. Mindy couldn't stand up by herself, much less lunge.

He swung the crowbar with all his might, following it with the lantern. The arc of flame revealed a glimpse of a grimacing black mask of a face with bared teeth gleaming.

Then a huge weight sent him plummeting backward. His skull slammed into the dirt floor—hard. Pain blinded him. A dreadful growling filled his ears.

He tried to roll away, but the monster rolled with him, trailed by a strange orange light. He blinked. It was a man—a very big black man with his hair on fire.

The man shook his head, flinging drops of hot oil onto Deke's face, and propelled himself toward the spring. He dunked his head, frantically trying to douse the flames.

Deke retrieved his crowbar and followed him. Awkwardly, he gripped the crowbar, wishing he was left-handed, and drew his arm back.

When the man lifted his head, Deke leaped, swinging. The crowbar connected with a loud crack.

The man dropped like a stone, and Deke's momentum carried him right over him. He landed sideways on his injured arm. He clamped his jaw and hissed.

Breathing hard, he got his feet under him and crouched over the unconscious man. He patted him down and hit pay dirt. A portable Taser—dripping wet.

Deke grabbed it. Just looking at it tightened his muscles in involuntary reaction. He shook it and dried it on his pants, then examined it. He started to turn it on, but on second thought he decided to give it time to dry out.

Pocketing it, he dropped to his haunches. He needed a couple of minutes to rest before he headed back toward the hotel.

After a few deep breaths and a swallow of water, he headed across the spring. He eyed the tunnels for a moment, then turned and looked at the rusted car that held the dynamite.

A sense of inevitability settled on his shoulders. As dangerous as it was, he had to carry the old, unstable explosive back to the hotel. He had to blow the two remaining entrances to the mine. He couldn't take the chance that James might escape through them, or force Mindy back into this dark abyss.

He swayed and had to steady himself against the wall. He clenched his teeth, refusing to give in to the fever that was trying to take him down. He couldn't. He had to keep going.

This time, if he failed, Mindy would die, and so would his son.

CHAPTER NINE

THE PITCH-BLACK TUNNEL seemed endless. Deke trudged along, carefully balancing the dynamite and blasting caps in the crude sling he'd made from the musty blanket, and using the crowbar as a walking stick. It was a sobering thought that he was carrying his own mode of destruction. He was literally a walking, ticking bomb.

But the dynamite wasn't his biggest worry. His biggest worry was that he wouldn't make it. He was having a hard time putting one foot in front of the other. And he felt cold and hot at the same time.

In a part of his brain he was trying to ignore, he knew what was wrong. His arm was bleeding again. The knife wound ached with a stomach-churning pain that turned the edge of his vision black. When he'd looked at it, he'd seen the red line running up his arm. It was an artery, and it was infected. If that line got much closer to his heart, he'd be in real danger of dying.

He'd tried Mindy's home remedy for stanching the bleeding. He'd gathered up spiderwebs and pressed them into the oozing gash on his arm. Then he'd rebandaged it. Not surprisingly, they'd helped for a while. And if he'd been able to immobilize his arm, they probably would have stopped the bleeding entirely, just like Mindy had said they would.

He'd stopped trying to use his arm, working hard

to keep it still. He'd draped it over the dynamite-filled blanket, and occasionally he felt the faint tickle of a drop of blood running down his wrist to drip slowly off his fingers.

He stumbled over a rock, catching himself just in time, cringing as he had to adjust the blanket containing the dynamite. The misstep jarred his arm and turned the darkness in front of his eyes into a bright fireworks show. He ducked his head and braced himself against the wall. He needed to shut his eyes for just a few moments, until the fireworks went away.

WHEN HE OPENED his eyes again, he was crouched against the wall. He'd fallen asleep—or passed out, for no telling how long. At least the blanket was still in place, slung over his shoulder.

Breathing through his mouth, trying to settle his racing heart, he lifted his head and blinked.

Was he still woozy, or was that a real light in front of him? It didn't dance around, and it wasn't the same bright yellow as his internal fireworks show.

This light was dim and pale and vaguely rectangular. A lump of relief closed the back of his throat and stung his eyes.

It was the end of the tunnel. Where Mindy was. Just a few yards farther. He covered half the remaining distance before he had to stop.

He pressed his back to the wall and rested his head against it for a moment. With his eyes closed, he pictured the small anteroom that connected the tunnels with the hotel basement. He'd returned the way he'd gone, back through the south tunnel—had it just been yesterday?

He was less than two yards from the anteroom. He

had to work fast. He carefully placed the blanket-covered dynamite on the floor just inside the tunnel entrance. He'd already attached one of the blasting caps and a length of fuse to the sticks. So all he had to do was unroll the fuse and light it.

He started working, but he kept losing focus. What the hell was the matter with him? His legs were heavy and slow. Sweat rolled down his face, chilling his skin. He shuddered and concentrated on making it to the south wall. He slid along it, keeping to the shadows until he reached the framed doorway. Then he stopped and listened.

Nothing.

To the east was the trapdoor, and on the north wall was the massive wooden door through which James had disappeared.

Before he positioned the fuse, he had something he wanted to check out. After listening again and hearing nothing, he moved from the dirt wall to the timbers that framed the tunnel opening. He angled around quickly, sweeping the room quickly with his gaze, then ducked back behind the timbers.

He looked at the trapdoor through which he'd crawled earlier. He'd discarded it because Mindy would never be able to crawl through the small opening.

But the thing that had puzzled him ever since he first knocked on that wood still held his interest. Sixty years ago, this alcove had obviously provided a passage from the hotel and the building to the north into the mine from the two buildings. That trapdoor must have once been a full-size doorway.

Deke gripped the crowbar in his hand and examined the wooden planks carefully. Whereas the other side looked like a door, this side appeared to be a rough-hewn planked wall, except that the planks above the trapdoor looked newer than the rest.

There *was* a door there. Relief stung his throat and turned the back of his neck clammy. With the noise he was about to make, he figured he had two minutes at the most before one of James's men saw or heard him.

He attached the fuse to the dynamite and ran it along the wall to the north door. There was barely enough to reach. He didn't know much about detonation. That was Brock's specialty. But he knew that fuse burned rapidly, so he figured he had about enough to last five minutes.

Five minutes to get Mindy outside to safety. If she was in there. Through the haze in his brain, Deke tried to remember why he was sure that was where Frank was holding her. He couldn't. But it hardly mattered. It could be their only chance.

He set the end of the fuse down at the edge of the inner door, praying he'd be able to come back and light it. He patted his jeans pocket, where the disposable lighter was.

That much dynamite would blow this whole basement area to smithereens, if the fuse stayed lit.

Then he turned to the door. He had maybe three minutes before the noise of prying the planks away from the door alerted James.

Here goes. He started with the planks at knee level, just above the top of the trapdoor. The nails screeched and the wood creaked. But within thirty seconds he had two of the twelve-inch-wide planks off and had started on a third.

Sure enough, the wood behind the cross-nailed planks was just like the wood he'd kicked in to get through the trapdoor. He figured with one or two well-placed kicks he could have an opening that was thirty inches wide and about three and a half to four feet tall. Plenty of room for Mindy to get through. If he had the strength to kick the boards away.

By the time the third plank let go, he was reeling from exhaustion. Fever from loss of blood, he was sure. He gulped in a lungful of air, hoping it would fortify him for another few seconds. He reared back and kicked the door. Wood splintered loudly.

At that moment, the north door opened and two soldiers in desert camo grabbed him, jerking the crowbar out of his hands and wrenching his arms behind his back. He groaned out loud at the screaming pain in his right arm.

Somehow, the pain heightened his senses. Suddenly, he was hyperaware of everything around him. The bright light from the open door. The air that swirled about him, evaporating the sweat and cooling his skin. The loud, sawing breathing of the two guards.

They shoved him through the door into a narrow foyer. He directed all his strength toward staying aware of everything around him. There were three doors in the tiny foyer. Besides the one they'd pushed him through, there was a door to his left and one directly in front of him. He was about to find out where at least one of those doors led.

A guard pushed open the door in front of him. Across a short expanse of rough flooring, lit by a single bare bulb, he saw Mindy. Tied up and gagged.

His heart slammed against his chest with a ferocity that left him breathless.

"Mindy," he rasped. His throat closed up and his eyes

stung with relief. He hadn't let himself even think of the possibility that she wasn't behind the door. But now, seeing her, he knew he'd feared just that.

She shook her head violently. He nodded slightly, hoping to send her the message that he knew James was waiting for him. That he was prepared.

By the look in her wide, frightened eyes he knew he wasn't fooling her. With one quick glance, she saw how sick he was. How weak.

She knew that he wasn't prepared. That he wasn't even sure how much longer he could stay upright.

Her gaze dropped to his right hand and back to meet his eyes. She knew how long it had been since James had cut his arm. He could see in her eyes that she was calculating the amount of blood he'd lost and how far along the infection was. She shook her head again.

He sent her what he hoped was an encouraging smile and took a step forward.

With a *whoosh* of noise, spotlights flared, blinding him. Immediately, the sound of weapons being raised hit his ears. And slowly, as the red spots from the lights faded, the outlines of three men coalesced. They were dressed in military fatigues and boots, and were aiming their weapons at his head.

The smallest man slung his rifle over his shoulder and stepped over to Mindy's side. He extracted a 9 mm handgun from a side holster and pointed it at the side of her head.

"Nice of you to join us. What were you doing out there, tearing through the wall? Trying to get away and leave your pretty girl behind? That's cold."

Deke's gaze snapped to the speaker. The accompanying movement of his head made the edges of his vision turn dark again.

Still, there was no mistaking who the speaker was. It was Frank James—without his bandanna. No question. As he thought, the face was so close to the sketch of Novus as to almost be identical.

Deke blinked to clear his vision and studied James's face. Somehow, without the bandanna covering his lower face, his eyes seemed more pronounced.

And familiar.

"Hey, Min. You feeling better?" he said casually, inwardly wincing at the sound of his voice. It wouldn't fool an infant, much less a roomful of trained combatants.

Mindy nodded, but her face was still drawn and pale, and she looked exhausted. Worse, if he could judge by the look in her eyes, she was worried about *him*.

"She's doing just fine, Cunningham. When we found her where you'd abandoned her, she was in a lot of pain. But thanks to some friends of ours, we were able to figure out what was wrong and correct it."

Correct it? Bile churned in Deke's stomach. "I swear to God," he said hoarsely, "if you hurt her, or—"

"Calm down, Cunningham. The drug we gave her is a medication that's commonly used for preterm labor. Ask your wife."

"You've got a gun to her head. What do you think she's going to say?" He met Mindy's gaze, and saw that James was telling the truth. *If* he could still read her as well as he once could.

"You'll see that she's no longer in labor. And she's feeling fine, which is more than I can say for you right now."

Deke shook his head and concentrated on the pipsqueak's words. He was well aware of the blood slowly oozing out of his wounded arm, and the clammy sweat prickling his forehead and neck. It infuriated him that he was letting a little knife wound affect him.

"Don't worry about me," he growled.

"I'm not. Trust me." James grinned, and the thing that had been bothering Deke ever since the first time he'd seen the fake cowboy suddenly came clear.

Of course Frank James was Novus Ordo's brother. But looking at him, Deke realized something else. Those eyes had looked at him from behind the shemagh every day while he was held prisoner by Novus.

It was Novus himself who'd held the gun to Deke's head, who'd grinned at him when he'd ordered him to rise to his knees. His eyes were older and more sinister than James's, but they were the same eyes.

James nodded his head. The three guards stepped toward Deke in unison, their weapons still raised.

Deke noticed that they were—to a man—Middle Eastern in appearance. Novus's men who'd infiltrated the United States. A chill ran through him. The implications were ominous.

On a few days' notice, Novus Ordo had brought together a half dozen armed and trained zealots to carry out a plan he was creating on the fly.

At least a half dozen. Probably more.

"What do you want from me, James?"

"Okay, Cunningham. Time to do a little business."

"You've heard my offer. It hasn't changed."

"Sure. I know your offer. I let your wife—'scuse me, *ex*-wife—go, and you'll answer all my questions. And I'm sure you're telling the truth—you'll answer my questions. But all your answers will be lies." He shook his head, laughing. "Now I'm sure that you've practiced 'em until they sound just as good as the truth—even while you're being tortured."

"Nnh," Mindy moaned and struggled, and shook her head. "Nnnh—nhh."

He knew exactly what she was saying. *Tell them*. He loved her for caring whether they hurt him. But there was far more at stake here than the lives of two people.

"I'll tell you the truth," he said quietly.

Mindy couldn't take her eyes off Deke. She was so glad he was here. And so worried about him.

Spots of color stained his cheeks, standing out against his pale skin and pinched mouth. His right hand hung useless at his side, and a drop of blood shimmered on the end of one finger. Also, one end of the bandage she'd made out of his shirt dangled from the sleeve of his shearling jacket. It, too, looked soaked with blood.

Mindy's stomach churned. It had been doing flip-flops ever since the nurse had given her the injection of magnesium sulfate.

Deke must have lost at least a pint of blood, maybe more. She wondered how long the wound had been actively bleeding. She'd wrapped it as well as she could, but she'd known it would eventually come loose and separate the edges of the cut. She'd intended to be there to rewrap it.

No, truthfully, she'd hoped they would be out of here safe and sound by now, and he'd have a stitched-up arm and a course of antibiotics for the infection.

Acrid saliva filled her mouth. She swallowed and focused all her strength on not giving in to the nausea. Magnesium sulfate was excellent for slowing premature labor, but it was also excellent for causing nausea. She clenched her teeth against the queasiness, praying that she wouldn't throw up while her mouth was gagged.

At least these terrorists had a health professional in their group. Although the idea that they had soldiers and nurses and God only knew who else available inside the United States was a sobering one.

"Just let Mindy go," Deke muttered. His words sounded slurred.

Frank James laughed.

As calmly as she could, Mindy assessed their situation. Not good.

Judging by the lack of color in his face and the way he was swaying, it was a miracle that he was still upright.

A miracle and a testament to his strength of will and his determination. He needed lots of fluids, and probably a blood transfusion.

His skin looked tight and drawn across his cheekbones. His mouth was compressed into a thin line, and his nostrils and the corners of his lips were white and pinched. Sweat glistened on his forehead and neck.

Stay with me, Deke. Don't quit now, she wanted to say. But that wasn't fair. He was the strongest man she'd ever met. He would die for an innocent. She knew he'd endure anything for his son. But he'd pushed himself further than any normal human being could have. He'd pushed himself past his body's limits, and it was shutting down.

The idea that he was mortal, that there was a point beyond which even his steely resolve couldn't push, sent a soul-deep terror searing through her like a spark touching a line of gasoline. The terror manifested itself physically as paralyzing nausea.

Her throat was too dry to swallow, so she squeezed her eyes shut and waited until the red haze of intense queasiness passed.

At that instant, Sprout kicked her, as if to remind her that everything she did, everything she felt, affected him, too.

For the moment, the magsulfate had done its job. But every few moments, she felt little aftershocks of contractions.

At eight-plus months, Sprout was capable of surviving on his own. With her knowledge and experience, she'd bet money that Deke's son would be born within the next twenty-four hours.

She did not want him born in an underground mine, held hostage by terrorists. And she certainly did not want him born an orphan.

She had to come up with a plan.

"You sound sincere, Cunningham. But then you always do. Even with a gun at *your* head, you still lie."

The gun barrel pressed against Mindy's head dug into her flesh. She couldn't see James, but she could see Deke.

His pallor had taken on a gray tinge, and his eyes weren't focused on anything. He took a stumbling step forward.

A soldier stepped in front of him and swung the butt of his gun at his head. The impact sounded like a gunshot.

Deke slumped to the ground.

"No!" Mindy screamed through her gag.

"Get up!" the guard growled in a heavy accent. He raised the gun butt again.

"Stop!" she cried desperately.

"Hold it," James snapped. "Careful. He's no good to us dead. Pull his head up. I want him to see this."

The guard grabbed a handful of Deke's hair and jerked his head up.

Deke rose to his knees, swaying. He squeezed his eyes shut, then blinked several times. The guard's blow hadn't broken the skin, but he was going to have a black eye and one hell of a headache.

Don't fight them, she begged silently.

"Let's see if you can lie while there's a gun at your wife's head. Is it loaded? Is it not?" He cocked the hammer of the .45. Mindy closed her eyes.

"What do you think, Mrs. Cunningham?" He jerked the bandanna away from her mouth.

She winced, and felt Sprout move in reaction to her pain. She licked her dry, chapped lips.

He wasn't going to kill her. He couldn't. If James killed her, he'd never get anything out of Deke. Somehow, her argument didn't make her feel better, considering the gun barrel pressed to her temple.

Deke's jaw clenched and his chin ratcheted up a notch. His face was pale as death. "Wait—" he muttered.

"Deke, no," she gasped. "He won't do it. He needs me."

"You think so?" James mumbled, easing the pressure of the barrel against her temple.

Mindy held her breath.

"I don't know whether Rook is alive—"

James pushed the gun's barrel against her head again.

"I don't know," Deke said quickly, "but I know the most likely place he'd be."

"You know where he might be if he were alive, which

you don't know." James barked a short derisive laugh. "Sorry, I just don't buy it. You're not quite ready to tell the truth." He squeezed the trigger, and the hammer clicked—a hollow sound that seemed to hover in the air.

Mindy's chest was tight with tension. She struggled for breath, as Sprout moved restlessly inside her. Fine tremors rippled through her limbs.

James made a gesture that she could barely see out of the corner of her eye. Two guards rushed toward Deke and jerked him upright. He didn't speak. Mindy had no idea if it was stoicism or pain and exhaustion.

His head lolled on his neck. He could hardly stand on his own.

"All right, Cunningham. Let's see how much stamina you've got. Every hour on the hour I'm gonna stick one live round into this gun, spin the chamber and put it against your wife's head and—bam!" He grinned. "Or not. Every hour on the half hour, I'm gonna break one of your fingers. So don't count on being able to handle a weapon." He nodded to the guards.

The two men pulled Deke to his feet and began to half drag him to a door in the back of the room.

"By the way, Cunningham. There's only one thing we want to know. You lead us to Castle, and we'll make sure your wife and baby are safe."

Deke muttered a curse aimed at James.

The fake cowboy just chuckled.

Mindy hoped that in his dazed and injured state, Deke knew what she knew.

Frank James had shown his face to them. There was no way he was going to let them live.

CHAPTER TEN

THERE WAS A clock on the wall, put there on purpose, Mindy was sure, so she could watch the minute hand go around. So she could anticipate, minute by minute, second by second, the instant when the guards would break one of Deke's fingers.

Then she'd have to watch the crawling hand for another half hour as she waited for James to come in, stand in front of her and load the single bullet into the revolver. Then he'd spin the chamber, press the barrel to her head and pull the trigger.

A twinge—like a miniature contraction, tightened her abdominal muscles for an instant.

Settle down, Sprout. You stay put. Mommy needs time to figure out a way to save your daddy.

There had to be a trick to it. Didn't there? As long as Novus believed Deke had the information he needed, he wouldn't kill her. Nor would he leave her life or death—or anything else he could control—to chance. So the bullet in the spinning chamber had to be a fake.

The minute hand bumped forward. Her heart bumped against her chest. It was eleven twenty-nine. One minute until they broke Deke's finger.

She opened her mouth and screamed. She didn't know why James had removed the gag, but she was thankful that he had.

"Don't do it!" she yelled. "Stop! I'll make him talk! I swear! Just don't hurt him!"

She stopped, holding her breath, but the only thing she heard was the silence.

"Don't hurt him!" Her eyes were glued to the clock. The minute hand quivered.

"Please!" she whispered in desperation, as tears welled in her eyes.

It jerked forward. And centered on the six.

"No!" she screamed as the tears streamed down her face. "No! Please!"

The door behind her opened.

She twisted, straining to see who'd entered the room. "Who is it? Is that you, James?"

The man who called himself Frank James stepped into her field of vision. "What are you yelling about?" he asked in an impatient tone.

"Where's Deke? Is he all right? Did you—"

James held up his hand. "Slow down. Try to stay calm. Now what are you saying?"

Mindy glared at the man who held Deke's well-being and the fate of her child in his hands. "Please bring Deke back in here, or take me to him. I'll make him tell you the truth."

James assessed her. "Has he told you the truth?"

She did her best not to look away from his staring eyes, but she couldn't stop herself from blinking.

"So he has. Well, the truth is the truth, no matter who delivers it. Why don't you tell me what he told you?"

She dropped her gaze then, wondering what Deke would want her to say.

He took a step toward her. "Mrs. Cunningham?"

"He told me he doesn't know where Rook is." She looked up at the fake cowboy.

James's beady eyes studied her face for a long moment. She could see the little wheels in his little brain turning, and hear what he was thinking. He had to decide if he believed her.

She tried to keep her expression bland, even as her mind raced. Ever since James had captured her she'd known this moment would come. But she still hadn't figured out what she was going to tell him.

She knew one thing though. If she admitted to James that Deke had no idea where Rook was, then James would come to the same conclusion she had. *They'd be of no more use to him.*

Finally he spoke. "Do you believe him?"

Slowly, deliberately, she met Frank James's gaze. "No," she said.

James's eyes twinkled and his mouth twitched. For the life of her Mindy couldn't figure out if he was amused by her or pleased that he'd gotten her to tell the truth.

"Why should I believe you?"

"Men care about country. About honor. About freedom. They will die for any of those things." She took a long breath. "But I'm a woman. There are only two things I would die for," she said evenly, as she cradled her stomach. "My child and Deke. And I don't want to die."

James laughed. "Well said, Mrs. Cunningham."

"So you'll bring Deke to me?"

"I'll let you know." James turned and left through the door.

"Wait!" she cried. "You're underestimating me. I can make him tell. Please wait!"

But the door closed with an unmistakable finality. James wasn't coming back. Not anytime soon.

DEKE RAISED HIS HEAD, wondering if he'd been asleep or if he'd passed out. Either way, his head felt heavy and swollen, and his eyes stung with the clammy sweat that poured off his forehead.

For a couple of seconds, he wasn't sure where he was. He tried to lift a hand to wipe his face, and found out he couldn't. He was tied up—again.

The memories came back. He and Mindy were prisoners of a ridiculous costumed cowboy who called himself Frank James, and who so far hadn't admitted that he was working for Novus Ordo. He was, though. Deke was sure of it.

He almost laughed. Were these knots going to be as easy to undo as the others were? Not a chance. As weak and sick as he felt, he wouldn't be able to untie a birthday bow.

He was sitting in a hard wooden chair behind a desk. He looked down and saw that his left hand was tied to the chair's arm.

He glanced at his right hand, which was lashed to the opposite chair arm. It was red with blood from the slash on his forearm. He stared at the bandaged wound.

How had that happened? He had a vague recollection of a hand slashing through the air and burning pain, but that was all. No face. No name.

He did remember the bandage. It was his shirt—a brand-new white dress shirt. Mindy had torn it apart to fashion the makeshift bandage.

It had served fairly well. The material still partially covered the wound, but here and there, where the blood-soaked strips had slipped, he could see the jagged, inflamed edges of the wound.

He blinked, trying to clear the stinging sweat from his eyes, and noticed that his fingers were moving. Was he doing that? He really didn't know.

He looked up, seeking the source of light in the room. It was a lamp, with only one bare bulb in it, sitting on the scarred wooden desk. It provided very little light—just enough for him to make out what was around him.

The big desk, of course, which sat directly across the room from the door. And the lamp, an old-fashioned leather desk blotter that held a 1959 calendar from Sundance Printing Company, and a pen stand with a wooden fountain pen. There were several ink stains on the polished surface of the desk.

Heavy, dark curtains covered the windows behind him, so he assumed he was aboveground. Probably the mine foreman's office, or maybe the office of the hotel manager.

On either side of the door were ancient, dusty barrister bookcases stuffed full of old books, folders and stacks of paper. Mindy would have a fit. She loved old books.

His mouth turned up in a wry smile. Mindy. He'd have to tell her about the bookcases, once they were safe.

All at once, the significance of those last words hit him. *Once they were safe.* That meant they weren't—Mindy wasn't.

Now he remembered, and all his scattered thoughts began to coalesce. He'd come here to rescue Mindy. They'd been trapped in an abandoned mine, and Frank James had cut him with his own knife.

More memories assaulted his brain. He'd gone looking for a way out of the mine, but he'd run into a cave-in. Then when he got back to where he'd left Mindy, she was gone, captured again by Frank James.

The sound of the hammer clicking against metal rang in his ears. The sound of one more day.

No. Not one more day. One more *hour.*

He didn't have a day because within a few minutes someone was going to walk in here with a heavy hammer and smash one of his fingers.

Then a half hour after that, they were going to play Russian roulette with Mindy again.

He wished he knew how long he'd been here. If he hadn't passed out, maybe he could have figured out a plan to get out of here and save Mindy.

Mindy didn't deserve any of this. She was innocent. As innocent as a newborn baby.

Baby. Deke blinked slowly and felt himself drifting off to sleep again.

If he could just wipe his eyes. They stung and itched like fire, until he couldn't think of anything else.

He lifted his hand and rediscovered that it wouldn't lift. He wiggled his fingers, idly wondering which one they'd break first. He shuddered with anticipated pain.

It hardly mattered. He just wished they'd come and get it over with. Then he could stop worrying about it and think about rescuing Mindy.

He drummed his fingers, one at a time, on the wooden desk and sleepily chanted, "One, two, three four five. Once I caught a fish alive." He started over. "Six, seven, eight nine ten. Then I let him go again. One, two—"

He heard something and froze, with his third, fourth and fifth fingers in the air.

He didn't move for a long time, but nothing else happened. It must have been the wooden beams creaking, or a clod of dirt falling.

One, two, three four five—

He shook his head. He had to get that annoying nursery rhyme out of his head.

Maybe he should search the room for hidden cameras. He wasn't sure what good finding them would do him, but at least he'd be doing something, rather than drifting off into unconsciousness.

While they were in the air force, Matt Parker had developed a foolproof visual search grid for assessing the danger points in a specified terrain. Maybe he could use the same principle to search this room for a camera.

He quelled the voice in his head that kept trying to chant the nursery rhyme and concentrated on the grid. He was almost done when he heard the doorknob rattle.

The wooden door swung open with a loud creak.

It was Frank James. And one of the soldiers was with him. The soldier held a hammer.

"Here we are, Cunningham. Ready to make good on our promise." James grinned, showing crooked teeth. "Got anything to say? Or should we just get to it."

"By all means, go ahead," Deke said hoarsely. "I've got nothing to say."

James nodded at the other man, who stepped up to the chair. He was holding a small sledgehammer—probably six pounds. Enough to make mush out of his fingers.

The soldier took a balanced stance, then reared back

like a baseball player, holding the hammer in both hands, and prepared to swing.

Deke wanted more than anything in the world to look James in the eye as the hammer came down on his hand, but he couldn't stop himself from cringing.

He closed his eyes and clenched his jaw so he wouldn't scream.

"Wait!"

Deke jerked at the single explosive word. Sweat rolled off his forehead and into his eyes.

James had stopped the soldier.

A painful spasm of reaction shrieked through his arm, from the shoulder all the way down to his fingers.

"Sorry about that, Cunningham, I almost forgot something." James smiled. "How would you like to see your wife?"

Deke swallowed bile and opened his eyes to a slit. "What are you talking about?" he asked, his stomach churning with worry. What was James up to now?

"I'm asking you a simple question. Your wife begged me not to break your fingers. Begged me to let her see you. She said she had something to say to you."

There was no way Deke was going to trust James. "What did you do to her?" He sat up as straight as he could and clenched his teeth against the dizziness that threatened to spin his head right off.

"Do to her? Me? Nothing. I told you my plan. You know exactly what I planned to do. But Mrs. Cunningham is so sweet and lovely, I couldn't deny her request."

"Great. I want to see her, too." Deke spoke in a toneless, measured voice. He wasn't sure what James was up to, but whatever it was, he knew it was designed to get him to waver.

And it had probably been planned by Novus.

Rather than ask James more questions, Deke closed his eyes. "I'm not feeling too good, so whatever you've got planned, can you hurry up? I'm pretty sure I'm in danger of bleeding to death, and I would definitely like to see my wife before I die."

"Your ex-wife," James corrected him. He nodded at the soldier who set the sledgehammer down and left the room.

"I've got a message for you to give Novus," Deke said, as soon as the man left.

James waved a hand dismissively. "I have no idea what you're talking about, but fine. Give me the message. I'm sure it'll be funny."

"You tell Novus Ordo he made a mistake when he targeted my friends and my wife. He's dealt with me before and he knows I mean what I say. Tell him if it's the last thing I do on this earth, I'm coming to get him."

James chuckled. "That is funny. You're talking about Novus Ordo, the international terrorist? That's some imagination you've got."

James bent down until he was mere inches away from Deke's face. "Now let me give you a message. You think you're so smart? You don't know anything. Treating me like I'm nobody? You'll soon find out just who I am, and when you do, I'm going to be right here, in your face. And I'll make you sorry you didn't respect me."

Through the haze that kept drifting in front of his eyes, Deke stared at James's thin, weaselly face and dark, beady eyes.

He closed his eyes, trying to give James the impression that he was totally bored with his threat while he drew on his memory, conjuring up the likeness of Novus

Ordo that Rook had described to the facial recognition artist for the CIA.

James had to be related to Novus. Deke could believe he *was* Novus, except that Novus was too smart to place himself smack in the middle of a terrorist plot in the U.S.

He squeezed his eyes shut tighter, and a splash of reddish stars appeared before his closed eyelids. He squinted open one eye and saw that James had straightened and was watching him with a vicious hatred.

He drew a deep breath, then another, trying to ward off the loss of consciousness with an overload of oxygen. It helped a little.

The doorknob turned, and the soldier was back with Mindy in tow. Her hands were still tied behind her back.

When she saw Deke, her face turned white and she swayed. The soldier tightened his hold on her arm.

"Deke. Did he—?" Her eyes flew to his bound hands, then to his face. As soon as she looked into his eyes, she relaxed. "Oh, thank God."

James gestured to a straight-backed chair on the other side of the desk. "Here you are, Mrs. Cunningham."

"For heaven's sake, give my husband some water," Mindy cried. "He's about to pass out. He's lost too much blood. He needs fluids. Where's that nurse of yours?"

James nodded at the soldier, who turned and left the room.

"Are you okay?" Deke asked her.

"For now," she said. "The medication they gave me did stop the contractions, at least so far."

The man dressed in desert camo was back almost immediately with a big jar of water. James took it from him and held it to Deke's lips. He wasn't careful, and a lot of the liquid spilled down Deke's bare chest and torso, but Deke managed to gulp down at least a pint's worth.

He did feel better immediately. It washed the haze from his brain and the heaviness from his eyelids and limbs.

"Now that we've provided *room service,* take her and tie her to that straight-backed chair," James instructed his sidekick.

"Please don't," she begged him. "I'm so sick. If the contractions start again, I'll need to lie down. Tie my hands in front of me, but please don't tie me to that chair. If I go into labor, I have to be able to move or—" Her eyes filled with tears. "Or," she sobbed. "I'm going to lose my baby."

James rolled his eyes. "Fine. You'll have your hands tied in front and you won't be tied down. So let me save you some trouble, Mrs. Cunningham. There's no need for you to go exploring around the room. It's been completely cleaned out. There's nothing in here you can use as a weapon. Nothing that you can cut your ropes with. I'd hate for anything to happen to your kid. I've only got so much patience. If you or Cunningham try anything, I'll go back to my original plan—with one change."

He looked at Deke, then at her. "Instead of breaking his fingers, I think I'll just go ahead and cut 'em off. I've got a cigar cutter that ought to do the trick just fine."

Mindy swayed. Only the man's hand on her arm kept her from falling.

"For God's sake, James. What did you bring her here for? There's no reason she has to go through this."

"I'll let her tell you why she's here." He turned to his sidekick. "Tie her hands in front of her."

"Not tie to the chair?" the man asked in broken English.

"No." James half turned toward the door. "Goodbye, Mrs. Cunningham. I'll be looking forward to talking with you. I'll see both of you in one hour."

The door closed quietly behind them as they left.

Mindy opened her mouth to speak, but Deke shook his head.

"Wait," he mouthed.

She nodded.

Deke waited a full five minutes—probably more. He counted to sixty five times, then added another sixty for a buffer, in case he'd counted too fast.

Meeting Mindy's gaze, he motioned with his head for her to come over to his chair.

She slowly pushed herself up out of the straight-backed chair and walked over to stand in front of him.

"Lean down," he whispered.

As soon as he smelled her tangerine scent and felt her hair soft and tickly against his lips, he whispered, "I've grid-searched the room. I'm pretty sure there are no cameras, but there could be recording devices. So play along with the things I say out loud, and whisper to answer my whispers. Do you still have the knife?"

She nodded, pointing to her breasts where she'd hidden it before.

"Good girl." Then he said aloud, "Why did James say he'd let you tell me why he brought you here?"

"Deke, please," Mindy answered, as she worked to retrieve the knife with her bound hands. "I was so worried about you. I was afraid they'd broken your fingers. Tell him what he wants to know. He'll let us go."

She finally had the knife in her hands. She pushed the button that snicked the blade into place.

Deke indicated his hands with a nod. "I *was* telling the truth. Are you saying you don't believe me?"

Mindy quickly cut the ropes binding his hands to the chair. He flexed his left hand, then his right.

"How can I believe you? You've lied to me over and over again." Mindy's eyes filled with tears and she shook her head.

Deke knew she was apologizing for saying those things to him, but he also knew he deserved them. He hadn't lied overtly to her, but he'd lied by omission, time and time again.

"I'm sorry, Min. I never meant to hurt you."

She blinked and the tears fell down her cheeks.

Taking the knife, he slipped it between her hands and cut the ropes binding her.

"Deke, tell me what you know. I know you haven't been truthful with James. Why would you, after what he's done to us?"

"You think I know something about Rook? Hell, Mindy. He was my best friend, and Novus had him killed. Even if I did know anything, I wouldn't tell that slimy terrorist."

She leaned closer. "What now?" she whispered.

"Do you know what time it is?" he whispered back to her.

She looked at him in surprise. "About three-thirty. Why?"

He shook his head. He wasn't about to tell her what he had planned. "And today is Saturday?"

She nodded in answer. "But, Deke," she said out

loud, "if Novus had Rook killed, why is he doing this? Why does he think Rook might still be alive?"

"The same reason Irina couldn't give up. Because they never recovered a body. Novus must not trust his sniper's aim. Besides, don't you think if Rook were still alive, he'd have contacted Irina? Do you think he'd have let her believe he was dead all this time?"

Mindy stared at Deke. She'd never thought about that before. What if Rook were alive? "He could have been horribly wounded and didn't want her to see him. Or maybe he has amnesia."

Deke frowned at her, but made a sound like a laugh. "All right, Mindy. Back off the romancing."

But her brain was racing. If Novus's man had killed Rook, wouldn't he have known it? Wouldn't the body have surfaced eventually? "Maybe Rook *is* hiding. Maybe he's alive, but he wants Novus to think he's dead. Maybe he's out there searching for Novus."

Deke pulled his right arm into his side and sent a scowl her way. "What was in that medicine they gave you? You're getting ridiculous. Rook is dead, and Novus holding a gun to my head or yours isn't going to change that."

CHAPTER ELEVEN

"Okay, it's done. I've worked out a way to get past security and into the house. It's going to be very tricky, though, so we probably ought to use it as a last resort."

"Last resort? What good is a last resort if we don't have a first resort?"

"That's just it. I'm working on something else. It'll be much cleaner and less risky. Tomorrow is Irina's regular monthly visit to the Children's Burn Center. She never misses going when she's in town. She'll probably get one of the specialists to drive her. I'm sure that's how Cunningham told her to handle it."

"So what's your big plan?"

"Shoot the specialist—wound him—just enough to put him in the hospital for a day or two. That buys us another couple of days. If one of her employees is in the hospital, she'll be there every day."

"That's your big plan? There are holes big enough to drive a semitrailer through."

"Yeah? You have a better idea?"

The voice on the other end of the line was silent for a few seconds. "You think I've got sharpshooters sitting around waiting for something to do? Keep working on a way to get past security. That spread is huge. There's got to be a few feet that are undefended."

"What about Cunningham?"

The man on the phone cursed in Arabic. "He's still swearing that Rook is dead. Even when he's alone with his wife."

"You think Cunningham doesn't suspect that you have every corner of every room bugged? Stop fooling with them. Stop just threatening the wife. Do some real damage."

A frustrated growl echoed through the phone. "I'm not sure Elliott has the stomach for that."

He sympathized with the man on the phone. He understood family loyalty, too, all too well. But it was sounding more and more like Elliott was a coward.

"Maybe you should have somebody in there that does have the stomach."

Sudden silence crackled across the miles. He sat there, watching his hand shake. Had he gone too far? He'd just given one of the most dangerous men on the planet a surefire plan to assassinate him—or one of his teammates.

"You just deliver Irina Castle to me. I'll take care of Cunningham."

"Don't make the mistake of underestimating him. Whatever else he is, I can guarantee you he's not stupid."

"WHAT ARE WE going to do, Deke?" Mindy whispered. "He's coming back, and when he does, he's going to cut—" she shuddered as nausea swelled inside her "—cut off—" She couldn't say it. "I can't let them do that. What can you tell them that will satisfy them?"

Deke took her hand and put his lips to her ear. "Listen to me, Mindy. I swear I'd rather die myself than scare you, but you've got to understand what's going on here. There's *nothing* I can say that they'll be satisfied with. Nothing. Whatever I say, the end result is going to be the same."

Mindy's heart leapt into her throat. "End result?" she whispered brokenly. "What do you mean?"

He shook his head. "You know what I mean. Can you act like you're sleepy? We can't keep up this talking for their benefit. I've got something I need to do."

Mindy sat up straight and spoke aloud. "I guess all this is catching up to me. I'm so tired, and I'm feeling some minor contractions."

"Contractions?" Deke said. "You're not going into labor, are you?"

"The drug is still working, but I do need to rest. Do you think it's okay if I sit down in the chair and try to sleep a little?"

He nodded, then quirked his mouth. "Sure, hon," he drawled. "You've got about forty minutes to nap until they come back to cut off my finger."

Even though she knew he was talking for whoever was listening, the words still made her wince.

"Deke, I didn't—"

"Drag the chair over here," he said. "You won't be able to sleep sitting straight up in that chair. At least over here you can lean against me."

"That's very nice of you," she said stiffly. "I'll do that. And just so you know, I really don't want them to hurt you."

"Hmph. Good to know. Thanks."

She made a face at him and dragged the chair, slowly and loudly, over beside his desk chair, which was just opposite the door, and made a production of sitting down in it.

"Oh," she sighed. "I am so tired. You're sweet to let me lean on you."

Once she was settled in the chair, Deke whispered, "Did they bring you in here through that foyer?"

She nodded.

"So this room is the third door?"

"Yes, why?"

"I may have a way for us to escape."

Mindy's hand flew to her mouth. She couldn't help it. She'd tried hard not to think about their fate, but when she heard Deke's words, she realized that a large part of her had actually believed that they wouldn't live through this.

He put his hand on top of hers and shook his head. "Not foolproof. It's extremely dangerous. We could die."

And there it was. The one thing she'd counted on was Deke's strength and confidence. But if he thought they could die—

She felt the blood drain from her face, felt a hideous chill run down her spine. "Okay," she whispered.

"I'll do everything I can to make sure you're safe."

"*We're* safe."

He nodded, but he didn't look at her.

"So what do I need to do?"

"Go into labor."

A short, sharp laugh escaped her lips.

He held up a warning hand. "Mindy, you okay?" he said aloud.

"Oh," she responded. "What? I was asleep."

"You were dreaming. Go back to sleep."

"Go into labor?" she mouthed. Had she heard him right? He was whispering so softly she couldn't be sure.

He nodded. "I need a distraction so I can get the drop on them when they come into the room."

"Deke, you're injured and weak as a kitten. I doubt you could get the drop on a mouse."

His turn to make a face. "Well, I'm your only hope."

"Tell me what your plan is." She waited while he scrutinized her.

"I'm going to blow up the tunnel."

This time she clamped both hands over her mouth and stared at him over her fingers.

He put his hand over hers and held it there. "Dynamite," he mouthed.

She started to speak, but he shook his head. "Don't even ask. Just do what I say."

"But if you blow it up—" Her brain was filled with visions of smoke and rocks and dirt and body parts.

"And don't tell me you can't run. When I say run, you run. Your job is to save your—our—Sprout there."

Her hands flew to her tummy.

"They'll be in any minute." He scooped up the cut ropes they'd used to bind her hands. "Sit. Put your hands in your lap."

She did as he instructed, and within a few seconds he had the ropes arranged so she looked like she was still tied up.

Then he leaned back down and whispered in her ear. "There. That'll fool them on first glance. Once I take them down, we'll have about thirty seconds. Now, start faking labor."

She turned her head until her mouth was next to his ear. As much as she wanted to lay her cheek against his, just for a second, she knew she had to stay strong. "What are you going to do?"

"Hide behind the door."

"And do what? Slam it on them?"

Deke shook his head. "I've got the knife and a Taser. As soon as I take them down, you run out the south door into the foyer. I pried some boards off the trap door before they heard me and stopped me. Then get up the stairs and out. Remember what I said about my car?"

She nodded, feeling stunned. As far as she was concerned, he was telling her a fairy tale. There was no way she could climb through the trap door, run up the basement stairs and out to his car—not in her condition. But she'd try. She'd die trying, if that was her only chance.

As long as Deke didn't give up, she wasn't going to.

"Remember what I told you? If Irina's men aren't there yet, there's a cell phone under the driver's seat with the keys. Press Call for Irina's number, then turn the car around and drive away from the house as fast as you can."

"What about you?"

"I can take care of myself." Deke turned and placed himself behind the door, so that when it swung open, he'd be in the perfect position to get the drop on their attackers. He held the portable Taser in his weaker right hand and the knife in his left.

As she watched, he adjusted the dial on the Taser down and held it against his hand. He hit the switch. His fingers contracted.

He looked up with a small smile on his face. "It works."

She gave him a thumbs-up.

He twisted the dial up to maximum, then paused and sighed. He raised his gaze. "Mindy—" His whisper carried across the distance between them. "Don't—give up on me, okay?"

Her eyes filled with tears that spilled down her cheeks. "I never have. I never would," she whispered.

"Okay, ready?" he asked.

"Should I talk out loud?"

He shrugged. "Whatever you think will convince them."

Mindy started moaning, as if in her sleep.

Deke stood behind the door, balanced on the balls of his feet in attack mode. He watched Mindy in admiration. She scrunched her face up, as if in pain, and began blowing air out through her mouth. She was acting just like she had when she'd gone into premature labor down in the mine.

A chill slid down his spine. What if she really went into labor? He had no idea what a woman in labor could or couldn't do, but he was pretty sure climbing stairs and running was way down on the list.

She groaned louder and started pushing air through her mouth in little bursts.

Deke waited. He wished he knew what time it was, and how long it would be before James burst in. He normally had a good sense of time, but there were too many factors working against him here.

He was weak and shaky from blood loss and infection, and for the first time in his life he was questioning his own judgment. He had no idea whether he could hold his own against James and his soldiers.

And then there was Mindy. He looked over at her. Her hair was tangled and stringy. Her eyes had deep shadows underneath them. The skin of her face was tight and drawn across her cheekbones. She was still the most beautiful thing he'd ever laid eyes on.

She was as brave as any soldier he'd fought alongside,

but bravery alone didn't win battles. He knew she would push to the ends of her endurance to save the baby she cradled within her, but he was desperately afraid that wouldn't be enough. And he was terrified that he was asking too much of her.

He wasn't sure if he could survive if something happened to her or to his son.

His son. He had a son to fight for. A piece of him. His own flesh and blood.

He straightened his back and tightened his fists around the Taser and the knife. He had one chance to prove himself worthy of being a father. He would win, or he'd go down fighting for his wife and child.

"Deke? I'm getting worried. My contractions are getting stronger." She spoke aloud.

"Try to hang in there. Do you need to lie down?"

"I—may in a few—minutes," she gasped.

"Hey! James!" he shouted at the ceiling. "My wife's in labor. Help!"

He rocked up to the balls of his feet and readied himself. He knew James wouldn't come in here alone, and he fully expected that he and whoever came with him would be armed.

Glancing over at Mindy as she simulated the sounds and actions of a woman in labor, he saw his fear reflected in her eyes. He quirked his mouth in a smile, hoping to reassure her.

She wasn't fooled.

Then he heard footsteps outside the door. He caught her gaze and gestured toward the door with his head. "Here they are," he mouthed. He tensed, ready to spring—not on the first man. That would be suicide.

He had to wait for the second, and hope there were only two.

The door slammed open and he flattened himself against the wall so it wouldn't hit him. Frank James walked in, followed by a soldier with a rifle cradled casually in his arms. The soldier had barely cleared the edge of the door by the time James realized that Deke wasn't in the desk chair.

"What's going on—?" he started.

The soldier reacted almost as fast. He raised the rifle.

As he did, Deke reached out and looped his left arm through the rifle's sling and jerked as hard as he could. He jabbed the Taser into the soldier's solar plexus and zapped him with a whopping dose of electric current.

The soldier shrieked and collapsed.

Deke jerked the rifle out of the soldier's limp hands and, in a single sweeping motion, swung it in an arc, slamming the butt into James's shoulder and knocking him aside.

He saw the flash of silver as James tumbled and immediately righted himself. He held a revolver.

"Get out, Mindy!" he yelled, as he lunged toward the gun. If James was still playing his game of Russian roulette, Deke might be able to overpower the fake cowboy before he could fire enough times to get to the live round. Or he might go down on the first pull of the trigger.

"Deke!" Mindy cried.

"Go, damn it."

He couldn't afford two seconds to turn his head and make sure she made it safely out the door. He got a good grip on the rifle and pushed the barrel into James's chest.

"I'll blow your heart right out of your chest, you sadistic bastard."

James's eyes widened in terror, but his shaky hand pulled the trigger on the revolver.

Even as Deke cringed, waiting for the hollow click of the hammer or the impact of the bullet, he bent down and Tasered James in the neck. As the hammer clicked impotently, James's body arched then went limp.

Deke grabbed the revolver.

He whirled and headed toward the door. As he stepped over the soldier, the man reached out and grabbed his boot.

He almost stumbled, but recovered himself and kicked backward, dislodging the soldier's hand.

Damn, with the dose of current he'd used, he'd have thought both of them would have been out of commission for several minutes at least.

The soldier tried to push himself up, but his arms collapsed. He screamed in a language Deke didn't understand, but the meaning was clear.

He was calling for help. Any second now, his buddies would burst in.

Deke had to get out of there.

He zapped the soldier again, but from the sound and the soldier's diminished reaction, he knew the Taser was almost out of juice. So he rammed the butt of the rifle into the man's head. At this point Deke didn't care whether any of them survived or not. They were terrorists. Enemies of the United States. And they'd tried to hurt Mindy.

Still carrying both the revolver and the automatic rifle, Deke rushed through the door.

He didn't see Mindy anywhere. "Mindy!" he called.

Nothing. Dear God, he hoped she'd gotten out and up the stairs. "Min!" he yelled. "Run!"

He slammed the door into the foyer, wishing he had something to block it with. But there was no time for wishes.

He ran to the abandoned tunnel, carefully scooped up a double handful of blasting caps and slid them across the dirt floor to the foyer door. He ducked back into the tunnel as they clattered against the door. None of them went off from the impact.

Leaning back against the wall, he gulped in a huge breath, hoping it would clear his head. His arm burned, and he felt so sleepy. If he could just close his eyes for a couple of minutes…

No! Closing his eyes was giving up. Whatever strength he had left in him would go to making sure Mindy got to safety. He hadn't told her, but he was afraid Frank's men might have found his car, or that Irina might not have been able to zero in on his shoulder chip.

That car was her only chance. He needed her to trust that it was safe.

Digging in his pocket, he pulled out the disposable lighter and flicked it with his thumb. Spark but no flame.

Not now! He flicked it again, and again. *Light, damn it! I did not use all the butane!*

Finally a weak flame appeared. He paused. Had Mindy made it out of the building?

Please, God.

He waited a few more seconds—as long as he dared, before lighting the fuse, holding his breath with apprehension until it caught.

Then he rushed for the trapdoor.

Shouts and thundering footsteps filled his ears. He dove through the opening into the hotel's basement and right into the path of two soldiers careering down the stairs.

One of them grabbed him by the collar, and the other pointed a combat rifle at him and shouted something in a foreign language.

Deke raised his hands. The soldier holding his collar kicked him behind the knees and he fell to the ground.

"Dynamite!" he yelled. "Back there."

Whoever was in the foyer was banging on the door, trying to get through.

The soldier holding him yelled a warning at him and prodded his back with the rifle.

Deke didn't have to know the language to understand what the guy was saying.

Shut up or die.

"Back there!" he shouted again. "Boom boom!" Wasn't *boom* the same in every language?

The sound of splintering wood told him that the soldiers had broken through the door to the foyer. He held his breath, and squeezed his eyes shut, trying not to think about what all those blasting caps would do when stepped on.

Sure enough, explosions like the sounds of giant firecrackers filled the air, followed by screams and shouts and the smell of gunpowder and burned metal.

In the next second, the hand on his collar let go, and both soldiers hit the ground.

Deke used their surprise and fear to push himself forward, toward the stairs. The dynamite was going to blow soon. He had to get out. If one of the soldiers recovered his wits and shot him, then so be it.

At least he'd die believing that Mindy had made it to safety.

He hit the stairs running, but with every step he climbed, his legs got heavier and slower.

A soldier yelled, and Deke instinctively flattened himself against the stairs. A bullet took a huge chunk out of the step near his head. He knew the man's next shot would be on target.

"Boom!" he yelled desperately. "Much more booms! Run!" Enveloped in a haze of drowsiness, he pulled together the last frayed threads of his strength and threw himself up the remaining steps.

A volley of bullets followed him. He stumbled through the door and spotted a patch of sunlight to his left. Was that the back door he'd told Mindy to look for? Or was just the flashing lights in his head signaling that he was about to pass out?

Didn't matter. Whatever the light was, it was his only hope for survival, because he heard heavy footsteps on the stairs behind him.

He staggered toward the light, noticing that it got brighter and dimmer at the same time. He shook his head, hoping he wasn't hallucinating, and grabbed at what looked like a door facing.

The light was bright and hot. And out in the distance, he saw two large uniformed men with a small figure in tow.

Mindy! They'd captured her.

He propelled himself forward just as a huge rumbling noise rose behind him and a blast of hot air slammed against his back, burning his skin.

It was over.

Tell Mindy I'm sorry.

CHAPTER TWELVE

"MINDY, I'M SORRY," Deke whispered brokenly through lips that wouldn't move. His mouth felt stuffed with cotton, and his head felt like it was made of lead. Helpless tears filled his eyes.

He hadn't wanted it to end like this. He would have gladly given his life for Mindy and their baby, but he had hoped he could have seen his son before he died.

"Mr. Cunningham?" A voice he didn't recognize was speaking very close to his ear. "Mr. Cunningham, are you awake? You need to wake up."

He wanted to swat at the annoying voice and sink back into oblivion, but he couldn't move his arm.

"We can't let you leave recovery until you wake up. Can you talk to me?"

Whoever was bothering him wasn't going to give up. He opened bleary eyes and then closed them immediately. The light was too bright. "Where's Mindy?"

"Mr. Cunningham, I need you to talk to *me*."

"Leave me alone."

He heard a soft chuckle. "Well, that's something, I guess. Now open your eyes. Do you know where you are?"

Deke growled under his breath. If he couldn't see Mindy, he wanted to be left alone. He felt helpless—and feeling helpless pissed him off.

"In hell?" he muttered.

Another chuckle. "Not quite. You're in the recovery room, but now that I've got your attention, I'll make arrangements for you to be taken to your room. See this?"

He forced his eyes open and saw a blue plastic container that looked like it was made to hold a kidney. "I'm setting it right here beside you. If you feel sick, use it."

Whatever the woman was talking about, it didn't interest Deke in the least. All he cared about was finding Mindy. He sat up—or tried to. As soon as he raised his head, his vision went black.

Mindy! he screamed, but nobody answered.

DEKE OPENED HIS EYES. The last thing he remembered was the blast of exploding dynamite against his back.

No. There was something else he remembered—an annoying voice, but he couldn't place it.

He took a careful breath and was surprised at what he smelled. No heat, no burning cloth or wood—or flesh.

He smelled bleach, and something fresh and medicinal. He opened his eyes to a narrow slit. Everything was a muted green color.

Hospital! He was in a hospital. Suddenly he was wide-awake. That meant he hadn't been blown up when the dynamite exploded. And that meant—

Did that mean that Mindy was all right? And the baby?

He looked at himself. His left arm was bandaged from elbow to wrist. There was a blood pressure cuff on his right upper arm and a needle sticking out of his wrist.

But not for long. He'd put in an IV port before, in the field. He could take one out.

And he did, with a little difficulty, hampered by the bandage on his right arm. The stick point bled a little, but he'd seen worse. Hell, he'd bled worse.

He slipped his arm out of the blood pressure cuff and sat up on the side of the bed—and discovered he had nothing on but the flimsy, open-backed hospital gown. He stood slowly, careful to give himself time to make sure his head was clear, then checked the closet and drawers. His clothes weren't there—not surprising. They'd been tattered and filthy. With a little digging, he found a set of scrubs—probably for him to wear when they discharged him.

He yanked off the gown and pulled on the scrub pants, stopping a time or two when his head began to spin.

By the time he got the pants on and the drawstring tied he was out of breath again. He took a long drink from a plastic water jug, letting a little of it drizzle down over his neck and chest. After rubbing it into his skin, he poured some in his hand and splashed his face.

Fortified by the water, he left his hospital room and headed down the hall to the nurse's station.

By the time he got there he was out of breath.

The ward clerk looked up from the orders she was transcribing. "Yes?" she said. "What room?"

"Where's my wife?" he demanded.

The clerk sighed. "What's your name and date of birth, please?"

"My room's right back there."

The clerk glanced past him. Deke turned and saw a security officer coming toward him.

"Take me to Mindy Cunningham," he demanded.

"Now Mr. Cunningham, I've been directed to see that you stay in your room. We need to make sure—"

"I need to make sure my *wife* is all right. Take me to her."

The guard held up his hands. "Now settle down—"

"No, you settle!" Deke's head was spinning again, but he took a step forward and got in the guard's face. "My wife was in labor. She'd better be here somewhere." He lowered his head and glared at the security guard from under his brows. "Take me to her—now!"

The guard nodded past him at the ward clerk.

The clerk typed a few keystrokes on a computer. "Room 410," she said.

"Where are the elevators?" Deke put a hand out to the wall to steady himself.

"Hold it. The only way you're going to leave this floor is in a wheelchair pushed by me. I have my orders."

"From who?"

The guard gestured at a nurse, who pushed a wheelchair up behind Deke. The guard put a hand on Deke's chest. Deke sank into the chair without a protest.

"From Irina Castle."

That shut Deke up for a few seconds. As the guard pushed him into the elevator, he finally found his voice. "Irina told you to make me use a wheelchair?" he asked suspiciously.

The security guard didn't answer him directly. He leaned forward and punched the button labeled 4. "She warned me that you'd be stubborn and difficult."

Deke watched the display as it showed 2, then 3 and finally 4. "Here we are."

"Stay put. You don't get to walk."

As the guard pushed Deke out onto the fourth floor, he realized it was the maternity ward. The sight of yellow ducks and pink and blue elephants on the walls and the smell of baby powder rendered him speechless and paralyzed with fear.

Had Mindy had her baby? His baby?

Their baby?

The halls were filled with hospital employees dressed in pink and yellow and blue printed scrubs, carrying stacks of snowy-white linens, armfuls of tubing, pushing medication carts—he even saw one carrying an infant.

Then he saw the rooms and the numbers on the doors.

"Stop!"

The guard kept pushing the chair.

"Stop!" Deke put his bare foot out to try and stop the chair. He groped along the side until he found the lever that threw the brake.

"Hey!" the guard said.

"There's room 410," Deke snapped.

"Right. That's where we're headed."

Deke turned his head and looked up at the guard from under his brows. "I'm not going in there in a wheelchair. She will *not* see me in a wheelchair, do you understand?"

He saw the guard's Adam's apple bob as he swallowed. "Yes."

Deke stood. He had on nothing but green cotton pants and a bandage on his right arm, but at least he was standing on his own two feet.

It took him a couple of seconds to be sure he was steady enough to walk. The guard reached out a hand, but he shook his head.

A nurse walked up. "Are you Mr. Cunningham?" she asked.

He nodded. "Is my— Is Mindy—?"

The nurse smiled. "She just got back to her room."

"And the—"

"The baby is just fine. We'll be bringing him to her in a few minutes."

Deke's throat closed up.

The nurse patted his arm. "You can go on in."

He nodded.

The guard clasped him on the shoulder. "Congratulations, son."

Deke frowned at him for a second, then nodded. He waited until the nurse and the guard left before he stepped up to the closed door.

He put out his hand, but stopped short of pushing the door open. It wasn't fair to her to barge in on her without her permission.

Nothing had changed. Not really.

Mindy had never deserved what he'd put her through. His life was and always had been a train wreck, and she'd been dragged along with him for far too long.

She deserved to have the safe, normal life she'd always wanted.

He drew his hand back and wiped his face. One thing had changed. Him. At least now he could see how bad he was for her. What kind of danger she was in because of him.

Hell, if he had any courage at all, he'd turn and walk away.

THE OBSTETRICIAN HAD been very clear.

Relax! I want you to sleep at least twelve hours a day if not more. Every time your baby sleeps, you sleep.

Easy for you to say, she'd responded. She was too tired—and too tense to sleep. After three days of unrelenting fear and tension as she and Deke ran from terrorists, she'd barely had enough strength to assist in her Sprout's birth.

The doctor had threatened several times to do a Caesarian, but she'd refused every time.

"I'm fine," she'd puffed in the middle of her contractions. "I want to have him naturally. I want to see him the very instant he comes out, and I cannot be confined to bed."

The doctor hadn't been happy, but Mindy had won. She'd told the doctor the truth, but not the whole truth. There was no way she'd let the doctor cut on her because as soon as she was able, she was going to find Deke.

In fact, she was just about to get up now. She took a deep breath that turned into a jaw-cracking yawn. She closed her eyes. After a couple of minutes of rest, she was definitely going to go searching for Deke.

The last glimpse she'd had of him was when he'd stumbled out the back door of the old hotel. In the very next instant, he'd disappeared in a cloud of black smoke as the building behind him had exploded.

She'd screamed and tried to run toward the burning building, but men in black secret service jackets had forced her into their SUV and rushed her with sirens wailing to Crook County Hospital's Maternity Ward. She'd screamed in protest until one of them made a call and verified for her that Deke was alive and on the way to the same hospital.

By the time Sprout had made his appearance, Mindy had made such a pest of herself that one of the labor and delivery nurses had checked with hospital admissions and found that he'd been admitted and rushed into surgery.

And that was all she'd been able to find out. Everyone seemed much more concerned with her resting and getting plenty of IV fluids.

She knew the nurses were going to be bringing little Sprout in to her within the hour, and her arms and heart ached to hold him. But she *knew* her baby was fine. She'd seen him briefly, and the doctor had reassured her that he had all the requisite fingers and toes.

She had no idea how Deke was. She had to find out if he was all right.

Dear God, please let him be all right. Let him be whole and well. And don't scar him any more than you have to, God.

Tears seeped out from underneath her closed lids. She knew scars wouldn't matter to him. She could hear him now. He'd say that the scars on the outside were a good match for the scars inside.

He'd endured so much. Been through so many trials, and kept his sanity and his goodness. If anybody in the world had earned the right to be happy, he had.

But his childhood had left such a mark on him. He was so afraid that he wasn't worthy of being a father. So afraid of being like his own father.

She wished she could convince him that he was nothing like Jim Cunningham. Deke's father had been a sick, lonely old man who'd wallowed in his own misery. He might have been a good man once, but he'd let drink and bitterness overwhelm him until he was consumed by self-hatred.

Deke had never let anything—not alcohol, not torture, not even heartbreak, overwhelm him. His innate goodness, combined with the love and trust of his friends, had kept him from veering onto the path his father had taken.

She just wished he believed in himself as much as

everyone believed in him. Deke was a hero. He just
didn't know it.

Mindy let her head recline back on the pillow, not
caring that tears slid down her cheeks and neck. She'd
never been able to break through the armor he'd built
around his heart. Never been able to convince him of
the kind of man he was. What made her think that she
could now? It broke her heart that he might never accept
that he deserved to be a part of his son's life or, more
important, how much his son needed and deserved to
have him as a father.

"You're a hero, Deke. Your son needs you, and so
do I."

The door to her room eased open with a small
squeak.

It was the nurse bringing her baby. Mindy smiled
and pushed herself up in the bed.

"Come in," she called. "I've been wait—"

The hand that grasped the edge of the door was not a
nurse's hand. It was big and long-fingered, with ragged
nails, scraped knuckles and specks of dried blood coat-
ing its back.

Mindy couldn't breathe as the door swung open and
Deke stepped into the room.

He had on nothing but green scrub pants that hung
low on his lean hips. His right arm was bandaged and
the cut on his forehead was striped with sterile strips.
His torso was an abstract painting in blues and purples
and greens.

He looked exhausted and sick and scared. His blue
eyes glittered in contrast to his pale face.

To Mindy, he'd always been larger than life. At over
six feet, he towered over her five feet seven inches. But

the physical difference between them had paled in comparison to his *presence*.

Now, however, standing half-naked in front of her, with all his hurts exposed, he seemed smaller, thinner. He looked human and breakable.

And she loved him so much that the mere sight of him stole her breath and hurt her heart.

She held out her hand. "Deke."

Deke stared at Mindy, unable to move. Hardly able to breathe. To his hazy brain, she looked like an angel, lying in the glow of the dim light that shone down from over the head of her bed. Her hair lay against the pale green sheets like dark angel wings.

He swallowed. "Can I—come in?" he said hoarsely.

She stared at him for a few seconds. Then her tongue flicked out to moisten her lips and his heart skipped a beat.

She nodded, still holding out her hand.

He stepped over to the side of the bed and took her hand in his. This close he could see the purple shadows under her eyes and the drawn translucence of her skin.

"Where's Sprout? I mean, have you—?"

She nodded. "They'll be bringing him in here in a few minutes."

A hot flash of pure panic ripped through him. "I should go."

Mindy's hand tightened on his. "Oh, no, you don't," she said. "You're not getting away that easily. Sit down here and tell me what happened."

He nodded. Sitting down would be a good idea right now. He gingerly perched on the edge of the bed, wincing as the movement made his bandaged arm ache.

"How's your arm?"

"I think it's going to be okay. I was supposed to wait for the doctor to come talk to me, but I needed to find you."

Mindy's eyes turned bright with tears. "That's funny. I was just about to go looking for you," she whispered. Her fingers slid back and forth across his knuckles. "The hotel blew up."

"Dynamite."

"What about James, and—?"

He shook his head, his lips flattened into a straight grim line. "I don't know."

Her hand squeezed his. "It had to be done, Deke."

"I know." He looked down at their hands. "Min, I'm glad you're okay. You and the baby." He paused, almost overwhelmed by all the emotions swirling through him. Love, fear, relief, sadness. "Really glad."

"I'm glad you're okay, too. I was so afraid—"

He nodded. "Do you remember how we got to the hospital?"

"Your car was surrounded by black SUVs when I got outside. I was terrified, but the men said they were Secret Service. I had no choice but to believe them. I got the feeling they would have gotten me into one of the vehicles one way or another."

"Secret Service. Aaron must have given them my location. Or maybe Rafe tracked me by the chip." He rubbed his shoulder.

"Chip?" Mindy's eyes widened. "You told me—"

A sharp rap at the door made them both jump.

"Hi, Mindy," a cheerful voice said. "You've got a little visitor." The overhead light came on, chasing every last shadow from the room.

Deke's chest tightened. He had an overwhelming desire to bolt; to run as fast as he could somewhere—anywhere—as long as it was far away from the tiny baby that he was about to see.

He vaulted to his feet and backed away from the bed.

"Oh, hello," the nurse said. "You must be Mr. Cunningham. Congratulations."

All Deke could manage was a brief nod. He was too busy staring at the tiny baby the nurse was placing in Mindy's arms.

How could such a little thing cause so much of a stir? The whole room was alive with its presence. Mindy was glowing like a real angel. Her face was filled with a love and serenity he'd never seen before. He almost had to turn away from her beauty and happiness.

The nurse glanced from Deke to Mindy. She cleared her throat. "Well, why don't I come back in about a half hour? I can help you get started nursing him." She backed out of the room, turning off the glaring overhead light as she left.

Mindy smiled at her little Sprout. She'd held him for a few minutes in the delivery room, but there had been doctors and nurses all around, rattling instruments, cleaning and talking, and obviously impatient to clear the room and bring in the next delivery.

Now it was just him and her—and Deke. She touched the little nose, the impossibly soft cheek. She held a finger for him to wrap his tiny fist around.

"Deke, look at his little fingernails." She kissed his fingers and rubbed her nose on his brand-new little arm. "He's so soft. So perfect."

She looked up at her ex-husband, and her heart twisted painfully in her chest. He'd been pale before, but now he looked positively ashen. If this were a sitcom, the audience would be laughing, she thought. But it wasn't a sitcom. This was real life, and Deke Cunningham had finally met his match.

"Come look at him," she coaxed, sending him a smile.

But he seemed to be frozen in place. His throat moved as he swallowed. His eyes looked huge and terrified.

Just moments before, Mindy had been worried about how he would react to their baby. But now that he was standing here in front of her, enveloped in paralyzing fear that not even the threat of death—not even the threat of *her* death—had raised in him, she was furious.

"Is this it, then?" she whispered fiercely, trying not to disturb the baby. "With everything that you've faced, the great, brave Deke Cunningham is going to be taken down by a six-pound newborn?"

She pressed her cheek against the top of her son's head for an instant, reassuring him.

Deke didn't move. He just stared at her.

"You're a coward. If you don't know by now what a wonderful father you'd make, then maybe you don't deserve him. Look at him. How could a bad person produce such a beautiful baby?"

"My father—" he started, but she cut him off.

"You know what? I know your dad hurt you, physically and emotionally. But my guess is he did the best he could. He just wasn't as strong as you. Maybe you got your strength from your mother. Or maybe something broke inside him." She took a shaky breath to try and calm her racing heart.

"I'm not excusing him, but maybe he couldn't handle life alone after your mother left. I don't know. What

I do know is you are not your father. You are a hero, and the bravest man I've ever known. But if you can't face fatherhood, then I guess you're not as brave as I thought you were."

Had she gone too far? Too late now. She lifted her chin and met Deke's gaze. He either believed in himself or he didn't. The next few seconds might decide the rest of their lives.

He swallowed again and glanced down at the baby cradled in her arms, then looked back up to meet her gaze. "What—what do I do?"

"Come over here and sit down." Her scalp burned with relief, and her hands shook. But she wasn't about to show him how worried she'd been that he'd turn and bolt. She sat up a little straighter.

Deke looked like he was taking the last two steps to the gallows. But he finally sat down on the edge of the bed.

"Here," she said. "Take him in your left arm. Tuck his head right in the bend of your elbow."

Deke took the baby in the crook of his arm. His head was bowed and his hair covered his face. All she could tell was that he was looking at their son.

"He's little," he whispered.

"Thank goodness," Mindy said.

She heard him chuckle. Then he bent his head and pressed a kiss to his son's temple.

"You're almost as beautiful as your mother," he whispered. "I love you, Sprout."

Mindy's heart melted. He'd told his son he loved him, and the hitch in his voice let Mindy know that he'd never meant anything so much in his life.

He was going to be okay.

She watched him staring at his son. She could make it without Deke now. Now that she knew there was one person who'd broken through the wall around his heart. Knowing how much he loved their son was enough—almost.

LESS THAN TWELVE hours later, Deke sat in a borrowed conference room at the hospital, facing Mike Taylor, the new Secret Service agent in charge of the security detail assigned to Castle Ranch. He'd arrived just after Aimee Vick's baby was kidnapped.

He'd tried his damnedest to get discharged, but the nurses had told him he couldn't leave for another twenty-four hours.

In the chair next to Deke, looking as if she'd seen a ghost, sat Irina. On her left was Brock O'Neill. His carefully stiff demeanor, combined with the Bluetooth device in his ear, made him look more like a Secret Service agent than the casually dressed Taylor. On the other hand, the black patch over one eye made him look like a pirate.

But it was Taylor who had just dropped the bombshell. He'd just told Deke in his soft, careful voice that someone had tried to kill Irina.

"Tried?" Deke echoed. He reached out and touched Irina's arm. "Are you okay?" he asked her while at the same time looking over her shoulder at Brock O'Neill.

She nodded, but he could feel the fine tremors that shook her body.

Brock's black gaze flickered. He had something to say, and he wanted to say it to Deke alone.

"What happened—and when?"

"I'm okay," she said quietly. "As soon as I heard

that they'd found you and Mindy, I wanted to come and see you—"

"Thirty-five minutes ago," Taylor said. "Bastard was bold enough. It happened in the parking lot of the hospital."

Deke sat up, cradling his bandaged arm. "Here? I didn't hear anything."

"You wouldn't. Nobody did. It was a sniper, from who knows how far away. I've got men out searching for his nest, but—" Taylor shook his head.

Deke understood perfectly. He knew the range of the weapons he'd shot, and it was expansive. "Can you estimate the trajectory? The height? I can help—"

"Deke," Irina said, laying a hand on his left arm. "That's not all."

Her voice was tight. He met her gaze and saw tears.

"What? Who was shot?"

She shook her head. "Brock tried to talk me out of coming, but Rafe told me he'd come with me. So Brock told Rafe and Aaron both to bring me."

Deke met Brock's gaze again and knew he'd been right to trust the ex-navy SEAL. Brock knew what Deke knew. Either Aaron or Rafe was Novus's mole.

"What happened?" He directed that question at Mike.

"Rafiq Jackson was shot. The shooter got off three rounds, then disappeared. Got Jackson in the meaty part of his thigh. Missed the artery. Damn lucky."

Damn good shot, Deke thought. "What about Aaron?" he asked.

"Narrow miss. The bullet grazed the skin right behind his temple. Both Gold and Jackson handled things well. The third round ricocheted off the top of Mrs. Castle's car. Your specialists both stated that a fifth of a second sooner and she'd have been hit between the eyes." Mike sent Irina a quick apologetic glance. "Sorry, Mrs. Castle."

She shook her head.

"Where's Rafe? And Aaron?"

"Jackson was rushed right up to surgery. Gold is in the emergency room. I'm about to go down there and debrief him."

Deke looked at Irina. "Would you like to go see Mindy and the baby for a few minutes?"

Irina's eyes darkened and she started to say something. But within a split second, she changed her mind and decided to do what Deke asked.

"I'll talk to you later," she said pointedly.

Deke nodded, suppressing a small smile. She was as gutsy as she'd always been.

He waited until she was out of the room

"What the hell?" he asked Brock. "Which one?"

Taylor stayed quiet, but he was all ears.

Brock shook his head a fraction of an inch in each direction. "They're both spooked. Jackson was sure his femoral artery had been sliced. Gold knows he was about two millimeters from being toast."

"I know there are some sharpshooters out there, but you think those two shots were on target?"

Brock snorted.

Deke sent the Secret Service agent a sidelong glance.

"What?" Taylor demanded.

"This man could have nicked Jackson's femoral and given Gold a pierced ear," Brock said.

Taylor's mouth turned up slightly. "I heard you were good, Cunningham. I get the message. How do you want to handle it?"

"How many men can you put on my specialists while they're here at the hospital?" Deke asked.

Mike opened his mouth, but he waved his hand. "Figure it out, and figure out how many more you can place on the ranch. Novus is getting desperate and careless. He's failed twice—first Matt and now me. This sniper attack is showing us that he's willing to go to any lengths to get Irina." Deke paused. He didn't want to say anything more out loud. There was no telling who might be listening.

"Get Irina back to the ranch, and put every man you've got available on security. I'll be out to talk to you later today."

Taylor shifted uncomfortably. "I say we take Mrs. Castle to Washington, where we can ensure her safety."

Brock folded his arms across his chest.

Deke shook his head. "We'll lose Novus if we do that. She's got to be here."

"You're using her as *bait?*"

Deke couldn't explain the real reason he needed to keep Irina close. So he nodded. "Find where the sniper's nest was. As soon as I get out of here I want to see it. I might be able to tell you who it was."

He turned to Brock. "Will you wait here until Rafe's out of surgery?"

Brock nodded and left the room.

Taylor watched him until the door closed behind him, then he turned to Deke. "I'd sure like to know why you're able to command this much manpower from this high up in the government."

Deke didn't acknowledge his question. "Don't let Irina out of your sight, please. And I mean *your* sight, until she's safely back at the ranch. I'll be out of here this afternoon. I'll want to talk to you after dark."

Taylor gave Deke a brief nod and left the room.

Deke looked around the room. On a side table in the far corner of the large room was a telephone. For an instant, Deke considered using it. But it would be too dangerous.

He left the conference room and stepped over to a receptionist's desk. "Are there still pay phones anywhere around here?"

The young woman looked up and smiled. "Yes, sir," she said. "In the elevator lobby." She nodded toward her right.

The telephone kiosks were hardly private, but that was okay. All he was going to do was listen. He entered a memorized phone card number, then entered the number he wanted to call.

After six rings, he heard a click.

One message.

Deke's heart rate sped up. He entered a six-digit PIN. After a few more clicks, he heard the message.

He pushed his breath out in a huge whooshing sigh. Then he entered the code for Repeat and listened again.

Then pressed Delete and hung up.

For a second, he closed his eyes and leaned against the tiny metal frame around the phone. Then he wiped a hand down his face and punched the elevator call button.

Irina was coming out of Mindy's room when he got there. She had tears in her eyes.

"You are so blessed," she said, her voice a mixture of joy and tears. "Don't you dare mess this up."

He pulled back, not wanting to look her in the eye,

but knowing she'd be suspicious if he didn't. "Yes, ma'am." He smiled.

But it didn't fool her for a second. Her brows drew down in a frown. "What's the matter? Is Rafe all right?"

"He's fine." Dear God, he wanted to tell her what he'd just found out. But he couldn't. No way. Even with everything that had happened, the worst still wasn't over.

In fact, the real battle hadn't even started, although it was about to.

Irina held his gaze for a beat, then nodded. "Good. Now get in there with your wife and son."

As Irina walked away, he rapped lightly on the open door, then stepped inside.

And stopped dead in his tracks.

Mindy was holding their son—nursing him.

"I'll— I can come back later," he stammered, awed and intimidated by the sight before him.

Mindy looked up and smiled. "Our little boy was very hungry."

He swallowed hard.

She laughed softly. "He's almost done. Want to hold him?"

Deke meant to shake his head no, but somehow it bobbed up and down instead.

"Come sit here."

He sat on the edge of the bed. "I don't know—"

"Don't worry. He's less fragile than he looks. I'm going to put one hand under his head and one under his body. You take him the same way."

Deke did, amazed at how tiny and perfect he was. "Six pounds?" he whispered, staring at the tiny, scrunched-up face.

"And three ounces. He looks like you."

"How can you tell?"

"Oh, I can tell."

When Deke looked at her, his heart swelled so much he was sure it would burst out of his chest. "You are so beautiful."

"Liar." She touched her hair and smiled sheepishly.

"No," he said solemnly. "I've always thought you were the most beautiful thing I'd ever seen, although you may have a rival here." He nodded toward the precious baby he held. "But I don't think you've ever been as beautiful to me as you are right now. Min, I've broken too many promises. And God knows I don't deserve another chance, but—"

Mindy's eyes grew wide, but she didn't say anything.

"I want to *be* your husband. His father. Can we at least talk about it?"

For a long time she didn't say anything.

That's it then, he thought, bracing himself. He held Sprout closer to his chest.

"There's nothing to talk about," she whispered breathlessly.

Fear and dread certainty hit him like a blow. "There's not?"

She shook her head. "You *are* my husband. You *are* his father. You are my hero."

While Deke was still processing what she'd said, she lay her palm against his stubbled cheek and raised her head to kiss him.

He kissed her back, holding their brand-new son between them.

* * * * *

We hope you enjoyed reading this
special collection from Harlequin® books.

If you liked reading these stories,
then you will love
Harlequin Intrigue® books!

You crave excitement!
Harlequin Intrigue stories deal in serious
romantic suspense, keeping you on the edge
of your seat as resourceful, true-to-life women
and strong, fearless men fight for survival.

Enjoy six *new* stories from
Harlequin Intrigue every month!

Available wherever books and
ebooks are sold.

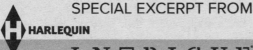
Read on for an excerpt from
MIDNIGHT RIDER
The latest installment in the
BIG "D" DADS: THE DALTONS *series*
by Joanna Wayne

When her search for a killer leads to danger and bull rider
Cannon Dalton, homicide detective Brittany Garner will
face her toughest case yet: catch her long-lost twin's killer,
and try not to fall for the man who might be her infant
niece's father…

"The woman in Greenleaf Bar was you?"

"You don't remember?"

"Vaguely."

He struggled to put things in perspective. That had been a hell of a night. He'd stopped at the first bar he'd come to after leaving the rodeo. A blonde had sat down next to him. As best he remembered, he'd given her an earful about the rodeo, life and death as he'd become more and more inebriated.

She must have offered him a ride back to his hotel since his truck had still been at the bar when he'd gone looking for it the next morning. If Brit was telling the truth, the woman must have gone into the motel with him and they'd ended up doing the deed.

If so, he'd been a total jerk. She'd been as drunk as him and driven or she'd willingly taken a huge risk.

Hard to imagine the woman staring at him now ever

being that careless or impulsive.

"Is that your normal pattern, Mr. Dalton?" Brit asked. "Use a woman to satisfy your physical needs and then ride off to the next rodeo?"

"That's a little like the armadillo calling the squirrel roadkill, isn't it? I'm sure I didn't coerce you into my bed if I was so drunk I can't remember the experience."

"I can assure you that you're nowhere near that irresistible. I have never been in your bed."

"Whew. That's a relief. I'd have probably died of frostbite."

"This isn't a joking matter."

"I'm well aware. But I'm not the enemy here, so you can quit talking to me like I just climbed out from under a slimy rock. If you're not Kimmie's mother, who is?"

"My twin sister, Sylvie Hamm."

Twin sisters. That explained Brit's attitude. Probably considered her sister a victim of the drunken sex urges he didn't remember. It also explained why Brit Garner looked familiar.

"So why is it I'm not having this conversation with Sylvie?"

"She's dead."

Find out what happens next in
MIDNIGHT RIDER
by Joanna Wayne,
available January 2015 wherever
Harlequin Intrigue® books and ebooks are sold.

—

HIEXP69806R

SPECIAL EXCERPT FROM

HARLEQUIN

INTRIGUE

Read on for an excerpt from
THE SHERIFF
The first installment in the
WEST TEXAS WATCHMEN *series*
by Angi Morgan

Mysterious lights, a missing woman, a life-long secret
revealed…all under a star-studded West Texas sky.
Sheriff Pete Morrison must protect a gorgeous witness,
Andrea Allen, from gun smugglers and…herself.

"We've got to get you out of here."

"I am not helpless, Pete. I've been in self-defense courses my entire life. And I know how to shoot. My gun's in the bag we left outside."

Good to know, but he wasn't letting her near that bag. He dropped the key ring on the floor near her hands. "Find one that looks like it's to a regular inside door. Like a broom closet. I'm going to lock you inside."

"Are you sure they're still out there?"

"The chopper's on the ground. The blades are still rotating. No telling how many were already here ready to ambush us." He watched two shadows cross the patio. "Let's move. Next to the snack bar, there's a maintenance door. Run. I'll lay down cover if we need it."

They ran. He could see the shadows but no one followed. Hopefully they didn't have eyes on him or Andrea. He heard the keys and a couple of curses behind him, then a door swung open enough for his charge to squeeze through.

He saw the glint of sun off a mirror outside. They were watching.

"Can you lock the door? Will it lock without the key?"

"I think so."

"Keep the keys with you. I don't need them. Less risky." Bullets could work as a key to unlock, but they might not risk injuring Andrea. He was counting on that.

"But, Pete—"

"Let me do my job, Andrea. Once you're inside, see if you can get into the crawl space. They just saw you open the door. Hide till the cavalry arrives."

"You mean the navy. He won't let us down," she said from the other side of the door. "This is his thing, after all."

Pete had done all he could do to hide her. Now he needed to protect her.

Find out what happens next in
THE SHERIFF
by Angi Morgan,
available January 2015 wherever
Harlequin Intrigue® books and ebooks are sold.